PRAISE FOR THE AUTHORS

"A striking portrayal of the society from the gutters to the royal palace, as gaudy and vivid as a Hogarth print in its writing about the underbelly of society and living there. The characters were utterly human, trying to do their best in a world which was far from perfect, and the conclusion left me wanting more."
Genevieve Cogman, author of *The Invisible Library*

"The world of Resurrectionist is tantalisingly real, the prose is breathlessly witty, and the characters are impossible to avoid loving (or loathing, in a few noteworthy cases). If you've ever called yourself a goth, played 7th Sea, or wished that Pride & Prejudice had magical ink-bees in it, you need this book."
Tyler Hayes, author of *The Imaginary Corpse*

"The Resurrectionist of Caligo is gothic fantasy in the extreme. Its pages are packed with fog shrouded streets, eerie blood magic, grave-robbing, court intrigue, bitter rivalries, shattered hearts, faded dreams, elegant clothing, and perhaps the strangest literary mushrooms since Alice in Wonderland."
Dan Stout, author of *Titanshade*

"I loved the characters, the world-building, the tight plot and the emotional payoff. One of my favorites of the summer!"
Patrice Sarath, author of *The Sisters Mederos* and *Fog Season*

WENDY TRIMBOLI & ALICIA ZALOGA

THE RESURRECTIONIST
OF CALIGO

ANGRY
ROBOT

ANGRY ROBOT
An imprint of Watkins Media Ltd

Unit 11, Shepperton House
89 Shepperton Road
London N1 3DF
UK

angryrobotbooks.com
twitter.com/angryrobotbooks
Blood & Mushrooms

An Angry Robot paperback original, 2019

Cover by John Coulthart
Edited by Lottie Llewelyn-Wells and Paul Simpson
Set in Adobe Garamond

ISBN 978 0 85766 826 4
Ebook ISBN 978 0 85766 827 1

Printed and bound in the United Kingdom by TJ International.

9 8 7 6 5 4 3 2 1

For my mother
– W. T.

To my loved ones: passed,
present, and who will be.
– A. Z.

1

Gaslamps bobbed like faerie lights in the foul wind sweeping down from Greyanchor Necropolis. Roger Weathersby adjusted his topcoat to conceal the rope and rolled-up sheet slung over his shoulder. Thrusting his moth-eaten gloves in his pockets, he inventoried his supplies with his fingertips: candles, tinderbox, lockpicks, folding candlehood, and a reassuring – if useless – garlic bulb.

"You're lookin' a mite wet, Roger love," crooned a painted doxy from a lodging house doorway. Her skirt clung to her thighs like rotten leaves. "Still no coin? Discount for that handsome face."

Roger cast her a regretful look and tucked his chin behind his collar. "Try me again tomorrow. You'll hear my pockets jangling all the way from Mouthstreet."

Veering off Goatmonger Street, he headed toward a looming hill, swollen with centuries of bones. He lost his hat in a mad shimmy over the necropolis wall but didn't waste time searching. Enveloped by fog, Roger relied on water-filled wheel ruts left by a hearse to find his way through the forty-acre necropolis. On the previous day, he had trailed a funeral through the gate, and noticed the simplicity of the affair: a single gentleman mourner and an anonymous mute clad in the traditional crape and mourning mask. Such closefisted families never bothered to hire a night watchman.

This corpse would be ripe for the plucking.

Dolorous Avenue, where Caligo's most venerable families were interred, descended trench-like into the ground, a sliver of sky visible through the encroaching flora. The ivy-sheathed family crypts stood in rows like townhouses. Flagstone paths led to wrought-iron porticoes that shielded crypt doors from the weather. Tiny glowing ghostcandle mushrooms sprouted from chinks between the stones, and the statue of some long-dead queen clawed the air with marble fingers. Decades of rain had streaked sooty tears down her face.

Roger drew the garlic from his pocket. He tore off a clove, peeled it, and popped it in his mouth. Chewing slowly, he knelt before the metal door of the Smith crypt, then tossed another garlic clove at the statue for good measure. A decorative iron curlicue blocked the keyhole, meant to deter amateurs. Roger gave the obstruction a practiced twist and slid it aside.

"May the foul Caligo mists blacken my lungs long afore the were-beasts get me." The sound of his voice banished fear – a little.

He glanced over his shoulder at the marble queen. Had she moved? Roger stood and approached her, watching her stone fingers as if they might conjure sparks, or fountains of ink, or whatever illusory faerie-rubbish the royals waved about as proof of their superiority.

"Poor jammy tartlet." Roger passed a hand over her marble cheek. "Having to witness my transgressions. You won't sell me out, will you, your highness?"

He gave a mock bow and retreated to the crypt door. Lifting a surgeon's charm from beneath his shirt, he kissed the shard of skull embedded in pewter for luck. He selected a tension wrench and, working by feel, torqued the lock's internal cylinder, then manipulated the tumbler pins with a diamond pick.

"May Reason drive out the hags and warlocks who sell their unicorn paste on Mouthstreet to the unschooled masses," he whispered. The internal mechanism clicked. Close. So close. And then…

Pang. Pang. Pang.

Roger froze. Metal struck metal – three times, then silence.

"I refuse," he whispered as cold sweat dribbled down his forehead, "as a man of science, to acknowledge witchcraft, spirits, vampyres, polterghosts, goblins, fae, volcanic subdragons, saint-sprites, mermaids, miracles–"

Pang. Pang. Pang.

The sound came from Roger's right. Shadows enveloped the portico. Behind him, he could make out the gray, rain-washed cobbles of Dolorous Avenue and the silhouette of the stone queen.

A faint blue light floated in the dark before his eyes. His stomach twisted.

Wary of watchmen, Roger hadn't bothered with a light. Now, arrest by a flesh-and-blood man seemed almost… welcoming. Roger fumbled in his pocket for a candle. He struck frantically with his flint and iron, struggling to light the damp tinder, then the wick. At last the flame flared up.

With a shaking hand, Roger raised the candle toward the shadows. He nearly fainted at the sight. A child swayed in the grass, a pale girl-like thing in a puff of white nightdress. Her hands clasped a bouquet of glowing mushrooms – the hovering light. Her white sliver of neck ended in a blob of darkness. No head, no face.

The candle rolled from Roger's fingers. "By the Lady's nethers!" He couldn't rise from his knees, nor unclasp his hands.

Whaaaaaatddddiiiiidyouuuuuuubringmeeeeeeee???

Roger pressed his palms to his face. Garlic oil coated his fingertips. He pulled the second bulb from his pocket, lobbed it at where the girl-thing's head should have been, then grabbed the candle. It hadn't gone out.

The being crouched and caught the garlic bulb when it bounced off the wall. A face like a half-moon appeared above her neck, as if she'd swung back a mop of dark hair. Her mouth made a thin line. No eyes, just black holes.

Hottttttttcroossssssssbuuuuuunssssss!

She tore at the garlic, defying all that superstitious nonsense of its protective qualities. A clove hit his shoulder. His chin. His eye. He heard a shriek. Her? Or himself?

Roger lurched to his feet. His head smacked a curl of wrought-iron lattice. The holes in the being's face filled his vision. All went dark.

Garlic – strong and fresh – tickled his nose. He felt ill.

"You ain't dead." A voice. A girl's voice, lit with annoyance but otherwise normal. "If your legs work now, then run. Afore I fetch someone bigger."

Roger lay on his back. He struggled to sit up. A girl crouched over him holding the candle. He wiped crushed garlic from his upper lip, blinking. She was a normal-looking girl with a soaked, otherwise normal-looking face.

"See?" she said. "I washed off the flour an' the coal. You ain't being hauled off to hell just yet."

"That were… you?"

"I like scaring scoundrels, not killing 'em. But breaking locks, graverobbing and such, you near deserve it. Besides, I saw the prison brand on your neck. Get nabbed again, and you'll hang."

Roger Weathersby, man of science, faced with this more-or-less logical explanation for his paranormal experience, laughed. It hurt. His head throbbed. Self-consciously he retied his neckcloth to cover the black, crenellated wall tattoo that marked him as an ex-convict. Warm blood plastered his hair to his forehead. "So, what?" he said at last. "You the caretaker's lass or some such?"

The girl thrust the candle flame at Roger's nose. "A minute ago you was begging for mercy. I won't let you forget it. Who am I? My mother is a night-walking pixie and Queen of Crumpets. I work in a laundry during the day while she sleeps, and at night she turns into a faerie. She brings me hot cross buns."

She paused. "What's that look for? You think I'm mad?"

"You mean your mother is a street-walking doxy and Queen of Strumpets, right? She lets the dead watch you while her room is busy, eh? Got a cozy nest in a hollowed-out crypt somewhere? Smart lady, your mother." Roger had apprenticed for an undertaker and seen what could befall a nine year-old girl fending for herself on the streets.

"Nasty graverobber. A pox on you."

"Pox ain't no curse you can call down on people for no reason. It's a disease that spreads in certain nasty, preventable ways. And, as I'm enlightened, I know how to keep immune." He touched his pewter medal. "Now stand aside, dollymop. There's a gentlewoman behind this door crying out to be released from an eternity of useless rot. And I'll be the one to free her." He set the hood over the candle, so it wouldn't be seen from the avenue.

"There ain't no crying lady," said the girl with a snort. She eyed the iron crypt door. "Is there? Why would anyone send for the likes of *you*?" Still, she stood aside and handed Roger one of the lockpicks he'd thrown into the grass in his terror.

"How'd she die?" asked the girl while Roger fiddled with the lock. He could hear the pins clicking into place.

"Hot cross buns." Roger removed his coat and set it aside. He took out the long, beaked leather mask and placed it over his head. Disks of red glass set into the mask's circular eyelets turned the candlelight a blood-red hue.

"You look like the vulture at Marlowe's Menagerie," snickered the girl. "What's the use of that thing?"

"In case she smells." So much for instilling respect. He pried back the mask and put another garlic clove in his mouth.

The girl stuck out her tongue. "And that?"

"In case she's not dead. Want one?"

"Blech."

"Also cures ulcers, warts, and helps you see in the dark."

The latch slid back with a clang, and Roger pulled at the crypt door's handle.

"You, little ghost," he said to the girl, his voice muffled behind the mask, "are not to step foot in that bone box."

"Don't tell me what to do."

"Hysteria ain't healthy for young ladies."

"Who said I'm a lady? The name's Ada, but you can call me Ghostofmary. That's what the boys call me, ever since I danced in the moonlight on the tomb of Sir Bentley Morris and set 'em all screaming–"

"Ada, you stay out here."

"So you go in then," said Ada, folding her arms. "I'll close the door behind you. Maybe I'll lock it."

Roger grimaced. "You're in league with the devil. Hold the candle then. I'll test for traps – sometimes the nicer crypts are rigged with a spring-gun and tripwire. Here, stand back." He cut a long strand of ivy from the wall and flicked it through the entrance like a whip, using the door as cover. "Safe as fishes. No wire, or the ivy would have snagged it. Couldn't afford one, I expect." He held out the battered metal flask he kept in his waistcoat pocket. "Now take a sip of this. It helps ready you for… the looking part."

Ada took a swig, coughed, and handed it back. "Gin?"

Roger nodded. He tossed back a mouthful and eased the door open.

Most noble family vaults housed a modest row of ornate coffins, but this one held a jumbled two dozen at least. The older ones had been stacked three high, packed so tightly that he couldn't see the back wall. The newest coffin, a cheap varnished pine box, was identifiable by its dustless lid. There were no flowers, nor the usual incense burners left by mourners.

Roger shook out the linen sheet he'd carried under his topcoat. He had Ada spread it on the ground while he pried out the nails fastening the coffin lid.

"You do all this alone?" asked the girl. "I thought bodysnatchers ran in gangs."

"I'm a vault man. You need more hands for digging up graves. But with a locked vault and a light lady corpse, I'd rather do it myself. Don't need to split the payment, neither. But we must leave the place as we find it. If family comes to visit, they can't guess by looking that we was here – unless they open the coffin itself."

"Must have had a big family once."

"And now they've lost their grand fortune, based on the sorry state of the funeral." Roger loosened the final nail and pried the coffin lid open just a crack.

"I thought it would smell worse." Ada sounded disappointed. To Roger's amusement, she hid her face, peering through the gaps between her fingers. Then darker thoughts distracted him.

What horrors might he find within? After several years as a bodysnatcher, he still hadn't lost his terror of this moment. A half-rotted ghoul? A writhing nest of rats? Violent mutilation? He took another swig of gin. A long one this time, letting it burn all the way down his gullet.

Roger pulled at the lid and forced his eyes open, then recoiled in shock. He'd never seen anything like this.

Ada shrieked and bolted out of the crypt. Roger heard her sobbing under the portico, but now was no time for emotion. The barrier of his mask gave him a much-needed feeling of separation.

She lay there, a woman so newly dead that sweat still glistened on her forehead. A woman whose face he recognized. But from where? How? He couldn't think. Her wide, lifeless eyes stared up at him, and her mouth formed a silent gaping scream – an expression no worthy undertaker would tolerate. The shredded remains of a bouquet lay scattered over her red taffeta dress. Her black lace veil had ripped. Most unnerving of all were the long vertical rips in the satin lining of the coffin's lid, made by a live woman's fingernails.

This woman had been dead a few hours at most.

A chill crept up his spine. *Did* he recognize her? Her waxen face bore an inhuman pallor. She looked about thirty. He had a flash of memory: this woman in a white cook's apron and cap. Perhaps he'd seen her in the royal kitchen where he'd been a scullion years ago. No, he must be mistaken. A cook could never marry so grand as to find rest on Dolorous Avenue. The shock must have triggered strange associations in his brain.

Roger wiped his sleeve across his soaked brow. He lifted her hand and pressed a finger into the vein of her wrist. She was dead now, at any rate. Accidental premature burial was not unknown. It was not his fault. Though a resurrectionist in name, he could not actually bring the dead back.

"I'm sorry," he mouthed. "Sorry I were but an hour too late."

If not for his dire need of wages, he'd gladly have shut the vault and gone straight home. Or to the Fox & Weasel for a pint or three. But he had his overdue rent to think of, the odd creditor, and the distant twinkle of a true medical career – though perhaps he'd have to resort to highway robbery first. *Pretend she's a statue*, he told himself as he tied a handkerchief around her face. A cold marble statue. Or a clay one, as rigor mortis had not yet set in.

It only took a few minutes to lay the corpse on the sheet. He removed her veil, dress, a small gold ring, a programme for *The Reluctant Milliner*, and a red monogrammed hair ribbon.

Her bare stomach appeared mottled with strange spots of a blue-green sheen that caught his eye in the dark, but the candlelight proved too dim for a deeper inspection of the body's condition. Probably mildew – he'd encountered all colors of corpse-mold before, from powder-blue to luminous orange, but never so soon after death, and especially not in winter.

However, this was no time to ponder the science of decomposition. He lowered her eyelids, and then placed her possessions back into the coffin. A corpse, according to the law, belonged to no one, but stealing even a tattered bit of shroud was punishable by hanging.

His hats would be the death of him, he thought. Swiped from the dead. His only vice, aside from gin.

Roger drew up the knees of the corpse and bundled it – he forbade himself to continue thinking "her" – in the sheet and slung it over his shoulder. Outside, the girl had recovered somewhat. She gathered up Roger's lockpicks, which he tucked away in his pockets with his other supplies.

"I need to make this delivery before dawn." Roger glanced toward the horizon, but it was obscured by fog. "Can I escort you to town?"

Ada shook her head. "I meet Ma at the bottom of the hill after the clock strikes six. But I've got a velvety coffin to sleep in, next door to Sir Bentley Morris. Mine's empty of course, 'cept for me. My day clothes are there. And Ma always brings me a hot cross bun."

"Keep the candle, then."

As Roger offered Ada the waxy stub, something fell from the folds of his corpse-bundle and lay glinting on the gravel. Some personal effect must have been cleverly hidden, for Roger took care in checking his wares and had never before missed an artifact.

Ada scrambled after it, but Roger kicked it away and snatched it up first.

"Hands off, you sack-'em-up man!" Ada snarled as she tried to pry open his fist.

"That belongs to my stiff, you imp." Roger yanked his hand out of her reach and studied the object, a decorative hatpin with a small pearl centered in a swirl of petals.

Ada clawed at his coat. "Give it back! What does a stiff care about a pretty metal flower?" She tried to climb him like a tree, but he held her firmly by the wrist.

"The constables find that on you, and you'll be the one hanging, or locked up at the very least. I can't return it now. But I'll drop it in the Mudtyne soon as I can. You'll thank me later, little ghost. Now be off with you."

Roger crossed a field of headstones. When he reached the trees he looked for Ada but she had disappeared. Loaded down as he was, he cleared the necropolis wall with difficulty. He didn't find his hat. Feeling naked without it, he headed for town.

He trundled his freight up Goatmonger Street in a handcart he kept stashed in a shed at the bottom of Greyanchor Hill. It could have been a coal delivery, or firewood, laundry, any number of things. As he turned onto Mouthstreet, the bell at St Colthorpe's sounded four languid tolls.

Entering Eldridge's College of Barber-Surgeons by the back courtyard, Roger rang for the night porter.

"Have you brought a specimen, Mr Weathersby?" Instead of the porter, old Dr Eldridge himself had sat up overnight to welcome the deliveries. "Good weather for it, with the fog. Blackett just brought a hanged man fresh off the gibbet. He's not got mass enough on him to use for my lecture on musculature, but he'll do for the digestion talk."

Roger unwrapped his bundle for the physician to examine. "I've brought a lady, sir. I know you was looking for a lady, for that series on female health. I scouted her funeral yesterday."

Dr Eldridge pressed his palms together in delight. "I'll give you nine for her. Has she her teeth? Then ten."

As Roger fumbled to check this, he noticed purple bruising around her throat. He hadn't seen these marks back in the dark crypt. Someone had forced her into that coffin against her will. Even worse, she had a hard belly with odd, soft raised bumps in her abdominal wall. A wave of nausea passed over him.

9

Second thoughts plagued Roger about passing off this corpse as a medical specimen after suffering such an unusual death. And here he was, tampering with what looked like evidence.

Roger tossed the sheet over the corpse and pressed his hands to his thighs. "I confess, sir. I can't take money for this one. Now I've seen her in the light, I fear her death were… not right. But can I leave her in the cellar, just for a time? I have some asking 'round to do. You can keep her as you like, but I don't want to bring you trouble, and I can't very well summon the constables to look into the matter."

"Constables? Certainly not." The doctor rested a wrinkled hand on Roger's shoulder. "This one will keep for a time in the cold cellar. My female series starts next week, and I always take the most discreet precautions. The face will be covered as usual, along with identifying marks. She'll be put to worthy scientific use. No one will be able to trace her to you, that I promise." Dr Eldridge counted out ten Myrcnian shells and tucked them into Roger's pocket. Begrudgingly, he added an eleventh. "For your discretion. To think I was on the verge of cancelling the series. They don't hang enough women in this city. Lucky for me I have a bold lad like you who goes beyond the easy pickings of the Old Grim gibbet. Well done. I'll see you tomorrow evening, Mr Weathersby. The hanged man needs to be readied for my next lecture, and I think it's high time you did a full dissection by yourself."

"Me? I – well, thank you, sir." Roger knew he should have felt grateful and flattered at this last pronouncement, but recent events had dampened his enthusiasm for hands-on practice. "Tomorrow evening it is."

2

On the first of every month since her expulsion from the palace, Princess Sibylla's cousin Prince Edgar sent a chocolate box roughly thirty miles from Myrcnia's capital of Caligo to Helmscliff estate in Tyanny Valley. For three-odd years, these boxes of violet-and-rose filled chocolates had been delivered to warm her to the idea of marrying her younger cousin, yet his obligatory wooing had a chilling effect instead. After all, Edgar had no more interest in wedding her than she him. It was their grandmother, the Queen of Myrcnia, who wanted to force the match. Only when Sibylla agreed to the royal union between cousins – a prosaic tradition to strengthen their family's magic – would she be welcomed back at the palace.

Her mouth salivated as her fingers hovered over the sweets, but despite being a favored treat, she had never eaten one of the fondant-filled bribes, certain that ingesting a single chocolate meant saying "I will" in church.

She tucked her feet into her slippers, and resealed the box of confections for a second delivery. Outside her room, heavy tapestries lined a stone corridor where cold morning air seeped through the seams of her dress and little clouds formed from her breath. She only knocked once before bursting into Captain Starkley's room.

"Harrod, a moment of your time."

The captain paused in the middle of fastening the gold buttons of his naval frock coat. He watched wryly as she shut his bedroom door behind her and inclined his head. "Your highness."

Sibylla flung herself into a wingback chair near the meager fireplace and tossed the rose-colored chocolate box at Harrod. He caught it and raised a curious eyebrow, then finished buttoning his uniform one-handed. Though only thirty years old, her warden protector fussed over his uniform like an aged valet. Scrutinizing himself in the mirror, he straightened the skirt of his jacket over well-ironed trousers, pinning on his most important medal last.

"Is her highness in ill spirits this morning? Or is this her way of protesting my departure?" He jiggled the chocolate box. "Rose and violet? I'd sooner eat a bowl of begonia and clover."

Sibylla exhaled unhappily. "Give them to your replacement if you don't wish to eat them. He's already sent word that he'll be arriving this afternoon."

After assuming the previous warden protector's post, Captain Starkley had been trapped with Sibylla at Helmscliff for two years. A different kind of officer might have enjoyed the stationing – one who preferred taking walks in the garden to hunting down rogues on the open ocean. Harrod was not that man.

"You sound angry." Harrod lifted the lid of the chocolate box and wrinkled his nose. "Shouldn't your highness be thanking me for my service rendered? Perhaps you might offer some additional remuneration."

Sibylla flicked wool lint into the hissing firewood. "Be grateful I don't blackmail you to stay on another two years." Having grown up without siblings – not counting the bastard half-brother she couldn't mention in mixed company – she'd enjoyed every one of Harrod's exasperations with her these past few years, and often teased him in return.

"I see your highness' renowned humor is intact."

"It's no jest." She slipped out of her shoes to warm the soles of her stockings. "I know all about your time aboard the HMS *Whalestooth*."

"Ah yes, my thrilling experience as the master gunner. Did you know the cannons of a warship must be cleaned by hand six times a day to prevent salt corrosion? It was non-stop adventure on the high seas, your highness. I became an expert in the various grades of chamois cloth to best bring out the sheen."

"You *became* an expert in pineapple piracy."

Harrod feigned a look of wounded dignity. "Piracy, your highness? Me?"

"After 'escorting' a merchant ship carrying her royal majesty's pineapples to an Ibnovan port, the captain claimed the cargo lost at sea in a storm, then turned around and sold them to the port's mayor. A certain master gunner, I hear, bartered the fruit's price to double its worth."

"How did you–" Harrod cleared his throat. "Your highness was barely fourteen."

Sibylla grinned. "One must learn the art of intrigue sooner rather than later."

Harrod compressed the corners of the rose-colored box in his hands, but gave no other sign of discomfort. "I acted under the orders of my commander."

"Who now serves as Admiral of the Fleet. I doubt *the* Lord Harlum would be held accountable while you're at hand."

"Wasn't it your highness who once trounced all the young ladies at some poetry competition in Derbershin by writing an elegy for the fall of man's morality?" Harrod shook his head as though aggrieved. He removed a dark chocolate from the box and popped it in his mouth. "To think that little girl has grown into a blackmailer."

He was teasing her now. So much for her threat.

"Perhaps we might take one last tea together? Do you still have that chicory from Lipthveria?"

Harrod pitched a log onto the fire. "I'll ring for the maid."

While they waited, Sibylla flexed her fingers. She'd have liked to return to Caligo with the captain, but she was only permitted to leave Helmscliff when her chapel's monstrance required a fresh supply of "divine fluids." Despite all of Myrcnia's noble houses bearing magic blood, only the royal family was worshipped. Most fervent Myrcnians believed the queen, her children, and grandchildren were divine, and, as such, on her sixteenth birthday Sibylla had been brought to St Myrtle's cathedral to bless her own chapel. Her blood was drawn and placed in a large gold monstrance for commoners to venerate. Even exiled she was expected to perform her spiritual duties.

"What will you do first when you return to Caligo?" asked Sibylla, knowing Harrod hadn't taken a day of leave during his stationing.

"I intend to catch a man who is plummeting off the precipice of social respectability. I'll try, anyway." He twisted his mouth. "You may recall a certain Roger Weathersby."

Sibylla jolted upright, but Harrod crossed his legs without a care.

He swallowed a second chocolate before noticing her interest. "So you *are* curious about what's become of him?"

Sibylla's throat tightened, and she answered in a reedy voice. "Of course not." She hadn't seen that two-faced liar in years, not since she spied him locking lips with a certain royal attendant beneath the weeping ash in the palace gardens. Once she'd even let that blackguard sit beside her on the ash's gnarled roots and amuse her with rambling yarns that ended in cringeworthy puns.

"Your highness doesn't wish for me to deliver some private correspondence, then?" Harrod leaned back in his chair with a smirk. "You could clear the air between the two of you, as it were."

Sibylla's tongue curled. "If you provoke me further, you'll find inking isn't my only talent."

Her magical gifts had emerged between the ages of twelve and fourteen, passed down through her parents. From her mother's House of Cornin, Sibylla had inherited an inking trait that allowed her to manipulate black fluid that bloomed beneath her fingernails, while from her royal father Prince Henry, she'd inherited a touch of bioluminescence and her great-grandfather King Rupert's whistle-click – a shrill burst of air shaped by her tongue that could upturn a collar or make a person's ears ring.

"Shall I give you a taste of old King Rupert's ear-shattering whistle?"

Harrod grimaced and dropped the subject. He reached for the poker and prodded a half-charred log. "Blast. How long does it take to bring up some damned tea?" He squeezed her shoulder before leaving to fetch the tea himself.

Sibylla suppressed a laugh at how quickly his patience broke. Here at Helmscliff, none of the staff relished their duties – not the maids who left the stairs dusty and the foyer pocked with muddy boot-prints, nor her lady-in-waiting whose only interest lay in teaching her to play the concertina. Technically, she shouldn't come and go from Harrod's room as she pleased either, but after a mere month, he'd stopped caring whether she behaved like a proper lady or not.

Her brow wrinkled in dismay. Though she'd certainly miss his model ships, engraved pistols, and the atlas she loved perusing in the evenings, she would mourn the absence of her favorite person most of all.

Sibylla pulled the chair closer to the fire, her eyes drifting to the secretary desk in the corner of the room. Should she write Roger after all? Invent some exotic ailment, perhaps, to lure him from his medical studies in Caligo. She imagined him arriving in a neat frock coat and hat, an auscultation scope around his neck and a shiny leather bag at his side. "Dr Weathersby, at your service," he'd say. "Tell me where it hurts."

Such foolishness! She sat on her hands as she tried to let the desire pass by, but after a few crackles from the pitiful flames she stood with a huff. Removing parchment from the slender desk drawer, she flexed her fingers. Her own magic rendered ink and quill obsolete. What had first manifested as an ability to release dark ink-clouds into the air similar to a squid's underwater escape she'd perfected into precise manipulations.

As bodily ink pooled beneath her fingernails, black letters appeared on the sheet as though penned by quill.

Dear Roger,

Her pinkie twitched, and a line of ink sliced through his name as though skewering the man himself.

Dear Snotsniffer,

Too mean? The nickname had a certain sentimental value if only for its ability to elicit a rise out of him. She encircled the salutation in a slender daisy chain.

I couldn't say I've given you much thought until today. After you departed with full pockets from a royal bribe, it was clear the mistake I made in trusting you. When I learned you'd lost your mother, I thought to send you a letter, but found myself in an unfavorable position. Although I had once imagined you and I carrying on for some time, I never knew how black your heart could be.

I regret having stolen those kitchen scraps for you when I was eight, and playing hog-the-wash with Lady Esther's skivvies in the yard. I should have never taught you to read and write so you could send love letters to other ladies too old for you by far. The first kiss I gave you, your mouth tasted like smoked haddock.

Did you know I spied you with Dorinda the night before you vanished? And afterwards she showed me your treasured physician's medal as proof of your dalliance with her. A gift that demonstrated how you treated her with more kindness than you did me. At least with the funds you were given you'll have no recourse for regret. A generosity I wish I'd been shown.

Was it worth it? Do you have your own practice now? Or perhaps you're still in residency as a medical student. I never did receive any apology, though I waited on the docks and behind Mrs Pennystack's hay barn. If I'd meant anything to you, you'd have given me one already. At least then I could have forgiven you.

Dodge, you really are the most awful man I've ever known.

With warmest regards,
Sibylla

Without a single word asking Roger to liberate her from Helmscliff, the letter read more like a whipping than a wish for reconciliation. She was still angry after five years.

She sighed as the ink beneath her fingernails thinned. She had little control over her marriage prospects, and Roger had known that. But he left without a word – and for money, too. He should have suffered a half-hearted farewell, if only to spare her feelings. At least, he might have written. She'd taught that man to write. He had no excuse.

She crumpled the parchment into a ball and tossed it toward the damp fireplace.

When Harrod finally entered with a silver tray in his hands, she'd returned to her chair. As her personal bodyguard, he had often doubled as an attendant over the last two years. While the tea steeped, he slipped a small box next to her cup.

She lifted it. "What is this?"

He cleared his throat and avoided eye contact. "A parting gift."

Inside, housed in blue velvet, lay a locket – silver with an oval etching of a ship. She cracked it open with her fingernail. No picture, no lock of hair, just a slip of heavy white paper waiting to be inked. She raised her eyebrows.

He waved her off. "Just magic whatever you want in there."

"How sentimental, Harrod." Smiling, she took a sip of tea.

Without removing the cardstock from the locket, Sibylla used her magic to ink a portrait of a man. When she'd finished, she blew onto the ink to make it dry faster. Harrod leaned over to get a closer look, but Sibylla snapped the locket shut before he could see her handiwork.

"Don't worry," said Sibylla. "It's not of you."

Sibylla's bedroom window afforded her a view of the front yard where Harrod stood, making final adjustments to his saddle. Snow stuck to his uniform like cotton gauze and in a matter of minutes his hat and shoulders had turned solid white. The muscular bay gelding huffed steam while its master mounted. Sibylla pressed her hand against the glass. Branches of ice covered the bottom of the pane. She half-hoped the horse would rear up and throw him, so he might stay one day more at Helmscliff.

By the time she stepped away from the window, only the horse's hoof prints remained in the snow. Seeking solace from the sudden emptiness at Helmscliff, she retrieved her copy of Salston's *The Barnmaid of Bareth* from beneath her pillow and threw herself into his sinuous tale. Curled next to the fireplace, she devised a way to trap the lecherous priest in the first act and outsmart the lascivious opera singer of the second. She was deep into the third act, where the heroic lawyer rescues the barnmaid from falling into the clutches of the randy ventriloquist, when a knock on the door startled her. She'd forgotten to take her luncheon, and a maid must have thought to deliver her meal.

Instead, an unfamiliar young man entered with a tray in one hand. He wore the uniform of the queen's light cavalry, a cranberry-colored pelisse over a jacket, and riding breeches in deep marine blue. His blond mustache seasoned his face, and Sibylla admitted he was amiably good-looking compared to the hoary regulars posted at Helmscliff.

He managed an elegant bow while keeping the tray upright. "Lieutenant Quincy Calloway – yes, those Calloways – at your service. I have been graced with the honor of being appointed your highness' warden protector."

Sibylla suppressed her opinion about the nature of that service beneath a polite smile. Young aristocratic sons often received plum positions on account of their names, their poor aptitudes notwithstanding. Still, this one might not be a complete bore. She'd heard Calloways could guess an object's shape and size while blindfolded by clicking their jaws. That could be fun.

Sibylla took her book to where the lieutenant settled his tray on a card table in the center of her room. He'd brought her lunch: crusty bread with what looked like cow's liver jelly, and sautéed spinach.

"I usually dine in the hall," Sibylla said, setting her book beside the lavender plate.

Lieutenant Calloway placed a scandalized hand to his mouth. "I saw guards dining there earlier – men who hadn't purchased their commissions. What if one of them were to sit across from your highness and try to speak with you?" His eyes fixed on her dress. "And is this all you've been provided to wear?"

Sibylla glanced down at her simple wool dress. The cut was sharp, militaristic even, with no unnecessary lace or pleats, in a dark gray that suited her. It never caught on brambles during the spring thaw when she walked the fields surrounding Helmscliff, or picked up soot from the fireplace, or ink specks from her magic.

"My dress is not your concern, lieutenant."

"Your highness' well-being is my *only* concern. To think so little attention has been paid to your station."

Sibylla disregarded his apparent horror at her living arrangements and ruefully eyed the soggy spinach on her plate. "I assure you, I am very comfortable."

His gaze wandered to the table. "*The Barnmaid of Bareth?*"

A dash of hope sparked in Sibylla. "Are you familiar with Salston's works?" If nothing else, she had longed for a partner to discuss her favorite author. Harrod had as much interest in books as he did in croquet, and Lady Wayfeather, her lady-in-waiting, preferred to hum concertina ballads than discuss lascivious dramas.

"Unfathomable. No one's considered your reading materials either. My predecessor's military honors might have given him a touch of class, but there's really no substitute for good breeding. Rumor is that his mother was a lady's maid. Can you imagine? I'll bring your highness something suitable to read directly."

That lustrous mustache hid a viperous tongue. Lieutenant Calloway reached for her book, but Sibylla slammed her palm on the cover. Her cheeks heated in anger. "Your hand," she prompted, expecting its removal. Her shoulders stiffened as she took on an air of authority that always won out over guardsmen's occasional objections.

"Not until after I've had a word with Lady Wayfeather."

"She's never once objected to my reading materials. And I hardly think a lieutenant in her majesty's–"

"As the son of General Calloway – Viscount of Highspits and commander to the queen's Kettlebay guards – I'm well-versed in the proper education of distinguished ladies, such as your highness. I'm sixty-ninth in line for the crown myself, you see."

Sibylla's lady-in-waiting, a mere baroness, might put up a fuss on Sibylla's behalf, but she'd ultimately have to acquiesce to this man, or jeopardize her comfortable position at Helmscliff. A man with influential connections really was as dangerous as a battalion when waging a war of positions.

Sibylla snatched her arm away, cooling her face with the backs of her fingers while the lieutenant gathered the book triumphantly to his chest. She now wondered if this lieutenant hadn't been deliberately sent by her grandmother to cow her into matrimony. Well, she had no intention of letting either her cousin or this young fop have his way with her and her belongings. If he didn't return her book, then she'd gleefully resort to theft. She might not have the Calloway's jaw click to locate her belongings in the dark, but she still had a trick or two up her puffed sleeves.

3

Roger's night of corpse-snatching failed to dampen his appetite. He ventured out at noon wearing a threadbare cloth cap and breakfasted on cold jellied eels from a waxed paper cone. The market teemed with girls hawking carrots and steaming mutton pies from handcarts, while coachmen hustled loudly for genteel fares. The crowds churned the street into a slop of mud, manure, and anything the locals tossed from their windows at night. No ordinances against that sort of thing existed here in the lower quarters.

Passers-by dropped coins into the hat of an Ibnovan performer with a chin-puff beard who jiggled a string of wooden dolls in ballroom finery, making them dance. The man touched his cap, and Roger noticed his missing little finger, a sign he'd once attempted "street magic" – putting whole eggs into narrow-necked bottles, or breathing fire using a match and a mouthful of starch. Street magic was just science, but Myrcnians mistrusted foreigners who attempted such heretical feats. Certain gangs still held to the tradition of scarring these so-called "false prophets" who faked royal magic. A lopped finger meant this performer had gotten off easy.

Roger's thoughts turned again to the woman in the crypt. If he'd just arrived an hour earlier, he might have saved her life. But as for selling her remains – he didn't believe in desecration. Consigning the dead to science gave them immortality, of sorts. In that respect, he'd done her a favor.

He was trudging up Hamtruckle Way when a poster plastered to a dingy brick wall caught his eye.

Roger stopped and stared. The likeness of a young Princess Sibylla smiled down at him, offering a silver tray of sweets. Her gown was hand-painted in cherry, and behind her stood an aproned chocolatier, tying a red ribbon into the princess' hair.

Sibet.

Sibet, her highness Princess Sibylla, had been his childhood partner in crime. Or rather, he'd been hers. Sidekick, stuntsman, scapegoat, whipping boy, and eventually the eager object of her affections. But the folktales had lied. A servant couldn't love a princess. Not if he wanted to keep his head. After his banishment he'd scaled the palace walls intending to explain to her why he'd taken the queen's money – his mother's illness, physician bills – and earned a prison stint for his pains, along with a broken nose. Maybe one day he'd meet her again at some banquet held by the Royal College of Surgeons, as a self-employed medical man with his name painted above the door of his own practice.

What was he doing, dredging up Sibet after all this time? He'd drive himself mad. He had dismissed that pie-in-the-sky long ago.

He forced his eyes off the poster princess, and onto the chocolatier behind her instead. His breath quickened. That corpse he'd liberated from its useless fate shared the face of this chocolate shop proprietress. The close likeness gave him gooseflesh. He scanned the poster for more.

Claudette's Chocolate Delights & Princess Nougats
Propr. Mistress Claudine
Visit us in Stargazy Lane.

He'd heard of Claudette's. It was one of those chocolate shops for toffs somewhere north of the Thimble District. Other thoughts piled into his aching head. A trip to Claudette's might provide closure. Or answers. He could still pay his respects – even if he had sold her body for eleven shells.

Roger didn't dare show up looking like a common workman. He searched the second-hand shops for a suitable hat to replace his lost one, and rationalized spending Dr Eldridge's payment on a silk neckcloth. Now he had an excuse to splurge. He plucked a few winter roses from a churchyard, bought a black ribbon from a girl for a half-winkle, and retied his unraveling cravat.

The confectionery shop was a cozy corner affair with a tatty black rosette nailed to the door and flimsy mourning silk dangling from the gold-trimmed sign. The front window displayed a selection of sweets: dark chocolate skulls, sugared fans of brown jelly, black rose marzipans.

A bell on the door jangled too cheerily as Roger entered. Black crape drapes swathed the windows and the marble counter stacked with cocoa coffin cakes. Children chewed licorice bows while their governesses gossiped over dainty cups of hot chocolate. The pair of shopgirls at the counter glanced his way. Their eyes traveled from his new hat, to his silk cravat, to his face. Then they broke into smiles.

"How can we help you?" trilled the first girl. "A box of princess creams for a lady friend?"

"Or perhaps a hot chocolate toddy?" added the second. "With a jot of whiskey, as you please."

Roger swiped his hat from his head. It should have been a rakish move but came off clumsily due to nerves. "I- I heard word of Mistress Smith. Right sad it was," he said and offered the flowers.

The girls stared.

"Only Smith 'round here is the man who brings the coals."

Roger tried a sheepish smile. "Perhaps Smith were her maiden name. I mean to pay my respects to the proprietress... Claudine?"

The girls exchanged a grave glance.

"Aye, a right nasty affair. Mistress was always fair to us, weren't she Mabel?"

"That's why you're here, isn't it?" Mabel asked. "You saw the broadsheets and want to hear the full story. Well, it'll cost you two winkles."

Roger felt in his pocket and slid two coins across the counter.

Mabel nodded, then leaned close and whispered. "The Greyanchor Strangler got her. She'd been ill, see, and wanted to take the healing waters at Fillsbirth."

"The Greyanchor Strangler preys on them that falls ill," added the first girl in a grisly undertone.

"That so?" Roger feigned nonchalance.

23

"We thought she'd gone on holiday, but she turned up dead in her bed two nights ago. The housemaid found her with marks on her throat and the window thrown wide. They buried her yesterday, when we had to work. Didn't even get to kiss her goodbye."

The first girl eyed the black ribbon on Roger's bouquet. "You a gentleman friend, then?"

"Friend," he echoed, regretting the flowers. He hid them behind his back. "Yes. Old friend."

Roger's head spun. Tales of some strangler chap had been circulating for months, in those cheap penny broadsheets that sold grisly headlines for entertainment. Mothers warned their children to be home when the lamp-lighters appeared, lest they be choked. He'd never taken broadsheet rumors seriously before, but now he'd seen that bruise on Claudine's throat. Suppose she'd been choked unconscious, then boxed before she was quite dead…

His thoughts trailed off as Mabel impatiently cleared her throat, and Roger realized a queue had formed behind him.

"So, mister, what can I get you?"

"How much for the chocolate drink with whiskey?" he asked.

Mabel told him.

Roger left the shop empty-handed and tossed the flowers on the nearest windowsill. Maybe that Claudine woman *could* afford her prestigious resting spot with those prices. "You can squeeze every penny out of them wealthy drips, but you'll get no shelling to line your coffin from me," he muttered.

He was chasing a shadow. People died every day in Caligo, and many were barely missed. Time to forget and move on.

The sun had set, and a single gaslamp illuminated the courtyard behind Eldridge's College of Barber-Surgeons. Roger stood at the pump, scouring his bloodstained hands with sand. He had just finished preparing a hanged man's cadaver for tomorrow's lecture on the digestion system, which had left him spattered with gore.

"Aesophagus," he recited. "Muscularis externa of the stomach.

Pyloric sphincter. The greater and lesser entrails."

Roger had eviscerated the body, cleaned and painted the relevant organs with bright pigments, then packed everything back into place. Meanwhile, Dr Eldridge looked on, helpfully pointing out the different structures. As a physician he rarely touched dead flesh, relying on surgeons and assistants for such menial tasks. Dr Eldridge's fingers had stiffened with age, and he was an instructor now, not a practitioner.

"The liver filters the blood, the spleen vents chemicals of anger, and the pancreas… is bloody useless."

Roger was not a physician, nor surgeon, nor even a proper student. The price of a medical education, even the required surgeon's toolkit alone, went far beyond Roger's means. Medical students came from the upper middle and merchant classes, and did not generally claim a background of scullion, undertaker's apprentice, and convict. However, physicians throughout the city had taken a shine to Roger once he proved he could wrestle a body cut from the gallows to any discreet anatomist with coin to spend. Dr Eldridge had taken him on as an unofficial dogsbody in exchange for off-the-record tutelage in the medical arts. After two years, Roger had experience in cutting, stitching, lancing, and injecting. He'd even performed an amputation – though not on a living patient. Yet.

"Delivery for Mr Roger Weathersby, man of science," said a sardonic voice behind Roger, startling him. "And you don't just wear the science on your sleeve, I see. You've smeared it all over yourself."

Roger spun around, still drying his hands on his bloodied apron. A man stood under the courtyard gaslamp, face obscured behind goggles and a dust mask. He wore a mud-spattered military uniform, knee-high riding boots, and a striking medal on his breast: the Order of the Kraken, the queen's highest honor for nautical service.

From a yawn-inducing history book Sibet had foisted on him, Roger recalled one rare interesting anecdote. A century ago, massive tentacles slid out of the sea foam in Kettlebay to wrap around a fisherman's dinghy. The fisherman had lopped off one tentacle and narrowly escaped with his life, then brought it to the palace packed in ice where the king – or queen? Roger couldn't keep the royal lot of them straight – made the fisherman the first recipient of the Order of the Kraken. Since then, the monarchy never permitted more than ten living members, military or civilian. The lopped tentacle was rumored to still be on display at the Anathema Club, a social hub for men of science.

"Sir." Roger wadded up his bloody apron and bowed. All citizens under the rank of baronet had to show respect to shiny medals, Kraken or otherwise – the lower one's station, the deeper the bow.

"Lovely," said the messenger. His voice rasped, as if he'd contracted a sore throat. "I didn't realize you were capable of bowing. I'll be sure to let her highness know."

"Do I know you?" Roger stared hard at the man. "When you say her highness, do you mean…" He couldn't bring himself to say the princess' name out loud.

The messenger adjusted his dust mask but did not reply.

Roger hid the apron behind his back, imagining the messenger's disgust. "You said there's a delivery, sir? Or do you expect a… a tip first?"

"I expect you to invite me inside. All transactions are to be done in private. I have her highness' express instructions to receive in hand your written reply. I am to proofread as needed or take dictation. And," he added, "do not insult me with a tip."

"I write my own private letters, thank you, sir." Roger bowed again and led the messenger inside to the preparation room. He lit a lamp on a little writing desk near the window. A scalpel, drill, bone saw, and other recently-cleaned instruments lay out to dry on the dissection table. Jars of wet preparations like malformed pickles lined the shelves, alongside varnished bones and sheaves of papery dried muscle.

"Please don't mind the smell, sir," said Roger to fill the awkward silence. "I swabbed the place down with wine spirits a short time ago."

The messenger glanced around the room. "I was expecting more corpses."

"Oh," said Roger as he unrolled his sleeves. "Well, we don't leave 'em out overnight. Rats, drunken medical students, that sort of thing. Everything is kept clean as the royal kitchens."

"And that?" The messenger pointed at the mask shaped like a crow's head that hung from a hook on the wall. "Is this for some vulgar masquerade?"

"It's a plague doctor's mask," said Roger, eager to show off. He took down the mask and handed it over. "During the Doomsday Miasma two hundred years ago, doctors would fill the beaks with nice-smelling herbs. They often died anyway, but these masks still have their uses. Can't even smell the stomach swill of a four day-old stiff when you wear it."

The messenger turned the mask in his hands, then passed it back to Roger. "I trust you won't wear it out on the street. It might remind people how scientists once started a plague, meddling in their laboratories with King Indulf's divine fingernail clippings. Half of Caligo died because some natural philosophers exhorted the unification of magic and science."

"There's no proof science caused the Doomsday Miasma." Roger struggled to control his irritation as he tucked the mask away in a cupboard. "In the old days, they used to blame disasters on heresy. Now it's science. Any scapegoat'll do."

"Is that so?" The messenger pulled his dust mask tighter over his face and handed over an envelope. "Perhaps I'll wait outside after all. Call me if you have a spelling question." He turned on his heel.

Roger examined the folded parchment, rumpled from its journey. One corner was stained black. He turned it over and his pulse raced – Princess Sibylla's handwriting. Did she want to see him again, to pick up where they'd left off? He glanced down at his bloodstained shirt and waistcoat. He should have had a broadcloth suit by now to match his silken neckcloth. A set of his own scalpels in a monogrammed box. The past five years had not gone as planned.

He sniffed the letter, catching a whiff of violets tinged with smoke. At last he opened it and read the first line of her looping script. He frowned. Snotsniffer? As children they'd teased one another, but she'd always treated him like a person, if not exactly an equal. He read the rest of the letter, his hackles rising, then sat at the writing desk with a pen and inkpot and scribbled furiously. When he'd filled a page, he proofread his handiwork. Finishing the second draft, he fumbled in his pockets and extracted the flower hatpin Ada had taken from the Smith crypt. The pin was the prettiest thing he had on hand, and dropping it in the Mudtyne would be a waste. He folded the pin inside the letter and sealed it with candle wax stamped with his physician's medallion.

Roger found the messenger studying an unlit cigar in the courtyard. He marched up and offered the envelope, but as the messenger reached for it, Roger wrenched off the man's dust mask and goggles.

"Harrod." Roger spat at the ground. "I thought it were you. You never told me you'd gotten the Order of the Kraken. And I thought you insufferable before, with your fancy schooling and navy togs. But now you're an even more arrogant twit."

"You never asked. Brother."

"And I bowed to you. Twice!"

"You'll bow again. When I leave."

"I won't make that mistake again."

Harrod crossed his arms. "I had hoped on my return to find you'd overcome your youthful folly. You could have had a life of service, military or otherwise. Service of the domestic sort was good enough for our mother. And your father." His voice had lost its previous hoarseness. He must have disguised it on purpose. "But you, Roger, respect nothing. Not laws, nor etiquette, nor your betters. And, I see, not even the sanctity of the dead goes undefiled at your hands. My own brother turns out to be a bodysnatcher and butcher of human flesh!"

Harrod had never said so many words to Roger at once. He'd been away since Roger was a boy, and the seven years between them in age made for awkward interactions during Harrod's rare shore leave. Once, as a midshipman, Harrod had taken him for a row on the Mudtyne, hoping to entice him into the sailors' life. But Roger, ten at the time, had turned green almost immediately and been sick all over himself. Harrod, always efficient, tossed him overboard for "disrespecting the ship." Though he'd quickly hauled him up again, Roger refused to speak to his brother for the rest of his shore leave and hadn't set foot on a boat since.

"I'm not–" Roger began, but his brother cut him off.

"You could have started off as I did, in the lowly yet respectable role of quarter-gunner."

"Easily done when you're the bastard son of a toff and learned to talk all posh-like at Donnellan." Roger's father certainly couldn't afford such schooling.

"You might still make a decent footman, if you watch your tongue. I did my duty at sea, earned a commission, honors, a ship, and lately a much sought-after post alongside royalty." Harrod's lip curled. "And now I've returned to Caligo for the present, as naval liaison to the Ordnance Board. Good things come to those who know their place."

Roger had stopped listening halfway through Harrod's speech. "To think, all this time I thought you was off pickling yourself in the briny deeps. How long have you been working for Sibet? You're her letter-carrier now? What kind of navy post is that?"

"Sibet? You still presume to address her highness by a nickname?" Harrod shook his head disapprovingly.

Roger gripped his letter so hard it crinkled. "I suppose your high opinion of me matches hers. Scrape me off your shoe with a stick, why don't you?"

"You speak of her highness as if you considered yourself her *peer*." Harrod expelled this last word like a bit of gristle. "A pity, that. I'd hoped to find you... contrite. I thought her letter might make you reconsider your future. It wasn't easy, but I've arranged a footman's position for you in a respectable household. You'll have room, board, and work better suited to your–"

"These class differences you harp upon ain't real!" Roger shouted. "No human is better than another. I've cut up enough of 'em, and we all look more or less the same on the inside. We all rot when we're dead. A smart man may have a small brain, or the other way 'round. Royals claim their faerie magic, but it's all smoke and mirrors. I grovel only so I don't hang. Enjoy your golden chains and your charmed life, and leave me alone."

"Look at yourself, Roger," barked Harrod. "Your hands are stained with blood. You have Lady-knows-what all over your shirt. And do I smell gin on your breath? Have you bathed in a fortnight? If our mother were alive, you'd have killed her seven times over."

"And maybe if I'd had surgeon's training back then, she never would have died. My last shelling paid for the physician who arrived too late to treat her consumption, though he did all he could. If anyone killed her it was you, for having a jolly time at sea during her final weeks, though I must have sent a dozen letters. I fixed her tea, and plumped her pillows, and wiped the blood from her chin. You only paid for the funeral."

Harrod's expression softened, and his tone became that of an adult explaining to a child why treacle pudding was to be eaten only after supper. "And now that I'm stationed in Caligo, Roger, I mean to intercede as our mother would have wished. I want to help you divert your many energies toward a more… socially respectable end. But you are far beyond help. Perhaps I've made a mistake in coming here."

"Says the high and mighty postman." Roger's hands had curled into fists. Now his eyes, to his profound horror, blurred with tears. "I could just hit you."

"Remember what happened last time. When you were, what, fifteen?" Harrod tapped his medal. "May I suggest you see me off with a bow instead? It's for your own good."

Roger swung. He'd built up his arms during his midnight cemetery raids and had confidence in his own strength. He should have knocked Harrod's mouth clean of teeth, but his brother dodged nimbly aside. Harrod grabbed Roger by the collar and retaliated with a cross-jab of his own. His knuckles struck below Roger's left eye. Sparks burst across his vision. He fought to keep his balance, but Harrod swept his legs out from under him with a well-timed kick. He slammed Roger facedown on the ground and held him there.

"Don't tell her about this," Roger gasped when he could breathe again. "Please."

"Give me the letter."

Roger blinked. The letter lay between the ground and his face. His hat, now dented, had rolled to one side. Blood dripped from his mouth onto the paper.

"No. I need to rewrite it…"

"Absolutely not. I'm not waiting another two hours for you to decide which end of the pen to dip into the ink." Harrod snatched up the letter. With a grimace, he tucked it inside his leather satchel.

"I won't bow."

Harrod glanced down his nose at Roger. "As long as you're down there, it's close enough for me."

4

Your Most Royal Highness,

Were I a gentleman, Id have returned your letter unread. You called me that dire nickname from long ago. It would take both my hands to count the years since I were a scruffy lad with a headcold. But I were just one of many running about Malmouth Palace, and Im certain all us sickly lads got struck with your same insults, and your kisses, like we was one and the same. Could you even pick out my face from the others after all this time?

I laugh at your suggestion that I had aught to do with a Mistress Dorinda Deer. If you was of lower birth, Id think you was jealous. Werent she the queens almighty maid back then? All I know is I only spoke to her when she had me take washing to the line. Has boredom driven you to fits?

Yes, I am a Professional now, and my own man. Through my medical work I lay eyes and hands on all matter of Curious, Morbid things. This week a woman who suffered premature burial lay upon our hospital slab. Some poor Miss Smith she were, and had a most unhappy look about her as I dare not further describe to a lady. But imagine the thoughts one would have upon waking in a dark box, ones friends and family thinking one dead! Her face looked somewhat like that Dorinda you seem so jealous of.

Pray tell, your Majesticness, is my own brother Harrod back in

Caligo for good? I saw him last eight years ago. He were always the lapdog around you royal lot. A decade at sea has made him a right pickled pilchard. Still after me to take a job licking some toff's boots, I expect. If he returns with a plum eye and no teeth, it were me. I shall take the hangmans noose afore I let him run my life.

My hand hurts from this awful writing. Beg pardon if I havent kept in touch, Your Imenint Majesty, as my betters wont allow it. Mayhap your not as priggish as you pretend. Id have visited, but theyd bash my head in even if I wore clean socks. By the sound of it, you would, too. Please accept the enclosed token as befits your Generous Condescension.

Your most Humble and Obedient Servant,
Roger X. Weathersby, a Man of Science

Harrod. Sibylla took a deep breath to calm herself as she set her empty teacup aside. She'd thrown that letter she'd inked to Roger into the fire. Somehow the captain had rescued and delivered it, crumpled like rubbish as it had been.

She flipped over Roger's reply. She didn't want to see any more of it. Reading his handwriting felt like divining wax drippings. She'd expected his penmanship to improve after so many years. It hadn't. Harrod had always warned her if she ever sought Roger again she'd soon regret her sentimentality, and oh, how he loved a good object lesson.

Whether she liked it or not, Roger had turned into one of the most ostentatious writers she'd ever had the displeasure to come across, as in love with his own words as he was with his transgressions. Sighing, she flexed her fingers. Black ink-bees flew from her fingertips, a habit of idle pondering, weaving through the air like insects until her mind wandered and they diffused in inky puffs.

Her other hand fiddled with the pin he'd sent, a peach-blossom hatpin she knew from somewhere. Perhaps she'd seen it on a baronetess, or in a shop. As she tried to recall the memory, another bee took flight, and then another, creating a swarm that threatened to engulf the room. Just then, a cluster of bees careened into the windowpane, leaving a slur of ink that reminded Sibylla of a scene in *The Reluctant Milliner* where the titular character was tarred and feathered on stage.

As a child, she'd attended a holiday production of that black-hearted comedy where a then-ingénue Angeline had performed as Madam Barstowe. The hatpin was a piece of her costume. Sibylla studied it up close when her mother took her to meet the actors backstage. Now the self-styled *Dame* Angeline had a different reputation. She was as well known for her charities as for her salon, where she played matchmaker between lonely noblemen and her curated collection of beautiful yet desperate young women. Sibylla dropped the pin onto the table, and the bees above her left hand scattered and dispersed into the air.

Why had Roger sent her such a thing, and how should she respond? In a fit of bitterness, Sibylla smashed the teacup on the table. The porcelain shattered, and a sliver of blood appeared on her thumb where a piece had nicked her skin.

Lieutenant Calloway, always a breath outside her door, burst into her room. His cheery eyes narrowed on the broken teacup as Sibylla shifted her skirts to hide the pin.

"My dear highness, you mustn't budge." Lieutenant Calloway dashed across the room and swept up the broken teacup with meticulous speed.

Unlike Harrod, who addressed her out of an ingrained respect for formality, Lieutenant Calloway relished her title like a sugar cube melting on his tongue. As sixth in line to inherit the crown, Sibylla had grown accustomed to the phrase "your highness," her title a cold barrier to the people and things she wanted. She'd had the unique pleasure of forgetting she was the daughter of a duke while at Helmscliff – until this lieutenant had arrived to remind her in the most irritating manner.

After he'd wrapped the teacup shards in his handkerchief, Lieutenant Calloway reached for Sibylla's hands to check for cuts. Fearful of the fuss he'd make over a mere nick, she hastily retreated her hands to her lap. His cheeks blushed in response. Perhaps he mistook her reaction for coquetry.

"The teacup slipped," she explained.

"Your highness must feel nervous."

"Why would I be nervous?" Sibylla checked whether, if by some mishap of her mind, she'd left Roger's letter in plain sight. Slowly, she released a relieved breath. The correspondence lay hidden beneath a stack of music sheets for the concertina.

"I know of no respectable gentleman or lady who enjoys the company of doctors," said Lieutenant Calloway matter-of-factly. "And with the new royal physician visiting tomorrow, you must be in a state."

Sibylla's brow crinkled. "I wasn't aware of a new royal physician."

Lieutenant Calloway beamed. He loved to gossip, but Helmscliff provided him few opportunities. Lady Wayfeather was of no interest to him and most of the soldiers stationed at the estate were on the verge of retirement. That left only the footmen, housemaids, and chef, each as dull to him as a Glaskin Street clockmaker.

"Apparently, during her royal majesty the queen's royal tour of the sloping moors, she suffered a terrible malady, and this country doctor saved her life. However, no one seems to be able to account for his family or place of birth. I assure you I would never be so presumptuous as to question her royal majesty, but to knight a man of such profession, and from such low stock…" Lieutenant Calloway clucked and shook his head disapprovingly, then added, "If it were within my power, I wouldn't allow him within a breath of you."

"I imagine it would be difficult to treat one's patients without seeing them."

Sibylla tugged her sleeve's carnation ruffle. True to his word, Lieutenant Calloway had "rectified" her wardrobe by replacing her charcoal and brown dresses with enough frilly, pastel frocks that she couldn't look at a macaron without shuddering. At least today, the numerous folds of her sugary gown were useful in hiding a certain insulting hatpin.

Sibylla glanced at the lieutenant. If he wanted to continue idling here, he could at least assuage her curiosity over how Roger might have come to possess Angeline's costume trinket. "Have you ever been to Dame Angeline's salon?" she asked.

Lieutenant Calloway sucked in his breath. "Some gentlemen might enjoy the company of a questionable lady from time to time, but I would never attend that kind of salon. I've heard, of course, that nothing too shameful happens there, and you shouldn't worry over any comparisons."

"Comparisons?"

"I mean to say comparisons between a proper lady and one who might be found in such a place. You're more beautiful than even the least clothed of women. While they may be of measured caliber, they are not noble-blooded, like you and I."

"You said you'd never been there," Sibylla reminded him. "Do you know whether Dame Angeline still wears her old theater costumes? I remember she had a certain floral hatpin that was quite exquisite. I may have noticed someone carrying it recently and wondered whether she gave such trinkets to all her admirers these days."

Lieutenant Calloway fidgeted and averted his eyes. "Her salon's ladies have been known to give certain hatpins as promise gifts to handsome men who win their hearts, but such pins are hardly awarded to any old jacksnipe. However if you've happened to glimpse a few, say, tucked inside a distinguished gentleman's upturned hat, there's no need to be concerned. Many loves are one-sided, so rest assured your highness, that simply because a man collects such pins, it doesn't mean his heart is taken."

"So these pins are produced en masse, and men who frequent Dame Angeline's establishment are known to collect them." Sibylla continued to fuss with her sleeve. She didn't know whether to feel better or worse that Roger had given her a common trinket. "Wouldn't a man who visits need to be wealthy?"

"Considerably so. Only the best gentlemen are allowed through that salon's front door. People of means. People of birth."

"Or at least people who can talk their way in." Roger had always been able to talk his way into her room, and apparently plenty of others. Inwardly she fumed. If he intended to crow about his conquests by attaching a disreputable pin to his letter, then he was a bigger fool than she remembered. An object lesson indeed.

"Even then, one would have to show considerable charm to receive such a gift." Lieutenant Calloway smoothed the ends of his mustache. "Should I take it jewels are the way to your highness' heart?"

Sibylla sighed, but cut off a sharp retort. The lieutenant might be annoying, but aside from Lady Wayfeather, no one at Helmscliff said more than "yes, ma'am" or "no, ma'am" to her. At least Lieutenant Calloway provided her a connection to the city she missed – lurid tales of the Greyanchor Strangler's latest victim, descriptions of the plaid bonnets popular in the capital, the latest beau of Earl Granden's winsome niece. And for that, she could swallow some bitter tea.

"I prefer sweets actually. Didn't you say the latest Greyanchor victim was a purveyor of chocolates?"

Lieutenant Calloway's eyes brightened at the chance to relay some scandal. "I heard the man had one hand about her throat with the other stuffed in a box of truffles."

"One wonders, then," Sibylla mused, "why the constables haven't caught him in the act."

If she'd been in the city, she'd have arranged a reward for information leading to this monster's capture. With access to the palace's paper stores, she'd ink posters warning women to lock their doors and kick suspicious strangers in the shin. After all, her inking magic and skill at reproductions rivaled a printing press. She might even convince the queen she had more to offer Myrcnia than becoming her cousin's wife.

Later that night, she sat on the edge of her bed, Roger's letter in hand. The candlewick had long since burnt out, and now she had no light save her own. As she concentrated, prickles of energy flickered through her, turning her fair skin a translucent blue. Her veins bled a purple-violet glow, and her hair and eyelashes turned white. Every part of her radiated like a human jellyfish.

Sibylla's glow, shared by her father, grandmother, and great-grandfather, had been part of the royal family bloodline since Saint-Queen Ingrid. After a snowstorm stranded an expedition of miners in the mountain pass between Myrcnia and neighboring Haupentaup, Queen Ingrid alone rode into the night to find them, radiating light from her veins, and thus earned the title of Saint-Queen. Sibylla stared at her own purple-violet glow. She'd done nothing more heroic than light her way to the palace kitchens without wasting a candle.

But as the royal line of Muir considered their magic divine, a blessing to set them above the commoners and their counterparts in other nations, Sibylla was still expected to embody those old legends. Even among the magically gifted noble houses, the royals alone had cathedrals built in their names. Unfortunately, she'd only ever cared for the family legend explaining the origins of their magic, especially when her father sat beside her bed at night with light in his veins and the candles blown out.

He'd begin: centuries ago, from the whirlpool off Fillsbirth's coast, a fisherman caught a water sprite. In exchange for her freedom, she granted him three wishes. First, he asked to be king, second for a ladylove, and the final wish he saved. One morning, this fisherman-turned-king met a beautiful woman on the strand and begged her to marry him. She would only say yes if every full moon he allowed her to leave him for one night. The king agreed and the royal couple had five princes, all blessed with magic. According to her father, this marked the founding of the royal Muir line, and Sibylla was a descendant of the eldest prince.

One might think with five princes, Myrcnia would have been overrun with magic by now, but that wasn't the case. The gifts often died out after a few generations, and noble houses that lost their magic entirely would have their titles removed. However, the royal Muir line never wavered in its strength. The church called it divine, but perhaps pressuring granddaughters to marry their cousins, along with the careful culling of bastards, had something to do with the "miracle."

The next part of the story was Sibylla's favorite. A drunken knight visiting from a neighboring kingdom pointed out that trusting one's wife with mysterious agreements was never a good idea. So on the next full moon, the king followed the queen to the shore where, as Sibylla's father relished telling, he found his bathing wife splashing with the tail of a grayling fish. The sprite cried for the king to forgive her falsehood, but instead he used his last wish to curse his wife back to the whirlpool whence she came.

As stated in the church's genealogical records, Sibylla was the descendant of a half-fish faerie who lived in a whirlpool and had blessed her descendants with magic. And so Sibylla had believed when she came of age, her legs would fuse together into a silver-red tail and she'd swim to the whirlpool to be reunited with the water sprite.

At age twelve, she'd been disappointed when her first gift manifested as the same translucent skin with glowing veins her father and grandmother displayed in country festivals. She and Roger had been hiding in a closet from the head steward, sitting with their knees touching. They'd snatched a jar of candied peach slices from the kitchen, and she divided them up, first popping one into her own mouth, then holding one out for him. He bit into the slice, then his lips closed around her sugarcoated fingers. She yelped in surprise, and a ripple of bluish light coursed through her veins, illuminating the dark closet in one bright flash. Roger shrieked. She revived him with a pinch on his neck.

For months afterward, she persuaded him to follow her whims by threatening to light up in the dark. It wasn't her fault he was such a milksop. As teenagers, his eagerness to kiss her had eventually subsumed his fear of her gifts – she hadn't been so reluctant herself.

The tip of her finger traced his signature. Was this letter really written by that same lad? She suspected years of reading dry books about anatomy had done him more harm than good.

Before she dealt with the younger brother, she had a few words for the older. With fresh paper in one hand, black ink bloomed beneath her fingernails. She'd covered two pages with complaints for Captain Harrod Starkley – beginning with his unsanctioned turn as postman and ending with his unbearable replacement, Lieutenant Calloway. Then she curled up on her side and pulled the blanket snug around her shoulders. Dame Angeline's salon pin rested on the table beside her bed, and she still couldn't imagine what had possessed Roger to send such an inappropriate memento. By the time Sibylla had conceived of a response to his letter, it was morning's glow, not her own, lighting the paper.

5

The following afternoon, Roger scouted out the Tenderbone Internment Ground, a cemetery for paupers and prostitutes, intending to unearth another corpse later that night. He was still short on cash to pay for his rent, never mind a proper medical education.

He put on his worker's cap, stuck a surveyor's folding ruler in his pocket, and let himself in by the crooked lychgate. Scouting in the daylight made for easier hauls after dark.

Tenderbone had been a churchyard since ancient times, but its church had gone to ruin long ago. Now more potter's field than cemetery, the dead were buried anonymously in trenches. Every new excavation churned up bone fragments and splinters of rotten coffin-wood, to be picked over by the ragmen and sold for a few winkles a bucketful.

The most recent burial trench had been dug two weeks ago, which meant it would be almost full now. Bodies were placed in the trenches gradually, topped with layers of thick clay and cobbles to deter bodysnatchers. But diggers, eager to pack in as many layers as possible, often skimped on the topmost corpses, covering them with barely a foot of earth – easy pickings for a resurrectionist working alone.

Roger strode about with a bundle of flagged stakes under his arm, loudly counting his steps, meanwhile casing the area for newly disturbed earth. This proved difficult, as most of the churchyard had a wet, tilled look. If there had been a trench, it was filled in completely.

As expected, the sexton from the adjacent Chapel of St Celia the Devout – a wooden hut in the shadow of the church ruins – wandered over to chat.

"Where's Mr Mortlocke?" asked the sexton. "Kicked the bucket at last?"

"Oh, I hope not sir." Roger unfolded his ruler, pretending to measure the distance between his randomly placed stakes. "Last I heard he was in bed with the bottle-ache."

"Well, one can hope. We could use an industrious lad like you to do the surveying. Usually by the time Mr Mortlocke pops by, our digger is jimmying the last few stiffs into the ground with a crowbar." The sexton clapped Roger heartily on the shoulder. "You might want to move your stakes about ten paces left. We only dug here last month. Best to wait a few more weeks before digging again."

"Very good sir, as you say," Roger grinned.

After the sexton returned to his chapel, Roger hammered in a flagged stake where he stood so he could find the spot later that night. Gathering up his equipment, he made for home to catch a nap before the real work began. However, the clouds scudded west after sunset, and a full moon was forecast to rise by midnight – bad conditions for a resurrectionist. Perhaps a night off would be best, as the shock from his Greyanchor outing hadn't yet worn off.

In the end, he enjoyed a supper of mutton pie and ale at the Fox & Weasel, and a hornpipe to impress the pubkeeper's daughter. The girl had laughed at first, then told him to stop or he'd make himself ill. Blood seeped intermittently from his nose where Harrod had struck him. He begged off early at a quarter to midnight due to a splitting headache.

Roger awoke next morning in just his trousers and boots, with a wad of wet flannel pressed to his nose. Nail, the undertaker's apprentice, stood over him. He was a tall, red-haired youth with a dour expression mimicked from a death mask.

"Mr Grausam has a job fer you," said Nail, whisking the blanket off Roger's cot.

Roger groaned. "I thought *you* were there to mix up Mr Grausam's preserving fluids and upholster his coffins, not me. I don't take no half-shelling for pallbearing neither. I'm a professional now. You tell him." He grabbed at the blanket, but Nail flicked it out of his reach.

Nail wrinkled his nose. He eyed the pail near the door containing a dead cat – Roger had tried and failed to revive the poor thing after it ate a poisoned rat. He had intended to keep it for a practice dissection, but time had gotten away from him and now it stunk.

"Aye, you've really moved up in the world, Mr Weathersby, Esquire. Mr Grausam said your night-owling would get you retired to Ol' Grim fer good."

"And you woke me up for that?" Roger stood – a difficult business in his cramped garret with its angled ceiling – and cast about for a shirt less filthy than the one he'd worn the day before. His only shirt without bloodstains was rusty with cemetery clay. He had two shirts in total. This was a problem. "I don't pinch Grausam's stiffs no more, and he already fired me twice, but that's water under the scaffold as it were. What does he care about how I spend my nights?" A thought crossed Roger's mind. He frowned. "He's not looking to buy my wares, is he?"

"I think not." Nail tossed the blanket at Roger. "We're a tad short on mutes. Funeral fer that actress, Lady Margalotte. Didn't you hear?"

Mutes were professional mourners hired to attend funeral processions for stiffs who'd left enough coin behind to afford them. They wore swaths of black crape, trailing hatbands, and miserable expressions, due more to the grim weather than grief.

Nail handed Roger two slips of paper. "The top one is a map to the home of the bereaved. Be there by noon tomorrow, and plan to stay till the funeral procession at dusk. That other paper there is yer laundry receipt fer the black togs. I'm to say you'll be fully ree-imb-arsed."

"A mute, hey?" Roger opted for his bloodstained shirt – less stiff than the clay-caked one. If he could remember to keep his coat buttoned until he had a new shirt, it would serve well enough. "That's worse than a pallbearer. What'll I get, five winkles? Four?"

Nail scratched an old smallpox scar on his cheekbone. "Beggars can't be choosers, Mr Weathersby. But there might be hot punch if the air is chill. I hear there'll be a right supply of fair women present, Angeline's upper-class salon girls. Margalotte was one herself, they say, before the poor lamb was strangled." The apprentice grinned. "You heard of her?"

"No." Roger buttoned his shirt. "And tell Mr Grausam I'm doing him a favor by not tempting myself to bag your latest stiff." In truth, he was sorely tempted. This fresh stiff would bring a good price at Eldridge's. Still, he knew better than to admit his interest to an undertaker.

Nail shrugged and moved for the door. "When you change your mind, you know where to go." He doffed his hat with a smirk. "I'll see you tomorrow at noon. An' don't forget the mask. Your face has the look of a blueberry pie soakin' through the top crust."

After Nail had gone, Roger opened a leather-bound journal and flipped past dozens of drawings to the first blank page. While he found journaling a nuisance, he documented his practice dissections with diagrams and terms he wanted to remember. Most recently the butcher's wife had given him a sheep's heart, and he'd sketched it in charcoal, annotating the chambers and tubes.

He finally had time to get to the cat. At the top of his page he wrote "digestive system." He set the journal on the bed and prepared his anatomy space. His table was made of stacked crates with a cupboard door laid across them, and on this he set a wooden tray, an old scalpel and other donated rusted instruments Dr Eldridge had spared from the rubbish heap. First he cut down the length of his specimen's abdomen, and found the bony tube of the trachea with his fingers. Gently, he peeled the skin back, prying away thin webs of underlying tissue to reveal the viscera beneath. He traced the digestive system just as he had during the dissection at Eldridge's. As he unraveled the intestines with his fingers, a creak on the stairs made him turn.

"Am I interrupting your breakfast, man of science?" Harrod, wearing a hooded oilskin raincoat, stood in the doorway with a letter in his gloved hand. "What a smell."

"What do you want?" Roger stuffed the entrails back into the abdominal cavity and jabbed the scalpel into the dead cat's thigh, where it stuck like a tiny harpoon. "Don't you have better things to do?" He plunged his hands into a basin of rainwater and dried them on his only spare shirt – it was filthy anyway. If Harrod expected him to bow, he could break his back first.

Instead, Harrod handed him a letter. "Please limit your response to a page. I don't have much time to spare."

Roger tore the princess' seal. The hatpin he'd sent fell from the letter. He skimmed the contents.

Dear Roger,

Since you have no fondness for childhood nicknames, I'll reserve them for all those other boys whom I so cruelly abused with my kisses, as they might wish to hear from my lips more than you obviously do.

What I find truly remarkable, however, is your audacity in sending me a pin from Dame Angeline's salon. If you meant to imply that I am at all like Dame Angeline, collecting the poor to pad my heart, then I'm sickened to think of the feelings I once expressed toward you, as they were shamefully genuine. The only thing more astonishing is how you might have come by such a trinket, having neither the title nor wealth her salon demands. But then I suppose you have experience in wearing down the fairer sex with your charms. In the future, perhaps you should avoid finely dressed women altogether.

Lastly, as concerns your brother, you may wish to reconsider your opinion. Unless, judging by the blood upon your last letter, you simply enjoy a good beating. He's one of the few men I've seen to land a blow over Cotton Mouth McCleary in the ring, and that is no small feat. He's hardly some despicable lout. Harrod's reasons for being long at sea are as pitiable as they are commendable, and one day I hope you discover how mistaken you've been in your pettifogging. Even when he has good cause to resent his position in life, he holds himself above reproach. He's not the kind to force one into wearing despicable clothes or make one read insipid gardening books. His two years as my warden protector are the closest I'll ever have to what you so abjectly take for granted.

Sincerely,
Sibylla

All Roger saw was one backhanded insult after another, reminding him of his place beneath her, Harrod, this high-class Angeline lady, and finely dressed people in general. He crumpled the letter in his fist.

"A gentleman always drafts his response before disposing of his correspondence," said Harrod. "Not that you are one. Do you even have the means to respond?" His eyes swept the room as though paper couldn't possibly exist there.

"I ain't responding to that."

"My mistake. The squalor of your abode is beyond the pale. Living alongside dead cats and disgusting jars of floating rubbish. How she ever looked your way, with her bearing and wits, is beyond my comprehension. But I suppose your third-rate letters provide her amusement. You've no idea how bored she is."

Roger discreetly closed his journal and slid it under the cot. He returned the cat to its bucket, his concentration ruined. "Some of us do actual work for the betterment of society," he spat. "You can go right back to the palace to tell her I'm too busy to write."

"Princess Sibylla is not currently at the palace. She has been away these past two years, not that it is any concern of yours."

"You're right. It's no concern of mine. And I'm no concern of hers." To hell with the lot of them uppercrust pies. No matter how Harrod and Sibylla harassed him, Roger couldn't care less what they thought. He didn't regret making his first dissection, unearthing that first stiff, or leaving the palace. And certainly not changing his name to Weathersby.

"But you're *my* concern." When Roger didn't respond, Harrod shrugged and inspected the slips of paper Nail had left. "At least you are not entirely devoid of worthy employment opportunities."

"That mute job ain't worth my time."

"Your time? I could scrape two shellings together, and your time would be worth less than the metal shavings. As for *my* time, I've wasted enough." He turned to leave.

"I changed my mind." Roger retrieved his journal and tore out the last page. He scribbled a terse note with his stick of charcoal.

I thank your highness for putting me in my place. I will stay far from wellborn ladies since you say so. Now leave me alone.

Yr most hmbl & obt svt,
rxw

He folded the page into a tight square and thrust it at Harrod. "Be sure to give her a nice deep bow from me."

"Ever the petulant child." Harrod set a shelling on the table. "Go buy yourself a more palatable meal than whatever is in your bucket."

Roger ran to the door and threw the coin down the stairs, but Harrod had already rounded the corner. It struck the wall and tinkled against the metal railings.

A door on the landing below opened with a creak, and Mrs Carver, the butcher's wife, called up to him. "Who was that dapper naval man? Not your brother to visit you at last?"

"No, ma'am," he called down in as calm a voice as he could manage. "Just a man to tell me my brother's been lost at sea." The force of Roger slamming the door shut sent Nail's receipts fluttering to the floor. As Roger stared down at them, something Nail had said floated to the surface.

Angeline's ladies even, as Margalotte was one herself, they say, before the poor lamb was strangled.

Another strangling.

He thought of the woman he had resurrected a few days ago. Could the two be connected? Seemed unlikely… but then again…

Curiosity got the best of him. He was a man of science after all. He could at least ensure Margalotte wasn't buried alive. That settled it. He would take the mute job, and maybe discover clues to Claudine's

45

mysterious death. Perhaps he'd even figure out why the hatpin he'd found in her casket had offended the princess so.

Roger hid the deplorable state of his dissecting-room clothes under his greatcoat. He'd intended to buy new garments with his recent earnings, but first he'd paid Mrs Carver two months of back rent while promising this month's payment within the week, bought a round for the regulars at the Fox & Weasel and acquired that flashy new hat to replace the one he'd lost. He figured he'd rather go about town without his trousers than without a hat.

Out on the street, Roger spent a few winkles on hot cross buns, eating two and pocketing one for later. He felt better with food in his stomach. More coins disappeared into the pocket of the boy who gave Roger's boots a much-needed shine. From what was left of Dr Eldridge's payment, Roger had just enough to pay the laundry to lease him the mute costume. He'd have to go without cash until he settled with Mr Grausam on the morrow. One missed supper wouldn't do him in.

He found the laundry in a dingy side street he didn't frequent much. The building was cramped with washtubs where girls churned the clothes with large wooden paddles.

"Ahoy hoy!" called Roger. The smell of ash-lye rekindled his headache. "I'm here for a set, all black."

"Mute, are you?" The head laundress, with arms like a stoker's, snatched the ticket from his hand. "Girl! Bring out that set of afflictions for the–" She looked Roger up and down, pausing at his new hat and his contused face. "–for the *man*." He was unworthy of the prefix "gentle", apparently.

The girl appeared from the back room, staggering under the mound of black material. "Your afflictions, sir." She placed the articles on an ironing table as the head laundress read them off the list.

"Frock coat, half-cape, silk cravat, wool trousers, crape hatband, calico weskit, all in black. That will be one and five, mister."

"Much obliged, mistress. And you, young miss."

Roger's heart leapt to his throat when he met the girl's eye. It was Ada. From the cemetery.

She wore her dark hair pinned up, and a shapeless green smock that made her look like a single onion in a sack made for two dozen. "Or should I say… Ghostofmary."

The head laundress growled. "I tolerate no oaths under this roof."

"Apologies, mistress. Have you a spare room where I might trade out my togs? I'd hoped to leave my own to be cleaned, but I have no other change."

"You might make do in the yard. Ada will show you."

"You look a sad drip today, Ghostofmary," whispered Roger as Ada preceded him wordlessly into the courtyard. His breath formed a white cloud. "You make a livelier ghost than a laundress. Give us a smile. Don't you remember me?"

"Here's your changing curtain, mister sack-'em-up man." Ada scowled and pointed to a sheet with two corners pinned to a clothesline. "Or whatever your name is, as you never did bother to tell."

"It's Roger." He tossed her his hat, then ducked behind the sheet and unbuttoned his coat. "Roger Weathersby. I'm sorry if I forgot to tell you before. Is that why you're glum?"

The other laundresses had noticed Roger's entrance to the courtyard. Their muffled laughter grew, and a few bolder ones tried to peek behind the curtain while he was removing his shirt.

"Roger, yeah?" called one lass with wild red curls. "Oh, I bet you do!"

The girls burst into fresh peals of laughter. "Rogerin' Roger!"

Through a gap between the hanging sheets, Roger glimpsed Ada tossing a pebble at the laundry window. The head laundress emerged wielding a dolly stick and brought the yard to order. She herded the girls inside, leaving only Ada alone to hold the sheet so it wouldn't billow in the wind.

"They was trying to see your smallclothes," said Ada in her same lifeless tone. "But I knows you haven't got any."

"What?" Roger shivered. Quickly, he fastened the fall-front of the black trousers and pulled on the black shirt that smelled faintly of lye. "You didn't see nothing. I was very discreet."

"I don't have to see to know. You've a streak of dandy in you, mister sack-'em-up. If a working man spends his metal on silk hats an' scarves, he must go as a pauper elsewhere. That's what my mother taught me, anyhow." At the mention of her mother, Ada sniffled.

Roger let his half-tied cravat unravel from his neck. He knelt before the girl and clasped her hands between his.

"What's wrong, Ada?"

Ada ducked her face away. "Your type waits with his shovel ready for them as falls ill."

"Ada!" Roger placed an awkward hand on her shoulder, but she shoved him off.

"You'll trade her in for a tailored weskit, won't you? Like a scrap of tin jewelry to pawn." On this last word Ada thumped Roger hard in the chest, then sobbed into her hands. This time when Roger gathered her to him, she pressed her tear-streaked face into his shoulder.

"I'm sorry… about damping… your afflictions…" Ada moaned.

"Mourning clothes are meant to be cried upon." Roger laid a hand on her head. "There now, take a deep breath. Better? Tell me about your mother. Where is she now?"

Ada sniffed and wiped her face on her sleeve. "At Miss Estella's."

"Is she a relative?"

"A friend. From her work. But Ma's got the burning. They won't let her be a night faerie no more, because of what's in her."

"Has a physician been sent for?"

Ada glared at Roger as if he'd offered to get his shovel. Her words crackled like musket shots. "Doctors. Won't. See. Whores. That is the *law*."

Roger flinched. "I could see her," he suggested before he knew what he was saying.

"Lots of gentlemen see her. Just not doctors. And you ain't neither."

"No, but see, I'm learning to be one – a doctor I mean. You can take your gentlemen and hang 'em."

"You'll be the one hanging," snuffled Ada, but she gave a weak smile.

Roger tried to remember what medical instruments lay strewn about his room, and whether they'd been recently cleaned. But he had no medicines, not even gin. From the sound of it, some tincture to ease the pain might be the only thing to do much good.

"After this mute job, I'll look for you at the necropolis gate. We'll see your ma together. Gentlemen aren't the only ones who know how to treat a lady, you'll see." Roger rummaged through the pockets of his old clothes. "Until tonight, here's a hot cross bun for Ghostofmary. May she only haunt me half-heartedly."

"Dirty graverobber." Ada knocked him hard in the shoulder, smiling, then devoured the bun in three bites.

6

Sibylla stiffened as Dr Lundfrigg, the new royal physician, set his bag on the card table and wet his fingers in a porcelain bowl of icewater. He flicked his fingers before removing the lower tube of his medical cane in a few practiced twists. While Lady Wayfeather acted as chaperone, watching from the corner of Sibylla's bedroom for signs of gentlemanly misbehavior, the doctor attached the removable bell to an earpiece and constructed his stethoscope.

By the cut of Dr Lundfrigg's suit, Sibylla could tell he'd been knighted and given a well-paid position at court but had no idea how to dress. She jealously studied him, curious what the queen valued so much in this new doctor as to remove the previous royal physician from his post.

His peach waistcoat bunched above his sallow pigskin trousers as he fiddled with his instruments, and he wore a cravat so festooned with lace and ruffles it looked like a swan had been stuffed neck-first down his collar. While obviously he had spent a considerable fortune at Butterwick's Emporium for Gentlemen, he'd never fit in with the noble crowd. How mercilessly her cousins must mock him behind closed doors.

"Are we feeling sprightly today, your highness?" He bowed, waiting for permission to approach. "No aches or sniffles? Any recent bouts of listlessness or hysteria that I should know of?"

"None," Sibylla said. "I'm sorry you had to make the journey from Caligo – I doubt you'll find any maladies to excite you here. When I require a physician, I send for one."

Dr Lundfrigg leaned his ear toward Sibylla's chest before remembering the apparatus in his hands. She breathed in and out at his command while counting the ridges in her room's molding. The doctor hummed as he jotted notations into a slender black book that reminded her of journals Roger had once used to copy pages from medical texts she'd lent him from the royal library.

"Ah, yes," he said. "A lovely set of lungs indeed."

He lowered his stethoscope to her abdomen to listen to her internals. She doubted he'd hear anything through the layers of muslin and silk.

"Have you been eating well? Do you have trouble sleeping?" A pocket mirror angled sunlight into her pupils. "Could you open your mouth, dear? Let's have a look at that silver tongue of yours."

At last he pronounced her physical complete, then removed a box from his bag, opening it to reveal a syringe. Sibylla swallowed. The needle spanned the length of a palm, and the glass vial was the width of a jam jar.

"I've no need of painkillers," she interjected.

"Oh no. Your highness misunderstands," Dr Lundfrigg smiled. "I'll merely be borrowing a sample of your blood."

Sibylla slipped back a step. "Why would you need such a thing?"

She had enough bloodletting in her life already. With her chapel's monstrance being used by bishops to give absolutions – spring, summer, autumn, and winter – drops of her blood mixed in wine graced the lips of countless Myrcnians, from cheating husbands and unfaithful wives to children who had lied about stealing pies.

She must have grimaced, for Dr Lundfrigg attempted to reassure her. "As the royal physician, I am most keen to investigate the divine sanguine spirit. King Indulf was the last of your highness' forbearers to embrace scientific advancements, and in the two hundred years since his reign, foolish superstition has stymied many fields of research. But I foresee the dawn of a new age of reason, where educated minds like yours will lead the people out of this darkness."

"While I appreciate your enthusiasm–" Sibylla took a step toward Lady Wayfeather "–let's not hastily forget our lessons. King Indulf gave his hair and blood to his chemists to develop a healing potion, but instead the Doomsday Miasma was unleashed." A permanent stain on magic and science relations took root in the royal court following the city's fires. Even the office of royal physician had disappeared for over a century, to be reinstated at last by her great-great-grandmother Queen Mildred over the protests of the archbishop.

"Surely your highness feels a moral obligation to the people beyond the mere parroting of ancient misunderstandings. The Miasma's true causes are shrouded in history, and all primary accounts of the events are lost. Besides, modern research methods have advanced well beyond potion-brewing. Even her royal majesty the queen understands that."

Dr Lundfrigg may have been right to question the stories, but Sibylla's stomach still churned with her recollection of last winter when blood ran down her skin in globs before the archbishop had collected enough to refill her chapel's monstrance. As Dr Lundfrigg raised his needle, her tongue curled. Before she could stop herself, she snapped a shrill whistle-click with her tongue. A blast of sound shot from her lips like an arrow released from a bow and burst the vial of Dr Lundfrigg's syringe. She'd meant to buffet his hand, not shatter the glass. When panicked her body often reacted defensively. Now shards littered the floor, and Dr Lundfrigg rubbed at his ear in obvious discomfort.

Sibylla bit her lip. Unlike her glow and inking, she had less control over her whistle-click. The trait hadn't shown itself in the family since her great-grandfather, so none of her relations could explain how to manipulate it. The queen herself had forbidden Sibylla from using it in the palace as she still remembered how her own father, King Rupert, whistle-clicked his mother, Queen Mildred, deaf during an argument over teacakes. Fortunately, Dr Lundfrigg appeared unscathed.

He turned to Lady Wayfeather. "Madam, does her highness always react so negatively to sharp instruments?"

He seemed more curious than angry, and Sibylla wondered if he'd ever witnessed magic up close. As the new royal physician, he must have examined her entire family by now. If only she'd inherited her father Prince Henry's knack for tracking people over her great-grandfather King Rupert's whistle-click, she wouldn't be staring at a mess of broken glass. She watched with a twinge of compunction as Dr Lundfrigg retrieved the pieces from the carpet. A look of fascination lingered on his face until an interruption at the door startled them both.

"If you please, your highness, she's ready for you." Lieutenant Calloway's voice came from the other side of the door.

"You didn't come alone?"

Still searching for errant glass shards, Dr Lundfrigg remained on one knee as though not wishing to tax himself by standing. "Not as such, I'm afraid."

Sibylla attempted to bury her excitement over the prospect of an unannounced visit. Her mother Lady Brigitte had been promising for months she'd pop by.

"Should I tell her you're not finished?" Lady Wayfeather's mouth pinched as though she'd bitten into a salted prune. Telling royalty to wait rarely ended well.

Dr Lundfrigg's eyes flicked to his disassembled cane. Sibylla could see vials of drugs hidden inside its longest tube and wondered if he required the medical cane to walk. He hadn't limped earlier. How odd to use secret compartments to carry supplies instead of his monogrammed physician's bag.

Nevertheless, she offered her hand to help him stand, but before she could touch him, he sprung nimbly to his feet.

"Very unfortunate indeed." Dr Lundfrigg brushed the dust from his trousers. His cheeks flushed red. "I thought I had more time with her highness, but perhaps we could finish on another day."

Lady Wayfeather fastened her hands to her waist and fixed Dr Lundfrigg with her most apologetic expression. "I suppose I could have a room prepared for an overnight stay. If you'll wait in the parlor, I'll see the cook about refreshments."

Dr Lundfrigg lifted his watch from a velvet ribbon at his waist. He shook his head. "I regret I must conclude my visit. I've certain other blooms to attend to back in the city. As it stands, I'll be riding through the night simply to arrive on schedule for my morning rounds at St Colthorpe's charity ward."

As he reassembled his cane, he lowered his voice so no one but Sibylla could hear. "Should we meet again, your highness, I can promise a most interesting discussion. What a waste to be languishing out here, when you obviously have so much to offer."

He bent into a polite bow before following Lady Wayfeather into the hall.

Despite the urgency of Dr Lundfrigg's departure, it was some time before anyone came to see Sibylla. She pulled at the cream lace pleated around her waist while her insides wore into frayed knots. Sibylla had not seen her mother since she'd been banished to Helmscliff, as Lady Brigitte considered Tyanny Valley too close to be of interest and too far to be worth a day trip. Sibylla's latest correspondence – a collection of puns extolling the virtues of mothers and daughters – must have finally persuaded Lady Brigitte to visit.

Sibylla contemplated the appropriate greeting for a mother she hadn't seen in years, but hadn't decided between a kiss and a curtsy when a knock at the door brought her hands to her sides. A woman entered wearing a green wool cloak mottled by melted snow.

At once, Sibylla recognized the queen's hand, for Dorinda was much more than a maid. She was her royal majesty's Straybound. This grotesque tradition of indenturing murderers to individual members of the royal family had existed long before Caligo's cobbled streets. For centuries, kings, queens, princes, and princesses had all used these unfortunate tools to carry out their sordid ambitions. But unlike countless other Straybound, discarded per royal exigency or whim, Dorinda had accompanied the queen for a full decade now, outliving her predecessors by years.

This cold wraith of a woman spoke with the queen's authority, even when addressing a princess. She was also the woman who had kissed Roger beneath the weeping ash and stuffed a royal bribe into his trousers. She must have been in her thirties by now. Though petite in size, her presence – rather like a wasp that had flown into a crowded room – was impossible to ignore.

An uncontrollable glow lit Sibylla's veins. She feared whatever reason the queen had sent Dorinda to Helmscliff. Straybound never went far from their masters, as they were bound by the church to serve their patrons through ancient blood rites. If those rites weren't renewed daily, then the Straybound risked a painful death. The queen must have taken drastic measures for Dorinda to make the two-day round trip to Helmscliff. Somewhere on Dorinda's immaculate person would be a flask of the queen's blood for her to ingest.

Dorinda tugged off her cloak, uncovering her blonde, tightly-pinned hair and a white blouse buttoned up to her neck to hide the tattoo of royal indentureship. Though the tattoo branding could be easily revealed, Straybound usually assisted their magical patrons privately, often conducting themselves outside the law, and committing on behalf of their owners all manner of sins, like seducing the princess' paramour and convincing him to abandon her. They could be anyone: the corner shop butcher who chatted over cuts of veal or the queen's assistant who managed the daily schedule of maids. Only when they chose to reveal their tattooed necks, usually when nabbed by the law for conducting illegal activities on behalf of their royal owner, did the constables and guardsmen know to look the other way.

Dorinda answered to no one save the queen herself, and as such she seemed to enjoy the discomfort she caused Sibylla. She perched on the settee, smiling. "Shall you at least greet me properly, your highness?" Years of serving as the queen's voice in all matters had made Dorinda immune to protocol.

"No one mentioned you'd be visiting." Sibylla stood, as though height gave her the upper hand. "Why did Grandmother send you?"

"Why on earth *would* her royal majesty send me?"

"Perhaps she's given up on the idea of holding me here until I agree to marry Edgar," Sibylla shrugged. Dorinda would only say as much as she wanted, whether Sibylla stamped her feet or filled the room with screams. To counter this, Sibylla had perfected the art of dismissive oblige.

"Perhaps you are right." Dorinda scanned the interior of Sibylla's room. "Your highness might finally have become more valuable than your doting ditherer of a cousin." Her voice took on a mocking tone she used only in private. Sibylla could almost believe the queen sat in front of her. "Maybe her majesty has decided to marry you to some lower nobleman whose estate she's looking to purchase. Like that lieutenant I encountered earlier."

Sibylla's nonchalance weakened at the idea, and she sat down. "You're not telling me something."

Dorinda smoothed her hands in her lap. "You should be pleased. How long have you been here? A few months?" Dorinda knew well enough how long Sibylla had been at Helmscliff.

"There must be some reason, some motive, and for Grandmother to send you, it must be something strange."

"Asking questions and acting as you wish is the kind of behavior that no one likes to see in a princess." Sibylla considered inking the dry smile off Dorinda's lips, but Dorinda broke her focus by leaning in conspiratorially, lowering her voice so it wouldn't carry beyond the bedroom's walls. "Have you met *your brother* lately?"

Sibylla's jaw tensed, but she kept the fading glow in her veins from brightening. Under her control, the light winked out beneath her skin.

Half-brother, she silently corrected.

Why was the queen concerning herself with that old rumor? Sibylla's father, Prince Henry, had produced exactly one child with her mother, Lady Brigitte, and it was well known throughout the palace that Lady Brigitte had been rendered barren in the process. Any other child would be a bastard.

Until a century ago, monarchs killed all bastards for fear of magic spreading throughout the common population. In the civilized modern era, they only did away with those who showed signs of having the gift. It wouldn't do for some commoner to come knocking at the palace gates with an ill-begotten magic spark in his fingers and an armed horde at his back.

Sibylla knew first-hand the difficulty in hiding one's magic. Fortunately, magical bastards were as rare as a King Melvin vermillion postage stamp, and those who survived into adulthood rarer still. Properly noble parents produced "divinely blessed" infants, but outside such pairings, only bastard sons had the slimmest odds of demonstrating any talent.

As a child, Sibylla had protected her half-brother's existence to earn her father's good opinion, his rare praise more valuable than Celia the Devout's pearl prayer beads. Then she'd remained silent because her half-brother gave her gifts whenever he saw her, tokens of affection she cherished over the queen's scoldings. Now she kept the secret not only out of filial love, but also because she understood the queen would toss her illegitimate brother, should she discover his identity, into the bastards' well beneath Fitzroy Muir's ledgerstone at St Harailt's church. There he would molder with the bones of his brethren.

Sibylla scrutinized Dorinda. No half-brother of hers would meet Dorinda and face execution. "As her royal majesty is well aware, I haven't the pleasure of siblings."

Dorinda smiled all too pleasantly as she rose from her seat. "Well then." She clapped her hands. "I've already discussed matters with Lady Wayfeather, and she will make the necessary arrangements. Her royal majesty's stagecoach will arrive in three days' time to collect you. After your departure, the remainder of your belongings will be sent along to Malmouth at the end of the week, such as they are."

"So this will be a permanent stay?" Sibylla couldn't deny the appeal of returning to the palace.

"Isn't that your wish? Or perhaps you look forward to the daily headcold associated with spring weather in this forsaken valley."

Sibylla didn't understand the reason for this reprieve when, as far as she knew, she still hadn't agreed to marry her cousin Edgar. Still, the queen's motive would unveil itself soon enough, and though Sibylla had no desire to see Edgar, the crown prince, or her grandmother, she *had* been longing for Caligo's beef and kidney stew. More to the point, she'd be able to have a proper word with her father, Prince Henry, about the queen's renewed interest in looking for a certain surviving bastard. Perhaps it was again time her brother fled the country. She'd been abroad. She must have *some* useful contacts. And once she returned to Caligo, she'd have other resources at her disposal. No matter the queen's agenda, Sibylla planned to sail her own course and use her limited power for good, royal currents be damned.

7

After leaving the laundry, Roger collected the rest of his mourner's kit at Mr Grausam's Undertaking and Coffining Services. Per tradition, he was expected to carry a staff draped with black linen and conceal his face behind the mourner's porcelain mask, shaped like the upper half of a skull. He refused the battered cocked hat offered by Nail and tied the trailing hatband around his own new topper instead.

By late morning, the weather had taken a turn for the worse. A stiff wind blew cold drizzle into Roger's eyes as he ambled up Mouthstreet with half a dozen other mutes, staffs hefted on shoulders and masks hanging from necks to show they were not yet on duty. Even Nail had donned black and joined their ranks. Anticipating hours in the cold, some had already filled themselves with gin and expected Lady Margalotte's bereaved family to supply them with more.

They trudged up Mouthstreet past Eldridge's College of Barber-Surgeons. A placard hung on the door, advertising the start of a lecture series on basic surgery to begin the following week. A pasted-on addendum read:

Now featuring a new Special Lecture on the afflictions particular to the Feminine Personage, to include a demonstration of basic surgical techniques required by the Modern Medical Gentleman, with anatomization of a Verified Lady Specimen.

A note at the bottom clarified that only current medical students and licensed surgeons or physicians would be allowed in the door.

"You're havin' those devilish thoughts again." Nail matched Roger's stride. "I saw you eyein' that monstrous surgeon school back there. If you're con-temple-atin' makin' a snatch fer our lady croaker, I've my eye on you. Measures have been taken to protect the lady against the sack-'em-up gentlemen. She paid a pretty penny fer it, too. I won't even tell you how much."

"Don't be daft, man." Roger affected a wounded tone. "I'm learning proper surgery nowadays." Still, the idea of resurrecting Lady Margalotte niggled at him. Society disapproved of "violating" a corpse by dissection, and only executed criminals could be legally used. But how was leaving a dead body to putrefy in a box any better? Such sentimentality, if it could be called that, was lost on Roger. Executions alone couldn't meet the growing needs of the expanding medical district. At least a resurrected corpse could provide a last service to the living, if one fewer surgeon botched a cut on a living patient because he'd practiced on a dead one first. "What sorts of measures did she pay for?"

"One of them sealable iron coffins an' a welded mortsafe that won't be removed until… until the lady's mortal husk be of less interest to the common snatcher. It is an uncommonly useful invention, the patent mortsafe." He bestowed a significant glare on Roger. "As an undertaker, my clients demand eternal rest. No one wants to wake up dead on some medical student's table. But you wouldn't know nothing 'bout that, would you?"

"Me? Of course not. Though if that mortsafe of yours can be removed at all, maybe it ain't so snatcher-proof." Roger walked briskly on.

"If that don't stop him, then the sealed coffin will."

"Nail, man, if you want widows giving you kisses and cash, you may wish to lay off the talk of mortsafes and coffins." Roger hoped to fluster his rival. "They don't find that very romantic."

Nail's face flushed to match his fiery hair. "Just because I talk shop to you don't mean I can't impress a lass when I wants, widow or no."

"Good. Let's have a bet. Which of us can convince a member of the female persuasion to press her lips against his own first?"

"What, as mutes? That's like askin' a lady to kiss a day-old haddock, that is."

"Speak for yourself. We'll be masked. You'll have an advantage there."

"I want nothing to do with your bet if we're wagering stiffs..." Nail trailed off as they arrived at their destination.

The glossy black door of Margalotte's three-story townhome swung open to reveal a tall man in his fifties with thick sideburns extending nearly to his chin. A pair of silver spectacles hung on a thin chain attached to his lapel, and under his arm he carried a leather-bound ledger. In contrast to the mutes' second- and third-hand afflictions, this man's ebony-colored tailcoat had been fitted with lines sharp enough to cut butter. A high clubbed collar covered his entire neck and seemed to disappear into his jawline.

The man surveyed the length of the walkway. From the top of the steps, he glowered at the mutes.

"There are only seven of you." He affixed his spectacles to his narrow nose. "I – at the behest of the dearly departed – specifically requested ten. Nail, where is Mr Grausam?"

It was a well-known fact that the more mutes in attendance, the deeper the pockets of the deceased. A full platoon of fifty mutes had marched in the vigil parade for Queen Mildred, and toffs still tried to imitate her a hundred years later.

"He's late, Mr Murray sir, but I can speak for him." Nail removed his hat and pressed it to his chest. His red hair stood up like a candle flame. "Mr Grausam an' I determined that ten mutes is a highly unlucky number. Seven is more oss-pishos for such an undertaking, if you'll pardon the pun, sir."

Roger recognized the name. Mr Murray was a bigwig barrister who had risen to fame over a decade ago, securing an acquittal for the infamous Scrimshaw Highwayman. The case was especially popular among ladies of a certain age, what with the highwayman being a handsome rogue and his lawyer a dashing orator. Apparently Mr Murray dabbled in probates as well as criminal law.

"Don't spout that superstitious rubbish at me. As Lady Margalotte's executor I know her ladyship's will backwards, forwards, and crossways.

The number 'ten' is written here on page forty-three." Mr Murray tapped the page with his pencil. "Neither you nor your master will be paid unless the terms of our contract are fulfilled. Several of your men are so drunk they're having trouble standing. Disgraceful."

"They are but prepared to stand five hours inna cold without relief, sir," said Nail cheerfully. "Mr Grausam is rounding up a few more of us as we speak, if you are still insisting on the most unlucky number of ten."

"I do insist on it." Mr Murray studied the mutes with distaste, lingering a tad too long on Roger. "Line up along the path. Let's have a look at you lot. You're enough to frighten off the friends and family. Brush off that dust. Untangle those sashes. You'll need to act a few shades more mournful if you expect payment. I can only hope that this cold weather will bring on said attitude soon enough. Now, affix your masks. Henceforth, you are officially mute." The lawyer turned to go, then paused. "By the by, you there with the dented hat. I'd like to speak with you."

Roger raised a questioning finger.

Mr Murray raked him with his eyes. "Yes, you. Follow me." He turned toward the house.

Roger handed his staff to Nail and ascended the steps. He paused on the threshold before setting his hobnailed boot on the checkerboard of tiles in the foyer. Gaslit sconces flickered on the walls as he moved through the gloomy hall. The curtains had been closed as tradition required and would not be drawn until after the burial.

He followed the lawyer past the front parlor where he glimpsed the coffin, and a frizzle of blonde hair among the lilies. Mr Murray entered a study and sat behind a mahogany desk. Roger, not invited to avail himself of a chair, remained standing.

"Remove your mask."

Roger obeyed. The flesh around his eye throbbed, courtesy of Harrod.

Mr Murray narrowed his eyes. "I've seen you somewhere before, and quite recently, but I can't place where. What is your name?"

Roger said nothing. It was common practice to try to trick mutes into speaking to dock their pay.

"For the next few minutes, you are excused from official muteness.

Your name." This time it was not a question.

"Roger Weathersby, at your service."

"From the look of you, you've been running with the wrong crowd, Mr Weathersby."

"Oh, my crowd is alright, as such. My own family ain't been so kind." Roger attempted an insolent grin, but a scab at the corner of his mouth began to split.

"And do you mute often at funerals?"

"Not lately, sir."

"Have you suffered your own loss recently?"

"Not as such, sir."

"How singular." The lawyer leaned forward on his elbows, nearly spilling the inkpot. "Now that I've gotten a good look at you, I'm convinced I saw you in Greyanchor Necropolis, trailing a funeral party at an... unusual distance."

Roger's hackles went up. "You're mistaken. Perhaps I were visiting my mother there."

"Perhaps. Though not on Dolorous Avenue, I'd reckon." Mr Murray wiped his spectacles with a cloth. "There's some other force at work, bringing you in proximity of the dead. They say criminals always revisit their crimes. What do you think, Mr Weathersby?"

"I'm just here to make some extra coin." Roger disliked this man's prying questions and sly tone. "As are plenty of others."

"Of course. Another starving medical student, I'll wager. And I can guess what else you do in your spare time."

Roger bit his tongue to prevent saying something reckless. Now that he thought of it, Mr Murray's face did look familiar. He had been the solitary mourner at that Smith funeral.

The man was onto him. Roger swallowed hard. "Oh, right, sir. I did follow a hearse once. Didn't mean nothing by it. Thought I knew the lady as was to be buried. But it turned out to be a Miss Smith, where I'd thought it were a Mistress White. Right daft I felt, once I saw that fine old crypt. Sorry if I caused distress. Is that all, sir?"

A flash of calculation sharpened Mr Murray's features. He replaced his spectacles on the bridge of his nose as though to hide some dark intention. A chill passed through Roger.

"For now, yes," said Mr Murray, his tone flat as before. "Though since you are here, I encourage you to pay your respects to the deceased. Let the visitors see your mournful face. They'll start arriving at any moment."

"I really don't–"

"I insist." Mr Murray rose with great aplomb, and Roger had no choice but to follow him into the parlor. "Once you come into a house of mourning, you can't leave without spending a few moments contemplating your own mortality. That's not the way things work in Caligo."

Servants moved wraithlike along the walls, setting a buffet with stacks of silver plates, finger sandwiches, and a cauldron of hot mulled punch. A black-clad woman sat watch over the deceased, her face hidden behind a lace veil.

Roger shuffled forward, hat in hand, trying to look sufficiently mournful. Mr Grausam had done good work on the deceased. Lady Margalotte's hands lay calm and folded in her lap; they would not shred the coffin lining to pieces. A wide satin choker hid any possible strangle marks around her neck. She was clad in scarlet and gold, her fair hair haloing her face. A glint of pink caught his eye. A flower hatpin adorned the woman's dress like a brooch, identical to the pin he'd taken from that thieving ghost Ada.

This was strange indeed.

Roger bowed to the veiled woman. Then, as if overcome with grief, he leaned over the coffin and grasped Lady Margalotte's hands in his own. As a mute, such extravagant displays of emotion were expected, allowing him to check the inside of her wrist for a pulse. While he counted to ten in his head, something caught his notice. Where her folded hands had concealed her stomach, shallow lumps the width of peach pits raised the red satin of her dress. The same as Claudine. He wished he might pull back her dress to examine the oddity more closely, but that was out of the question. From his brief undertaker apprenticeship, he knew that overworked city coroners often skipped autopsies if they deemed the cause of death "obvious" at a glance. If only he were a true surgeon, in a starched cravat and carrying a satchel of instruments, he'd demand a proper examination. As a mute, he had less influence than the punchbowl.

Reluctantly, he settled Margalotte's hands in her lap.

Mr Murray's bespectacled gaze never faltered. "Now, replace your mask." He directed Roger outside. "You are again mute. Don't forget the price of talking out of turn."

The lawyer made Roger's flesh crawl. He wanted to throw Mr Murray's disapproval of bodysnatching right back in his face. After the door closed behind him, the mutes on the cold front steps became decidedly less mute.

Nail beckoned Roger over. "Don't tell me he's engaging your services."

"Come off it, Nail." Roger wasn't interested in foolish jokes. "That lady. You're the undertaker here. Didn't you notice anything peculiar when you were preparing her for the coffin?"

Nail raised an eyebrow. "We at Grausam's Undertaking Services strive fer absolute priv-assy in the affairs of our clients. Hold a derringer to my skull, an' I'll tell you the same."

Roger shrugged, feigning nonchalance. He didn't need Nail to tell him anything he could see for himself. The coffin would have to be in the ground before he'd get any answers. And that, of course, required digging her up again.

The mourners arrived at last, materializing out of the frozen mist that slicked the ground. Men with tall hats and traditional mourning masks helped solemn women in trailing black veils out of hansom cabs. They advanced up the walk with lowered heads. The mutes, even the tipsy ones, fell into dutiful silence, affecting sorrowful poses until the guests disappeared indoors.

Roger rubbed his hands to keep warm and tucked them under his armpits while bouncing on numbed toes. Now that the festivities were underway, the house livened. Liquid spirits loosened tongues and displaced ghostly thoughts. The frost on the windows began to melt.

A pair of arms, disembodied by the closed curtains, opened a window, and a gush of warm air and conversation spilled out. Roger edged toward the window until he stood just below it. The air was warmer still here and soon the other mutes huddled beside him, their teeth chattering and vapor spouting from the nose-gaps in their masks.

Up in the parlor, an older woman's husky voice moved near the window, continuing some conversation from before.

"She's the ninth to die, they say. Just like the ones before her." Her voice was almost too soft for Roger to catch. "The daily papers don't report it for fear of scandalizing visitors, what with that Cabbage King of Khalishka on his way. Can't say I blame them."

Nine women? Roger stretched his neck upward to hear the rest of it.

"One expects such ends for women of the slums, but not actresses and respectable shopkeepers. I admit, reading gruesome broadsheet headlines is a diversion of mine – don't tell my dear Tobias…" The speaker moved away from the window, and Roger cursed his luck.

To keep his mind off the cold, he pestered the other mutes for information on the Greyanchor Strangler. No one agreed on who – or what – the fiend was: a soldier gone mad in the border wars, a sexual deviant, a demon. One account they did agree on: all his victims had taken ill first.

Then another knot of conversation moved to the window, and a familiar name caught Roger off guard.

"I'm not superstitious, but I'm taking my daughters to Lady Sibylla's chapel for a blessing of protection. Can't be too careful in times like these."

Roger scoffed at the idea that a trip to Sibet's chapel would keep illness – or this Greyanchor Strangler – at bay. He'd once been closer to her than anyone, and still his mother had fallen to consumption.

"Whatever will the Emperor of Khalishka say when he visits our fair city?" asked a lush young man. "He'll think us a regular backwater, no more capable of maintaining public safety in our streets than that troll-village in *Housewench of the Haunted Hearth*. By the by, did you happen to get that invitation from your brother-in-law's second cousin?"

"No luck, dear. Not even Dame Angeline has made the guest list. With all the fuss over this emperor, the Royal Heritage Ball has become *the* ticket of the season."

"I say, that is a shock considering those two darling princes are at her salon nearly as often as the lady herself…"

A stiff elbow to the ribs interrupted Roger's eavesdropping. An amused mute pointed to the front door where Nail argued futilely with the butler.

"Up your arse with solemn duties, sir! We demand hot toddies an' punch, sir!"

"The venerable Mr Murray suggests you jump up and down to keep warm, as that is good enough for others of your class." The butler slammed the door in Nail's face.

"They can't expect *mutes* to jump up and down," fumed Nail. "We'd look regular asses."

Roger clapped an arm around Nail. "Maybe one of us already does."

"My, my," interrupted the silky voice of a woman used to projecting without deigning to something so common as shouting. She advanced from the main street. "I believe there is a scene in *The Whipping Mistress of Whipperton* where a mute, failing to silence himself during the prince consort's funeral procession, has his tongue summarily sliced from his mouth."

Roger and Nail glanced at one another. Behind them, the other mutes shuffled into their mourning poses. This woman alone, had arrived unaccompanied. A simple square of gauze veil hung from her plain black hat. Shards of scarlet trim adorned the black bodice that peeked from under her fur-trimmed cloak. Her half-mask, too, was feathered with black and red plumes.

Nail bowed extravagantly, then launched into his repertoire of silent sobs. Meanwhile Roger turned his face to the side. He'd been told he had a strong chin and looked best in profile.

"The pair of you would have made wonderful clowns at the Highbarrow Public Hall," said the woman as she stalked past. Navigating the front steps, skirts clutched high, her buttoned boot caught a patch of ice. Her hands flew up and she gave a girlish shriek. Roger threw his staff to the ground and lunged for the foot of the steps, arms outstretched. Nail, running up from the side, slammed into him. They crashed in a heap on the path.

The woman managed to pitch herself forward on her hands instead of tumbling fatally backward. She pressed herself into a sitting position on the top step, brushing ice and gravel from her gloves.

"I survived a three-story fall during the balcony scene of *Sirens in Flight*, my dear." The woman rose to her feet unaided. "Men say I'm not easily broken." Without further delay, she disappeared inside.

By the time the massive hearse drawn by four plumed black horses arrived, Roger's feet had become wooden pegs. As he assembled with his fellow mutes in the street for the torchlight funeral procession, the red-and-black veiled woman emerged from the house to take the place of honor beside the hearse's driver.

Nail elbowed Roger in the ribs. "Now, if you'd managed to get a kiss from Dame Angeline herself, maybe I'd give you them mortsafe keys after all."

Roger nearly set the crape staff alight with his torch. "That were *the* Dame Angeline?" The woman's name had been a fixture of their conversation all evening, but he hadn't guessed she was one of the mourners.

"It were. You've never been to the theater, have you? Her *Whipping Mistress* is the one to see."

By Nail's account, Dame Angeline ran an elite salon for men with expensive tastes – the sort of establishment that served flutes of sparkling wine, where ladies in ruffled undergarments peeled grapes and frolicked about scattering rose petals. Roger suspected he'd suffer more than a stiff kick to his nether parts if he dared place a finger on the salon's stained-glass doors.

All along the funeral route passersby joined them, it being bad luck to cross paths with a hearse. The procession arrived before sundown on the north ridge of Greyanchor hill. Lady Margalotte would find rest among the immodest stones and pillars of the upper middle class. Six of the soberest mutes, Roger included, lowered the coffin into a deep grave, then helped shovel it over while the guests wiped their eyes and headed home.

The mutes were each given a few winkles and told they'd get the rest when they turned in their afflictions. Assuming the role of undertaker, Nail pulled a tarpaulin off a cart to reveal a coffin-sized iron cage – the mortsafe as promised – and directed a group of workmen as to its installation. Roger lingered nearby, just close enough to glimpse the locks. To resurrect Margalotte, he'd have to simultaneously open two locks on either end of the cage, each likely requiring a different key. Difficult, but not impossible…

"Getting a good look, are we, Mr Weathersby? I can only imagine what fiendish fancies run through your mind," said Mr Murray in a low, menacing voice. He'd snuck up from behind and now clamped a hand on Roger's shoulder. "Besides a mortsafe, Mr Grausam has supplied a pair of armed watchmen to guard the dearly departed. I'm afraid this one will have to remain where she is."

"Sir." Roger ducked his head. "I was just on my way home." He might pry the locks, but guards would not be so easily manipulated. He stuffed his hands in his pockets. So much for his planned autopsy of Margalotte and the satisfying weight of Dr Eldridge's shells in his pocket.

He could try again later. Corpses didn't rot away in a single night, and watchmen might get drunk. Besides, Roger had other engagements. He'd promised Ada to check in on her mother, and with the sun setting, she'd have left the laundry by now.

Roger hurried toward the arched lychgate. The caretaker closed its wrought iron doors at dusk to everyone except undertakers, and he didn't relish the idea of scaling the wall without his rope while lugging this hideous crape staff, too expensive to abandon.

Outside the necropolis gate, he spotted Ada. She must have hidden in shadow, for she appeared suddenly on the path as if out of nowhere, still clad in her shapeless laundress smock.

"Ghost."

She darted up and kicked his shin. "You're late, sack-'em-up man."

"Have you eaten?"

Ada eyed him skeptically, so Roger produced the payment from his mute job.

"Tell you what. You take these winkles and get yourself a stargazy pie down at the Fox & Weasel. Know where that is?" She nodded and snatched the coins from his hand as quick as any pickpocket. "Once I've popped back to my room to lose this bleeding staff and fetch my surgical instruments, I'll find you at the pub, and you'll show me to your ma. Is it a plan?"

"You better not be late again." Ada pocketed the coins. "Or else I'll boil your clothes into lye mush."

8

It would be another two days before the royal stagecoach arrived to take Sibylla to Caligo. After a vicious overnight cold snap, fireplaces burned in every room. The air smelled of cinders, and a hot haze now blanketed the hall. As Lieutenant Calloway escorted her to her morning concertina lesson, sweat soaked the lace of Sibylla's collar. If she'd been born with her Aunt Esther's ability to blow water globes, she'd have doused the flames by now.

"It's an outrage." The lieutenant had been sulking about one thing or another since he learned of his imminent shift from warden protector to ordinary cavalryman. "I've word of a stir up in the barracks. We're to prepare for an absolute horde of visiting foreigners and their gruesome warlord. My tailor's written to say he's fallen behind on monogramming my silk cravats. Not that I care. Why should anyone care to make themselves presentable for that nasty beast?"

"You mean the Emperor of Khalishka," Sibylla corrected. "As I recall, you took part in a few border skirmishes. Did you happen to glimpse the emperor among his men? He's never been on a diplomatic tour, so his visage is still a mystery to those of us outside the military." She'd often wondered if the most powerful man on the continent did indeed look like a "warlord" as the lieutenant suggested.

Lieutenant Calloway pretended to stroke an imaginary waist-length beard, then grimaced. "Oh, I saw him. His face is as gnarled as a withered old root, and he smells of sour cabbage and horse sweat.

Nevermind that he keeps his mistresses' teeth in a belt around his belly."

As inhospitable as the lieutenant presented its emperor, the nation of Khalishka could be a powerful ally. Currently, no Myrcnian embassy existed there. Sibylla inked a winged horse – the symbol of the Khalishkan Empire – to gallop between specks of dust caught in the afternoon light. No embassy meant no ambassador. She wondered how difficult it would be to convince the emperor to take on a foreign diplomat. She'd been concocting plausible harbors for her bastard half-brother ever since her visit with Dorinda.

He could board a merchant ship and disappear on a year-long sail of the Andorna Seas, but she could not. Nor could she write to remote villages without drawing attention. Sibylla knew she was selfish, wishing to hide her brother somewhere she'd be able to send letters and royal packages. Yet she didn't know how else to live. She was fortunate to see her parents two or three times a year – less since she'd been banished to Helmscliff. In truth, her brother was the only family member who made her feel of consequence, and she couldn't even acknowledge him. At least, on occasion, she might visit an embassy.

Lost in her head, she had forgotten Lieutenant Calloway rattling on beside her until he leaned close enough that his mustache tickled her neck. Startled, she fell against a foxhunt tapestry, whereupon the lieutenant reached out to steady her.

Sibylla avoided his assistance altogether by adjusting the numerous folds of her skirt. "This dress you recommended is too many layers of silk, satin, and wool. If I'm not tripping, I'm waddling."

Unfortunately, the lieutenant remained oblivious to her pointed commentary on his choice of garments for her, and shoved a book wrapped in brown paper in her direction.

Curious, she tugged at the string, but before she could peel back the wrapping, he declared, "It's a first edition of the preeminent field guide on the collection and preservation of seaweed, and it's yours. It won't be sold in Caligo for another five months, but my family knows the publisher personally."

Not once in her life had she cared a whit about seaweed. She could muster a mild excitement over the sea, but she preferred the docks where vendors sold fresh oysters and men played dice games for money.

"This is a very fine book," she said after an uncomfortable stretch of silence.

His eyes brimmed with pleasure as he tenderly grasped her wrists. She expected her veins to ripple with bluish light the way they once had when a certain roguish kitchen boy used to tug her hand and guide her down to the tidal mudflats along the Mudtyne. Lieutenant Calloway's touch didn't elicit even a glimmer. How disappointing that the lieutenant's amiable face didn't stir her heart.

Sibylla left him standing in the hall with the seaweed guide in hand while she slipped into the music room for her concertina lesson. As the door shut behind her, a cold shiver prickled down her neck. Instead of Lady Wayfeather at her music stand, Dorinda stood at the window, sharp as glass.

The queen's Straybound pulled the curtains closed, and turned to Sibylla with a mirthless smile. "Shall we continue our conversation, your highness?"

Sibylla didn't answer at first – the silence of the room was heavy and dangerous. How foolish she'd been to drop her guard without confirming that Dorinda had indeed left Helmscliff empty-handed. Sibylla took a seat to appear comfortable with the impromptu second meeting, though her face heated with worry. Finally, she asked, "How many times must it be said? I have no brother."

Dorinda produced an envelope with eerily familiar script. For a moment, Sibylla wished it was her illicit missive to Roger, but instead recognized the express postmark. She'd arranged for a letter to be sent to her father, Prince Henry, after her encounter with Dorinda, alerting him to the queen's renewed interest in bastards.

"We already know about him," said Dorinda coolly. "There's no reason to hide what's been uncovered. Her majesty merely wishes to preserve his safety and set him up with a respectable title for propriety's sake."

Sibylla smoothed her skirt to the side. She and her father had always used coded language when discussing her half-brother. If Dorinda thought she could bluff her way to the truth, she'd be disappointed. "I have nothing to say."

Dorinda approached Sibylla and in one swift motion tore the letter in half. She let the two halves fall to the ground. "Amnesty. The crown will grant your half-brother a lifelong reprieve."

A raspy laugh escaped Sibylla's lips. "I know what happens to royal bastards in this country. If they're lucky, they're offered poison, and if not, it's a long and nasty trip to the bottom of the bastards' well in St Harailt's."

Sibylla couldn't count the times she'd sat at dinner while the queen, after several goblets of wine, extolled the virtues of abstinence and the dangers of wanton lust. No bastard born during her reign had lived past two days. As far as she knew.

"What a spiteful princess. Her royal majesty is offering your brother a blessed drop of her mercy, and you spit upon her hand."

Sibylla didn't believe a word of it. Dorinda was the queen's Straybound, and murder dwelt within her bones. If the queen truly intended to offer Sibylla's half-brother mercy, then she would not have sent her weapon.

She made to stand, but Dorinda forced her down. Her fingers dug into the frilly layers of Sibylla's dress until Sibylla could feel Dorinda's sharp nails through her thick puffed sleeve. She had no intention of letting Dorinda best her. After all, a Straybound was no match for a princess with magic. Flexing her right hand, she flung a cloud of ink into the air between them. The inkblot swelled outward to coat the front half of Dorinda's white blouse black. Rivulets dripped down her buttoned chest.

Dorinda jumped back. "How dare you!" She thrust her arm through the dispersing ink cloud to yank Sibylla by the wrist. "See what happens if you don't take her majesty up on this offer."

Sibylla raised her other hand to the bridge of Dorinda's nose. Black ink flowed from beneath her fingernails as though poured from an inkwell, stretching into a blindfold across Dorinda's face. Dorinda scarcely shut her eyes in time to avoid injury.

Ink dripped from Sibylla's fingers as she escaped into the hall, spreading into a black pool on the tile floor outside the music room. Let Dorinda give chase and smack her head against the slick ground. Sibylla straightened; she'd done the right thing. There were other ways to win over the queen. She wouldn't bargain her brother to gain the Crown's approval.

But just how long would it be before the queen, through Dorinda, used more than carrots to find Prince Henry's bastard son? Sibylla hated Straybound for this very reason, their single-minded devotion to achieving the will of their owners. For now, with her brother in Caligo and herself in Helmscliff, she could only remain silent for him. However, once she returned to the capital, she intended to play a good game. Not only would she protect her brother, but she'd also prove to the queen once and for all that she could accomplish the impossible: prevent her majesty from having her way.

9

Roger followed Ada along sinuous avenues woven through some of Caligo's worst slums. Oddly, the most destitute neighborhoods often backed up to fashionable streets, separated by a single row of houses. The ancient city of Caligo resisted urban renewal with the steadfastness of a small child facing a washtub. Locals knew where they belonged, and ventured into more-or-less advantaged areas at their own peril.

Off one well-lit boulevard, Ada turned into an alley so narrow and dark Roger would have missed it had he been traveling alone.

"This here's Will-o'-the-Wisp Lane."

Upper stories leaned in over the street, with a sliver of sky visible above. Doxies swished their canary and vermillion frocks from doorways. Though seedy, the district had a touch more class than Roger's haunts on Goatmonger Street.

"That one." Ada pulled his coat and pointed. A faded clapboard sign read *Eglantine's Den of Delights*. "Ask for Miss Estella. She'll take you up, like the regular gent you ain't."

"What of you, Ghostofmary? Don't you want to see your ma?"

Ada shook her thick mop of hair. "She don't want me here. I'll wait outside." She climbed onto the lid of a rain barrel set back in an alcove. Concealed in shadow, she again looked more ghost than girl.

Roger hid his instrument case – a knife roll he'd once nicked from the royal kitchens – under his coat. With a last glance at Ada, he straightened his posture and entered the bawdyhouse. Inside, he found a drawing room upholstered in dingy red velvet. The air smelled musky and feminine. A few girls slouched in threadbare chairs, heels kicked up to show off their calves, and one of them plucked an out-of-tune harp. Half a dozen bored faces tracked Roger's movements. He hoped they didn't care he was dressed for a funeral.

"Is there a Miss Estella?" He forced a confidence into his voice that came out with an awkward shrillness. "I understand I'm expected."

The harp twanged as the woman abruptly stood. "Come with me, sir. If you're here about the two-for-one, we shan't disappoint." A rougher accent seeped through her posh diction. She was tall, with broad shoulders and a pinched waist under a plum-colored taffeta gown. Her dark hair hung in stiff curls to her shoulders like loosed springs. "Weathersby?" Estella asked, lighting a candle from the gas font.

"Aye, miss." Roger noticed lines under her face-powder, suggesting she wasn't quite the lily-fresh girl as advertised by the cut of her dress.

"Tell me you didn't bring the mudlark." She led him up winding spiral stairs.

"She's waiting outside. Out of sight."

"Good. Some patrons here have certain tastes. We don't want them getting the wrong idea about that one."

They ascended to the third floor and walked the length of a low hallway to the final door.

"Thank you for agreeing to come, doctor. We rarely get your type here. The bleeding-heart eager to break the law on our account, that is. Since the queen passed her ban, most doctors we see are the ones ribboning their maypole."

Roger forced a smile and passed a hand over the roll of medical instruments hidden in his coat. "First do no harm, as they say."

Estella tapped on the door. "Celeste, it's that man you were waiting for." She nudged Roger into the room and slid in behind him.

The chamber was small but cozy. A canopy bed with dark red curtains took up most of the floor. Roger had expected to find an invalid tucked under a coverlet. Instead he faced a woman of about thirty years with hair black as a mourning veil. She wore only a blue corset and a frill of lace undergarments, and sat in a wingback chair before a tiny lit fireplace. At first glance she seemed healthy enough, but as Roger approached he noticed her jaundiced skin, her knobby elbows, and the dark bruises under her eyes,

"You should be wrapped in a warm blanket, lying in bed," he insisted.

She glanced up from the book in her hands. "*Oh doctor, come to stuff my mind with platitudes, and my bosom with thy antidotes, root out instead the wormwood of thine own rotten blood. I know how thou cravest the whip.*"

Roger stood awkwardly before her, wishing for an outfit more professional than these afflictions. At least he wasn't wearing his bloodstained shirt. And anyway, plenty of physicians wore black. "Is that a quote from a novel, miss?"

"A play, Dr Weathersby. *The Whipping Mistress of Whipperton* to be precise, by Myrcnia's own eminent playwright Richard Salston. You haven't read it, I take it." She flashed pearly teeth, made whiter by the sallow skin she tried to conceal under powder.

"I've… heard the name in conversation, miss. Celeste, is it?"

"And how did you manage to win over my little Adelaide, Mr Weathersby?" Celeste lay her book down and motioned that he sit on the bed near her. "Just what kind of friend do you profess to be?" She took Roger's face in her hand and looked straight into his eyes, as if daring him to look away, which he did.

"She's worried about her ma," he managed. "And what with the rumors, I couldn't rightly blame her either."

"To think she hasn't knifed you yet." Celeste released him with a laugh. "But you've seen the dark. I can tell. You know why a mother should be concerned for her only child."

"Aye, miss."

"And if you're here to merely play pretend doctor, I shall not be amused." She attempted to push herself upright but ended up slumped against the wing of the chair.

Reminded of his own mother's illness, Roger rallied to focus on the ailing woman before him. He removed his mute's frockcoat, hoping he looked more like a medical man in just his waistcoat. "I work at a top institution. You've heard of Eldridge's College. Do I have your leave to perform an external exam?"

"You're the first man to ever ask permission." Celeste bit her lip as she sized him up. "Estella will be chaperoning. But yes, I'm ready. How do you want me, doctor?"

"I'm but a surgeon," Roger said, then clamped his mouth shut before he could add "in training." He rolled up his shirtsleeves. Why had he expected a living patient to be as inert and malleable as his uncomplaining cadavers? He'd handled corpses who had died of every imaginable ailment, many with signs of venereal disease and the treatments that came too little, too late. Now he could feel his confidence waning.

"I could lie on the bed, love."

"No!" Roger shoved away the unhelpful image of her writhing on the coverlet. "I mean… the chair is fine."

Estella brought a basin of warm water. Roger added a slosh of gin from his flask – it made things smell cleaner – then washed his hands.

"I'll start with a palpation. Sorry for the cold hands." He crouched before Celeste's petticoat-covered knees and tried to remember his medical texts. "Tell me of your symptoms. When did they begin?"

"Fevers. Chills." Celeste uncrossed her legs. "A month ago, though it was slight at the start. I thought I'd caught the Ibnovan disease from a gent, but that fades in a few weeks. Then, the cramping started last week, like jellied eels slithering about my belly. Don't tell me I'm with child. I've had one. I know."

"I see." Roger held his breath as he ran his fingers down her cheeks and throat, searching for the telltale lumps of syphilis and finding none.

She undid her corset so he could check her abdomen – her stomach felt too firm, and as he moved his fingers across, there was a dip, and then another, like soft pit marks in a hardened cheese. She winced and bit into the upholstery to muffle a shriek. As his fingers pressed into one of those strange divots, he tried recalling Hemon's *Studies of Medical Phenomena and Their Surgical Treatments*, but couldn't think of a passage to fit this symptom – a hard *and* soft belly.

Her eyes, like her skin, seemed yellow, and her gums pale. He had no scope for auscultation, but when he pressed his ear to her back he could hear her shallow breaths. The weak pulse in her wrist proved difficult to find and stuttered rapidly under his fingertips. Roger tried to think of what to say next and remembered the questions the doctor had asked at his own mother's bedside.

"Has your daily regimen changed in the last month? Eating habits, perhaps? Medicaments?"

Celeste shook her head. "Not as such. We always use the sheep-gut sleeves with the gentlemen, as the law requires. Although a client of mine gave me some fancy wine, a morelle mauvingnon. But we finished that off weeks ago."

"We?" Roger asked. "You and Estella? Is she sick as well?"

"Of course we both drank it," Estella spoke up. "We always share our spoils. But there's nothing wrong with me, doctor, if you'd like a peek…" Her voice trailed off seductively.

A mushroom wine seemed an expensive gift for anyone who was neither a toff nor an overpriced salon girl. Roger associated the stuff with royal religious rites, and one bottle of it cost as much as a carriage. He hardly saw the point of drinking it. Still, it was strange.

"Your humors do appear out of balance." Roger repeated the diplomatic phrasing physicians used to tell patients something was definitely wrong. He thought back to the stiffs he'd encountered on his slab, bellies slit and gaping. "I'll wager it's gallstones or the like."

Suddenly Celeste grabbed Roger's hair with a painful, throaty moan.

"Miss!" Roger struggled to hold her wrists. "Miss, are you all right?"

"Another spasm." Celeste released him. She lay back in her chair, heaving. "They come and go, these past few days. If you'd been a regular customer, I'd have twisted your giblets."

"And I'd have deserved it," said Roger to lighten the mood. "If you don't mind me saying, you seem rather high class for Will-o'-the-Wisp Lane."

Celeste gave a wan smile and laid a hand on Roger's shoulder. "Don't think I was always to be found in such a rum district as this. Oh no. Not to boast, but I once played the courtesan in Dame Angeline's famous salon. Sometimes we put on saucy renditions of Salston in our underclothes. The officers and gentlemen couldn't get enough."

"I imagine not." Roger's face burned, and he prayed she couldn't tell in the meager light. That Angeline again. "Seems a popular place."

Celeste wistfully tugged the ends of her hair. "Many friends found marriages to fulfill their contracts with Dame Angeline. I was engaged – that was enough for the contract – but Ada's untimely arrival ended that. Estella here didn't pass the salon's physical, though back then she turned far more gentlemen's heads with her looks than I. Still does."

A tear streaked Estella's cheek. "My poor chaffinch. The years have not been kind to either of us."

Celeste sighed and stroked Roger's hair. He started warming in stiff and decidedly awkward places, and delicately removed her hand. "Please, I'm determined to stay professional."

"As if a little pleasure could ruin a *man*." She dropped her hand into her lap. "Gallstones, you said? Is there treatment for that?"

Roger hesitated. He knew of some surgeries performed, but they'd been experimental and risky. Although gallstones seemed like a reasonable guess, he wasn't certain. He couldn't entirely rule out the pox based on her strange symptoms, or even arsenic poisoning. This was impossible; he made a worthless "doctor." He sighed inwardly. Corpses were simple to diagnose – cutting them open revealed their secrets. But Celeste was a living woman with a daughter, and he had to figure out what ailed her, before she ended up like his own mother, dead and buried.

"You'll at least bleed me," she said. "There's something inside me that must be let out."

"Of course." Roger rose and washed his hands. "That's a surgeon's bread and butter."

He prepared his fleam and basin, then tied a ribbon around Celeste's upper arm to find the vein. When he nicked her skin, instead of a bright red spurt, thick black blood dribbled down her forearm.

"Is something the matter?" she asked.

"You may want to take more fluids." He'd never seen anything like her blood, not even in a corpse. It looked like licorice syrup.

This just added to an already confusing list of possible illnesses: the pox due to her stomach pains, dropsy for her distended stomach, jaundice from her yellowish skin. Or it could be the green sickness, brought about by a lack of iron in the diet. Poison. Cancer. An internal infection. One ailment he could rule out for certain was consumption. His mother had died of it, but Celeste wasn't coughing or spitting blood. Still, nothing added up.

He poured the blood from the basin into an empty chemist's vial, to examine later.

As he rinsed his fleam, he offered Celeste instructions, not knowing if they'd do any good. "For now, eat nothing you don't prepare yourself. No face-powder or rouge, in case metals are leeching through the skin. Drink water from a different pump than usual. Stay in bed and avoid cold drafts. I've brought no medicaments today, but tomorrow I'll return with a treatment." That would give him time to take a closer look at the blood at Eldridge's College.

"How fortunate Ada dragged you here, Dr Weathersby," said Estella as Roger dressed to depart. "If surgery doesn't pan out, you might consider a change of career. You seem to have very good hands." She winked. "Some wealthy woman might gladly pay to lie back and let *you* do the work."

Roger flushed and turned to Celeste. "Shouldn't I send Ada up to see you?"

Celeste gravely shook her head. "The girl should not be here at night. I'll meet her in the morning, if I'm up for a walk."

Roger exited through the back and found Ada's alcove, but she no longer perched on the barrel. He searched a side alley used by coalmen, then checked in the windows of Eglantine's Den of Delights. There was no sign of her.

"Ada? Ada!" He was afraid to say her name too loud.

A gent in a tall hat and well-cut coat stood in front of the brothel, peering up at a tiny ornamental balcony on the side of the building.

"Come down, little cat," the man crooned. "Good kittens get the cream."

Roger froze, overcome with revulsion. A huddled figure, barely more than a bundle of clothes, was visible between the balcony rails. Ghostofmary.

A pale face under a mop of black hair appeared. "Go rot in the sewer with the other filth-rats!" she shrieked.

"I'm here, Ghost," Roger shouted. "Thought the goblins got you."

The gentleman glared.

"I ain't coming down."

Roger held out his hands. "I'll catch you."

"Bet you couldn't catch the pox from an open sore," she snarled, but then stepped over the rail.

Roger caught Ada and held her to his chest. "Your mother loves you, Ghost," he whispered in her ear. "I'll return tomorrow with medicaments. I promise you. I'm going to do all I can to heal her."

She slapped his face and squirmed out of his grasp. "A pox on the cat man, and on you too, sack-'em-up!" She sprinted into the darkness.

The gentleman looked Roger over and winked. "Bad luck. But I could show you a house with the most nubile tartlets."

Roger didn't wait to hear more. He fled in the direction Ada had gone, searching the shadows for her. By the time he emerged from the tangled alleys onto a wider gaslit street, he had given up hope of catching her. So much for keeping an eye on the girl. He didn't like her sleeping in a mausoleum while human monsters prowled Greyanchor at night. The Strangler was just one of a dozen potential threats – a young girl could fetch a good price, alive or not. Even his garret would be safer. But he could hardly blame Ada for not trusting him.

Roger dismissed the idea of sleep. He made for the medical district and arrived out of breath at the back entrance of Eldridge's College of Barber-Surgeons. He pulled the bell, hopping impatiently in the freezing dark. At last the door creaked, and Dr Eldridge peered out.

"It's early for you to be poking your nose in here, lad." Dr Eldridge eyed Roger's mute clothes without comment. "Not even midnight yet. Have you brought me another lovely stiff?"

"Sorry to come 'round empty-handed, doctor. Not that I didn't try. I'd hoped to borrow some instruments, a microscope, maybe glance at your medical journals, if you'll pardon the intrusion. Need to get a leg up on my studying." In truth he needed to diagnose Celeste, but without embroiling the old physician in his illegal house call to a prostitute.

Dr Eldridge gestured for Roger to follow him into one of the dissection rooms. "I keep a Darby model in the cabinet here." After some rummaging, Dr Eldridge produced a wooden case. "I don't like students getting their fingerprints on it, so I trust you'll keep its existence to yourself."

Dr Eldridge's hands faltered as he tried to assemble the brass pieces, so Roger took over for him, screwing the stand into the wooden base. Three cylindrical lenses composed the brass pillar, and a swivel mirror caught lamplight to illuminate a specimen – just what Roger needed.

"There's a box of glass slides in the cabinet, and anything else you might need." Dr Eldridge gave Roger's shoulder a paternal squeeze. "I'll be in my study shuffling papers. After hours is the only time anyone leaves me alone. If you're still here in the morning, and you give the lecture hall a good scrub, I could use an assistant for my female anatomization lecture."

"With pleasure." Roger had hoped Dr Eldridge might ask him. His assistants did all the hands-on dissection work – much preferable to sneaking in with the medical students and auditing the class while hiding in the back.

Once alone, Roger pulled the vial of Celeste's blood from his pocket. Dabbing a handkerchief in gin, he cleaned a row of glass plates. Then, recalling how he used pigments to dye the organs and vessels in cadavers to make the structures easier to see, he mixed a droplet of carmine solution with a smear of Celeste's blood on the glass plate.

Though he'd prepared plenty of slides for Dr Eldridge's laboratory classes, Roger had never looked through a microscope. When he lowered his face to the eyepiece, he saw a jumbled mess of shapes in varying shades of red. Roger knew blood contained disc-shaped red cells, called corpuscles, floating in a yellowish brine. White globules, believed to be a form of pus, might be glimpsed among the more numerous red cells. If only he knew how to tell what he was looking at.

A thought struck him. He needed another blood sample for comparison. Preparing his fleam, he slit the pad of one finger and let his blood – a fresh brilliant red – flow onto a slide. Again he mixed it with carmine and smeared the droplet thin. Examining his blood under the scope proved equally fruitless. This collection of pink shapes looked different, but he still couldn't tell how to distinguish the healthy blood from bad.

How stupid to assume a microscope alone would solve his problems. The container of glass plates caught his eye – a repurposed biscuit tin whose girlish princess decoration had nearly worn off. Sibylla's voice came to him: "If you don't know a thing, Dodge, find a book that does. Then sit down and read it."

Dr Eldridge's tiny library consisted primarily of rickety old shelves groaning with back issues of Caligo's oldest medical journal, *The Speculum*, dating back over a century. He flipped through the most recent issues, his eyes scanning the pages for the word "blood."

An hour later, with a half-dozen relevant articles read, it seemed to Roger no pair of physicians agreed on the purpose of the blood. Many opinionated men engaged in verbal fisticuffs within *The Speculum*'s pages, including the royal physician to the queen, Dr Finch Lundfrigg, whom Roger had once glimpsed in Dr Eldridge's lecture hall surrounded by students begging him to autograph their textbooks.

While other physicians theorized blood behaved like a series of water pipes to modulate temperature, or distributed minerals to the extremities, Dr Lundfrigg insisted the blood was an "internal fingerprint" that informed the nature of one's physical appearance and mental capacities.

Roger left the library more daunted than ever. Still, he'd determined healthy blood looked a certain way, thanks to Dr Lundfrigg's sketches. Once he understood how to describe what was wrong with Celeste's blood, he could ask Dr Eldridge his opinion without exposing the particulars of the case.

He returned to the dissection room and fixed a slide of his own blood to the microscope. Lowering his face to the eyepiece, he adjusted the lenses, focusing the bright red smear into a pale field of poppy-red buds – the corpuscles.

He swapped out the slide of his own blood for Celeste's sample. Now that he knew what he was looking at, the differences between the two samples were plain to see. Celeste's corpuscles appeared oddly bunched and stacked. Clotting, perhaps, since her blood wasn't as fresh. As he stared into the lens, his eyes dry from forgetting to blink, he noticed a strange presence in the space between the red cells. Numerous pus globules, more than he'd seen in his own blood, clumped around tiny black speckles of foreign material. Those black speckles hadn't been in his blood.

Celeste was ill, but he'd never seen her particular symptoms before. Except... he *had*. Celeste wasn't the first woman with a strange abdominal wall he'd come across. No, he'd observed something similar twice before, though his other "patients" had been dead when he examined them. The strange bumps beneath Lady Margalotte's dress and that odd pimpling on Claudine – there had to be a connection.

Both women had been sick when they'd died. Perhaps this Greyanchor Strangler fellow had a twisted sense of empathy, or perhaps he had something to do with what plagued them. Now Roger feared a darker pattern.

If he could check their blood for foreign specks that matched Celeste's, he might be on to something. Margalotte lay under a mortsafe, but Claudine was in the basement awaiting her special lecture.

Roger raced for the cellars where the stiffs were kept at night. Once he had confirmed his suspicions, he would return to Will-o'-the-Wisp Lane and tell Celeste to move immediately. He'd offer up his room to her and Ada, he'd stand guard on the stairs. And if it meant keeping them safe, he'd even risk his own neck by calling the constables.

When he burst into the cellar, he ran to the first sheeted corpse – a hanged convict. He checked the other specimens, but Claudine was missing. Then he remembered Dr Eldridge had asked him to scrub down the lecture hall for the upcoming course on female anatomy. The "verified lady specimen" must have been moved to the dissection room adjoining the main hall.

And that's where Dr Eldridge intercepted Roger.

"Ah, Mr Weathersby, I've been looking all over for you." Dr Eldridge, his face glistening and red, propped himself against the doorframe to catch his breath. He leaned into the corridor as if searching for eavesdroppers, then left the door ajar.

"I wanted to thank you for lending me that microscope," said Roger. Something was amiss but he tried to pretend otherwise. "I'll have it shining like new as soon as I've finished my research. Then I'll start preparations on the lady corpse. I weren't about to skip out on you. Why don't you sit down?"

Dr Eldridge remained standing with his back to the door. The old man rarely stayed on his feet for so long. "That female corpse you brought the other day," he began.

"Right." Roger didn't like how Dr Eldridge blocked his only exit. Probably fatigue had made him paranoid. "About that lady stiff, sir. If I might just tap her for the tiniest dab of blood–"

"Can you tell me again how you came about her?" Dr Eldridge interrupted in a manner usually reserved for drunken students. "You seemed worried about her identity when you brought her in. If you'll just repeat your story, I think I might be able to solve our little problem."

"You didn't seem much interested last time." Puzzled, Roger studied the man's face. "I followed a hearse to the mourning chapel and sprung her from the crypt that night, afore the fog lifted. Standard crypt lock, plain pine box. But the lady didn't look right. You saw her."

"I did indeed." The doctor gave a sorrowful sigh, and Roger wondered if the corpse had touched his feelings in some way. "Unfortunately, some others also noticed." Dr Eldridge stepped back and pushed open the door. "And I'm afraid I cannot with good conscience employ you at my college any longer."

"You're giving me the sack?" Roger gripped the empty slab for support. "But that makes no sense. How many stiffs have I brought you? Them what died in their sleep, them who was hanged, old, young, always fresh. And this one does me in?"

The doctor pointed at the door. Roger tried to leave, but a figure blocked his way: a broad-shouldered man in a blue double-breasted coat and custodian helmet, cudgel in hand. A second blue-coated man moved in behind him. Constables.

The first advanced, pulling a pair of iron manacles from his belt. "Consider yourself under arrest for breaking and entering private property within state cemeteries, and unlawful trafficking of the deceased.

Everything you just said while we was listening outside the door will be used against you. Come quietly, and you might keep your teeth."

"Dr Eldridge, sir!" Roger backtracked hastily. When he met the resistance of brick, he flattened himself against it. "Tell them–"

"As far as the law is concerned, I acquire my specimens by legal means," said Dr Eldridge, speaking to the constables. "If the men bringing me the specimens are doing so illegally, I assert that I have no knowledge of their methods. This college must be above scandal." His voice darkened. "And certainly above people trying to dispose of murdered young women."

The pair of constables flanked Roger and grabbed his arms. He struggled as they pulled his hands in front of him and shackled his wrists. "Pinching stiffs is only a misdemeanor. I never took no property. I'm a man of science! You can't train doctors without stiffs." Roger's chest tightened. "You're not stupid enough to think I'm the Greyanchor Strangler, are you? There's more to this than–"

"What's this?" interrupted the first constable. Thin sideburns ran the length of his cheeks as if they'd been drawn with charcoal. He pulled the cravat from Roger's neck in one sharp tug, revealing the tattoo shaped like a crenellated wall, the one he'd gotten during his second stay at Old Grim.

"Lookee here. He's got the brand, Melbus. The lad's been jugged twice already." The constable chuckled. "You'll be in for quite a bit longer than you was before, son, mark my words."

Roger gave Dr Eldridge a beseeching look as he was dragged from the room.

"There were times when I thought of you like a son," mumbled Dr Eldridge from the doorway. He choked, yet continued, "But this college is my life. And I'd rather cut out my son than my own throat."

Roger's vision blurred as tears stung his eyes. "That makes two of you worthless blighters, don't it!" Rage coursed through his veins like the hot colored wax he injected into display cadavers. When he looked over his shoulder, Dr Eldridge had gone.

The constables brought Roger to Old Grim in a cab. During their ride through the foggy streets, Roger convinced himself a mistake had been made, a clerical error that would be corrected soon enough. It wasn't uncommon for the wrong man to be arrested and held for a day, sometimes even two or three. Nail had once been kept on suspicion for pickpocketing simply because the victim reported seeing a man with red hair.

The cab halted before a sunken ramp that led deep into the lower levels of Old Grim, levels Roger had never visited during his misdemeanor days. Back then he'd shared a large communal bay more like a barracks than a cell, and he and other fit youths his age were sent to work at the docks or the quarry, overseen by guards with truncheons.

"You've never been down here, have you?" said the constable with sideburns as they disembarked. "It's where we take the rapists and murderers. Not so many windows to climb out of, neither, and I don't just mean lit'ral ones."

"I might be a repeat offender, but you'll see… I'm no murderer."

Roger stumbled forward as the two constables frogmarched him down a muddy ramp. The ramp became a winding stone staircase slick with moss and ended in a gaslit office. A clerk sat behind a paper-strewn desk.

"Name?" he asked without looking up. "Offense?"

"I won't speak till I have legal counsel." Roger did his best to look innocent and affronted, but the constables jostled him roughly.

One of the constables volunteered the requested information instead. "His name's Roger Weathersby, and see this brand on his neck? Former convict, known corpse-trafficker, and I reckon a murderer to boot. You going to deny it again, son?"

Roger bit his tongue – better to remain silent than get tricked into a confession. The clerk shrugged. While the constables gave the particulars of the arrest and the clerk made notes in a ledger, Roger suppressed an urge to shout how wrong they were. They removed the manacles from his wrists, then shucked off his mute's frockcoat, his waistcoat, and searched his pockets to find only the laundry slip for his rented afflictions.

"Where's your coin, son?"

"I weren't yet paid for my last job. I won't be till this afternoon once I've returned my afflictions," said Roger. They'd taken everything but his shoes, trousers, and shirt. He wondered how far they intended to take this farce.

"We'll hold your belongings for now," said the clerk. He made a bundle of Roger's removed clothing and pinned a card to it. "Prisoners pay for their own meals and bedding if they want more than a biscuit and sackcloth – and I advise you to tip your jailer well. He'll clear out a holding cell for you."

Even if Roger wasn't broke, he refused to pay for basic decency.

"For now, you can stay in the counsel room till evening, when you'll be advised on legal matters."

"This won't take long, will it?" Roger's plea sounded tinny and far away, drowned by the constables' laughter. The cold, clammy air dampened his clothes, and he had the sensation of being dragged deep underwater, away from the light.

He didn't deserve this. Though he enjoyed bending the law on occasion, bodysnatching was illegal – barely – because the public feared stiffs and didn't understand how badly doctors needed them. Still, he couldn't afford to stay in jail, not with the real strangler out there and Celeste sick. Then there was Ada. She expected him to return with medicine, and he'd given his word to protect her. If he didn't meet the girl like he'd promised, she'd assume he was a lying bastard who'd forgotten her on purpose.

Worries filling his head, Roger was led to a vaulted room that had the look of an old wine cellar, but for the massive desk in its center. A metal ring was bolted to the floor before the desk, and to this Roger's chains were fettered so he could kneel, but not stand.

"What is this?" Roger shouted, as he was forced to crouch at the jailer's feet. He'd never faced this level of humiliation during his previous arrests. "I didn't kill no one! I have rights. This is no way to treat a suspect."

"If you're lucky, you'll have counsel when you stand afore the magistrate," said the jailer in a voice tinged with mock pity. "Just wait here all patient-like. I wouldn't expect no one before afternoon tea. Behave yourself now and don't make no disgraceful noises."

The jailer left him huddled in the dark.

At first, Roger beat the floor with his fists. Then he tried to contort his hands and slip them free of the iron bracelets, but he only managed to scrape his skin raw. This must be the beginning of the end. No one would find him here. The jailer might as well have tossed him into the deepest pit of Grim's lowest level, and everyone outside would forget he'd ever existed.

No. He arched his back and pulled himself upright. He couldn't give up now. Not with Ada out there, waiting for him. He knew first-hand how rotten it was to care for an ailing parent alone. He'd been eighteen when he'd buried his mother, but Ada wasn't more than ten. If Celeste died, she'd take it hard. And then what? The daughter of a doxy would surely become one, too.

Roger could do nothing while chained in this hole. But it could be worse. Though he was a repeat offender with a zigzag mark on his neck, that didn't mean he'd hang. There were no formal charges on his name yet, just hearsay. Evidence existed to pin him for a single resurrection. He wasn't a murderer, a housebreaker or a highwayman – all hanging crimes. One incident of bodysnatching meant the stocks or whipping post. He'd take his flogging and, as a repeat offender, a month of hard labor on one of the Mudtyne hulks. Ada was resourceful enough to take care of herself for that long, and then he'd start his life over. After all, he'd done it twice before.

He must have fallen asleep on the floor, for when he woke hours later, a pair of patent leather shoes gleamed before his eyes in the gaslight. Roger shifted onto his knees and looked up into the serious, spectacled face of Mr Murray. Beside Roger stood a jailer, idly thwacking a truncheon against his palm.

"Ah, Mr Weathersby," said the lawyer, a stack of papers in his hands. "We meet again, and so soon. I thought you rather evasive during our conversation yesterday, but truth and murder will out, as they say."

"Why do people keep bringing up murder?" Roger snapped.

Mr Murray sighed. "If you plan to argue innocence in a court of law, you'll find it very difficult."

Roger needed to stay calm to get through to this man. "I stole a stiff. I admit it. It's not uncommon, and if you don't steal nothing more, it's barely a crime. I'll take my lashes, that's the risk of the job. But there's no reason for doing me down like this. What haven't I been told, sir?"

Mr Murray sat at the desk and began to read from his papers. "One Roger Weathersby first appears in court records nearly five years ago, upon his release from three months of hard labor. Interestingly, there is no written documentation of his crime. In fact, there's no previous record of Roger Weathersby anywhere, not even a report of birth. But only a year after his release, an undertaker's apprentice named Roger Weathersby was accused by his own master Mr Grausam of eleven counts of resurrectionist activity. A court found him guilty and sentenced him to a flogging and six months of hard labor. On his release he was branded. A subsequent arrest will be the end of legal leniency."

Mr Murray shuffled his papers while Roger knelt with his face burning in rage. "That's none of your business."

"Just last week, this same Roger Weathersby sold the corpse of Claudine Walston to an unknowing physician at an anatomical college. Matters surrounding the woman's death, along with physical evidence, suggest that this Roger Weathersby had, motivated by coin and inhuman urges, suffocated the innocent lady by his own hand and violated her. Further evidence suggests he killed one Lady Margalotte in the same dastardly way, though he was thwarted before he could unearth her, too. In fact, there are a dozen such cases that might be linked to this man."

"Lies!" Roger pounded the floor. "You rotten lot of bastards. It's a frame job. I've been set up–" The jailer landed a kick on Roger's jaw and sent him sprawling.

"My words to you as your legal advisor," continued Mr Murray, "seeing as the evidence falls so hard against you, is to plead guilty and pray for a drop of her royal majesty's mercy."

Roger pushed himself up and spat out a mouthful of blood. "But I ain't guilty."

Mr Murray left his desk to stand over Roger with a leer. He leaned down and whispered, "Then you should have left Ms Walston's corpse alone. Unfortunately, someone must be held accountable. The people expect the Greyanchor Strangler to eventually be caught, and one must manage public expectations, as it were. Finding a suitable scapegoat can be nearly as tiring as arresting the culprit himself. You happen to have a vagabondish look about you. In the court of law, perception is everything."

"But she were dead when I found her! I can prove it, if you bloody imbeciles will let me speak." He had a lot more to say, too – about Celeste's blood and illness, and how none of this seemed right.

Mr Murray shook his head. "You'd do well to hold your tongue. Since it would be best that I handle your case myself, I will note here that you are not of your right mind. How could a man who strangles invalids be sane enough to stand trial? And so you see, your counsel is complete. I thank you for your time, Mr Weathersby."

10

Sibylla spent the morning packing her travel trunk while scheming how she might earn the queen's grace without divulging the identity of her bastard brother. So far her list of queen-endearing strategies included marrying her cousin, catching the Greyanchor Strangler, or plotting the assassination of an Arenberg head of state. After all, Arenberg's pragmatic policies toward its neighbors had soured everyone's good opinion of them, including her grandmother's. Certainly interfering with a foreign nation's government was more palatable than accepting her cousin's hand.

When the gilded stagecoach that would carry her back to civilization crested the hill, her fingers shook with nervous energy as she gathered up the seaweed guide that Lieutenant Calloway had redelivered to her bedroom. Hidden safely between *Chordaria flagelliformis* and *Cutleria multifida* were Roger's letters. She did not intend to let them leave her person until she arrived in Caligo, not after the calamity with Dorinda.

Offering his arm to Sibylla in the hallway, Lieutenant Calloway led her out into the courtyard where guards already flanked the royal carriage. Her feet halted in the snow, and she turned for a final look at Helmscliff estate. Its gray bricks and steepled towers loomed against the clouds. Her eyes swept the windows to glimpse Lady Wayfeather standing in the music room as if expecting Sibylla for lessons. Sibylla lifted her hand to wave, but Lady Wayfeather merely shut the curtains.

She turned back to the carriage where Captain Harrod Starkley was descending its folding step. He wore his dark blue uniform and a surly scowl. At his unexpected appearance, Sibylla had to stop herself from running to him in an unseemly manner. Lieutenant Calloway merely grunted and smoothed his mustache. The two men sized up one another. In spite of Harrod's distinguished naval honor and superior military rank, Lieutenant Calloway chose not to bow. As the son of a famous general and as a lower nobleman from Highspits, he must have decided Harrod was beneath him. Each man reached for Sibylla's hand to help her into the carriage.

Sibylla nearly toppled out again at the sight of her concertina's hexagonal case lurking on one of the benches. She'd always had a horrific time with the instrument, and her skills had never improved despite a decade's worth of practice. In fact, she had deliberately left the concertina sitting in a corner of the music room with the hope of never seeing, or hearing, it again. Lady Wayfeather herself must have placed it in the carriage as a misguided gesture of farewell, or perhaps she feared the ghost of Sibylla's languishing talent might haunt Helmscliff's dreary halls. Either way, the concertina could not arrive in Caligo intact.

Resigned, Sibylla sat beside it with her back to the driver, clutching the seaweed book in her lap. Harrod joined her, and the driver coaxed the horses into a trot.

"Is your highness in good condition?" asked Harrod.

"No one mentioned you'd be escorting me home. I'm so glad you're here, Harrod. I've had the worst visitor, and I mean to tell you everything." She'd only feel comfortable discussing Dorinda once some distance had been placed between her and Helmscliff. In the meantime, she slyly tapped the concertina case. "Do you think we could lose this thing on a particularly bumpy stretch of road?"

His disapproving scowl softened, and he cracked a genuine smile at her suggestion. "Ladies, yes. You really are terrible at that thing. But first, your highness, you'll be just delighted to read *his* reply."

Harrod handed her a scrap of paper crumpled with such little care that she'd have mistaken it for street-side rubbish. So Roger had written after all. Perhaps Harrod had said something to him about her impending return. She unwadded the paper, expecting a message of anticipation.

I thank your highness for putting me in my place. I will stay far from well-born ladies since you say so. Now leave me alone

yr most hmbl & obt svt
rxw

"Is that all?" It took less time to read than a signpost but upset her more than a bad performance of Salston. She dug her nails into her book's leather binding.

"Your highness shouldn't expect so much from my brother," said Harrod with a commiserating lilt.

Sibylla folded the uneven ends of Roger's "letter" together. To her surprise, when she lifted the cover of the seaweed guide to slip it inside, she found a piece of finely folded correspondence from Lieutenant Calloway awaiting her there.

My dearest lady,

I cannot stand to be parted. Each day will be a hollow mollusk without your face to look upon. Though our love must be kept a secret, my ardor swells greater for you each passing day.

I will live tirelessly to please you, to instruct you in the gentle tides of desire and the ebbs of adoration. Do not fret or struggle to know your worth to me. No other woman shall ever quench my thirst.

Once I have persuaded my father and you're finally rid of her royal majesty's rule, we will be together once more.

Your lieutenant and son of most honorable General Calloway,
Viscount of Highspits,
Quincy

Was the man insane? He'd concocted an imaginary love narrative between them that rivaled Salston's greatest tragicomedy: *The Whipping Mistress of Whipperton.* She cursed the salacious playwright, who'd surely inspired this ridiculousness, beneath her breath. At least Harrod would be amused. She was about to share another laugh with him when she realized he had been staring wretchedly at her the entire time.

By the look on his face, discussing Dorinda would have to wait. Sibylla tapped his knee. "Have out with it. We agreed to the concertina's unfortunate demise, so why do you look as though you're about to hear me play the abhorrent thing?"

"I haven't come from Caligo just to escort your highness home."

"Ah." Sibylla paused, listening to the slosh of snow, the squeak of wheels and clomp of hooves. White flakes melted on the windowpane. "Father sent you to warn me of the queen's search for illegitimate children. He's too late." She hesitated, afraid to openly broach the topic of her half-brother. Even carriage footmen had been known to divulge overheard conversations, given the right enticement. The queen herself had learned of the late Prince Consort's untoward relations with prostitutes from a similarly attended ride.

"Prince Henry said nothing to that effect." Harrod stared out the window, distracted by the cliffs overlooking Tyanny Valley. "But then, the queen has always been relentless. Your highness might consider it from her point of view. Myrcnia is a lovely country, but we don't command the massive armies of, say, Khalishka. Every ruler needs legitimacy. The Emperor of Khalishka has military might. Our own beloved regina has magic. Some might say that's all she has. Pardon me if I speak frankly, your highness, but a Myrcnia with a fractured royal bloodline, where any bastard with demonstrable magic could petition the church for legitimacy, would not remain a united Myrcnia for long. If I were in her royal majesty's shoes, I'd do the same."

"How exceedingly unhelpful. I suppose your recommendation is to tell her what she wants to know." Sibylla chafed at his iron love for crown and country.

"I hardly think your highness will do as her royal majesty pleases now, after holding out for so long."

Sibylla released an ink-bee into the air to ease her nervous tension, as she could take no other precautions to protect her secrets while inside a carriage. "At least you're assured. Then I take it you're accompanying me in order to apologize on behalf of a certain deplorable letter writer."

The bee flitted before Harrod's racked face before dispersing into the air.

"Your highness." Harrod jammed his hands between his knees and bowed. Positioned like a bowsprit, he spoke to her knees. "I need your help."

Sibylla flattened her back against the carriage cushion. "Are you soused with spruce liquor?"

"There's someone I know, a brother in arms of sorts, bound to hang from the yardarm by week's end. He's accused of murder." Harrod didn't move.

Sibylla squeezed the cushions. "If you don't stop bowing, I'm going to strike you with this book." She rapped the seaweed guide to emphasize her point. "It's heavy."

"Your highness, please."

"I'm not a barrister, and until you tell me what you want, I can't say yes."

He cleared his throat and straightened. The Order of the Kraken gleamed on his chest. "First, I have no illusions this man is innocent. But, it is beyond the realm of possibility that he would have committed all the crimes he's accused of. Second, I've used my connections, both in the navy and private sector, and no one, not even the Admiral of the Fleet, has been given leave to see the prisoner."

"You should give up hope, then. As much as I commend your responsibility to your comrade, there's nothing I can possibly do. My influence in the capital is sorely lacking."

"There is something." He hesitated. "A royal prerogative of service."

She sharply inhaled. Only recently, she'd seen Dorinda, herself a tattooed recipient of such a prerogative. Sibylla felt a wave of disgust. The royal prerogative of service was just a pretty term for contracting a Straybound. Sibylla had sworn she'd never stoop to take one herself, her royal claim be damned. She didn't need a murderer to carry out her duties. And Harrod knew this. He wouldn't dare ask for such a favor, even if his own brother were bound for the scaffold. Fortunately, Roger practiced medicine, not murder.

"A royal prerogative might untie the tightest of nooses," she said, "but it's hardly a pardon. I wouldn't wish such a fate on a close relative, not to mention your dubious cohort. He may live, but he'd be beholden to me. You've seen what it's like to be tossed about on royal whims."

"Dammit, I know."

"And I could discard, most permanently, this man if I wished. It often happens with the Straybound."

"Your highness." Harrod leaned forward, and for a moment, she thought he intended to bow again. Instead, he placed his hands over hers. "Sibylla, please. I'm asking you for this." He barely refrained from groveling.

Still, he'd never used her first name before. This brother in arms must have saved his life once – a debt Harrod now felt honor bound to repay. She freed her hands, took a breath, and stared at the carriage ceiling. Anyone else and she'd have refused. "Oh, Harrod. I'm going to be in so much trouble."

She opened the seaweed guide. Pressing her fingernail along the binding, she tore out the blank page at the end of the book, its expensive paper perfect for penning an official document.

She paused. Harrod had never asked anything of her in all their years of knowing one another. There was more to this than he let on. "Are you certain he's innocent?"

Harrod nodded stiffly, and she didn't have the heart to press him to unveil his secrets when she kept so many of her own. Sibylla flexed her fingers, black crescents of ink welling underneath her fingernails. She had seen royal prerogatives set behind glass in the palace depository, but reproducing one without the proper signet required steady concentration.

"The name?" she asked.

Harrod shifted forward. "Ah, best left until a justiciar is present. You have my word: he's innocent. And in need of a saving grace – even if that comes via Straybound branding."

She reviewed the paperwork. "Are you certain this is right?"

"Oh, quite, I've seen this done before. If you'll just indicate at the bottom that I'm acting as your executor, I promise your highness that when the matter is concluded, we'll find a suitable place for my... cohort in your service."

Sibylla handed Harrod the writ, but he remained half-bowed as if he'd just lost to a bruiser in the ring. Hoping to enliven his mood, she grabbed the leather handle of the concertina case and opened the carriage window. "Now there's only one matter left to attend to. What do you shout on the high seas? Man overboard!" She waited for his dry smile, then pitched the instrument into the dark.

The clop of horse hooves on paving stones woke her. The dim morning light flickered across Harrod's face as he snored. Pulling the blanket around her shoulders, Sibylla leaned against the window. The fog and brick of Caligo seemed colder and darker than her memories of painted stucco and gilded gates. How long before she could walk its narrow alleys again and buy oysters at the docks?

As they approached the palace, streets widened and gutters emptied until finally she didn't see anyone pissing or passing out.

The carriage slowed as the horses began the climb toward Broadbriar Street and the highest point of Caligo – Malmouth Palace. Her childhood home. Sibylla noted the excessive number of guards stationed along the exterior wall. She hunted for familiar faces, but they were all strange to her now. The palace, however, hadn't changed. After the death of the prince consort a decade ago, the royal grounds underwent an expensive refurbishment that included scouring the grim exterior, adding a wing, and restoring the century-old marble fountain by the famous sculptor Obden. And to garner favor with the public, a section of the gardens had opened for visitation.

Curious, she kicked Harrod's leg and he started awake. "Why are there so many guards?"

"For the Emperor of Khalishka's extended visit. All hands on deck, as it were. His imperial majesty – Emperor Timur – had so much fun touring his newest territories, he's decided to stroll along our coast as well. When the Cabbage King decides to swoop in for a visit, you can't very well say no. Besides, if we put on an impressive enough show, perhaps he'll lower the tariffs on Myrcnian cheese."

Sibylla hoped to gain more from the emperor's visit than a tax reduction. Emperor Timur's reputation for starting and ending wars in his favor did not paint him as an obvious solution to her worries, but a royal bastard could easily disappear into Khalishka's countryside. Her grandmother would never think to look for Prince Henry's illegitimate son in the lofty post of Ambassador Extraordinary, and Sibylla would still be able to contact him. And, if the queen *did* think to look for him there, he'd already have a host of connections abroad. Now she need only convince Khalishka they needed a Myrcnian embassy.

Unfortunately, diplomacy with Khalishka was mired with difficulties. When the Khalishkan Empire, long desirous of an eastern warm water port, annexed Arenbough – the slender country wedged between Myrcnia and Ulmondstedt – the queen signed a treaty of alliance with Ulmondstedt's parliament, which provoked the Khalishkan government to levy an extra import duty on Myrcnian cheese. Many considered this outcome a failure of the queen. Some even believed she should have officially renounced Ulmondstedt as an ally.

"What do you think of our relationship with Khalishka?" Sibylla tapped thoughtfully on the cover of her seaweed guide.

"Strained to say the least – our entire military has been on edge for months. But the emperor's procession is expected to go smoothly, and the queen is even planning one of her famous spark shows." Harrod shrugged. "A show of power for the powerful."

Whenever the queen wanted to impress the masses or foreign dignitaries, she trotted out her special recreation of King Roderick's Great Geese Feast.

Centuries ago, when a flood of the Mudtyne River threatened to decimate the city's population with famine, a desperate King Roderick sighted a large flock of geese migrating over the capital. He immediately took to Hangman's Tower where he shot forth sparks from his fingertips over the city. Fully cooked fowls fell from the sky, the famine was ended, and the people rejoiced. Nowadays, the queen used floating paper lamps instead of live birds, and the people collected the burnt ash in silver dishes.

It was not a good sign. Her grandmother hadn't bothered with the extravagant ceremony in years.

As they approached the palace's front gates, Sibylla nudged Harrod's foot. "After you've settled affairs, I expect to meet this fellow of yours. Well ahead of the Binding ceremony, if you please."

"Your highness knows that's impossible." Harrod lurched forward as a carriage wheel hitched into a divot. "Tradition dictates that until the Binding is completed, your highness shall be kept at a distance from the condemned. For your safety."

The Binding ceremony was the final pact in the Straybound contract and would take place within Sibylla's personal chapel inside St Myrtle's cathedral, presided over by Archbishop Tittlebury. Once completed, the convicted murderer would be reborn in the eyes of the church, absolved in the eyes of the law, and magically bound to their royal patron for life. Sibylla's stomach nervously turned.

"But if, as you said, the condemned in this case is an innocent man, I'd like to speak with him to ensure he understands the price."

Harrod averted his eyes. "Then I'll try to bring him by before his six days of probation are up."

As the carriage squeaked to a halt at the front of Malmouth Palace, Sibylla pondered Harrod's odd request. He wasn't the sort of man to be overtaken with sentimentality. His former comrade-in-arms must be special indeed. Why else would Harrod have begged her for such a cruel favor? Still, if this man *had* saved Harrod's life then she also owed him, though the thought of taking on a Straybound left her cold and shaken.

11

After his sham of a consultation with Mr Murray, Roger was hauled off to a private cell. The jailer removed his chains, reminded him that washing-up water would be provided once a week and food once a day unless he paid for extra privileges, then locked the iron door. Roger paced, glad at least to use his legs again. Just two strides wide and four strides long, the cell contained little more than a bucket, a wash basin, and burlap sacking on a stone ledge that served as a cot.

Roger wiped the blood from his face as best he could. Then he wrapped himself in the filthy burlap and slept for what felt like days. When he woke, he'd lost all sense of time. His shouts went unanswered, so he lay on his side and watched a smudge of gray, fog-filtered sunlight creep across his cell floor. Throughout the day he paced, sipped brackish water from the basin, and scraped his sore teeth against the impenetrable crust of a biscuit the jailer shoved through a hatch.

Just as the light-smudge reached the far wall, a folded parchment slid under his door. Roger pounced on the official-looking document and read:

Mr Roger Weathersby, though not fit to stand before the magistrate, was this morning convicted of ten counts of brutal and unnatural murder, vile acts of indecency, and resurrectionist activity. Despite every effort of the defense, the aforementioned Roger Weathersby has been justly sentenced to die tomorrow at noon. He will be hanged

by the neck and then removed while still conscious to be drawn,
castrated, and finally disemboweled. In consideration to the defense,
the burning of entrails and quartering will be waived in favor of
a public dissection, performed on his mortal remains in the Caligo
University main lecture hall, as a deterrent to the public for the
horrid crime of murder.

Disemboweled and castrated! Such punishment was reserved for traitors or those who defiled the royal family. Not even murderers had their tackle lopped off – they were simply and decently hanged. In principle, he believed in giving his *intact* body to science, but couldn't bear the thought of medical students recognizing him and laughing at his mangled, emasculated corpse. They'd probably carve off his fingers as keepsakes. He knew one young doctor who liked to show off the ear of Mortimer Stubbs, leader of the Highspits Plot, which he kept preserved in a jar – not for science, but to shock and disgust his colleagues.

This whole bloody affair didn't make any sense. Only the criminally insane – the kind who would throw their own filth at the barristers – didn't have a say at their trial. Everyone else had the right to speak in their defense. Twice before he'd stood in the prisoners' dock to address the magistrate, and both times he'd actually done what he'd been accused of. This time, when he finally had something to say on his own behalf, he had no way to present his case. They had him dead to rights.

The clack-clack of footsteps echoed in the corridor.

Roger threw himself at the door. "Hey! Talk to me man-to-man, you filthy lying bastards!" He shouted his throat hoarse and bruised his fists from pounding. When he stopped to catch his breath, he heard the jailer singing in a spiteful baritone:

When lamps are lit along the street
Beware if you should ever meet
A miscreant named Weathersby
Who murders girls most lustily.
He'll catch them in a stranglehold
– they say he likes his women cold.

But now he's caught, his time is through,
And soon, exposed to public view,
His anatomy shall be displayed,
As a lesson for all: laws must be obeyed.

The jailer halted outside Roger's cell and knocked twice before adding one last impromptu line to his ballad.

No evening gruel
For the Greyanchor ghoul.

Roger slumped against the door. If he'd had any food left in his stomach, he'd have lost it now. His name must have appeared in the criminal broadsheets, featured among Myrcnia's most gruesome accidents and crimes, and accompanied by a catchy verse and woodcut illustration. They sold for a winkle to morbid-minded carpenters and fishwives, who then spent their day singing "Justice Hoggs was found eaten by dogs" or "Take no gift from Poison Mary, cake or biscuit, peach or plum" set to popular melodies. Just last week, his landlady Mrs Carver had been singing "Poison Mary" while splitting chickens. She'd have seen his name in the broadsheets, maybe even rented out his room after sending for a deacon to purge his garret of evil.

And Ada. She might not read but, with others singing it on the street, she'd overhear soon enough. How monstrous he'd seem, filtered through a criminal's ballad. Everyone he'd ever known – including a certain princess – would remember him as a strangler and a violator of corpses. It might be simpler to make his shirt into a noose and hang himself. At least then he'd die with his bollocks intact. He got so far as unbuttoning his shirt when his fingers froze. He was alive, and he might still get free. He just needed to convince himself.

Sod it. No one ever escaped from Old Grim.

He lay sprawled on the stone ledge like a corpse on a slab, determined to sleep until he was dead.

The next morning Roger woke to a stale biscuit ricocheting off his forehead. He chipped a tooth biting into the thing and ended up pounding the biscuit to bits using the basin as a millstone. He added water to the crumbs to make a paste, which he licked off his fingers. When he'd finished, he realized the jailer had been watching him all along through the sliding hatch in the door.

"You've some visitors," said the jailer as he entered the cell. He was a thickset man in a long blue coat and official's cocked hat. By his baritone voice, he'd sung the ballad outside Roger's cell the day before. He manacled Roger's wrists together and fed the long chain through a ring on the cell wall. "Right distinguished ones. Mind yourself before the most holy liaisons or you'll be pressin' your face to the whipping post, mark my words."

Roger was made to sit on the floor with his back to the wall. His head throbbed, and any pressure to his left temple sent a knife-stab through his brain. It took a minute for the jailer's words to make sense.

"Liaisons? Holy?" Most likely the chaplain – well, he could go toast his eyebrows. The church thought a man's blood held his soul. Surgeons knew better. He spat on his fingers and raked them through his hair, rattling his chains.

"Aye. Come to absolve you of your sins before your guts is slit, I expect. Which reminds me. For ten shillings I'll procure for you the finest kidney pie as your last meal. Fitting, no?" The jailer grinned. "His grace might spot you the coin, if you remember to ask."

The jailer set a wooden chair inside the cell door. Footsteps rang in the corridor, and he doffed his hat and bowed.

But this was no chaplain.

Harrod entered the cell, and Roger sat up in shock. It couldn't be. His brother had traded his dusty traveler's coat for a pristine uniform with bicorn hat, and had tucked a riding crop under one arm.

"Brother," Roger gasped. The sight of a familiar face, even one as vexing as Harrod's, wrung a few humiliating tears from his eyes. Though days ago he'd vowed to pummel him at the earliest opportunity, Roger now felt an overwhelming urge to embrace him, even clasp his knees. The chain proved too short, however. Roger slumped to the ground. In all his imaginings of how he'd spend his final hours, Harrod had never crossed his mind.

"Leave us. I must prepare the prisoner to meet his grace," Harrod instructed the jailer, who bowed and retreated.

"How did you find me?" Roger spoke to the tops of Harrod's boots.

His brother tapped the riding crop against his shin. "Magic."

"My fault for asking."

How typical of Harrod to track him all the way down here. When Roger was a boy, Harrod had always known when and where to catch him red-handed and up to no good. His instincts – or intelligence sources – were uncanny.

Ignoring the chair, Harrod glowered at Roger. "So, I hear you're a convicted murderer now. Is there any truth to that?"

"I didn't murder no one. But why should you believe me? No one else does."

"Oh, I hardly think you capable of the arduous task of murder," Harrod laughed. "But when a man breaks laws as flagrantly as you do, he gets what's coming to him."

"A traitor's death is what's coming to me," Roger moaned.

"I hear the evidence against you couldn't sway the most merciful judge otherwise. But I know a louse like you can hardly curl his hand into a fist, let alone strangle anyone."

"If you would just listen. There's a strangler out there, but he ain't me. I'm telling you, that poor soul Claudine were buried alive. By Queen Mildred's knickers, if I'd only found her an hour sooner, none of this would be happening."

"Found her where? In her grave?" Harrod shot him a furious look. "All this could have been avoided, had you lived the respectable life our mother would have wished."

Roger winced. "I might deserve to rot in the jug for a good long while, but that don't change the fact that I never killed no one. If you came here to gloat then you can bugger off, you ass."

"Enough of your whinging." Harrod crouched and prodded Roger in the chest with the riding crop. "They won't hang you. Not yet. Some strings have been pulled, and you've been granted a divine intervention."

Roger could hardly believe his ears. "I've been pardoned?"

"Not exactly. You won't be gutted or emasculated. Though it comes at a steep price."

"Don't take on my debts, Harrod."

"I have nothing to do with it. You have the princess to thank."

Roger stared. Sibet's belittling letters had convinced him she'd lost all feeling for him.

A creaky voice interrupted them. "Innocent of heart, pure of charity." An elderly, clean-shaven gent stood in the doorway, wearing full church robes in white and gold. His tall hat nearly scraped the ceiling. He kissed his fingers and held them up like some cheap actor, muttering invocations beneath his breath. Harrod bowed deeply, as if greeting the queen herself.

"And who's this?" Roger squinted. The man's grand posturing was so out of place in this dingy cell, it had to be a cruel joke. "The Almighty Whomever himself, come to bail me out? You're having me on. There's no pardon. You toffs paid off the jailer to have a laugh at me."

"Silence." Harrod thrashed Roger's shoulders with the crop. Roger flinched and bit back a yelp. "I won't stand for your heresy. His grace the honorable Archbishop Tittlebury of Cropspin is present on behalf of her highness, the most merciful Princess Sibylla. I can assure you, no one here is amused."

Roger pressed his palms into the ground and gathered his thoughts. "That's truly the bleeding archbishop?"

Archbishop Tittlebury was the designated head of the Myrcnian Church, and officiated over state religious matters on behalf of the queen. Acting as the ruling monarch's 'divine conduit' to the commoners, his position sounded more like some sort of special gutter in which to upend royal chamber pots. As a palace footman, Roger had glimpsed the archbishop at official dinners in full regalia, which he recalled more clearly than the man's unremarkable face.

Harrod tapped his riding crop against his boot. "That is indeed the archbishop. You will refer to him as 'your grace,' and he is here for the sole purpose of saving your neck. Show some respect."

"Your grace." Roger sucked in a breath as if he might retroactively silence himself, and bowed his head toward the archbishop. Then he looked at Harrod. "You said there's a catch?"

Harrod's professional demeanor didn't crack. "Her highness Princess

Sibylla has elected to save you, a convicted murderer–" Roger bristled at the word "–from the scaffold by ordaining you into the Straybound. You will be sworn to her highness and given the rites of redemption through service. Can you comprehend the meaning of this?"

Harrod's choice of the word "service" put him on guard, and his relief at dodging a disgusting end faded only slightly as he realized a new type of noose would be fitted about his neck. As a dead man he wouldn't be fit to serve, so by his estimations he *might* be better off.

"I've heard the word before, sir. Along with a faerie story about bewitched slaves who do as they're commanded. Though," Roger added softly so Archbishop Tittlebury wouldn't hear, "I think it's mostly nonsense. A man's brain is his own. It can't be bridled or fitted with levers."

Harrod's face remained unreadable. "Today is the initial anointing. Your final Binding will take place at St Myrtle's Cathedral in six days' time. But as we can't have murderers serving the Divine Maiden straight out of Old Grim, or running loose in the streets scaring children, I will oversee your probation until such a time as you are fully bound, and your soul reclaimed. For the next week, I will prepare you for this most vital and blessed role."

Roger detected a sardonic curl to Harrod's lip. Now he understood which way the wheels in his brother's head turned.

"You've leashed me at last. With the nooseman at my door, one of you was bound to get a rope around my neck." He almost believed Harrod had orchestrated this entire murder conviction so he could smugly waltz into prison, snatch Roger from the scaffold's shadow, and bring him to heel once and for all.

To his surprise, Harrod placed a hand on his shoulder. "Roger – Mr Weathersby," he amended, a reluctant formality for the archbishop's benefit, no doubt. "We're here to spare your life and guide you down the proper path at last."

Roger stared at the moldy floor between his hands and didn't budge. "And how is that?"

"Think of Princess Sibylla as your gentle-hearted patron. After the archbishop anoints you, you'll spend your probation in preparation for the Binding. You'll be locked up at night, of course – until the Binding you remain a convicted murderer in the eyes of the law. But I'll feed you, ensure you are respectably dressed, and see that you adhere to your ceremonial fealty."

"Ceremonial fealty? You mean to enslave me. What devilish tripe!" shouted Roger.

Harrod brandished his crop. "You will not speak thusly in the presence of his grace."

Roger winced. By the sharp expression in Harrod's eyes, Roger knew if he protested again, he'd get worse than his brother's right hook. "Pardon the language, your grace." He ducked his head.

Harrod continued, "Myrcnia punishes criminals, it does not enslave innocents. All Straybound are pardoned murderers. They also have a reputation of extreme loyalty to their patrons. Something you'll come to understand in time."

Again, the archbishop kissed his fingers and raised them in the air. "Thou shouldst be grateful to be chosen by the most exalted princess for the ordination, young man. This Rite of Initiation by the ancient line of Muir dates to the first merciful pardoning of Angus the Foul, who exchanged an inevitable state of headlessness for the divine bindings of Priest-King Rupert the Webbed."

Roger had seen a reprint of an illuminated manuscript once, in a book Sibet had given him to read. The figure of a shirtless man lay bent over a chopping block, while around him gathered richly-clad spectators – some human, some with faerie wings or water sprite tails. One man held a golden knife above his head. Another offered a golden cup. Sibet had translated the caption in fancy Old Myrcnian script aloud for him: "The Binding of Angus the Foul, first Straybound to the King."

"I've seen the pictures, your reverence," Roger said.

Harrod swung his crop impatiently. "Never mind the history. Let's not keep his grace from his *many* important duties."

Archbishop Tittlebury nodded solemnly. "First, to become bound the sinner must surrender his autonomy into the hands of his patron with an act of supplication and a signature. This is the Rite of Contract. Angus the Foul signed his in blood, but nowadays we use red ink."

Harrod lay a hand on Roger's head. "Should you wish for the Divine

Maiden to spare you an excruciating death, you must perform a formal act of supplication. I've written a brief script for your convenience."

Roger sat up on his knees. Having little choice, he took Harrod's offered scrap of parchment and read aloud through gritted teeth: "I, Roger Weathersby, being found guilty by the magistrate for the heinous and vile crime of murder, do humbly beg the Divine Maiden Sibylla that my wretched life be spared by the power of her royal majesty the Queen's Exalted Bench."

"Now, there's only the matter of your signature." Harrod gave Roger's head a satisfied pat.

The archbishop held out an ivory box in his shaking hands. He lifted the lid, revealing a gold quill and crystal inkwell filled with the blood-colored ink. Harrod pressed the writing instrument to Roger's palm and pulled the chair over to serve as a table. Miniscule calligraphy covered the document they set before him, the text incomprehensible Old Myrcnian.

"Your signature," said Archbishop Tittlebury, "must be freely given. A Straybound's existence is as fleeting as a candle in a hurricane. Some say it is easier to simply die."

Roger balked. Formal supplication be damned, he didn't have to sign this hideous paper. He could tell Harrod to bugger off with his oppressive contract and enjoy a freeing, if excruciating, death on his own terms. Roger touched his neck, imagining the scratch of a hemp noose. A slit belly. Mutilated manhood. His own pickled eyeballs in a jar on some young surgeon's desk, forever winning staring contests with horrified patients.

On the other hand, Sibet had offered to save his life. She hadn't forgotten him. Swearing fealty to her couldn't be worse than death. He swallowed, then scribbled an X where Harrod pointed.

"Your full name," said Harrod sternly. "You might fool your jailers, but I know you can write."

Roger added the *Roger* and *Weathersby* to either side of the X.

The ink had barely dried when there was a commotion in the hall. A flush-faced Mr Murray slid into Roger's cell.

"Did you think you'd get away with this chicanery?" Mr Murray pulled his collar higher and stabbed his pen in Harrod's direction. "I think not, sir. I don't care what medals you wear, this man has been found guilty, convicted of the most heinous crimes, and will pay for it at the end of a rope."

Harrod adjusted his Order of the Kraken. "This man is no longer a concern of the court."

"I do insist on verifying this alleged legal claim. You may have put a blind man's mask on these constables, but I won't be fooled by so evident a sham. You'll be demoted and stripped of your station for committing perjury. Nothing short of a royal pardon by the queen herself could set this villain free."

"Fortunately, you are mistaken." The archbishop stepped forward, his tall hat falling slightly askew to reveal a tuft of silver hair.

"Archbishop Tittlebury." Mr Murray bowed his head respectfully, sucking in his breath as he affixed his spectacles to his nose. "I had no idea your grace was present here. I would have never dared to interrupt. But on whose authority…"

Archbishop Tittlebury cleared his throat. His shoulders hunched, but his chin rose, displaying a ceremonial gold mask little more than the width of his eyes that appeared melted to his face. "According to the Act of Righteous Authority, as a direct heir to the throne, the aforementioned signatory who will henceforth not be named has exercised privilege to this man's life in perpetuity."

"Perpetuity?" said Roger in alarm. It hadn't quite sunk in that he'd be in the princess' service for the rest of his life. But Sibet had mentioned the Act to him once when they were younger, in between complaining about her cousins and cursing the concertina. He hoped she hadn't planned this fate for him all along.

According to the Act of Righteous Authority, a member of the royal family was permitted to keep one Straybound at a time. As a palace footman he'd known they existed, but their identities were shrouded in mystery. There were rumors the Crown Prince changed his Straybound every few months, and, since they were sworn to him for life, that meant they must have died. The high turnover of palace staff made it difficult to determine who was a Straybound – if Straybound were palace staff at all. Sibet had teased him that any one of the maids could be a cold-hearted villain capable of killing him with a knitting needle up the nose, should he misbehave.

Mr Murray stared at the cracks in the floor. "As a proxy for her most honorable grace, might you not divulge the truth so I may offer my wisdom to the newly blessed?"

Archbishop Tittlebury merely kissed his fingers and shook them in the air. "As *you*, my dear fortunate, are already aware… per the Safekeeping and Privacy of Royals Act, no one royal shall presume authority over the property of another, or interfere in the acquisition of said property. All the details therein shall remain confidential."

Harrod snatched the pen that had assaulted him from Mr Murray's trembling hand and jabbed it at the lawyer's chest. "Not for you to know."

"And what is *your* name?" Mr Murray scoured Harrod's uniform for evidence.

Harrod leaned his head into the hall. "Jailer, remove the prisoner's restraints. And this man, too."

Mr Murray stood slack-jawed while Roger smirked. For once he wasn't the only victim of Harrod's officiousness.

12

Sibylla strode through the palace gardens until she reached the steep hillock at the furthest end. Malmouth grotto was only open to the public for one hour before dusk each day but the royal family had no such restrictions. Her father, Prince Henry, visited every morning, and the grotto would be the perfect place for them to discuss her half-brother's wellbeing, or lack thereof. The extreme measures the queen had taken to pry his identity from Sibylla – sending Dorinda to Helmscliff when the palace was busy preparing for the Khalishkan emperor's historic first visit – made her suspect the queen had recently gained proof her half-brother had survived into adulthood.

Passing beneath an archway covered in ivy, Sibylla descended a subterranean path excavated into the hill. The sound of her footsteps crunching gravel became hollow echoes of her soles on smooth stone. The architect Obden had created the grotto shrine nearly two centuries earlier to commemorate the end of the Doomsday Miasma. An inscription on the wall recalled how King Indulf rediscovered his faith in Myrcnia and the people of Caligo via their swift action against those who sought to blend science and magic to evil ends.

Sibylla bowed her head toward the small copper statue of the Lady of the Stream nestled beneath a protective awning on a limestone ledge. Her copper hair, polished daily by the priest who cared for the grotto, cascaded over an armored breastplate. Absinthe-green moss carpeted the stone ledges and crept up the statue's fishtail.

Beside a basin – the wavy shell of a giant clam mortared into the rock – hung a tin dipper. Visitors could wash their hands and drink from the healing waters after hanging their prayer plaques on a wall-sized iron trellis. Sibylla sipped from the dipper before peering down into the pool.

Its deep, clear water glowed blue even in ice-cold winter. A pair of silver ghost-carp spiraled lazily in the pool while gas fonts illuminated the grotto with a low, greenish light that rose and faded with the air currents. No one dropped coins into the pool out of respect for the royal family. Donations went in a large metal lockbox instead, and simple painted plaques of holy monarchs could be purchased for a few winkles. Most were simply carved and painted. The more desperate supplicants could buy grandiose gilded plaques at the cathedrals. Stealing the plaques, too, was rare. People in Caligo tended to believe in curses.

Sibylla removed her glove and dipped her hand into the water. Sensing a kindred creature, one of the ghost-carp swam up to brush her fingertips. She shook water droplets from her hand and wandered toward the trellis that held the prayer plaques.

Her father, Prince Henry, checked on the plaques daily. He believed it was his obligation to read the wishes written on the back of his likenesses. While Sibylla waited for him, she flipped the plaques over to read the various prayers. Someone had entreated Saint-Queen Ingrid for a sunny wedding day. Another, addressed to the current queen, begged a husband to stay true, while one of King Roderick's devotees had a simple hankering for a pork haunch. Each royal's reputation tended to guide the worshiper.

Sibylla glimpsed one plaque and gasped. An all-too-familiar face with rounded cheeks stared back. The likeness of herself was handsomely carved and painted by some novice priest as part of his training. Either that young priest had taken his vows as a joke or plaques bearing her face had become acceptable icons for saintly intercession during her absence.

She hunted through the others. While she found no depictions of her cousins, she collected a total of five "Divine Maiden Sibylla" plaques, fewer than Prince Henry but more than the crown prince.

Because money had been spent to leave them in her name, she

treated each as a delicate artifact. One by one, she read them: a man asking for her help to bed the barkeep's daughter; a woman wishing to heighten her husband's passion for her; another begging forgiveness for fornicating with the haberdasher's husband. Apparently, she'd attended one too many Salston productions for her reputation to come through unscathed.

But as Sibylla read the last two, her interest piqued.

Mabel says we owe it to mistress to ask for your help, so here I am writing to a princess after my shift when I'd rather be at home. You may have heard about the Greyanchor Strangler. Near everyone in our Quarter has.

Then, in tinier script as though the author suddenly realized she wouldn't be able to fit much else…

Well, maybe you haven't heard so far as the countryside, but here it is, Divine Maiden Sibylla, please have this man caught and quartered and displayed so I may spit upon him meself.

The final plaque – Mabel's? – displayed better legibility and more reverence.

Divine Maiden Sibylla, I beseech thee, on behalf of the good people of Caligo and as a devout Myrcnian, to smite the beast that hath taken our dear mistress, Claudine Walston, on her final carriage ride. She were a goodly and kind mistress, and loved your highness so.

"Quiet, isn't it?"

Startled, Sibylla's breath caught in her throat, and she clutched the plaques to her chest. She had read the Greyanchor Strangler's name and for a moment she believed she'd summoned him. Upon turning, she discovered her cousin Edgar marched stiffly toward her instead. He wore a black overcoat and a scarf wrapped three times around his neck. The eldest son of Crown Prince Elfred, Edgar never ventured far from his mother Lady Esther, or from Malmouth Palace. A favorite of the queen, Edgar usually got his way in all things, save Sibylla agreeing to marriage.

Sibylla forced a smile. "I didn't expect to meet you here."

Edgar scanned the iron trellis before his eyes narrowed on the plaques in her hand. "You've seen them, then." He sniffed. "Your plaques. They should have thought to copy a more honest portrait. I've been trying to halt the manufacture of those ridiculous things for months, but the commoners won't have it. At least the church is filling their coffers." Edgar looked as though he intended to snatch the plaques from Sibylla's hands. He was petty enough to do so, especially as no one had left any in his name.

Sibylla tucked the plaques neatly behind her back. "You appear in good health, cousin."

He ignored her compliment. "The idea of praying to a princess." He tsked. "I might have a word with the priest who makes them. If he favored a more realistic likeness, there'd be less interest. I hear they're being sent as far as the Fillsbirth grotto. The very idea…"

"I'm sure yours will be equally popular…" Sibylla glanced around the grotto. "…somewhere."

Even if her father showed his face at the grotto now there was no sense staying. She couldn't speak with him about her half-brother and risk Edgar reporting everything to the queen. Instead, she made her way toward the exit.

"But alas," she said, "I only came for a quick peek. Who but Grandmother would schedule a dress fitting so soon after an overnight carriage ride? You'll forgive me, but I'm certain I'll be missed."

"The plaques?" Edgar prompted. "I'll get rid of them for you."

"I simply must keep them. I am so sentimental, after all." She bowed her head. "Later then."

She veered around her cousin and hurried up the path. The gardens spread out in front of her and she chose the circuitous path back to Malmouth to avoid further interactions with Edgar. The idea of *anyone* marrying the man upset her. Her thumb traced one of the plaque's indentations. While she might not be able to grant everyone's prayers, she could look more closely into this Greyanchor Strangler. After all, those two shopgirls had cared so deeply for their mistress they'd made the trek to the palace grotto in the middle of winter.

While the queen practiced for the emperor's reception in two days' time by shooting sparks in the courtyard, Sibylla slipped unnoticed into Malmouth Palace. Once in her bedroom, she removed her coat and draped it over her traveling trunk, which the servants had delivered a short while earlier.

She hardly recognized her childhood haven with only its barest living necessities: a bed, wardrobe, and fusty chaise lounge. Her one remaining personal belonging was an oak writing desk that had belonged to her mother, filled with paper she'd collected from places as far as the milky seas of Andorna. Even the chairs from her reading nook were gone, and she was half-surprised no one had pried off the porcelain ivy-leaf moldings that wound up its walls.

As she set the prayer plaques on her desk, some writing on the picture-side of one caught her eye. She hadn't noticed it before. It was Mabel's plaque, and appeared to be a list of sorts, in a kind of shorthand, of six locations, each accompanied by a date. The final date lined up with Mabel's mistress' death. Helpfully, this Mabel had also provided a partial list of the Greyanchor Strangler's victims along with the addresses where they'd met the murderer.

Sibylla removed paper from her desk and spread the blank sheets across the floor. A map of Caligo lived in her heart, with its familiar corners and cervices. She spread her fingers and let the ink flow until it stained her fingernails. Then, with a twist of her wrists, she touched the center of each sheet. Ink lines sinuously spread outward to form the arteries connecting Greyanchor Necropolis to the Medical district, Malmouth Palace to Brocade Circle, from one sheet to the next. The Mudtyne River formed a black spine of vertical bridges that eventually became the docks. At last the entire city lay unfurled before her, a black skeleton of streets on bone-white paper.

As Sibylla walked among the sheets of paper, she inked numbers upon the map to correspond, in order, with the locations where the

Greyanchor Strangler had claimed his victims: a humble flat above a tailor shop on Newbridge Street, a modest townhouse on Stargazy Lane, a pricy home near Skyes Park within view of the Starry Opera House, and so on. When she'd inked the six known crime scenes, she tried to discern a pattern, some preference in locale that might tell her where to send additional constables. But the six victims extended from one end of the city to the other, crossing the Mudtyne and back, in wealthy neighborhoods, slums, even two different hospitals.

She gripped the desk in frustration. *Nothing*. This Greyanchor Strangler might as well be drawing lots from a census. She glanced toward the prayer plaques. These two prayers deserved to be answered, but she didn't know how. The constabulary should have been on top of any patterns and clues. Still, those shopgirls had trusted her, even given her a lead. She didn't want to be a divine disappointment.

At the sound of footsteps in the hallway, she hurriedly gathered her drawings and stacked them facedown on her desk, lest someone think she had an unnatural obsession with murderers. She jumped when the queen arrived with an entourage in tow. She hadn't expected to see her grandmother until dinner.

Sibylla lowered her head. "Your Royal Highness, Grand Merciful Mother." She shifted her right foot behind her and placed her left hand over her heart.

As she held her curtsy, five of the queen's attendants filed inside the bedroom. Among them, Sibylla recognized Dorinda, wearing a high-collared blouse and sharp smile. Bringing up the rear, a girl pushed a cart laden with boiled quails' eggs, mustard tarts, and fresh milk. Sibylla waited for the nod that would indicate she could move, but the queen circled her twice before allowing her to relax.

"Your hair is too short." The queen's terse manner suggested a lack of sleep but her eyes brimmed with alertness. She had the look of a constant planner, ready for whatever the wind might blow onto the cold Myrcnian shores. As the queen tugged a lock of her graying hair, Sibylla noticed the horizontal scar across her left thumb – the telltale sign of performing Dorinda's Straybound devotionals. Only a cut repeated daily in the same place could escape the Muir bloodline's exceptional healing that quickly faded blemishes and scarring alike.

Since Sibylla had trimmed her hair several times without Harrod or Lady Wayfeather catching on, she wondered if they might be reprimanded in her stead. "It only appears short because it's pinned up."

"Take measurements for a new corset." The queen beckoned to a woman with a seamstress' chatelaine at her waist. "She is obviously in need of something stiffer with better boning. She'll require new gowns as well as shoes and gloves for the theater, several dinners, and a ball. Azalea pink, Tympen purple, and Lipthverian blue. Also something silver for the reception. Be sure it has sheen. The finer quality the better, but nothing too cloying. No sense swaddling the sow."

The seamstress pulled off Sibylla's wrinkled dress before she could object. With tape from the chatelaine she measured Sibylla's shoulders, waist, and bust. The queen had rarely cared what Sibylla wore. Even as a child, she had never been forced into heavy brocade dresses or elaborate tiaras and masks. Her gut twisted with every pinch of this personalized attention.

"Your face is nicely pale," said the queen, "and I assume you've kept up with the concertina."

Sibylla could still hear the crack of the instrument case, tossed out of the carriage from Helmscliff, but she kept silent lest she suffer a thorough dressing-down.

"She looks beautiful." Lady Brigitte, Sibylla's mother, appeared in the doorway, wearing a dusky blue dress and a hat so bedecked with carnations it would make a basket jealous.

Sibylla slipped free from the seamstress. After holding her tongue through the fittings, it was a relief to embrace her mother. Lady Brigitte smelled of jasmine and honeysuckle. Exhaling a deep breath, Sibylla's tension drained away as she squeezed her mother's waist. The rare sight of her parents always reduced her to an adoring child. Raised under the firm hand of the queen, she sometimes forgot their faces. When permitted to visit, her parents brought stories and gifts.

The queen snapped at a maid to move out of her way. "Lady Brigitte. You've finally returned. And no more punctual than your daughter, I see."

"I came through Fillsbirth last night." Lady Brigitte pulled hatpins from her hair.

"Have you informed your husband?"

"I will shortly, but as I haven't seen Sibylla since last spring, I thought I might indulge in a peek."

The queen scrutinized Lady Brigitte's face. "The baths have improved your complexion." She glanced back to Sibylla. "Dorinda, have a milk bath prepared for my granddaughter. We can't have her looking inferior to her mother. Brigitte, now you've had your… peek, shouldn't you be on your way?"

"As your royal majesty wills it." Lady Brigitte bowed her head before whispering in Sibylla's ear, "I have something for you, my dearest. After dinner, if you can make it to dessert without upsetting your grandmother. You'd never believe it, but feculent Fillsbirth has the most delightful shops."

Fillsbirth was an industrial town south of Caligo, known for its shipping industry and steady supply of import goods. Lady Brigitte travelled there once a season to stock up on hats, silks, and lavender soaps from abroad.

Sibylla kept an eye on the queen as she spoke to Lady Brigitte. "Could you tell Father I've a new song to play for him? 'The Ladies of the Stream.' The sooner he hears it, the likelier I'll remember the notes." The shanty was an old favorite of her half-brother's, and he'd often hummed it as a young man. Prince Henry would recognize the coded language as a warning. Perhaps she could finally get word to her father that they needed to speak, and soon.

"Of course, darling." Lady Brigitte swept out of the room, leaving a wake of jasmine perfume.

With Lady Brigitte gone, the seamstress reasserted her control, snatching Sibylla by the arm and positioning her in the center of the room. She produced a heavy bag of fabric swatches and held them one by one against Sibylla's face while the queen nodded or frowned. Sibylla's nerves frayed with the extra fuss, but she bit her lip to keep from pouting. The queen expected a princess, not a melancholy child. When the seamstress had packed her bag, and her grandmother finished criticizing Sibylla's physical condition, they all filed out of the room.

All except the queen.

"Let me see your glow." It was not customary for her grandmother to ask for a magical display, but her stiff command brooked no objection. Sibylla held up her arms, palms facing outward, as her skin became translucent and her veins lit up to make her flesh flush blue. She self-consciously held the proper pose until the queen nodded.

"You'll stand with the crown prince on the dais during the emperor's arrival."

Sibylla hated glowing in public. She'd caught her reflection once and thought the sight more ghastly than ethereal, and a few children always cried upon seeing their first royal "stars."

"Shouldn't Edgar be there?" asked Sibylla.

As the crown prince's eldest son, Prince Edgar was second in line to the crown. He would soon turn twenty-one, old enough to perform his religious duties as well as marry. By his age Sibylla had already blessed her chapel, given countless benedictions, and ridden in several festivals. A deep frown settled on the queen's face. She didn't answer Sibylla, and Sibylla couldn't ask her twice unless she wanted the queen to spark her earlobes. Instead, the queen trotted to the hallway where her attendants remained, and Sibylla was told to wait for the milk bath to be drawn.

The queen had never shown her favoritism before and had always praised Edgar as the future royal ruler to measure oneself against. Still, Sibylla had been holed up in Helmscliff too long. She knew nothing of the current palace politics. Perhaps Edgar had been caught bedding a maid. Or maybe the queen simply wanted to dazzle the emperor with the brightest collective family glow, and Edgar hadn't measured up. Regardless of the reason, Sibylla didn't relish taking Edgar's place on the stage.

13

Archbishop Tittlebury, Harrod, and Roger waited inside the cramped cell for the prison tattooist to arrive and apply the ritual Straybound ink.

Myrcnian tribes of old used to mark their skin with colors and designs. However, since the founding of the church and the royal Muir line, tattoos were used solely for identifying criminals. During his last hard labor sentence, Roger had encountered old men with brands or ink applied to their foreheads. Facial tattooing had been banned at the start of the current queen's reign, and now prisoners were marked on the neck – less disfiguring, easy enough for constables to check, and impossible to remove.

The tattooist painted the surface of a carved wooden block with ink, the stencil he'd use to apply the design. He chuckled when Roger unbuttoned his shirt, revealing his old black prison mark.

"Most men don't live to bear my handiwork twice." The tattooist pressed the cold ink stamp to Roger's neck. "Did we hold you down last time?"

Roger shook his head.

"Well, ain't you a tough lad," the man said with a leer. He laid out a selection of needles, then opened a case of artist's pigments in shades of blue, red, pink, and gold. "This'll hurt three times as much. I'll put the new one just above your zigzag. You ready?" He swabbed the side of Roger's neck with gin.

Roger gritted his teeth and nodded. He managed to stay conscious by counting a prior cell tenant's tallymarks etched in the stone. When the tattooist finally set his needle aside and closed his pigment box, Roger exhaled and let his taut shoulders slump.

Once his new tattoo had been cleaned, Roger was made to kneel before Archbishop Tittlebury, who held a golden hand mirror before his face. Roger beheld his new tattoo. A double-flowered rose in shades of red and violet, and topped with a golden coronet, adorned his neck just above his old prison zigzag. It looked more like an oil painting than a murderer's brand. The outlines glinted with a metallic sheen, like it had been dusted with gold. The pink skin beneath the new tattoo throbbed. He ran a finger across the red and gold pigments.

"The Straybound Stigma," intoned Archbishop Tittlebury, "marks you as both a murderer, and a redeemed man. By bearing the Muir Rose, you are transformed into an instrument of holy service until the day your Stigma – along with your mortal remains – shrivels to dust." He exchanged the mirror for an oilskin bandage with a waxy adhesive, which he affixed to Roger's tattoo. "The Stigma must remain covered throughout your probation, so the colors may set in time for the Binding. Should you uncover the Muir Rose too early, the colors and sheen will fade, and you'll be forced to repeat the rite. Change the bandage daily and apply a liniment. Do you understand, dear fortunate?"

Harrod prodded Roger with his riding crop until Roger nodded with reluctance.

"And should you break your probation in any way, or come to trouble with the law before the Binding, or should anyone see your unbandaged Stigma before her highness has taken charge of you, then your divine intervention, as it is, shall be revoked. Your execution will be carried out as before. Is that also clear to you, my lad? Speak up."

"It is clear, your grace." The seriousness of the ritual hadn't diluted Roger's bitterness toward this spiritualistic blather, though he wasn't about to argue.

Archbishop Tittlebury produced a stick of ambergris incense, which he waved over Roger in some purification rite. Tendrils of smoke swirled about Roger's face, making him cough. Next came an unintelligible invocation in the old Myrcnian dialect, which Roger recited back to the archbishop in halting snippets – for all he knew, he'd just promised to plait daisies into his hair. Behind him, Harrod's boot tapped impatiently on the stone floor.

At last Archbishop Tittlebury fell silent and placed an ambergris wafer between Roger's lips. As it melted on his tongue, the archbishop kissed his brow.

"Rise, thou Straybound, toward redemption. May you serve well." Archbishop Tittlebury leaned in and patted Roger's shoulder. "I'll see you in a week, at the Binding. If she hasn't changed her mind."

"Oh lovely, my bewitchment. I can't wait." An insolent grin spread across Roger's face. "Strange way to deal with murderers. I wouldn't trust me for a week, were I a killer. Which I'm not, point of fact." He'd grown too lightheaded now to mind his manners. This was all too ridiculous for words.

"That's six days of probation, to be precise," Archbishop Tittlebury said. "In order to complete your transformation from murderer to Straybound, you'll spend each day devoted to a single ideal: supplication, diligence, patience, reflection, and service, culminating in the sixth day, rebirth. Should you misstep, you will be hanged and mutilated as I said, and only have yourself to blame. Divine grace has its limits."

After ceremoniously binding Roger's hands with a strong silk cord, the archbishop handed the loose end to Harrod. "Captain Starkley, as an officer of her royal majesty's the Queen's Exalted Bench, I now turn over one Roger Weathersby to your keeping. You are charged with preparing the anointed for his Binding and have the power to punish him or terminate his probation at your discretion. Do you understand?"

"I do." Harrod bowed low, pulling Roger down with him.

After Archbishop Tittlebury had departed, Harrod escorted Roger out of Old Grim to a coach drawn by a pair of stout black horses. He helped Roger inside, then seated himself on the opposite bench. As the coach pulled away, Harrod cut the cord around Roger's wrists with a penknife.

"He makes it longer every time," Harrod grumbled.

Roger rubbed feeling back into his hands. Perhaps Harrod did believe in his innocence. Otherwise, he wouldn't have freed him. "What the deuce just happened to me? Other than you saving my neck." Roger swayed woozily. The sight of the afternoon sun confused him. He wanted nothing more than to return to his garret in Suet Street and sleep off this ordeal like a bad hangover. "Sorry for putting you out, brother. Just drop me at the corner. I'll find my own way home."

"Sorry for putting *me* out?" Harrod crossed his legs and flicked the toe of his boot with his riding crop. "Perhaps I was too hasty in cutting your bonds. Do you really think that Archbishop Tittlebury would show his face in Old Grim just so a profligate like you might go home to his blood-soaked clothes and rotting cats? I should be taking you to another dank cell, not escorting you to my house so you can fulfill your week of probation in comfort."

"I saw you back there, rolling your eyes and scowling as the old goat rambled on. You play the high and mighty hero, but I'll reckon you're no more pious than me."

"Allow me to disabuse you of that notion by sharing the formal guidelines." Harrod withdrew a booklet from his pocket and smacked Roger in the chest with it. "During probation," he recited without cracking its pages, "the anointed Straybound may assume that he or she is above the law. Should this attitude persist, it may be best to follow through with the suspended execution. The officer of the probation will challenge the anointed with tasks that prove he or she has mastered each daily ideal."

Roger sighed, leaned back and closed his eyes. His head spun from days of meager prison rations, his neck throbbed under the oilskin bandage, and his wrists stung where the manacles had worn through his skin.

"First day of probation: Day of Supplication," Harrod continued. "After the anointed has made an earnest and humble plea for the commutation of execution, the probation officer should encourage further expressions of humility and gratitude."

Roger opened his eyes. "Humility? Gratitude? Just because you rescued an innocent man? I'm no guiltier of those crimes than you, or even the high-and-holy princess herself. If you think I'm going to spend the next six days on my knees praying for forgiveness for something I didn't do, then you're a right bastard."

Roger swung a fist at his brother's face, but Harrod blocked the blow and seized his wrist.

"You will refer to her as *her highness*." Harrod twisted Roger's arm backward until he swore he heard his ulna crack. "Or Divine Maiden Sibylla if you're feeling religious." Harrod let go. "Your insolence will see you hanged yet."

Roger slumped back onto his bench. "You really are going to enforce this sham, aren't you? You said yourself I couldn't be a murderer."

"Sins always make debts, and someone always pays." Harrod studied Roger, from his bruised face down to his hobnail boots. "A few days in Old Grim really took the piss out of you. Look there." He tapped the carriage window. The coach was crossing Brandybones Square, where pale yellow ropes swung from a weathered scaffold. A sparse crowd gathered for the midday hangings, vying for the best viewing spots. "You can refuse her highness' merciful gesture, and the hangman will cheerfully fit you for a new rope cravat. You *are* a convicted murderer in the eyes of the law, whether I believe it or not. No court in the land can change that now." He raised the riding crop as if to tap on the window. "Let me stop the coach."

"No!" Roger didn't mean to shout with such desperation. He bent over his knees and hid his face in his hands.

"Don't be a child. Haven't you snatched a corpse off that very gibbet? You have a disgusting affinity for the dead. Perhaps you'd be happier joining them."

"I can't," Roger's voice rasped. "There are things I need to do. People to look after."

"I already regret coming to fetch you," Harrod interrupted. "There's only one person for you to look after. I'll explain in as few words as possible. You are now royal property, to be used as her highness Princess Sibylla wishes."

"I'm not some stargazy pie to be bought and sliced," Roger snapped, but the mention of food reminded him of his hunger now that he'd otherwise survived the morning.

Harrod rapped on the glass. "Turn back to Old Grim!"

Roger might have fallen to his knees if there'd been any room in the cramped coach. "Don't take me back. I beg you." He bowed his head. It was the best he could do.

Satisfied, Harrod opened the window. "Never mind, driver. Carry on."

The ache in his stomach prevented Roger from saying more. He thought of week-old corpses he'd dissected in the summer whose stomachs had begun to dissolve from the gastric juices, and wondered if his own neglected guts had started to putrefy in a similar manner. He clutched his side. Those prison biscuits had been full of weevils.

Harrod glanced at him. "Will you survive another half hour?"

"It's nothing."

Harrod leaned out the window and ordered the driver to halt. He left Roger doubled over in the coach and returned a few minutes later with a mug of warm spiced port bought from a street vendor. "Here, tip this down your gullet, man." Harrod supported Roger's shoulder and helped him raise the cup to his mouth.

Roger gulped the drink. He thought he might be sick, but once the coach started up again and cold air blasted his face through the window, he relaxed.

Harrod's hand still propped him up. Roger balked at the awkwardness of this physical contact. His brother's sudden kindness surprised him, especially after that theatrical turn with the riding crop. Now he felt even worse about his intent to abscond at the first opportunity. But he had to check on Ada and Celeste somehow.

"I'm sorry I tried to wallop you earlier," Roger said begrudgingly.

Harrod raised a dubious eyebrow. "I think you have sufficiently demonstrated the Straybound value of 'supplication' for today. You should rest." He crossed his arms and examined Roger. "However, I must get you into halfway respectable clothes. My valet can give you a barbering. You haven't shaved in over a week, have you? People will think you're a Khalishkan peasant from the visiting emperor's baggage train."

Roger self-consciously ran his finger along his jaw. "Never bothered me before."

The coach turned off the main road and bumped along a cobbled lane. They arrived at a row of townhouses with marble fronts and pillars before the doors. Painted shutters framed three stories of windows. How many corpses would he have to sell to live in such a fine neighborhood? The entire population of Caligo would have to die off first.

The coach halted. The driver opened the door, and Harrod helped Roger down.

"I suppose it's a bit cramped," said Harrod with a frown, "but I've had a private room prepared for you nonetheless. The archbishop would prefer I kept you in a cell, but I stand by my assertion that you couldn't strangle a worm."

Harrod guided his brother to the sunken stairwell used by tradesmen and servants. A muscular man with a sailor's weathered face greeted them at the door. His dark blue butler's coat was reminiscent of a naval uniform stripped of gold trim.

"This is my butler and valet, Samuel Dawson," said Harrod. "He was my quartermaster on the HMS *Whalestooth* until he sustained shrapnel to his knee during a skirmish with an Arenberg frigate. He only survived because our shipboard surgeon was blasted overboard and never had the chance to prod about with his filthy scalpel. Dawson, this sorry excuse for a man is Roger Weathersby. I don't want to see him again until he's presentable."

"Yes, captain." Dawson bowed to Harrod and passed a dubious glance over Roger. "Wherever did you find this one, sir?"

The crooked grin Roger loathed appeared on Harrod's face. "Hugging the yardarm with a rope around his neck." With a nod to Dawson, he left.

Dawson assessed Roger with an appraising eye. "Roger, eh? More like Shiner," he said, indicating Roger's contused face. "And are you wearing a mute's afflictions? By the state of 'em, that must've been some wake." He cackled and, rolling with the side-to-side gait of a man still at sea, showed Roger to a pump out back.

Roger hauled five buckets of cold water to a tub in the servants' washroom. Dawson poured in a kettle's worth of boiling water. Confiscating Roger's clothes, he left him to soak and scrub until the water turned a reddish-brown from the dirt and dried blood.

"Yer new clothes are on the chair, Shiner," said Dawson as Roger toweled himself off. "The captain said to make you presentable, and as manager of this household, I won't be having you besmirch his good name."

Roger lifted a pale blue livery coat with ridiculous orange floral trim that would make even a palace footman cringe. "Looks like it were sewn from curtains swiped from old Queen Mildred's court."

"Don't you speak of swiping from her royal majesty's forebearers. The captain said the coat is part of your probation. A 'test of submission' or somesuch. Put it on, man, or must I instruct you in the science of sleeves?"

Roger didn't relish the idea of promenading naked before Harrod, so he pulled on the garments without further comment.

Just as he finished dressing, Dawson returned with towels and shaving soap. The butler gave Roger's face a thorough going-over with his razor. He only nicked him once – deliberately, Roger was sure – but left him with nicely shaped sideburns. Though Dawson never commented on Roger's bandaged tattoo, his eyes flitted to it as he worked. When he tied Roger's new starched cravat in a mariner's knot, he took care to cover both.

"How smart you look," exclaimed Harrod as Roger was paraded before him like a prize racehorse. "To think there was a… man under all that grime. Dawson, don't let him venture down Kingsblood Street alone. The streetwalkers will be so keen on him they'll tear him to pieces."

"He's got the look of a footman, don't he?" said Dawson, admiring his handiwork.

Roger wished he'd stayed naked.

14

Not until late afternoon did Sibylla catch sight of Lady Brigitte again. Her mother sat ensconced in the drawing parlor, playing a game of Contemplation and Crisis with a deck of gold-leafed cards.

Disquieted by Prince Henry's continued absence, Sibylla loomed over Lady Brigitte's shoulder, suspicious of her message-passing abilities. "Did you tell Father I needed to see him?"

"He knows you've arrived." Lady Brigitte flipped the deck over. "But her royal majesty wanted to speak to him about some matter or another so he escaped to Glasspon Gardens around noon." She looked at the clock on the fireplace mantel. "Oh dear, I was supposed to meet him an hour ago."

"This is important," implored Sibylla. She wanted to reprimand Lady Brigitte for allowing Prince Henry to leave without seeing her first, but she couldn't be angry with her parents for flitting off, as she knew how uncomfortable they were under the queen's scrutiny.

Her grandmother had never approved of their marriage, and during family luncheons she would often remark on Lady Brigitte's inability to produce a second child. Still, Sibylla had news to share with Prince Henry, questions to ask, and the glimmer of a plan to keep her half-brother safe, if only her father would make the time for her. She couldn't shake a lingering doubt that, since her parents had less to do with her upbringing than the queen, they considered her more of a distant relative than a daughter – one they liked but needn't go out of their way to meet.

Lady Brigitte reached up to pat Sibylla's cheek. "Really, no need to fuss. When I see him, I'll tell him that, according to Sibet, the world will end if he doesn't speak with her straightaway." She stood and pecked Sibylla's cheek, her skirts swishing as she left her game unfinished and her cards strewn across the table.

Sibylla watched her go with a defeated sigh. As usual she hadn't been able to say half of what she wanted to her mother.

Since most of the staff didn't recognize her, she was able to make a quick jaunt from the royal family's private quarters to Malmouth's more public wing without the requisite parade of footmen.

After securing the royal library's copy of *Khalishkan Attitudes and Greetings: A Resource* from a shelf of foreign protocol books, Sibylla tucked herself into the deserted butler's pantry that was her second-favorite spot in Malmouth. She'd need to know more than how Khalishkans said hello if she wanted to persuade the emperor to permit a Myrcnian embassy within his country, but at least she could learn whether to bow, curtsy, or – she shuddered – embrace.

As she flipped open the book, the smell of food wafted in from the warming room. As a girl she had often spent the better part of a day in this abandoned nook, reading and avoiding her family or hiding with Roger. Located in a recess near the servant staircase, the pantry had redwood panels and shelves now empty of silver and porcelain. No matter the mood in the palace, Sibylla had always felt safe here.

Click-thud-thud click-thud-thud

At the sound of footsteps, Sibylla angled her head into the hall to see who approached. At the end of the corridor strutted Dr Lundfrigg, the royal physician she'd met at Helmscliff, once again dressed in a manner that affected wealth without understanding how to properly display it. This time he paired aubergine silk trousers with a pale blue wool waistcoat. His medical cane clicked in step with his black shoes.

What is he doing here? Sibylla snapped her book shut. She had no desire for another encounter with the royal physician but she was curious why he'd come to Malmouth. A sick royal family member, perhaps. He might even know the reason Edgar wouldn't be standing behind the queen during the emperor's greeting ceremony. Not that she'd be asking. She intended to avoid the gentleman.

Sibylla pressed herself toward the back of the nook, trying her best to dissolve into the red paneling.

Unfortunately Dr Lundfrigg had already noticed her. He stopped abruptly outside the pantry and bowed in her direction. "How fortunate to meet your highness."

Sibylla forced a smile and stepped out to greet him. "Dr Lundfrigg."

"Please, child. Your highness may think of me as you would an uncle. Or call me Finchy, as my closest friends do."

"One uncle is more than enough." She didn't exactly have a warm relationship with Crown Prince Elfred. When they did speak, he usually harped on family marriage traditions and how he looked forward to her eventual children with Edgar.

Dr Lundfrigg tapped his cane. "I have to say I'm elated to find you here. You've saved me a most inconvenient trip, as I had already begun preparations for another visit to Helmscliff to finish your examination."

If she had to converse with him after all, she might at least gather some useful gossip. "I'm unsure what needs examining, though I do wonder if you've come from seeing my cousin Edgar, or… the crown prince? Surely, you haven't journeyed all the way to Malmouth merely to admire its hallways."

Dr Lundfrigg leaned in close as if to divulge a secret, then answered coyly, "I've come for her royal majesty. A matter most private."

"I hope it's nothing serious."

"Everything concerning her royal majesty is serious." Dr Lundfrigg's expression bordered on playful. "I even had chance to mention that little trick of yours. I was quite charmed the other day by your… auditory air disturbance. I had to scour the records at St Harailt's just to discover which relative passed it on."

"I didn't realize the royal physician had such interest in divine blessings. Your predecessors made sure to concern themselves with our daily health, not our magic. Let Archbishop Tittlebury measure otherworldly affairs." Roger, too irreverent for his own good, had once argued with her biology tutor that the princess couldn't glow by the grace of divinity alone. Now, she found herself chiding Dr Lundfrigg with the same speech. "An old friend of mine would say, aren't you a man of science? Best to stay within your sphere, *doctor*."

Dr Lundfrigg stroked his cane. "Of course. Naturally such things are beyond our understanding. I would never say otherwise, certainly not within her royal majesty's walls. But alas, the pursuit of the unknown is my burden to bear, despite dangers of offending."

"Careful. In Myrcnia, offenses given are never taken lightly."

Questioning whether the royal family truly descended from a mythic water sprite could be construed as treason. She'd seen enough merfolk statues to reason a population must have existed under the sea long ago. Perhaps some had grown legs as she'd once dreamed of growing fins. But even she would never voice such an opinion.

"Yes, yes. I only say this because of your reputation as an intellect. At this rate I may have to visit Divine Maiden Sibylla's chapel if I wish to procure a sample of your highness' blood."

"Are you in need of absolution?" Sibylla raised her fingers toward the doctor's forehead. She kept her face dreadful and serious until Dr Lundfrigg met her eyes with a vehement stare.

"I thank your highness for the offer, but the only sin I've committed is my unwillingness to allow the poor to live untreated when there are so many advancements to be made on their behalf."

Sibylla fidgeted uneasily until a familiar aroma offered her a reprieve from Dr Lundfrigg's righteousness. "If I'm not mistaken, the gravy for this evening's dinner has nearly finished heating. Perhaps another time."

"Certainly, your highness. I hope soon to have a word about your mother's Donnellan School for boys. I'm most interested in looking up its alumni. I understand Lady Brigitte still holds luncheons with various former students in Caligo."

Sibylla studied Dr Lundfrigg with an unfaltering eye. His interest in Donnellan School for boys meant one thing: the queen had discovered where her half-brother had been educated. From what Sibylla had been told by Lady Brigitte, a respectable Myrcnian couple that had emigrated to Ibnova lent the royal bastard their name, and as far as school records were concerned, he was like any other son of a rich family living abroad. The couple had even passed away in the intervening years.

So why then did the queen think her royal physician could sniff out Sibylla's half-brother where Dorinda must have already failed? A list of names would tell Dr Lundfrigg nothing, and he couldn't exactly place a wooden depressor to their tongues and have them glow for him.

Sibylla stiffened her shoulders. "Unfortunately so many of the students don't attend."

"How tedious it will be, then, to give them all physicals." Dr Lundfrigg dragged his cane across the floor as if solving an equation, then dipped his head toward Sibylla. "Ah, but I shouldn't keep your highness from her dinner preparations."

As Dr Lundfrigg headed off, Sibylla nervously inked a bee that barely held its shape. Dr Lundfrigg seemed oddly keen for royal blood samples, and now she had a strong hunch that this "physical" of Donnellan alumni would involve drawing their blood, too. If this royal physician could discover a bastard's identity by blood alone, then he was far more dangerous than Dorinda. She inked a larger bee that scudded after Dr Lundfrigg's retreating figure. Let him try. She'd render him deaf before he could collect a drop of her brother's blood.

15

Harrod's butler Dawson escorted Roger to a simple, spacious room – at least compared to his garret – located in the servants' quarters of Harrod's townhome. As soon as he was alone, Roger tossed the hideous livery coat over a chair and threw himself on the narrow bed.

To demonstrate gratitude toward Sibylla for saving his neck, Harrod had given Roger a journal in which he was expected to write five pages each day of probation like some wayward schoolboy. Roger would rather have shoved those pencils up the real Strangler's nose. He flipped open the journal and stared at the blank page. In a flurry he scribbled: I AM NOT A MURDERER. He repeated the sentence until he met his page quota.

Meanwhile his thoughts drifted to his precarious situation. With only five days to clear his name, he had to convince the courts he was innocent beyond all doubt – or be bound to Princess Sibylla forever. Once he'd brought the real strangler to light, even the archbishop might change his tune. But, until then, one slip-up and he'd be hanged at Old Grim. He had to tread lightly. Perhaps playing Harrod's lackey wouldn't be so bad for a day or two, though he chafed to leave this prison. A man of science needed the freedom to investigate, even unearth a few stiffs, to figure out who had framed him before it was too late.

Nighttime was best for wily evasions so he slept through the rest of afternoon. By the time Dawson returned, the orange glare of the gaslamps shone in from the street below. The butler set a tray of tea, cabbage soup, and bread on the dresser.

Roger sat up on the bed and gave the butler a cheerful smile. "Thank you. My last jailer weren't so thoughtful."

Dawson ignored him. "I'll be locking you up fer the night."

"Locking me up? When I called you a jailer, I didn't mean it literally."

"Just normal procedure 'round here when we take in new help off the street. How do we know you won't steal off into the night with the silver?"

"Point taken," Roger muttered.

"If this were the *Whalestooth* brig, you'd get beetlecakes and saltwater tea," snapped Dawson. "Eat up. Tomorrow you start pulling yer weight 'round here." After shaking out and hanging Roger's crumpled livery coat, he left and locked the door behind him.

Roger sat on the edge of the bed and drank his soup straight from the bowl. As he chewed the bread broiled in garlic butter, the smell triggered a memory. He froze with the bread half in his mouth.

Ghostofmary. Ada. She'd have given up on him by now. He didn't doubt Ada could handle herself, but if she continued haunting graveyards and Will-o'-the-Wisp Lane, she'd end up more of a ghost than she already was. With the real Greyanchor Strangler still at large, Ada's mother was still in danger, too. Maybe he could scrounge up a hospital admittance slip for Celeste. She'd be under constant observation and receive better care than he could provide.

Night had fallen; his body was rested and his stomach full. Roger jammed the rest of the bread in his mouth and examined the door. If only the key had been in the lock, he might have pushed it out with a pin and caught it on the tray slid under the door. But it was not, and this lock mechanism required a more sophisticated tool, a diamond pick perhaps, to open. The window, however, was merely latched.

He opened the third-story window, then paused. Was he really planning to pull one over on Harrod so soon? He hadn't thought this through. His brother would be livid.

"*If* he finds out," Roger said between clenched teeth. Either way, Harrod would be more lenient than the law. He decided he'd rather be flogged for clandestine doctoring than executed for crimes he'd only partially committed.

Then there was the question of his clothes. He had only the servant garments Dawson had given him. The gaudy livery coat would draw attention in public. He lifted the coat from the chair and examined its black lining – by turning the garment inside-out he might be less noticeable. He pulled it on. Though he wouldn't be dressed for the weather, it would have to do.

Roger leaned precariously through a little window and reached for the crown molding that edged the roof. He held his breath and hauled his legs through the tight opening, letting them dangle free, then inched his hands along the gutter toward a lead pipe that channeled rainwater into a barrel below. He nearly lost his grip as his fingers went numb with cold. With a final swing he hurled himself at the pipe. His hands slipped on the wet metal and he careered down faster than expected. A yew bush broke his slide, and he landed uninjured in the back garden.

He glanced back at the lit windows. If he thought too hard about another arrest and his emasculated corpse on display, he'd turn back. He tucked his chin into his collar and headed in the direction of his garret. Once he'd rustled up some coin to pay for medicaments, he'd check in on Celeste at Eglantine's Den of Delights.

Within the hour Roger stood in front of the butcher's shop on Suet Street, in a dingy Caligo neighborhood far from the lamp-lined streets where Harrod lived. He craned his head up at his attic garret window. All was dark. The boards creaked under his feet as he ascended the winding stairs. When he reached the first landing, Mrs Carver's door opened a crack and the landlady peered suspiciously out at him. The smell of stewed beef liver drifted from her room.

"Mr Weathersby?" she whispered, as if afraid of being overheard. "You vanished days ago. Then I saw your name in the broadsheets, your likeness too. It said that a Roger Weathersby were the Greyanchor Strangler, sentenced to hang." A note of fear hung in her voice, and he imagined her holding a cleaver behind her back.

Though his pulse pounded his skull, Roger put on his most charming smile. "Do I look like a strangler shackled in a cell, Mrs Carver? I were only at my brother's funeral. You remember – that fancy naval man came by to say he was lost at sea. Besides, Weathersby's a common enough name, and half the men in Caligo are Roger something or other."

Mrs Carver thrust a folded broadsheet through the cracked door. "You'll agree the likeness is uncanny. It's even got your zigzag."

Roger touched the neckcloth covering his tattoos, wondering when Mrs Carver could have glimpsed his old prison mark. He unfolded the broadsheet to study the pen and ink portrait, purported to be Roger Weathersby, Greyanchor Strangler.

"A good likeness indeed," he said dryly. "They even remembered to add horns. But the chin is all wrong."

"You're right." She relaxed somewhat. "Weathersby is a common enough name. I'm sorry to have vexed you. My condolences about your brother."

"No bother, Mrs Carver. I bid you good night."

Roger turned to climb the stairs, but she clutched his sleeve.

"Not to cause more fuss, but there's been something… queer about your garret these past few nights."

"Queer? The unusual quiet has caused you alarm."

Mrs Carver opened her door wide enough to fit her shoulders through. "Oh no. I swear I've heard strange noises on the stairs. Miss Agnes next door said she saw a pale glow floating about in the window last night. I took a candle upstairs to see, but it were snuffed out by a draft. I then had such a feeling of dread, I rushed down straightaways. Something were chucking pebbles and such at my back. Be on your guard." She handed him a half-burned candle. "I shall stop by the Chapel of Solemnlych tomorrow, to ask for an exorcism," she whispered.

"That won't be necessary, Mrs Carver. You know I'm a man of science." Roger feigned nonchalance. "Though if you have any garlic on you, I'd be much obliged."

Mrs Carver nodded. She ducked inside and returned with a full bulb of garlic. Roger broke off a clove, peeled it, and placed it in his mouth.

"I'm sure it's nothing." He thanked her with a bow and continued up the stairs, candle in hand.

The stairwell spiraled into darkness, and he climbed with quiet footfalls. As he rounded the final curve, his eye caught something that gave him pause. The door to his garret was ajar. Hadn't he closed and locked it the last time he'd been here?

"Ahoy hoy!" he called.

No response. Those superstitious ladies must have caught a glimpse of his luminescent jars through the window and let their imaginations run to Greyanchor and back. Roger placed his hand on the door. He heard a rustling within – rats after his cat carcass? Maybe he'd left the window open by accident.

Roger bit down on the garlic and flung open the door. In the dull light of his candle, the room appeared in the same state he'd left it, with jars on shelves he'd fastened to the canted ceiling, and the blanket in a heap on his cot. Yet the smell of the place was off. Then he noticed the empty bucket beside the door. His dead cat must have wandered away on ghostly paws.

A weight attached itself to Roger's back. He dropped the candle and the room went dark. A rope pulled tight across his throat. He wrenched it free, but small hands and arms grasped his face and neck.

"I'll teach you to break your promises, sack-'em-up man!" shrieked a voice.

Roger threw himself on the cot. The sagging mattress smelled like lye and necropolis lavender.

"Have you been living in my room, Ghostofmary?" he said through the crook of his elbow as she pummeled his shoulders.

"Aye. And I sold your disgusting cat to the bone-rag man for a winkle."

"I planned to put that cat to use for science."

"It were rotten." Ada knocked Roger a final time, then collapsed on the cot next to him.

Roger fumbled for his tinderbox to light the candle. "Have you... heard anything about me, Ghost? In the broadsheets, or maybe songs?"

"I heard you was a poxy rotten slime-tongued liar who breaks his promises."

Roger exhaled in relief. Some day he'd thank the balladeer who'd chosen a lesser known tune to accompany his prose. "The Greyanchor Strangler" was no "Poison Mary."

"I've just come looking for coin to buy your mother's medicaments," he said, holding the orange candle flame between them. "I'm glad to find you. Thought you'd be at the necropolis."

"I ain't been up to Greyanchor these last few nights. You left your togs at the laundry, and your address on the slip, so I came to deliver 'em. I waited but you didn't return."

"Have you been here all this time?"

"Nights. I like it. The jars, they glow blue and green. Are they pickled ghosts?"

Roger pulled one of the jars from the shelf, a stout apothecary's glass sealed with a cork coated in wax. A translucent blob undulated inside, glowing a faint purple.

"They're jellyfish," he said, pleased at her interest. "Preserved in spirits of wine. The fishmongers at the harbor haul them in sometimes with their catch, and I'm one of the few that buys 'em. This one here is a moonstar jelly. That's an amber bowlflower there, and a chartreuse medusa." He pointed to the shelves. "I've also got a raven skull, seaweed dried on paper, and a cat skeleton I assembled with wire. Not to worry," he added when Ada balked. "Them human bits are teeth. I can wire 'em in, if folks is missing their own." He pointed to his own jaw. "I did this one here myself."

Ada cradled the jar with the moonstar jellyfish. "Where's the light from? Is it magic?"

"There ain't no magic. I dissected one, and the luminescence – the light – it rubs off on your fingers, like ink."

"They're nice to have in the dark."

Roger found the leather knife roll with his medical instruments. The furrows under the girl's eyes were a shade darker than he remembered, and she'd twisted strands of her hair into knots.

"I'm sorry I'm late, Ghost. You were right to be angry. But I'm here to keep my promise, whether I catch hell for it or not."

"You done dithering yet? You promised to come days ago. But then you had to get yourself arrested. For murder!"

Roger grimaced. So she did know. Best not to make a thing of it. He rummaged through his cupboards but found no coin or curatives, not even gin. He lingered for a few minutes before his small collection of books. Most were disintegrating cast-offs given to him by broke medical students as payment for doing their practicums. His hand hovered over the spine of Hemon's *Studies of Medical Phenomena and Their Surgical Treatments*. Sibet had given it to him, and even during his coldest, hungriest winters he hadn't brought himself to part with it. He could see her now, the glow in her eyes as she produced the book from behind her back, her delight in surprising him, her belief in his talents to do good…

She should have directed her efforts elsewhere. With its tooled leather cover, the book must have been expensive. He could get a decent price for it, enough to sustain him through one more house call. He'd read every page at least ten times, and made notes in his journal since he hadn't the courage to scrawl in the margins. The leather spine, soft from use, reminded him of her touch.

He scrunched his eyes shut. What had that sentimentality gotten him? If selling Sibet's book might save this girl from becoming an orphan, so be it. He plucked the book from the shelf.

His ripped topcoat hung by the door. He pulled it over his servant's clothes to better brave the cold. Then he slipped his pewter physicians' medal around his neck.

"You look scrubbed," Ada said as they tiptoed down the stairs. "I liked your face better before. But where's your hat? How will you look respectikal?"

"No time to worry about that. I'm late for a house call. Which reminds me… have you heard of any more stranglings since I've been gone?"

"Besides me strangling you? No."

Roger couldn't tell if that was her idea of a joke.

Mrs Carver heard them sneaking past and leaned her head out the door. "Mr Weathersby? I thought I heard some commotion."

"This is my… ah, niece, Adelaide. She'll be staying with me, so don't worry yourself if you hear noises. She's just a girl."

Mrs Carver squinted at Ada, who ducked behind Roger. "Your brother's girl? Well, tell the poor dear to sit with me for supper if she gets hungry. I could pass on some tips for taming that unruly hair."

When they reached the street, Ada pulled the hem of Roger's coat in the direction she wanted him to go.

"Don't get too eager, Ghost. I still need supplies. And for them, I need coin."

Roger headed in the opposite direction, and Ada ran to keep up. He pulled his collar up to hide his face and kept to the shadows, though the unconvincing likeness on Mrs Carver's broadsheet eased his fears somewhat. Two left turns later, they stood in front of Mr Grausam's Undertaking and Coffining Services. The red-haired apprentice Nail could be seen through the front window, filing the nails of a deceased gent who reclined in a handsome oak coffin.

"Wait here." Roger squeezed Ada's shoulder and entered the undertaker's shop. "So, friend Nail, do you have any extra stiffs lying around?" In lieu of a hat to doff, Roger raised his fingers to his temple.

The apprentice dropped his file and leapt up in surprise.

"You think I'm a ghost, man?" Roger stuck his hands in his pockets and grinned. "Maybe I am. Passed right through the walls of Old Grim to come haunt you."

"Bollocks. That daft Carver woman said your room were haunted after they arrested the Greyanchor Strangler, but I knew that Weathersby weren't you. I just figured you'd offed yourself or somesuch, from the shame of association."

"Offed myself? I were called away." Roger approached the coffin, feigning interest. "Nice-looking fellow there. I'm in the market for one of them."

"Get your thievin', coffin-vacatin' person out of my shop."

"This shop belongs to Mr Grausam. I'm here to collect payment from that mute job."

"Mr Grausam is indisposed," said Nail. "But I can tell you this. The crumbs you did earn went to Mr Grausam's coffers for them rented clothes you ap-skonded with. Never even returned the crape and staff, and them's worth more than a mutton pie."

Ada had probably sold the staff and crape he'd left in his garret along with his cat, and spent the earnings on hot cross buns.

Roger could tell by the stubborn jut of Nail's jaw that he would get no cash tonight. But he might get *something* out of him. He glimpsed the wraithlike Ada waiting in the shadows beyond the window. She patted her head, then pointed at the dead man's hat.

Roger turned back to Nail and shrugged. "A shame, that. You pester me to take your mute job, then won't pay me? If you and Grausam want to stiff me on my pay, I'll have to 'stiff' you right back, or starve." He leaned over the coffin and straightened the corpse's cravat. "I know this poor sod can't afford a mortsafe or a watchman. Not if he took you up on that 'display for a day, get a half-price coffin' deal. Lock up shop tonight at your peril. I'll have him to the anatomist's before you get home."

Nail's eyes widened at Roger's bluff. "I'll turn you in."

"If you can prove it were me. Or… you could help a mate out."

"Meaning what, extort-shun?"

Roger rattled his leather roll of medical instruments in Nail's face. "What if I told you I were headed to my first surgeoning job as a man of science, but seeing as I've lost my hat I'll get flung out on my ear?"

Nail's lip curled in a snarl. "Is that a payin' job?"

"Not if I get the boot. So, lose a whole stiff, or just the deader's hat?" Roger flashed his most innocent smile.

Nail heaved a defeated sigh. "Take it if you must. But you stay far from my shop, you hear?"

"You have my word." Roger crossed his heart and spit on the floor.

"Good enough. How 'bout instead of a stiff, I send you off with a stiff drink?" Nail reached under the counter and pulled out a bottle. "I heard rumors you was trainin' as a surgeon, but I figured it was lies. When have you ever looked so clean and scrubbed?"

Roger opened the empty flask he'd brought from his garret. "Gin?" he asked hopefully.

"Spirits of wine from the preservin' vat." Nail poured some into Roger's flask with a wink. "It's the best I can do, but it ain't watered down. Here's to your honest trade."

They both took long swigs of the burning ethyl alcohol, and Roger left the shop with a tip of his new hat.

In the street Ada grabbed his sleeve. "That hat looks well on you. But did you get your coin?"

He shook his head.

"Then how will you buy the medicaments for Ma?"

Roger pulled his hat low on his forehead. "A surgeon always has his resources." He grasped her hand and led her down the shadowy street.

They made their way to the Bookbinding District where Roger haggled up the price of Hemon's *Medical Phenomena*. His self-satisfied feeling fled when he glimpsed the pawnbroker gloating at him through the window on their departure. Roger wished he had stood his ground over the price of a princess' gift. That pawnbroker must have fleeced him good and proper.

At a chemist's in Mouthstreet, Roger purchased a bottle of laudanum and sow's butter, which the apothecary promised could cure innumerable female diseases to include hysteria, ulceration, monthly cramping, and wandering womb. It seemed like a reasonable catchall.

When they reached Will-o'-the-Wisp Lane, Roger made Ada promise not to move from her hiding place and to throw pebbles at the window if she needed him.

"Are you sure your ma still wants to see me?" Roger asked. "She won't report me to the magistrate, what with all the rumors?"

Ada shook her head. "She won't, but she said you'd be doing her a favor either way. You're to use the window this time, not the front door."

Smart lady, that Celeste.

Roger scrambled up the rusted drain spout, the old brick crumbling against his shoes. Estella helped him in through the window where he found Celeste in bed under a heap of crocheted blankets. Her jaundiced skin had darkened, and her cheeks were hollow bowls.

"I can't take callers with her like this." Estella lowered her voice so only Roger could hear. "We went to the hospital and I begged them to admit her, but they turned us away, us being what we are. Please don't think me cruel, Dr Weathersby, but I can't earn a living with an invalid in my bed. But you're influential. I'm sure you could put in a word for us." She kissed Celeste's wan cheek, then excused herself to "strum a back-alley ballad," as she put it.

Roger placed a hand on Celeste's forehead. "I wish I could say you looked well, but I'm not a good liar."

Celeste smiled weakly and clasped his wrist. She placed his hand on her throat.

"Is it you, sir, come at last to end my misery? I've been waiting. Say you'll spare my Ada, and I promise I won't cry out."

Roger inhaled sharply. "I'm no strangler, miss." He moved Celeste's hand to the coverlet. Her palms burned as if her blood simmered beneath her skin. "I've but come to administer your medicaments." Roger counted out drops of laudanum and fed her with a spoon. Celeste couldn't stay here in this state. "I need to move you to a hospital."

"The hospitals won't take me. Estella and I have tried. The private ones require tickets bought in advance, and the charity wards need references."

"Then leave it to me. I'll find a way." Roger worried he was again promising more than he could deliver. But he couldn't promise nothing.

"Thank you, doctor."

He observed the weak latches on the window and the paper-thin door. It had been easy enough for him to climb up the drain and gain access to her room. "Bar your door tonight, and the window, too." He strongly suspected that someone had done this to her. "Can you think of anyone who might mean you harm? A customer perhaps?"

Celeste shrugged under her mountain of blankets. "They all love me and hate me in equal measure."

"But think," Roger urged, before the laudanum took full effect and her senses grew muddled. "Perhaps someone threatened you."

Celeste laughed, bright and distant. "I'm threatened every time I refuse to marry a customer. So, most of them."

Any one of her customers could be the culprit, assuming the strangler was male. Roger noted her arm, still bruised from where he'd lanced her vein. Her black treacle-blood had disturbed him so. Perhaps a doctor might welcome Celeste into a hospital if he perceived in her a medical curiosity.

"Might I bleed you again?" Roger could do little else.

Celeste nodded her assent before her eyelids flickered closed. Her face relaxed as the laudanum entered her system, and her breathing slowed. Roger cleansed his fleam and set a basin beneath her arm. His nick produced the same thick, black blood as before. It dribbled out slowly, but he needed more this time if he wanted to catch a physician's attention. It could save her life.

He rubbed warmth into her icy hands and feet as the bowl slowly filled. She whimpered in her sleep. By the time Estella returned from her back-alley job, Roger had replaced the wine spirits in his flask with Celeste's blood and tucked her snugly back into bed.

16

The Coral Drawing Room had at one time been papered red-orange with a birds-of-paradise motif before the queen ordered its walls painted ivory, though the name had stuck. Silver candlesticks spiked the great fireplace's mantel where a painting depicted the end of the Doomsday Miasma – Caligo's gray skyline ablaze with sinewy red charcoal fires. The room's splotchy wool and silk carpet reminded Sibylla of a boxing ring post-match, and gold-leafed cornices held up a molded ceiling. Her encounter with Dr Lundfrigg had left her shaken. If not for the promise of seeing Prince Henry, she'd have found an excuse to miss the family dinner.

She signaled a footman to bring her an aperitif while she looked for signs of her parents: a half-full glass of juniper and whiskey, or a whiff of jasmine perfume.

Splayed across a blue sofa, Crown Prince Elfred clutched a pastille tin. After he slipped the tin's last lozenge between his lips, the empty container in his hand rusted away to a fine powder. He blew the pile of rust-colored dust from his palm in an orange plume, then lazed back with his eyes closed.

A high-pitched whistle stung Sibylla's ears.

Edgar.

Her cousin enjoyed taking advantage of her sensitivity to sound, and she knew better than to ignore him. She half-wondered if he wasn't already preparing some spiteful recourse after her refusal to relinquish the prayer plaques at the grotto. Once as a child she'd refused to join him in smashing ladybird beetles, and he'd removed her favorite gardener along with the rose bushes she'd helped plant. When she snubbed him at the Royal Hunt Ball by choosing Lord Howell's son as her first partner, Edgar had her best-loved reading chair taken to his own bedroom. Shortly after, Lord Howell's son broke his leg in an unfortunate croquet incident.

Wearing a meticulous brown suit and a shimmering gold cravat about his narrow neck, Edgar reminded Sibylla of an immature parsnip – long and bitter. Rolling an unlit cigarette between his fingers, he nodded curtly in her direction. "Cousin."

"I should thank you for the chocolates you sent to Helmscliff," said Sibylla, searching for the footman with her aperitif.

Edgar tilted his head. "Weren't you always stuffing your face with one treat or another?" He swiveled the cigarette between his fingers. "Anyhow, Edmund practically beseeched me to help finance the sweet shop when it opened, bribed me with his plaid cravat, too."

"Then I should be thanking Edmund." Luckily, Edgar didn't mention the marriage proposals.

"If you must thank someone, thank the lady whose skirts he wanted to get into. He had his eye on that tart of a proprietress ever since she worked at Dame Angeline's salon."

Seemingly on cue, Edgar's two brothers burst into the drawing room, batting each other over the head with badminton rackets. They'd recently turned sixteen and seventeen and Sibylla wondered at their childish behavior. Edmund and Edward charged between the furniture, jostling their father who clenched his armrests to keep from falling over. Crown Prince Elfred used to demonstrate a sturdier constitution and better reflexes.

"Uncle Elfred doesn't seem well," said Sibylla as she watched the crown prince fumble with his empty glass. "Perhaps he might benefit from Dr Lundfrigg's attention." At least then, Dr Lundfrigg would find less time to concern himself with bastards.

Edgar flicked the end of his unlit cigarette. "One too many Straybound. Took another just this week. Does that make five or six this season? I lost count after Old Gabe."

The church prohibited each member of the royal family from having more than one Straybound at a time but did nothing to prevent the deadly discardment of servants who failed to please their patrons. Revulsed by the crown prince's habit of replacing Straybound when he grew bored of them, Sibylla guided the conversation back to Dr Lundfrigg. "Don't you think it's strange how obsessed Dr Lundfrigg is with studying our 'sanguine spirit'? I'm surprised you haven't had him dismissed." Perhaps she might use Edgar's spitefulness for good.

"I still can't fathom why Grandmamma knighted the man, passionate old trout that she is. I preferred old Dr Hartlin myself. At least he had a respectable lineage and kept his examinations to gentlemanly conversation. Not that I have anything against Dr Lundfrigg, but he is a…" Edgar leaned in to Sibylla's ear, "…*hematologist*. Disgusting."

Sibylla bit her lip. Given Dr Lundfrigg's academic expertise, his interest in taking her blood at Helmscliff made more sense. Worse, he may really have some way to test whether someone belonged to the royal family or not.

"You haven't seen your parents, have you?" Edgar slipped a silver watch from his pocket, and Sibylla noticed his soft, unblemished hands. The most arduous thing he'd ever done with them was likely fanning his cards at his gentlemen's club. Despite his father Crown Prince Elfred's proclivity for remaking murderers into disposable servants, Edgar had yet to take a Straybound himself. No scars marred his left thumb. His morality, it seemed, remained intact.

The footman brought Sibylla her aperitif, which she downed in one gulp.

"If you drink like that your cheeks will turn an uglier hue." Edgar stole a glance at her thumb. A great deal could be gleaned by the age, depth, and quality of the thumb scar; whether, for example, the royal had bound a fresh Straybound or if they kept a long-faithful servant like Dorinda.

"That comb." Edgar pinched his cigarette.

Looking about the room, Sibylla found the object of his disdain. Lady Brigitte had slipped into the drawing room. Her gown, white lace with daringly wide folds of blue satin, rustled over the crackle of the fireplace, and an ivory comb inlaid with doves corralled her hair into a loose bun. Sibylla would have preferred to spend the evening alone with her mother, speaking Ibnovan and listening to the gossip from Fillsbirth than suffering seven courses of the queen's dinner evaluations.

"A foreign diplomat gave it to her," Edgar added. "Only someone raised in Ibnovan excess would think to accept such a thing. I'm glad *you* didn't suffer the misfortune of an upbringing abroad."

Sibylla doubled her efforts at smiling when she wished only to swear at him in Ibnovan. Lady Brigitte's parents came from the House of Cornin. Amongst the magicked nobility, Lady Brigitte's position was neither as low as the Viscount of Highspits – Lieutenant Calloway's father – nor as high as the Duchess of Guset, Edgar's mother Lady Esther's title before she married the crown prince. In fact, the Cornin family's inking magic made them respectable matches for royalty, though a direct marriage into the Muir family had eluded them for several generations.

Prince Henry called Lady Brigitte's parents travelers by trade. They spent more time in other countries than their own. On one of these holidays they took a house in the Ibnovan capital, where they settled for a decade before returning to Caligo in search of a suitable husband for young Brigitte. The effort had paid off handsomely, as Lady Brigitte's more pragmatic Ibnovan upbringing allowed her to befriend Prince Henry when other ladies would have turned shyly away.

Sibylla suspected Lady Brigitte's success at securing a royal union had to do with her tolerance of Prince Henry's bastard son by a palace maid, but her parents would never share the sordid details of their early courting. As the outcome of their unusual pairing, the queen had insisted early on that Sibylla marry her cousin, to reinforce traditional betrothals.

Before Edgar could offer more unwelcome opinions, the queen mercifully arrived. She surveyed the family like a collie shepherding a flock, searching for sheep that intended to stray – most notably Prince Henry who skulked into the drawing room after her, and Lady Esther who seemed to emerge from the wallpaper in an ill-fitted bodice made of tasseled fringe and over-large buttons.

At the dinner chime, Sibylla straightened her shoulders and the royal family, nine in all, percolated into the Grand Dining Hall behind the queen. The room's heavy drapes and long table had remained unchanged since Sibylla last took a meal there. She could name each of the portraits, and the china painted with tropical flowers reminded her of family functions. Even the silverware hadn't lost its luster.

She waited for her grandmother to sit at the table's head before she seated herself. The queen stared down the line of her relations, her expression full of discrimination. Like most of their family dinners, the courses were served in silent judgment. Crown Prince Elfred drank heavily. Prince Henry set his pocket watch on the table beside his plate and monitored it obsessively. Lady Brigitte, charming and talkative in most settings, took on a muted guise, while Lady Esther and Edgar sprinkled the queen with innocuous conversation.

Sibylla gnashed her teeth through a piece of lettuce in an effort to endure the company of her cousins, Edward and Edmund, seated on her left and right. They whispered behind her like an annoying crosswind. As Edward mouthed something to make Edmund titter, Sibylla set her fork down to prevent stabbing one or both of them.

"You're looking well, Weed-eyes." Edward jostled her chair.

"Isn't she?" Edmund's chortle rasped in her left ear. "Guess being locked up with a manservant did her nicely."

"Maybe he undid her buttons for her."

"Or maybe she undid his."

"You think she would?"

"I know if I had a fetching warden attending to my every day functions, I definitely would."

"You, dear sir, could unlace a lady with your hands tied behind your back."

"Teeth are made for tugging."

"I thought they were made for biting."

"Or nibbling. What do you think, Weed-eyes? Which would you like us to do to you?" Edmund winked while licking his upper teeth.

Sibylla pulled her hand back from the butter knife. "You do realize we're having dinner."

"Don't be stiff."

"Ladies should never be stiff."

"Although maybe she'd like him stiff." Edmund pulled his napkin taut.

"All into the conquest, eh?"

"Ladies first and nations second. Poor brother Edgar's about to lose his eel's nest."

"How quick do you think before *he* spreads her legs?"

They shared another awful snicker.

"No one will be spreading my legs any time soon," Sibylla spat. She curled her tongue as if to whistle-click when she remembered the rest of her family sitting at the other end of the table. The queen clanked the side of her water goblet. Her cousins snapped their mouths shut. Edward flashed an adorable smile and Edmund blinked innocently.

The queen's vexation had moved onto Sibylla, and she didn't know how to be dainty or charming. Instead, she shoved a forkful of butternut squash into her mouth. Even though she was confident she could avoid causing irreparable damage to her cousins, the queen's eyes narrowed as if waiting to see if she would dare use magic at the table.

When dessert came, she wanted to drown her sorrow in the silky folds of coconut custard. Sibylla hated to admit that sharing supper with Lieutenant Calloway, as he chattered on about sea birds off the coast of Ulmondstedt, had been preferable to the queen's constant appraisal of her table manners. She finished her bowl before anyone else.

The queen retired for the evening, and Edmund and Edward beat a hasty retreat, murmuring about Dame Angeline's newest coquette. Crown Prince Elfred wandered off soon after, while Lady Esther and Edgar continued their dinner discussion in the drawing room. Sibylla hurried to the end of the table where Prince Henry stood waiting. Her skirts tangled as she slipped behind a footman, and her father tapped the crown of her head when she stumbled to his side.

She'd waited all day to speak to him – searching the palace, sending coded messages through Lady Brigitte, and enduring dinner with her cousins. Now she fell silent. Unlike Lady Brigitte, Sibylla never knew how to address Prince Henry: Father, sir, or your highness. She awkwardly curtsied.

"No need to rush, Sibet." Prince Henry brushed lint from his black as steel-spice dinner jacket.

Sibylla tugged his arm. "Didn't you get word? About the sea shanty." Her breath caught in her throat.

Prince Henry stroked his chin. "Come along."

Sibylla followed him out of the Grand Dining Hall, down the corridor to the second wing's private library. She'd collected her favorite books there over the years. The glossy leather spines bounced candlelight across the room. Her half-brother had once lifted her by the waist so she could hide a bottle of spruce liquor on one of the shelves, behind some Salston plays. Sibylla joined Prince Henry to stand at one of the windows.

"How do they know about Donnellan?" Sibylla exhaled, out of breath. She'd been walking on cracked ice ever since Dorinda came to Helmscliff, and now she rushed to speak. "And since when did the queen decide he was alive? By the Lady's fins, she actually sent Dorinda to Tyanny Valley, as though I'd merrily give him up to be thrown down the bastards' well."

"Do lower your voice Sibet, dear." Prince Henry sheepishly tugged on his sleeves. "Several bottles of Blue Ogre and a cauldron of nutmeg soup may have loosened my tongue." He looked to still be considering whether this made him the guilty party. Sibylla bit back a rebuke. She couldn't reprimand her father any more than the queen.

Taking a deep breath to compose herself, she considered how to explain the seriousness of the situation. "I believe Dr Lundfrigg has a way to discover whether a person is related to us or not, and you're not at all worried."

"A man cannot open a vein and find a long-lost prince. There are limits to science, even for brilliant physicians. I do wonder if you haven't been reading *The Speculum* and filling your head with fads and fancies. Besides, the queen has greater concerns with Emperor Timur's visit. Imagine if he adds another import tax to our cheeses. A spark show won't end that diplomatic fracas."

"But–"

Prince Henry put his hand on her head. "Don't worry, little cuttlefish. I'll handle the doctor, you handle the queen."

But Sibylla *did* worry. Prince Henry made things simple for himself, but they didn't always remain that way for anyone else.

Long after he retired, Sibylla paced the library, flicking ink-bees into the air. She'd been five the first time she saw Prince Henry place his hand on a young man's head at the annual Founders' Banquet for the Donnellan School for boys. Only years later did she understand the relationship when the same young man rescued her after she became lost on a trip to the Caligo docks. In the corner of a gambling den he discovered her sopping with tears and offered her a winkle to stop crying. Once she composed herself, he let her bet the winkle on a game of dice before returning her to the palace.

When Prince Henry returned from Haupentaup he was furious. He knew all about how she'd gone missing, as well as the man who found her. She hadn't told anyone. Even an eight year-old could tell something was terribly strange, and Prince Henry reluctantly had her kneel beside the fireplace in his apartment and swear to never speak of the young man: her half-brother. Part of her hated Prince Henry for having to keep this secret, but the rest of her felt sorry for them both.

Pulling a ladder to one of the shelves, she climbed to the top. There, her fingers reached behind the collection of Salston's works – first editions of *The Barnmaid of Bareth*, *The Whipping Mistress of Whipperton*, and *The Housewench of the Haunted Hearth* – until she felt a smooth glass bottle. Apparently, no one else in the palace had a taste for great works of theater. She took the three volumes and liquor back to her bedroom where she threw herself on the bed and reached underneath the mattress. Thankfully, her silver corkscrew was still stuffed between two wooden slats. Uncorking the bottle of decades-old spruce liquor, she swilled it straight from the neck. After two years of tepid teas and lemon water, the heavy spirits were a burning philter in her chest.

Prince Henry may not think his bastard needed swift rescue from the queen, but Sibylla had read enough tragedies to know how illegitimate offspring fared on their own. Propped on her side, she alternated between drinking and flipping through her favorite bits in *The Housewench of the Haunted Hearth*. An easier solution than installing her half-brother at a foreign embassy might yet present itself.

The sound of shoes in the quiet hallway provoked her to hide the half-empty bottle between the nightstand and the bed for fear the queen might make another unannounced visit. After a knock, Lady Brigitte entered her bedroom. Sibylla's mother wore a nightgown and her hair hung loose around her neck.

"Aren't you tired of those books?" Lady Brigitte sat beside Sibylla on the bed.

"You can't tire of Salston."

"Seeing as you only mildly annoyed your grandmother, I brought you that little something from my trip to Fillsbirth, as promised." Lady Brigitte set a brass nautical sundial on the bed. "I know how you love the ocean."

Sibylla hefted the sundial, delighted by the serious weight of it in the palm of her hand. She loved practical objects crafted with an artistic eye, and the sundial reminded her of all the voyages she might still take in life. If only she could escape her day-to-day obligations. "I've been wondering," she said. "Do you know why the queen is having me participate in place of Edgar at the emperor's reception ceremony? He should be the one forced to glow for the masses."

"Why are ladies ever presented? To be seen, of course." Lady Brigitte took up a lock of Sibylla's hair and braided it through her fingers. "She's more willing to woo the emperor than I imagined." Lady Brigitte's smile brightened. "You never thought you'd pick your own husband, did you?"

It sunk in all at once: her cousins' dubious dinner conversation, the preparations around the palace, the queen's inspection, the seamstress and her swatches, and a Khalishkan delegation set to arrive in two days. She'd been so focused on Dorinda and her own plans for the emperor, she'd overlooked that the queen might have designs on him, too.

"The Emperor of Khalishka can't possibly look *here* for a wife." Sibylla tilted the nautical sundial on its side. "We haven't married outside Myrcnia in over three centuries. I was sent to Helmscliff for two long years because I wouldn't agree to Edgar. Now this. She's mad."

"You've always enjoyed studying statecraft," Lady Brigitte chided, spying the bottle tucked between the bed and side table. "Your grandmother's been corresponding for months, planting the seeds of this vibrant scheme. She's hoping the emperor won't focus on our uncomfortable alliance with Ulmondstedt when he has such a shiny jewel in front of him."

"But she'd never allow the marriage."

"That remains to be seen. Things are rather… tense."

"Enough to break a bloodline?" Prince Henry was right. The queen did have greater concerns.

Lady Brigitte flexed a finger and painted an ink dot in the air. "Marriage is something all ladies endure. I also thought marrying your father an impossible feat. His reputation for foolheartedness may have been worse than yours, but every branch grows in different directions." She flicked her hand, and black tendrils spiraled out from the tiny seed of ink. "Besides, I've heard the emperor is pleasing on the eyes – once you grow accustomed to the whole foreign look. And he's young. There will be time for you to take root in his heart." An ink flower bloomed before Sibylla's eyes to illustrate her mother's point.

Sibylla tapped on the compass set beneath the sundial. "Our two nations have so little to do with one another. Not to mention the sentiments within his own country. Khalishkans gather Myrcnian dolls for bonfires, thinking them bewitched." Marriage seemed like a reach, even more so than an ambassadorial position.

"You'd do well to keep those imaginations to yourself."

"And if I don't? I shall be sent packing back to Helmscliff." She flopped backward onto the bed. "Thank you for attending and goodbye forever."

"Theatricality can, on the rarest occasions, be quite pretty in a lady, but between a mother and daughter, it is not."

"As much as Grandmother wants security or a distraction or whatever she is thinking, no one can make a man fall in love."

Lady Brigitte smoothed Sibylla's hair. "You've read enough books to know not all marriages are about love."

"The happy ones are."

"That's simply what impoverished authors would have you believe."

"And are you happy with Father?"

"No amount of hysteria will change the next few days. Perhaps the emperor won't like you. After all, your charms are particular. And if the emperor does like you, would it be such a dire turn of events? Unless you'd like to see Edgar in your bed after all."

Sibylla didn't wish to marry Edgar, but she didn't wish to marry the emperor either. "So I'm to behave."

"I want you to be smart. I want you to do as you did this morning when your grandmother measured you for dresses, and you bowed and said nothing. There is a time for small rebellions, but now is not one of them." Lady Brigitte touched her daughter's cheek. "Be who you want afterward."

Lady Brigitte kissed Sibylla's brow before leaving. As the door shut behind her, Sibylla propped herself against the headboard. She watched the arrow on the compass wiggle north each time she turned it. She'd always believed she'd marry Edgar, no matter her efforts. If struck by some strange fortune, a Calloway or a Tittlebury. But a betrothal to the Emperor of Khalishka was as impossible as being with her first love.

"Timur."

Speaking his name aloud made her uncomfortable, as though she'd recited a foreign curse.

"Your imperial majesty." Better, but not quite right.

Sibylla huffed, exchanging the nautical sundial for the half-empty bottle of spruce liquor. In little more than a day, this Khalishkan emperor would arrive with his company of guards and advisors. She hadn't any idea of how to protect Myrcnia. If the queen was depending on her to distract him, then she'd sorely misjudged her granddaughter's inherent charm. Still, if the queen assumed Sibylla was actively courting the emperor, she could follow her own plan with regards to the royal bastard. Winning over Timur might provide her the ally necessary to thwart the queen. Through guile or luck, she'd do everything she could to gain a foreign embassy in which to safely hide her half-brother.

17

The following afternoon, Sibylla wandered the gardens while the household prepared for the emperor's forthcoming arrival. All her attempts to subdue her anxiety over the next day's festivities – reading Salston, inking fancy calling cards, stuffing olives in her cheeks – had failed. And now that Lady Brigitte had unveiled the queen's idea of foreign diplomacy, Sibylla had more to consider than securing an embassy and protecting her brother: might she break marriage traditions older than Queen Mildred?

The only calm she felt was in learning the Greyanchor Strangler had been caught, and without her personal intervention. She'd have liked to contribute something toward his apprehension, but at least Mabel's shopgirl friend would soon satisfy herself by spitting upon his visage.

Plum-colored helleborus peeked from lingering clumps of snow. Sibylla wound through the maze of barren paths until she found herself before a particular tree. Her stomach churned. The gardeners should have chopped the thing down by now.

The tree itself wasn't the problem. The weeping ash sat in a line of gnarled old pears that hadn't borne fruit since Prince Consort Barnaby died. Its branches drooped over the path, heavy with ice that forced her to duck if she didn't want a bruise. As a little girl, she'd watched children play around this tree with sticks in their hands, assailing ruffians or assaulting warlords. It was also where Roger had first kissed her.

A soft whistle-click to the back of Roger's neck had sent a stack of sun-bleached petticoats he'd taken off the clothesline billowing in the breeze. As he gathered the laundry, she spied her own bloomers in the grass. With a distressed shriek, she lunged for them. Roger must have thought she wanted to start a game of hog-the-wash because he grinned and sprinted after her, chasing her through the gardens. At last he'd cornered her against the weeping ash with the bloomers still clutched to her chest. He wound his fingers in the lacy frills, ready to tug, then froze. Her face burned hot and her veins pulsed with bluish light.

"These are mine," she said, her voice tight.

"I know." He stroked her hair and traced her cheek with a callused finger. She dropped the bloomers to the ground. Her fingernails dug into the tree bark as he leaned in to kiss her neck, then her mouth. His lips had been chapped and his tongue tasted of salted haddock, but she still closed her eyes to savor the moment.

The following summer, she'd met him again under the ash, this time to give him the royal library's only copy of Hemon's *Studies of Medical Phenomena and Their Surgical Treatments.*

Of course, that was before the queen had paid Roger quite a sum to end his dalliance with her. Her stomach soured. He'd had no difficulty kissing Dorinda beneath these same drooping branches – Sibylla had seen it all from a hollow beside a gooseberry bush. She wondered if he had ever discovered the value of that rare medical volume. Perhaps he wouldn't have agreed so hastily to the queen's terms if he'd known.

Sibylla kicked the ash's trunk, succeeding merely in scuffing her boot. Removing her gloves, she flexed her fingers and inked a spiral of bees around the ash tree in an attempt to keep her eyes from watering. Despite being told whom she *should* love, she'd only fallen once. Roger had taken her heart and run off with it. And soon she might wed a man just to lower the market price of cheese abroad. Tears prickled behind her eyelids.

Not that her first love had been all that forgiving. Over the years, she'd invented plenty of excuses for his silence, but now she had his letters – hateful, unremorseful boasts accompanied by inappropriate hatpins. With every pass around the tree her frustration grew until the branches of the weeping ash turned black from all the ink-bees drifting upward.

The sound of a man loping down the path threw her off guard.

Lieutenant Calloway's bright cranberry uniform stood out from the soft gray mist and the browns of empty branches. Relieved to be woken from her moping, Sibylla almost waved. He bounded over a hedge as if charging an imaginary battlefield, though he could have simply crossed the gravel path where it cut through the boxwood.

He'd settled his affairs at Helmscliff more quickly than she expected.

His riding boots crunched on the frosted grass as he approached. He blushed and swept her hands into his, squeezing her bare icy fingers.

Though not a cousin, nor servant, nor foreign diplomat, she admitted this young lieutenant did have a nice mustache. He'd even written her a love letter with impeccable penmanship. She absently wondered if it might be easier to run off with some soldier than to win over an emperor or cease pining after a medical student. She might kiss this man, and forget the others. Sibylla leaned in to find out.

She expected him to say something, but his eyes only widened. His mustache tangled in her lips. After a moment's hesitation, he kissed her back, his mouth insistent but gentle. She tasted a sweet sugar dusting on his blond bristles that suggested Lieutenant Calloway preferred breakfast in the Ibnovan style to the hearty veal sausage and white cheddar quiche she'd enjoyed that morning. Her fingers gripped his hips, and she allowed him to brazenly wrap his hands around her waist.

But it was no good. Her heart didn't burst in her chest, and his lips didn't blot out the other kisses she'd shared beneath the ash's bowed branches.

Stiffly, she slipped out of his arms. As she straightened the pin in her hair and adjusted her collar, her mind kept returning to Roger. She should have slapped the lieutenant, or just herself for using him as a crutch to forget.

Dazed, Lieutenant Calloway looked as if he'd been unseated from a horse. "I have the best news, my dear. But it's taken all morning to find you. The queen's Black Stallions will be in the parade." They were part of the household cavalry – elite, hand-selected guards of the royal family – so their inclusion shouldn't have been a surprise to the lieutenant.

"Is that so?" she said to humor him.

"I'll be fitted with the cuirass this afternoon, in time for the emperor's greeting procession."

Sibylla forced a smile. His bright, enthusiastic stare only confirmed she'd made a mistake out of weakness. Lieutenant Calloway moved closer, obviously wishing to continue their earlier sport, but Sibylla pressed a hand to his chest. His face turned such a bright red hue, she wondered what he imagined doing to her.

"Sibylla." A sudden call from across the frosted lawn interrupted them.

Her mother. Lady Brigitte used the same tone when disapproving of her reading choices, her penchant for eating sweets after midnight, or her excessive drinking of spruce liquor.

Lieutenant Calloway withdrew into a deferential bow. His flawless execution from ardent suitor to solicitous protector surpassed even Harrod's talent for deception.

"What a spitting image of your father, the great general of Mince." Lady Brigitte playfully took stock of the young man. "Highspits certainly produces men of vigor."

"May my duties allow me to guard our most precious princess for many years to come." Lieutenant Calloway clamped his fist to the chest of his jacket.

Lady Brigitte winked at Sibylla. "The princess will be ever grateful. Now might I have a private moment with my daughter?"

"As you wish, your grace." He turned to Sibylla and snuck a smile. "Your highness."

The exuberant officer bounded down the tree-lined path.

Lady Brigitte listened to his steps fade before speaking. "Even if he's prominently placed in the queen's Stallions, has an influential father, and is from one of the noble houses, try not to fall on your knees for him. I had no idea you had such affections."

The heat rose in Sibylla's cheeks. "I don't." She observed her mother's devilish smile. Lady Brigitte had seen them kissing by the tree.

"Come now," Lady Brigitte tsked. "Be proud you've finally mastered an instrument. Consider how difficult it is to find a man of his caliber. And his loyalty to you seems unyielding. You can always use good soldiers, Sibet."

Instead of defending herself, Sibylla dryly remarked, "Oh yes, I shall send him to conquer the color-chalked streets of Parney Avenue. He'll return with ribbons of blue and sage."

"Such theatrics. Really, how did I raise such a firebrand?" Lady Brigitte snapped a low-hanging twig off the weeping ash. "As long as you remember that chivalrous men don't bend. They break. And do take care how you address him in public." Lady Brigitte whispered into Sibylla's ear. "There's nothing wrong with letting an officer into your drawers, as long as he knows when to pull out."

Having spent a great deal of her childhood in Ibnova, Lady Brigitte was blunter than most, but having a forthright mother had its advantages. Sibylla would never be so traumatized after her wedding night that she couldn't attend public functions for a year.

"The parting of my thighs seems to be everyone's favorite topic of late."

Lady Brigitte brushed a bit of snow off her shoulder. "The curse of our sex, I suppose. In any case, do you know how many servants are searching the palace for you? You're late for your final fitting."

Sibylla had utterly forgotten.

"Apparently no one considered you daft enough to be out wandering in the cold. I, on the other hand, know you would happily roll around in the snow naked if it meant avoiding your duties as princess."

"The queen must be livid."

"Luckily for my daughter, the queen is otherwise occupied with preparations." Lady Brigitte flung her hands out to mimic the throwing of sparks. "The only one you're inconveniencing is Dorinda."

As Sibylla dashed off in the direction of the palace, the shearing wind cut cold threads through the seams of her overcoat. Inconveniencing Dorinda *was* inconveniencing the queen. While seamstresses worked night and day to finish her dress for the spark and glow ceremony, she planned to spend the evening ensuring she could hold a strong light for tomorrow. With Prince Henry handling Dr Lundfrigg, the queen attempting to entertain the emperor, and Harrod off rescuing a stranger from the gallows, she'd started to feel adrift: like a minnow swimming in an ocean of stingrays. Any moment she could be stung.

18

Having remembered to stash the lockpicks from his garret in his jacket, Roger effortlessly cracked Harrod's locked back door before dawn. If not for their uncomfortable relationship, he'd have suggested his brother install a more secure bolt. When Dawson unlocked the bedroom door at dawn, Roger was sprawled on his bed asleep.

Dawson first set him to work on the stairs. Roger was crouched in the morning sunlight rubbing walnut oil on the banister spindles when Harrod breezed past him without a glance, on his way to the Naval Office. Roger leapt to his feet.

"Captain Starkley, I know you're busy, but I must speak with you." Roger managed to add "sir" with barely a sneer.

Harrod flinched. He halted on the landing below and turned.

"I've a good idea who this strangler intends to murder next," Roger said. "And if you'll just help me find him – or her – I might clear my name. You know I'm no murderer, and I'm hardly a threat running loose on the street."

"Help you?" Harrod sniffed. "I expect you to grovel for forgiveness after what you pulled."

"After what I pulled?" Roger brandished his rag. "I'm here polishing your stairs, aren't I? Just as you've always dreamed of. If you're going to accuse me, then spit it out instead of prancing about like some fancy royal pony."

"I haven't time for this." Harrod sounded nearly as exhausted as

Roger felt. "I'll merely mention my disappointment in your nocturnal visits to a certain loathsome neighborhood. I'm more aware of your movements than you may think, and likewise your lecherous habits. I can't even trust you for one night to do as you're told, Merciful Mother help you. You still must survive five more days until the Binding. Don't press your luck."

Roger stiffened. "I'm the only one who seems to give a damn that there's still a killer on the streets. How long before he snuffs another precious life?"

"If you knew what I had to…" Harrod sighed. "Your elusive killer is nothing but some fishwives' fantasy, and not worth risking your neck. What must I do to get through to you?"

Roger stood tall and pulled his shoulders back. "Just flog me already and get it over with. I'll learn my rightful place eventually. Once I've brought the real strangler to justice."

"The archbishop was right. I should have locked you in the old basement coal-room. You'll only get yourself killed if you aren't literally tied down. That changes today. As for the flogging, there's only one way to deal with petulant little boys who disobey direct orders." Harrod stalked up the stairs toward him. "Only men get flogged."

He slapped Roger across the face with the flat of his palm, and all the force of a right hook. Roger reeled into the banister. His lungs stung like he'd breathed in a handful of iron filings.

Harrod spoke through a clenched jaw. "The second day of probation: diligence." He left Roger slumped on the stairs and clutching his oily rag.

Harrod's idea of diligence was an endless litany of chores to be completed by afternoon tea: scrubbing the front steps, beating the rugs, dusting the tops of bookshelves, scouring the pans – all under Dawson's ever-present eyes. In the afternoon, Dawson instructed him to wash up and put on his footman's livery. Harrod would be home for tea and Roger, as if living his worst nightmare, had to serve it. If Harrod thought this would put him off clearing his good name, he'd be disappointed soon enough.

Roger lay out the tea service in the drawing room. The mindless rhythm brought him back to Malmouth Palace when he'd been a footman. He'd had to memorize how all the royals took their tea, but only Sibet's remained in his head.

Harrod tossed a pile of missives onto the table before collapsing into a chair and peeling open the seals of his correspondence with a butter knife.

"May I pour the tea, sir?" Roger couldn't help sounding snide. He sidled up to Harrod's elbow and caught a glimpse of a lady's lacy script.

Focused on his reading, Harrod slid his teacup toward Roger, but angled the parchment away.

As he reached for a plate of almond cakes, Harrod accidentally nudged his stack of letters off the table. One of them fell near Roger's feet. He recognized Princess Sibylla's inked seal and stooped to retrieve it.

"Not that one." Harrod rose from his chair.

As Roger's fingers brushed the parchment, the captain trod on his hand.

Pinned to the ground, Roger was forced to look up at his brother. "I'm down here fetching your letters to be helpful. I didn't realize it were also a hanging offence, sir."

"The only reason I haven't strung you from the banister is because last night you somehow restrained yourself from visiting the necropolis, shovel in hand. Though that seems to be the only disgusting quarter you avoided." Harrod shifted his weight. "Perhaps if you lost something you truly cherished…"

The tendons of Roger's fingers rolled flat against the bones. If Harrod applied any more pressure they would snap. A surgeon deprived of his good hand was no surgeon at all.

"Enough!" he gasped. "I don't much care for societal respect, but I aid folks in pain. If you don't care to help me seek truth, then my after-hours business is none of yours. Your coin would be better spent on widows and orphans than hiring some blighter to follow me around."

Harrod snatched the letter off the floor. "Take a seat."

Hesitantly, Roger pulled out a chair.

"I don't waste funds tailing derelicts like you." Harrod took his place at the table and draped his napkin in his lap. "All I need do is think to myself, where has that louse gotten off to? You might call it a powerful hunch."

Roger rubbed his sore hand. "A hunch? More like you was parsing the wares in Will-o'-the-Wisp Lane yourself."

Harrod snapped a brittle biscuit and drowned it in his tea. "Before we lost our mother, couldn't I always track her down? Whether she'd gone to the garment district for new silks for her mistress, or the butcher's for a crown roast. Even when I was at sea, I had an intuition as to her whereabouts. Almost as if I was holding a map in my head. And you're just the same, Roger. I can find you anywhere."

"Now you're so desperate to control me, you're trying to make me believe you've got some 'magic' parlor tricks up your sleeve, just because you're some toff's bastard." Roger gave a bitter laugh.

"For a man of science, you have some fanciful notions. If you refuse to believe in magic, then yes, Roger, convince yourself I've hired a whole brigade to follow you about town and keep me abreast of your important doings. I used to think you particularly devoted to our mother's grave with all those cemetery visits, but now I know better. Hopefully, if you know *why* you cannot pull wool over my eyes, you will cease your ham-fisted attempts to do so. You're a Straybound now. In service to the princess. It's best you get comfortable with the idea."

"I'm not bound yet." Roger sat, his mind processing, mouth clamped to contain a flood of scornful words. While he didn't relish another humiliating slap, he wondered if his brother did worry for him, the way he'd worried for Ada when she'd vanished on Will-o'-the-Wisp Lane. And based on the broadsheets he'd glimpsed Dawson perusing, another girl had gone missing just last night – too young to be Celeste but close enough to set his heart racing with fear. This time no one suspected the Greyanchor Strangler; he was already arrested.

Harrod crossed his legs patiently, and Roger tried to mirror his brother's silence. He only lasted ten seconds.

"I have a life outside these walls. I may not be a surgeon but even so, people depend on my medical services. 'Diligence' means keeping promises and mending those that need it. The real murderer is still out there, and here you sit with that smug face for having brought me to heel. I doubt you care about anything else, or anyone but yourself."

Harrod tore a watercress sandwich in half. "After all I've done – the positions I've found for you in the service of well-born families and which you ignored. You're still sulking over boyish trivialities. What would her highness think?"

Roger calmed himself with a deep breath. "I don't want to sound ungrateful toward Sib… her highness, but I mean to do more than empty chamber pots as some bewitched slave. I'm a man of science like you said. And *she* knows I'm more than just a footman."

Harrod stared into his teacup. "I suppose the physician present at our mother's death made an impression on your malleable young mind. Is there something you find romantic about soaking your shirt in human blood?"

Roger sat up sharply. "That man weren't at fault for how she died, fighting for every breath like she were drowning. When he bled her, she woke one last time to tell me… never mind what. He did all he could, right to the end, as you'd have seen yourself, had you bothered to show. I paid him every last shelling that were stuffed into my pockets by the queen's maid for… you know. You always speak of doctors as 'human butchers,' as like to kill off their patients as heal them. There may be some crooks among them, but it's unfair to think physicians of every stripe are quacks. Setting a man's leg will change his life more than polishing his silver."

Harrod flipped the empty teacup and let a damp ring form on the tablecloth. "Don't think a pretty speech is going to wash away that tattoo. That'll never be removed. There was only one way to get you out of that cell, and I did what I thought best. But that doesn't mean I'll see her highness scarred by your necromantic, blood-spattered hobbies." He stood to leave and waited for Roger to bow.

Roger forced his body into a humble pose, and watched his brother turn his back, as unbreakable as a brick wall. Roger clenched his fists, but he'd lost the confidence to take a swing.

Later that night, Roger slipped into the study on the excuse of damping the fire. Harrod had convinced him of one thing. All of Caligo thought him guilty, save for the only person who'd believed in him all along.

The sight of parchment, ink, and quills laid out on Harrod's sturdy writing desk mobilized Roger into action. This could be his best chance. Dawson would soon come looking for him, to lock him in the old windowless coal room for the night – apparently Harrod hoped to prevent future nocturnal wanderings. Regretting his recent correspondence to Princess Sibylla, Roger sat at the desk and scribbled a letter. She'd saved his neck, so she must suspect his innocence. He owed her an honest thank you, but he couldn't bear the thought of Harrod reading it. He'd find a way to send it in secret.

Your Most Merciful Highness,

I cant help but trust that you know the truth of me, though I dont dare commit it to paper. Why else would you come to aid me in my darkest hour? I cant never express myself as best I should. Im but an Ingrate, an indebted one at that.

My late ordeal were like something in one of them thick books you like to read. Thanks to you, I have my neck. But its not the same neck as it was. Now I bear your mark. The Stigma of the Straybound. The Bishop mumbled his faerie incantations, they inked me, and my chains was removed. Harrod says Im to be bound to you in four days yet has near hysterics when I but mention your name. In your last letter you professed an admiration for him beyond my ability to understand. I dont wish to burden you with petty complaints (Im an Ingrate remember) but my brother needs reining in. Is it your wish that I bow to his every demand? You shall understand I require my Autonomy to excel in my chosen profession. Id serve you better as a surgeon than a drudge.

Dearest Sibet, I confess I have always been a bit afraid of you, for though I was always told you was as a delicate crystal vase, Ive long suspected that you would be the one to shatter me. I should cross that last part out. I wont. This letter wont never reach you anyway.

Your humble and contrited servant,
Roger X. Weathersby, Man of Science.
P.S. Have you not burned this yet? Hurry, I beg you!

Roger did not dare rewrite this letter, fearing he'd lose his nerve and destroy the thing. He decided not to use Harrod's seal and stamped the wax with the underside of his physician's amulet marked with the skull and lancet. On the front he wrote simply "Sibet." Adding a more formal name would raise unnecessary curiosity. There were multiple inappropriate sentiments written into that letter. Well, bollocks to them all.

Roger hadn't forgotten his other promise – to find a place in a hospital for Ada's mother – and a well-placed letter might solve that problem, too. Writing to Dr Eldridge was out of the question, but a certain physician from his research in *The Speculum* medical journal had fixed in his memory. A curious case like Celeste's could make careers, and history books if a physician cared for such a thing. That physician should be a notable blood scholar. He dipped his quill and started a second letter on a fresh page.

Dear Sir Finch S Lundfrigg, Royal College of Physicians,

I hope youll forgive a humble surgeon who begs your help in a matter befitting your expertise. As an eager student of your work I have read of your great interest in the bodys lifeblood. I have found a Case with many Symptoms which may be of interest. I beg you to admit this Case, a humble and devout widow, into St Colthorpes Charity Ward. At very least I hope you will permit me to ask what would cause blood to turn to thick ink. Please send your reply care of my brother, Captain Harrod Starkley, at 13 Burkeshire Gardens.

Your obedient servant,
Roger Starkley, a Man of Science

This time Roger closed the letter with Harrod's seal, hoping it and Harrod's opulent neighborhood would lend a certain authenticity. At the sound of Dawson's voice calling his name in the corridor, Roger stashed the letters in his pocket and ducked from the room. Tomorrow he'd find a way to send them, and with any luck he'd intercept their replies out from under Dawson's nose.

On the following morning, "Patience Day," Roger was made to face the wall in an unlit alcove and clean grout between bricks with a nailbrush. He'd been at work for hours when the sound of Harrod's footsteps on the stairs made him turn. The captain hurried past, clad in his formal dress uniform: a double-breasted tailcoat with fringed gold epaulets, ruffled shirt and jabot, and white knee breeches with matching silk stockings. A tasseled saber hung at his side. Across his chest he wore a sea-green sash and a sapphire-studded medal etched with a kraken and anchor. Between this ostentatious dress and the buzzing servants this morning, Roger knew there was something afoot in Caligo.

A few minutes later Dawson appeared, dressed in a less elaborate variant of Harrod's uniform. Roger dropped the nailbrush as he passed, catching the man's attention.

"There you are, Roger. First-rate news – the Emperor of Khalishka arrives today, an' I have orders to lock you in the coal room while the captain an' I attend the procession. You'll have plenty of boot-blacking to keep yer hands busy. And as I hear yer handy with a needle, there's a tablecloth for you to hem by hand, long enough to fit a table in Queen Mildred's great hall. If that don't take patience, I don't know what will. Don't get into no trouble. Captain Starkley says he'll be watching you." Excitement had softened Dawson's usual gruffness.

Roger nodded. Excitement led to confusion, and confusion cloaked as well as darkness when it came to moving unnoticed. A plan for delivering his letters formed in his brain.

"Procession? I'll be sorry to miss the spectacle. Will you have a chance to see the palace?"

Dawson nodded. "Aye. I'll fill you in later, if you behave yerself to the captain's satisfaction. Should be a grand show, hundreds of riders, cannons, and a ceremonial spark show by her royal majesty, I hear."

They descended to the old coal room. Roger patted the pocket of his coat where he'd stowed his letter to the princess and cleared his throat.

"There's a girl in the palace waiting for word of me."

Dawson cocked his head. "That so? A serving-girl sweetheart, I expect?"

"More or less." Roger reached into his pocket. "If it's no bother, I've a letter."

"But have you coin?" Dawson fixed him with the uneven gaze of his lazy eye, and Roger knew he was about to be fleeced. After a brief but passionate negotiation, they settled on an extra caddy of boots to black, and one tooth extraction to be performed at a time of Dawson's choosing.

Roger handed him the letter with a show of reluctance. "If you can't deliver it, tie a rock to it and throw it in the Mudtyne."

Dawson closed the door and turned the key.

One letter down. Unfortunately, he'd need to take care of the second one himself, as his use of the fake name – Roger Starkley – on the return address would certainly raise questions.

Per his probation, Roger practiced further "patience" by waiting for the commotion of Harrod's departure to settle before retrieving his lockpicks from the pocket of his topcoat. Harrod must have assumed that, since this old coal room had no window, it made a secure cell. He'd assumed wrong. Roger picked the lock with ease and tiptoed toward the servants' entrance.

Within the hour, Roger had anonymously delivered Dr Lundfrigg's letter to one of the clerks at St Colthorpe's Hospital and arrived in Suet Street. Though he relied on the atrocious strangler portraits in the broadsheets to keep people from recognizing him, he wore the hat from Nail low over his eyes to hide his face. Details about the latest missing girl remained sparse – specifically whether she'd had an unidentifiable illness. Perhaps Ada knew something about the men who'd met with Celeste before she'd taken ill, though the idea of asking her turned his stomach.

He climbed the stairs to his garret two at a time, his mouth dry from worry that she might not be there. And in case she was, he held a hand level with his throat to prevent her strangling him.

This time he knocked.

"I saw you coming down the street," she called from the other side of the door. "I got you a gift, Mr sack-'em-up man. Close your eyes and come in."

Roger's heart settled. He closed his eyes, arms braced against attack, and opened the door.

"Look."

Roger opened his eyes.

Ada held up a tray of the sort street vendors used to hawk carnations or buttered parchment potatoes. "Mrs Carver promised to make jellied veal of it, but I asked and she said you could cut it up for me first."

A fetal calf the size of a bread loaf lolled on the tray, front hooves splayed as if inviting an embrace.

"I'm sorry I sold your cat. I'd hoped you'd show me some insides."

Roger had expected Ada to ask about her mother, though he didn't know what to say when she did. He hadn't had to tell Celeste she was dying. She already knew. But did Ada? And if not, was it his responsibility to break such news?

No. Or at least, not today.

Perhaps he might cheer her in his own, admittedly morbid, way.

"A fetal calf, eh?" Roger let his face light up with interest. He plucked an old scalpel from a jar of coffin nails, charcoal sticks, and mismatched cutlery.

"Set the tray on the bed," he said. "Now hold the limbs like so, while I make the cuts. Watch them fingers." He dragged the tip of his knife down the center of the calf's belly, then made two crosswise incisions at either end so he could fold back the skin to reveal the organs underneath.

"Them looks like pickled eels."

"These are the entrails. Help me unravel them. See how long they are?"

"They feel slimy."

"We all have them inside us, you and me, too. When we eat, that's where it goes."

"Where's the stomach? Can it really burst if you eat too much?"

Roger explained the path of digestion as best he could, borrowing many of Dr Eldridge's words, then showed her the heart, lungs, and brain. He encouraged Ada to touch and even taste the different parts of anatomy just as Dr Eldridge had encouraged him.

"Nasty sack-'em-up."

"Horrid ghost."

Roger had saved hardboiled eggs and bread from his breakfast to give to Ada who, though she'd eaten breakfast with the Carvers, wolfed down the food. As Ada prepared to return the calf to Mrs Carver for the promised jelly, Roger took a deep breath, hating himself for what he was about to ask.

"Ghost, when your ma got sick, do you remember her talking about any strange customers, or…?" His voice trailed off at her deadpan expression. "I'm not asking for details, just–"

"Did a man with horns and a funny looking chin come knocking at her window?" She put a hand on her hip, but when she spoke, her voice cracked. "You think someone made her sick? Like that song Mrs Carver's always singing, 'Poison Mary.'"

"I don't know." Celeste hadn't acquired her ailment from a water pump or rotten grain; there'd be more bodies, an epidemic. Roger's current theory was she'd been infected by some foreign substance – a heavy metal or natural venom. "No one else has fallen sick at Eglantine's, or the laundry?" Ada shrugged no. Claudine, Margalotte, and now, Celeste; women roughly the same age, with hard-soft bellies, and different professions. No men so far.

Ada puffed up her chest and slugged Roger in the arm. "Don't worry, sack-'em-up. You bring the strangler to me. I'll pull his entrails out through his nose."

A series of explosions and whistles blared outside the window.

"Fireworks," said Roger. "The royal procession must be on. Shall we go see?"

They washed up at the public pump, then wandered several blocks toward the general sounds of chaos. As the crowds grew thicker, Roger hoisted Ada onto his shoulders.

"I see horses," she exclaimed, drumming her palms on his hat. Roger stood on a low rail that boosted his head above the crowds. A procession of mounted cavalry, the queen's Black Stallions, rode past in formation, the riders clad in vibrant berry-red coats and shining cuirasses. The horses trotted as one in a fancy, forward-kicking gait.

A dozen cannons rumbled by, each pulled by a feathery-hoofed draft horse.

"Look!" shouted Ada, yanking Roger by the ear. "It's a sailing ship on wheels."

"The navy likes to put on airs," he said. "They don't fight wars with ships like that. The wheels are just for show. Look at all them poor sailors who have to pull it along on ropes."

Ada dropped her voice to a whisper. "There's a man on the deck. I think he's staring."

Sails snapped as the craft rattled forward – it wasn't a full ship, and barely the length of an omnibus. In the bow stood Harrod, his eyes fixed on Roger amid the massive crowd. Might there be some truth to what he'd said about his uncanny hunches? Roger reached for his garlic.

"The high seas must be grand," sighed Ada.

"I'd say they're more apt to make one ill." Roger frowned. He shouldn't let his problems creep into his afternoon out with Ada. "Can you see the palace from up there, Ghost?" he said brightly to change the subject. "Are there any pretty princesses riding past?"

"None, 'cept for me," said Ada with pride and squeezed his neck.

19

Sibylla's gown of silver satin, quilted with white pearls, had been constructed for this occasion. As she stepped outside, her bodice refracted the sunlight like a crystal chandelier. One of the queen's Black Stallions escorted her to the main dais where she climbed the stairs to eager applause from the crowd. Families had arrived as early as dawn with their children, baskets of food, and small metal dishes to collect the falling ash. Afterward, they'd take the dishes home to display on their mantels, a blessing of bounty from the queen herself.

Sibylla stood at the queen's right while Crown Prince Elfred, in a silver-embroidered dress uniform, stood on the queen's left. The remaining royal family members had boxed seats on the palace's terrace. Myrcnian guards lined the main thoroughfare to keep the crowd from blocking the entry. No more people would be allowed inside the gates until the emperor's parade concluded its tour at the front of Malmouth Palace. Sibylla's fingers twitched nervously. She focused on *not* flinging ink-bees into the crowd, even though she considered her role here as entertainer.

Murmurs spread from the back of the throng forward. A general excitement settled in the air. Around the edges of the courtyard, palace servants prepared for the queen's signature recreation of King Roderick's Great Geese Feast by readying their matches to strike candlewicks. Applause trickled toward Sibylla before cheers at the back of the courtyard erupted with the emperor's arrival.

Six pale horses of a special breed from Arenbough drew the emperor's carriage, a reminder of Khalishka's recent annexation of the slender coastal country. The small retinue of foreign soldiers outshone its Myrcnian escort, riding in a staggered formation on wide, pitch-black horses. Clad in calf-length black coats, they drew their slightly curved, guardless blades in salute. As they halted before the queen, the unified snap of their swords being sheathed into wooden scabbards silenced the crowd.

Sibylla concentrated on breathing steadily as she waited for the emperor to exit his carriage. Her nerves won out and a small ink-bee slinked off her fingertips. She expected a bear of a man, with a thick beard and fingernails like claws, not the sleek and lithesome figure that jumped from the carriage. How unfamiliar he looked, in the traditional Khalishkan military dress uniform, without crown or sash. Instead of the jewels and ribbons favored by Myrcnian royals, Emperor Timur kept a pair of fighting knives sheathed in a timber box on one hip and a silver pistol on his right. He wore his thick, black hair in a topknot, and a well-manicured short beard that obscured his age, although Sibylla knew he was five years her senior. He was neither the tallest nor the shortest man, and hurried to the dais as if bored by the affair already.

He vaulted up the stairs and affectionately shook hands with the queen. Sibylla wondered if the exact measure of their greeting had been arranged in advance. He took position at the queen's right, holding his hands stiff behind his back. Not once did he attempt to make eye contact with Sibylla and she began to think the talk of their potential marriage was rather more fuss than fact. All the better for her to focus on what she wanted: a Myrcnian embassy on Khalishkan soil.

The queen raised her right arm for silence.

"On this day–" the queen's voice dipped and rose "–we welcome Emperor Timur and his countrymen. Long have we wished to strengthen our ties with noble Khalishka, and in celebration of this historic occasion we will offer the Blessing of King Roderick to those who have so benevolently gathered here today to wish us well. May this blessing represent to our guests Myrcnia's great generosity and bounty in the face of all adversities."

The crowd bobbed in elation.

At the sound of a shrill trumpet, servants around the courtyard released floating lamps made of paper soaked in tree gum resin and infused with rose essence, then dried and crafted into bird-shaped lanterns. The heat from stub-candles gave them lift. The paper lamps rose like a flock of petrels on the low wind, climbing above the heads of the crowd. As they drifted ever higher, even the emperor tilted his head to follow their ascent. The paper-birds blotted out the sun, and Sibylla followed the queen and Crown Prince Elfred's example in illuminating her skin with a royal glow.

Near the front of the crowd, a boy of about two or three fixed his eyes on her and wailed, his face mushed with tears and snot as he clutched his mother's arm. Sibylla winced, but no one else paid attention. All eyes were lifted to the sky.

Her translucent skin prickled from the growing electric charge in the air – wisps of hair, already turned white, stood on end. Beside her, the queen pulsed the muscles in her fists and raised her arms to form a "V". Once the paper lamps had drifted to the appropriate apex, the queen clapped her palms together in an explosive sizzle. White sparks crackled upward and set the paper-birds aflame. Ash blanketed the crowd, leaving behind the scent of smoked roses. The sky dimmed and the crowd stared, blank-faced with awe, at the royals glowing on stage.

Men wept. Ladies clapped. Scholars and farmers alike anxiously laughed. All the while, Sibylla waved her luminous hand until the ash settled and she dropped both arm and glow. For his part, the emperor did not stare at her like the boy near the front of the crowd, whose horror slowly turned to fascination as his mother stooped to scrape ash into a biscuit tin.

Sibylla was grateful when a Black Stallion came to escort her into the Great Gallery where formal introductions to the Khalishkan delegation had commenced. She curtsied to Emperor Timur without stumbling, but he still showed no marked interest in her and moved on to meet her cousins with a muted expression.

"What do you think, Weed-eyes?" Edmund hissed in her ear. "Are your loins girded?"

"Better watch out," Edward whispered from behind Edmund's back. "I heard the ol' Archbishop's commuted another felon, a true monster they say."

Edmund carried on in a singsong voice: "He'll catch you in a stranglehold, they say he likes his women cold."

"Old, he likes his women old."

"Old? Like Granny?" Edmund grabbed Edward's bum. "He *is* a monster. He'll grab as much queen as he can hold, I dare say he likes his women old!"

They tittered back and forth.

"Your highness. Mr Maokin, the Minister of Culture and Administration." The palace aide motioned Mr Maokin forward in the receiving line to meet her.

Sibylla ignored her idiot cousins and focused on the advisor. Easily one of the oldest Khalishkans there, Mr Maokin wore a lilac sash cinched around his waist and a pair of circular spectacles slouched across his nose. She needed to make a strong impression if she wanted to be taken seriously.

"May I?" he asked, lifting a tiny pink vial shaped like an orchid. "It's only water," he assured her.

Sibylla closed her eyes, and Mr Maokin splashed the vial's contents in her face. Water dripped down her chin.

Thank the Lady of the Stream, she'd read beforehand about the Khalishkan custom of "damping" a potential bride, or she might have reacted with a whistle-click to Mr Maokin's watery assault. Her cousins' giggles rang in her ears, but she refrained from smacking them both and kept her composure with a tight smile. The water was supposed to lay bare any concealments or unclean motivations she may have toward the emperor, though no magic existed in Khalishka to accomplish this feat. She was glad not to have her agenda exposed.

After Mr Maokin finished studying her face, he offered her a raw silk kerchief with a masterfully embroidered violet-blue iris in its square center. He tapped the inside of his wrist, and said, "Matches your colors, no?"

"Yes, it does. How kind." Sibylla admired the stitching, and at Mr

Maokin's prompting, dabbed the water on her face. If only she had something to offer him in return. Then it struck her. Recollecting a passage from her protocol guide, she stood on her toes and touched her cheek to his thrice, left, right, then left again, as a sign of friendship.

With a delighted smile, Mr Maokin squeezed her shoulder in return before he moved on to greet Edmund, who hid behind his hands while his brother Edward raised his fists like a boxer. How embarrassing for themselves and Myrcnia. It was a wonder the queen remained fond of them. But then, their behavior never had the consequences hers did. The rest of the introductions continued uneventfully, and by the time Sibylla smiled and nodded at the last Khalishkan, she had to change her dress for dinner.

As Sibylla finished preparing for dinner, an apologetic junior maid entered her room with a curtsy.

"Your highness." The maid lowered her head and shoved a letter forward.

Sibylla glanced at the envelope. Her pet name was well known throughout the palace. Close family members often called her Sibet, but none of them would have the gall to address a letter that way. Only one person would have dared thus.

Dismissing the maid, Sibylla took care to conceal any emotional reaction. Once alone, she rubbed her thumb across the macabre skull imprinted in the wax seal. Compared to this afternoon's performance, opening Roger's letter should have been easy, yet she trembled at the sight of his chaotic handwriting as if his words could bite.

The tips of her fingers whitened as she read, then her hands glimmered blue. The letter fell from her grasp.

Roger, her Straybound?

A joke. No, not even Roger could be so foolhardy to invent such a lie. She took a deep breath, but a glow spread throughout her veins, popping purple-violet beneath her once-again translucent skin. The tension she'd restrained all day flooded through her blood like a river of light. *Her* Roger was a Straybound. Impossible. He'd have to have killed someone – not accidentally, but with purpose.

"Ma'am?" A timid knock followed.

"A moment." Sibylla's chest rose and fell as the luminescence spread throughout her body. Another knock. She stamped the letter with the tip of her shoe and slid it beneath the side table. Sibylla squeezed her eyes shut. She took short, shallow breaths and at last opened her eyes.

She swung the door open before the maid called a second time and stepped into the hallway. Clenching her jaw, Sibylla tried to hold back frustrated tears.

The maid stumbled after her. "Din- dinner will be ser- served in the Grand Dining Hall," she stuttered, half out of breath.

Dusk had fallen and the hallway window captured Sibylla's frightening reflection, with her brightly lit organs and veins visible through her translucent skin. She had lost complete control. She offered the frightened maid a hand, but the girl flinched and disguised her fear with a hasty curtsy. Sibylla dismissed her with a wave and moved away. As she exhaled slowly, her skin lost its translucency until only a faint afterglow remained in her eyelashes.

Harrod had lied to her about Roger. Or at least, he hadn't told her the truth. She blamed herself for giving him that prerogative of service without understanding the full gravity of the matter. She'd been so giddy with her newfound freedom she'd not paid his words attention.

A Straybound was a convicted murderer. A Straybound was royal property. A Straybound could be discarded at a royal's whim or tortured on the moors. And somehow Roger, that milksop studying to be a surgeon, was *her* Straybound.

Hers.

Racked by these thoughts, she blundered into the dining hall without an escort. Startled footmen scurried to their positions. She paused, looking down the long table set with plates and polished silverware. She couldn't flee. If she did, she might not return.

One dinner: just another performance.

The footmen averted their stares as Sibylla circled the table in search of her seat. The emperor's place card sat at the head of the table and, dauntingly, Sibylla found her own card placed beside his. Mr Maokin would be seated to her right, while a Dr Kaishuk had been placed across from her. Guests trickled through the doors, and by the time the queen and emperor arrived, no one dared note her breach of protocol.

Once the emperor and the queen were seated, Sibylla swept the hem of her gown to the side and perched on the edge of her chair. Footmen served bowls of peeled grapes soaked in wine and drizzled with almond oil. To her right, Mr Maokin started a polite conversation with Lady Brigitte on seasonal vegetables, while the woman across from her remained silent. Hadn't a doctor been assigned that place? Her cousins' dirty jokes about female Khalishkan doctors sprung to mind. No wonder the woman looked put-upon. Female doctors were unheard of in Myrcnia.

Sibylla swallowed a grape. Sitting on Lady Esther's left, Edgar glared at her from the other side of the table. Only recently informed of the queen's unusual matchmaking designs, his ire seemed equally aimed at the emperor. Sibylla reached for another grape, then stopped. The queen gestured to her from the other end of the table, pointing to the emperor.

Sibylla nearly laughed. Apparently, she was expected to engage Emperor Timur in conversation immediately. People had fitted and stuffed her into gowns, but no one had briefed her on his interests. And living in an isolated valley had not, in fact, turned her into a social wit. Still, if she wanted to accomplish her own ends, she'd need to give it a try.

Dr Kaishuk, who was smashing grapes with the prongs of her fork, seemed to share Sibylla's lack of enthusiasm for small talk. She might make a better target than the emperor. Perhaps one conversation would start the other.

"Are you a reader, Dr Kaishuk?" Sibylla asked.

Dr Kaishuk's eyes narrowed. "I can read." She wore her hair in a bun, austere by Myrcnian standards. Her outfit, with its wide sleeves, brass buttons, and narrow epaulets, was more reminiscent of a chef's kirtle than any evening gown. "We have universities in my country. My accreditation is in the alchemical arts. What about your highness?"

"I've been extensively tutored."

"Ah, of course. Very practical." Dr Kaishuk squashed another grape beneath her fork. "Would her highness care to show us? Perhaps arrange the flowers or fold our napkins."

Dr Kaishuk's hostility left an uneasy knot in her throat. Sibylla glanced at the emperor. A black mark on her social performance tonight might hurt more than her standing with the queen. She'd try again – this time with something more exciting: plays.

"As a girl, I attended the Rose Theater in Minq where they were performing Lin's *Parade of a Thousand Sins*. It was my first Khalishkan play, and I've been addicted to them ever since. Have you been?" Not only was Minq the capital of Lipthveria, Khalishka's closest ally and southern cousin, but Lin's *Parade of a Thousand Sins* was also considered a true Khalishkan masterpiece – enjoyed by schoolchildren and scholars alike. If Dr Kaishuk had sentiment at all, she'd respond to one or the other.

"Strong words. I've never known anyone to care so much for our theater. Foreigners call it dry." The woman had no sentiment. "As a devotee of Khalishkan works, your highness must have a deep appreciation for the oppressed. And here I understood it was Myrcnian policy to ignore the plight of your lower classes, but your highness is practically a prawn's manure."

Mr Maokin censured Dr Kaishuk by harshly tapping his middle two fingers on the table in a distinctive one-two rap before slitting his throat with his other hand. As the cream of barley soup arrived, he turned to Sibylla to explain, "Your highness might not be aware of Talchi's poetry. She compliments your kindness."

"I'm aware of the poem." Sibylla lifted her spoon. If compliment in Khalishkan meant insult, then Mr Maokin may have been right. "The prawns' manure saves the village from starvation, but the villagers – blinded by the beauty of the golden rice fields – celebrate the sun. It's a testimony against giving false praise." No doubt a jab at Myrcnia's divine royal family.

"A poet most often overlooked by foreign readers. Especially Myrcnian princesses." The emperor's voice, deep and unreserved, startled her. "How diverting. I am also a fan of your theater. One playwright in particular: Richard Salston."

Sibylla's cheeks grew hot. Unless she believed in the Lady's providence, Emperor Timur *had* been briefed on her preferences. She should have been happy for the attention, but now felt uneasy at the prospect of an actual alliance. She took a long gulp of wine.

"If you enjoy tales of revenge," said the emperor after finishing his soup, "you must read *Curse of the Pretty Pelican*, the saga of a wronged whore and the man she sets out to destroy. Its ending is worth the effort." The emperor turned to Dr Kaishuk. "Has it been translated?"

Dr Kaishuk shook her head no. "Your imperial majesty can't expect a Myrcnian lady to appreciate such a treasure when those women are treated so poorly in her country."

"No society's laws are perfect, nor is any leader's will." Sibylla found herself defending her nation instead of currying their favor. Apparently, her tongue had an uncooperative mind of its own.

The emperor nodded as he flaked the newly arrived lemon-broiled cod with his fork. "At least your country's food is faultless, if not its ruler."

"I hope we have more to present your imperial majesty than good fish."

The emperor leveled his eyes at her. "Am I looking at what else she has to offer?"

"We also export a number of tantalizing sows," Sibylla answered. "And our cheeses, mustn't forget those." She caught his slight grin, though he quickly hid it behind a forkful of cod.

"I believe that's the next course," chimed in Lady Esther. She raised her thumb – scarred from performing Straybound devotionals – toward the approaching footmen, and nearly stabbed Edgar in the eye.

By the time the salad of thinly-sliced raw cabbage with fennel seeds and cherry tomatoes arrived, Dr Kaishuk's patience for Lady Esther's questions about Khalishkan winters had worn thin, and she turned to Sibylla almost affectionately. "At least your highness seems to believe in a measure of rationality when it comes to protecting the welfare of your people." Dr Kaishuk picked off the last tomato from her salad. "And yet your queen claims her right to rule by magic."

Sibylla had as little interest in delving into the historical merits of

Myrcnian divine rulership as she did in performing a concertina recital. If only dessert would arrive for them to stuff their mouths with sweets instead. Having failed to elicit a conversation on foreign embassies and ambassadorships, she'd given up on gaining ground with the emperor tonight.

Before she could answer Dr Kaishuk, Lady Esther slapped the table, sending a shiver through Sibylla's plate. "We have no reason to misrepresent ourselves." Her breath caught shrilly in her nostrils. "The honorable Muir bloodline has survived centuries longer than Khalishka's elective monarchy and lives strong within my husband and sons."

The emperor snorted. "How do you think your honorable magic would fare against iron and steel? I've seen many a 'sacred' man lose a leg or an arm to a cannonball. Let's see your son's magic stop my pistol."

"You all witnessed her royal majesty's display this afternoon," said a flustered Lady Esther.

Dr Kaishuk laughed for the first time. "As a doctor in the alchemical arts, I know when I've seen phosphorous. Although I admit, it was a… spectacle."

Sibylla cringed when Lady Esther elbowed Edgar beneath the table. She needn't lose her composure over a doubter. After all, Dr Kaishuk wasn't the first science-minded individual to question the royal family's magic, even though most did adjust their opinion after a live demonstration.

Lady Esther raised her voice. "My son's talent is no mere spectacle."

Boys tended to be late bloomers so Sibylla had never witnessed Edgar perform Crown Prince Elfred's signature rusting touch. Once, during a heated dinner conversation, the crown prince had tarnished every silver fork and knife in sight, including the silver serving trays of the footmen. Ever since, the queen had banned magic during mealtimes. Sibylla's cousins had never bragged about their divine gifts, and she'd seen Edmund spew water bubbles from his mouth only once – yesterday. He must take after Lady Esther. Did Edgar also, or had he inherited some generation-skipping oddity like her whistle-click? Sibylla eagerly looked on with the Khalishkans.

Edgar's expression tightened. He hesitated, searching his pockets for a snuff tin. He took a pinch and very slowly gulped his wine before lifting his hand. Instead of squeezing his fingers into a tight fist like the queen, Edgar rubbed his thumb back and forth against his fingertips until finally a few white sparks fizzled off his skin. This went on for a minute or so before Dr Kaishuk could no longer contain her laughter.

"How shocking." She snickered behind her napkin.

"I've been feeling under the weather," mumbled Edgar.

Sibylla stiffened. The emperor, too, had joined Dr Kaishuk in using a napkin to politely obscure a smile. At this rate, Edgar would make a fool of more than himself. Her chair scraped the floor as she stood. She had no intention of letting their self-satisfied smirks persist through dessert. With an exaggerated flourish, she lifted her right hand and flexed her fingers while the ink pooled beneath her nails. Growing in form, a snow crane took flight from her hand on wings of black ink. Then held in midflight like a painting, frozen – the slightest flutter in its black feathers left a blur of dissipating ink.

She tilted her head toward the emperor. "Naturally, this would not stop a bullet."

The emperor's eyes glimmered. "That would depend on who's firing the pistol."

The ink bird diffused into the air until only a slender section of tail remained. Sibylla bent over the table and blew the remaining ink away. She smiled as tiny flecks of black stuck to Dr Kaishuk's face like freckles. Dr Kaishuk glared while Sibylla seated herself in time for an uncomfortable footman to deliver the custard pie.

"Delicious," Emperor Timur said, though he had not yet tasted the pie. Instead, he studied Sibylla as if deciding, then and there, whether she was a songbird or a hawk.

Suddenly uncertain of which outcome she preferred, Sibylla used her napkin to blot the remaining ink beneath her fingernails. After the fingerbowls of cashews arrived to conclude the formal dinner, and the queen and emperor had set aside their napkins, an attendant rung a tiny bell to signal the meal's end. Gentlemen and ladies withdrew to opposite ends, but Sibylla dodged the queen, her mother, and digestifs by exiting through the servants' passage.

Eventually she found herself standing on the terrace. Overwhelmed by the day's events, she leaned into the cold wind that snapped at her face and provided relief from this evening's heat. She brushed her arms up and down to keep from freezing.

The emperor had not met her expectations of a perfidious monster who squashed his neighbors for his own pleasure and plotted to ruin the Myrcnian cheese industry. Even so, Khalishkans seemed no more enamored with Myrcnians than she'd been told, and with Edgar's dismal display at dinner, Sibylla didn't see how the queen could approve her marrying anyone but her cousin. Ceremonies had to be performed and magical abilities passed along. If Edgar couldn't rust, or spark, or even glow on cue, then Myrcnia needed someone who could. But she'd played enough Contemplation and Crisis to know one sunken path could open another. An embassy could yet be gained along with her grandmother's respect.

She bit into her lip.

Tomorrow held other trials. The first of her Straybound ceremonies loomed, knotting her stomach with dread. When it was some nameless convict she'd spared on Harrod's behalf, the Rite of Cleansing hadn't mattered to her. It was just another necessary step toward the eventual Binding. However, after this afternoon, her Straybound was no longer a faceless associate of Harrod's. He was Roger – the boy with a clever tongue, whom she'd kissed.

At morning's first light, Archbishop Tittlebury would ask her to read the accounts of her Straybound's misdeeds and absolve him spiritually of the sins that had legally convicted him. Sibylla had always trusted Harrod's judgment, yet doubt niggled in her heart. Not only had she never performed this rite, but now she worried that she couldn't go through with it.

20

After the parade, Roger saw Ada back to Suet Street before returning to Harrod's townhome. It was already late afternoon by the time he slipped through the servants' door. Fortunately his brother was still out.

He locked himself back into his room and had started polishing his fifth pair of shoes when someone thumped on his door. Then the lock rattled, and Mrs Confit the cook peered inside.

"There's some footman on the steps outside," she said breathlessly, wiping floured hands on her apron. "I spied him through the window when he rang the bell. I can't answer like this. Dawson's still out with the master, and the other servants haven't yet returned from the parade. You'll have to do, lad."

Roger pulled on his livery. "Aye, Mrs Confit. Right away." He buttoned his coat as he raced upstairs.

Balancing a silver tray in one hand, Roger opened the door to a footman in more subdued livery than his own.

"Delivery for Mr Starkley," said the footman, placing a letter on Roger's tray.

On the ivory parchment, in miniscule saw-toothed calligraphy, was written *Mr Roger Starkley, c/o Captain Harrod Starkley*. It must be Dr Lundfrigg's reply, and so soon. The tray wobbled in his unsteady hand.

"I'd warn you not to drop it, to avoid wearing the 'coat of shame,'" said the other footman with a wry grin, "but I see my advice'd come too late."

Roger dropped his eyes and waited impatiently for the man to leave so he could open the letter – his letter – in private. He closed the door and turned, nearly running into Dawson who stood behind him, still in his topcoat. He must have just returned by way of the servants' entrance.

"I'll take that," said the butler, snatching the letter off the tray. "An' you, Roger, can get the drawing room ready fer the captain's return." He glanced at Roger's fingers, streaked with boot polish. "But don't even bother until you scrub those hands. The cook will have a brush for getting the dirt off potatoes. Use that. And wear your white gloves next time."

"Yes, Mr Dawson."

Mrs Confit did indeed have a potato brush and had already brought her largest kettle to a roiling boil. Roger staggered up the stairs with the fluted copper tea urn and found that Dawson had stashed his correspondence out of sight. So much for intercepting it. He had a good idea who was going to read it first.

The butler was lighting the lamps in the drawing room. "It's cold as a Khalishkan ice-wind with no fire in the grate. But take off that nice coat before you smudge it with ash."

By the time Harrod arrived home, Roger was still crouched before the fireplace, his face smudged with soot, struggling to keep a flame burning.

"What's this?" exclaimed Harrod as he burst in, a wide grin on his drink-warmed face. His naval uniform reeked of cigars, and his breath of Admiral Oakberry cognac. He shouted over his shoulder, "Dawson, go draw a bath hotter than a bowl of Jameson's cock-a-leekie soup. I'll boil myself sober." Harrod clapped his hands as if summoning a dog. "Roger, come here."

Roger rose to his feet and gave his required bow. He'd never seen Harrod so sloshed before.

Harrod waved a folded parchment in Roger's face. "Dawson tells me he rescued this letter from your filthy fingers. He seems convinced you'd have opened it had he not intervened."

"I didn't realize it was illegal for a man to open his own letters, sir."

"What lark is this?" Harrod squinted at the tiny handwriting. His jovial expression returned, and he handed the letter to Roger with a nod. "Well, well. Mr Roger Starkley. Now who might that be? Why don't you deliver it to him?"

Roger didn't wait for his brother to change his mind. He slid his finger under the seal and cracked the wax.

Meanwhile Harrod collapsed sideways onto the settee and kicked his glistening military boots indecorously over the armrest. "The letter certainly looks authentic. I suppose you could have swiped quality paper from my bureau, but as for the handwriting, no. You couldn't manage that on your own. And the royal physician's seal tops it off. Go on, man. Read it out loud. I can't wait to hear what some mysterious person of means has to say to the likes of you."

If Harrod had been less drunk, the whole scene might have unfolded differently. Even if Roger didn't care to read the letter out loud, his gut told him to strike with Harrod in high spirits. In a wavering voice, Roger read:

My dear Sir,

As a fellow man of science, I would invite you to meet me at the Anathema Club, an exclusive haunt for science-minded gentlemen of society. It is located at 24 Brocade Circle, and I expect you at eight o'clock tomorrow evening. I will inform the servant at the door to let you in.

Yrs. Faithfully,
Sir Finch S Lundfrigg, M.D.
Fellow, Royal College of Physicians

Roger read the correspondent's signature twice over. He hadn't missed his brother's surprise, either. The famous Dr Lundfrigg! He'd finagled an audience with one of the leading names in the medical field, and the royal physician to boot. Using Harrod's seal and address had worked better than expected. No doubt the promise of a medical mystery had helped his chances. Now he just needed his probation officer's approval to attend.

"My good man," said Harrod with a boozy grin. "Of all the wild tales I heard today, this here is the most hysterical of them all."

"I intend to take Sir Finch up on his offer," said Roger quickly. "With or without your permission, sir."

"Of course you aren't going!" Harrod's voice rose to a shout. "You are mine to command. And even if I wanted to let you go, which I don't, my hands are tied. You have no idea the complexities of your situation."

"You're the one who's always harping on at me to better my society. A knight of the realm wants to speak to me after writing a very respecktical letter – addressed to *me* – and you forbid it. But what if I told you I'd clean his boots with my tongue. Would that change your mind, *sir*?"

For a second, Roger thought Harrod might slap him again. Instead, the captain rose to his feet with as much dignity as his intoxicated balance would allow, and turned his back to leave.

"Roger," barked Harrod over his shoulder. "My bath will have gone cold by now. Go refresh the water. I'll be up presently."

Roger climbed the stairs to Harrod's chambers, kettle in hand, wishing he could cram reason into his brother's legalistic skull. But he'd need more than a bonesaw for that.

He trod softly on the thick hallway runner, making for the bathing room at the end of the hall. Inside, a copper tub and gold-draped picture window lent the cramped space a royal magnificence. He wasn't about to refill the entire thing, no matter what the "master" said. A few scalding kettlefuls would suffice. When he'd made his third trip up from the kitchen, a somber-faced, rumpled Harrod leaned in unsteadily at the bathing room doorway. He waited for Roger's bow before speaking.

"What do you know of the Anathema Club?" Harrod sounded a notch more sober than he had downstairs.

"Not much. The well-heeled medical students have ether frolics in the smoking room. I used to hear their chatter in Eldridge's lecture hall. But that's not why I'm interested. Dr Lundfrigg is an expert in blood chemistry. I might discover some clue to clear my name." He didn't mention his primary goal of getting Celeste into a hospital bed. Harrod had already made his opinions of low-class doxies known.

"I know from experience that a pleasant day of shore leave makes shipboard life nigh unbearable, but if you're keen to suffer, I won't stop you." Harrod handed Sir Finch's letter back to Roger. "You made this appointment, and you'll keep it. Tomorrow is the fourth day of probation: reflection. That means you're to spend the day in silent adoration. I'm sending you to the Chapel of the Solemnlych for a day of silent prayer, but you'll be finished in time for your rendezvous. Perhaps this will be better than prayer. At least at this club you'll have someone to adore." Harrod clapped Roger's neck, and his Stigma, still raw and tender, throbbed. "If you get caught, we'll both be keelhauled. Maybe then you'll believe I did this for your benefit and not my own."

Dawson entered with a silken dressing gown and started unbuttoning the captain's jacket. Harrod waved him off.

"I'm not that intoxicated, man. I can undress myself. Go see what Mrs Confit left out for your supper." Harrod dipped his hand in the bathwater and sighed. "Dawson, let's leave the door of this rascal's room unlocked tonight, shall we? Perhaps he can keep himself in check when he has important people to see tomorrow."

At long last, things were looking up for Roger Weathersby, man of science. Not even the act of bowing himself from Harrod's presence stirred his ire.

21

Sibylla pulled low the brim of her hat. Eerie predawn light cast shadows on the faces of the statues residing in the corners of St Myrtle's cloister. An ancient stone firepit accented the middle of the lawn, guarded by the watchful stone eyes of the four saintliest monarchs in Myrcnian history – Saint-Queen Ingrid, Celia the Devout, King Roderick, and Priest-King Rupert the Webbed. Three stacked rings of weathered granite stones, each carved with Old Myrcnian symbols representing the history of the royal bloodline, encircled a sunken pit of neatly raked ash more than three centuries old.

Archbishop Tittlebury reverently lowered his head. "Your highness."

"I, Divine Maiden Sibylla, at morning's first light on my anointed Straybound's day of reflection, will now hear the crimes committed by the marked so I may judge, with sound knowledge and mind, his record of sinfulness against my grace."

The archbishop handed her a jewel-encrusted tinderbox while two attendant junior priests bearing court records and police documents waited to one side. Sibylla smoothed her dress and knelt before the stone pit. She took the iron pyrite in her left hand and the flint in her right. One priest placed a woven wreath of yew branches, studded with a flammable tinder fungus, in the center of the ring. Sibylla scraped flint across pyrite, producing a tinny scratch but no flame.

She would not be defeated by hard chalk and fool's gold. After a quarter-hour, however, the pit remained cold. Sparks showered off the stone, but not even a dull orange ember rewarded her efforts. Obscenities flew from her mouth. The queen could have set the pit ablaze with a clap of her hands.

The archbishop pulled a pouch from his belt. "A little gunpowder might help things along." He took a pinch of black powder and sprinkled the nearest tinder-mushroom. "Mind your skirts."

Sibylla tucked her loose petticoats back in place before taking up the flint and pyrite. This time the sparks ignited the yew in a flash, and the fire crackled and spread through the pit. Sibylla stumbled to her feet, the heat warming her face against the morning chill.

The archbishop nodded in approval. "As did Priest-King Rupert the Webbed with regards to Angus the Foul, today you will read out the crimes of your Straybound. Hereafter, your highness will have two days' time to weigh the merit of his soul and offer him eternal redemption, or allow his punishment to be carried out forthwith, that he may seek forgiveness in the afterlife."

"I understand."

He motioned one of the priests forward. "For the sake of brevity, and per the guidelines set forth by the Act of Reasonable Intent and Solvency, the church has prepared an abbreviated summary of each crime. Should your highness wish, the entirety of the documents held herein may be read at your leisure."

Sibylla nodded and Archbishop Tittlebury took the first of a curiously large stack of parchments carried by the younger priest.

"You will now read the sins of the condemned man." He handed her the document.

She read out loud: "Emma Jane, dearest daughter to the late Mr and Mrs Jane, was violently strangled by one Mr Roger Weathersby, a resurrectionist, whereupon liberties indecent were taken until dead."

At the sight of his name amid this unexpectedly vile crime, her throat tightened. Surely it was an exaggeration. Sibylla let the parchment fall into the sacred cleansing fire where it blackened and curled. She scanned the attached police file, as well as the court records, and one by one let them fall into the pit to be eaten by the "holy flames."

The destruction of evidence connected to the Straybound's crimes

– investigation reports, coroner's notes, even witness testimonies – was considered a vital step in the cleansing. It served partly to grant the Straybound an unblemished record in the eyes of society, but mostly so the royal could bestow a new identity. As with Dorinda, given a new name and position as household maid, nothing existed to connect her to the Murderess of Fraycable Street, save for hearsay, which faded after a few years of uneventful service.

Sibylla paused at the date of Emma Jane's murder, a month after she'd been sent to Helmscliff. Certainly, Roger hadn't committed any murders while they were together, but she knew little of his life after. A silly thought she tried to shake off as she finished burning the first folder of documents. The remaining records only deepened that niggling doubt, her confliction over his true guilt rising with each victim. The vast, horrific evidence couldn't have stuck to him purely by accident. Her breath rasped in her throat, and the fire whipped nasty black smoke into her eyes. After the recitation of the ninth victim, she took the last record from the archbishop's hand.

Her throat burned as she spoke. "Claudine Mary, wife of Daniel Walston, proprietress of Claudette's confectionery shop, was brutally strangled until dead, whereupon her corpse was buried beside her beloved husband, Plot 715 of Necropolis Hill, then resurrected by one Mr Roger Weathersby, a resurrectionist, so he could commit violations of a most foul passion upon her resting soul before selling her remains, in an ill and callous nature, for personal profit."

This last victim was the shopgirls' mistress. The two women had left prayer plaques in Sibylla's name, yet here she stood, answering them by destroying the evidence of Claudine's murder. Shame prickled her skin as she watched the final documents turn to ash, and the sun lit the sky in a grey haze of clouds. Was this how royals answered prayers?

Her shoulders shuddered despite the heat from the fire. Even after the pit had been cleared, she stood supporting herself against the statue of Saint-Queen Ingrid. The sculptor had attempted to capture her glow by chiseling veins into her neck and forehead, turning her expression severe. Sibylla empathized with the long-dead queen's misrepresentation.

Not only had Harrod failed to mention she'd be rescuing Roger, but he'd dubiously left out the horrific nature of the charges as well, perhaps in a misguided attempt to shield her. Now she had just two days to have a word with one brother or the other, else she'd be wearing an ill-fitting conscience to the final ceremony. The criminal who committed these crimes deserved to die, not be granted a reprieve and made Straybound – no matter his royal connections. Still, she couldn't reconcile her memories of Roger with the vileness she'd read. A real monster had murdered those women, and surely Roger hadn't become that.

Light rain sprinkled her cheeks and Sibylla tucked her braided hair into the collar of her coat. The smell of smoke permeated the air and Larksman Castle's towers rose before her like sharpened charcoal sticks above the rooftops. She made her way across the moat-bridge and under a raised iron-lattice portcullis. Harried-looking naval officers stalked in and out of heavy stone buildings.

The Ordnance Board's lacquered plaque stood next to an iron naval cannon in the courtyard. An ornate carriage waited near the entrance, its four black horses pawing and snorting impatiently. Workmen rolled barrels of gunpowder across the pavement toward Hangman's Tower for storage. In her years knowing him, she'd never beaten Harrod in a game of hide and seek, but after this morning she'd be damned if the first time she saw Roger again was at the Binding ceremony.

Stepping into the castle's foyer, she stopped the first ensign she encountered. With a flick of an ink-bee as proof of her nobility, she demanded Captain Harrod Starkley be brought to her. As she waited, a collection of sailors loitered in the adjoining hallway. Their heads turned to one another in discussion, and she half-expected them to form a queue for benedictions.

When the ensign finally returned without Harrod, his eyes were red and he appeared seasick. Running his hand through his hair, he stammered, "Yer highness, Captain Starkley is nowhere to be found. He reportedly… left for lunch."

"Before eleven?" Sibylla's fingers twitched at her side. "The captain is not that uncouth. Did he order you to say he's not here? I wonder that an order from a superior officer relieves a man of lying to a member of the royal family." The ensign nearly burst into tears, but breaking his spirit wouldn't solve anything. "If you would at least deliver a message?"

"Whatever pleases yer highness."

"Tell that poltroon that I am not above defacing this entire building with ink if he continues to behave like a childish caitiff. And ensign, I suggest you take a trip to church. Lying is a sin, no matter who ordered you to do so."

Flustered, the ensign kept nodding. "Yes, yer highness. I promise I'll go at lunch. No, sooner. I'll go now."

At this rate, he'd end up in the stockades for dereliction of duty. "I don't think that's necessary." Sibylla gently laid her hand on his shoulder. "Why hurry to an appointment that is always being kept for you?"

Tears fell from his eyes in wet streaks, and she realized her mistake when the ensign clutched her hand so tightly she thought her fingers might break. Barely the age of Edmund and Edward, sixteen or seventeen at most, he didn't let go. It was a mistake to scold him. Two years in Helmscliff had made her forget this could happen, *especially* with sailors.

He forced the words from his throat. "Forgive me, Divine Maiden Sibylla, please."

She winced at the title. She had no choice, now. Wriggling her hand free, she placed her thumb to the center of his forehead. "With mercy, I unburden thee." She slid her thumb down his nose to his lips. "May you swim in the glow of the sea." Closing his eyes, the ensign kissed her thumb. Before stepping back, she stroked his head as a mother might until his sniffles ceased.

What a disaster. Sibylla turned from the ensign to where a cluster of male onlookers jostled one another, trying to hide behind a horse's suit of armor. They peered over the shiny rump and Sibylla pretended not to notice, lest she spend her day blessing the rest of the keep.

"That's her? The princess?"

"Looks like maybe. You gone to her chapel, yet?"

"Not since we came to port, but Forks swears by her blessing of virility. Said after being anointed, he kept his shivers wet for more'n an hour without so much as a sip of Dr Groady's droop serum."

These buffoons had no idea how their voices echoed off the stone. As she passed, the men ducked behind the iron horse, their bodies visible between its legs.

Outside, the drizzle had stopped. Perhaps pursuing Harrod at his house might yield better results. If not Harrod, then she might find Roger on her own.

She veered left to avoid the carriage horses. She had an unfortunate past with the beasts. Her riding lessons always left her bruised with muddy skirts when her mount would throw her for no apparent reason. With her head in the fog, she nearly collided with a lithe gentleman dressed in embroidered blue silk.

"Watch where you step, girl," said an annoyed vice-admiral who accompanied the gentleman.

Sibylla adjusted her hat to keep her face hidden. One discomforting apology was enough for the day. Evidently the vice-admiral had other business on his mind, as he bustled on toward the carriage. The gentleman in blue, however, did not.

Before her, Emperor Timur stood without a hat – brazen by Caligo's customs – and gazed at her with curiosity.

Sibylla lowered her head. "Your imperial majesty." As she moved to one side to allow him to pass, he stepped to mirror her.

Meanwhile the vice-admiral waited beside the carriage with Dr Kaishuk. Neither of them had noticed her yet, and she'd rather not explain what she was doing at the keep, or who she'd come in search of, or why. If only the emperor would bow and turn away, she might escape relatively unnoted.

"What a welcome distraction," said the emperor in his deep, warm voice. "I was tired of listening to old men prattle. None of them have tasted blood since the War of Ships."

Sibylla smiled despite her desire to remain unnoticed. "Let us hope they grow older before partaking in another such culinary delight."

With a scowl, Dr Kaishuk puffed up her chest and called out, "The carriage is ready, sire. We've a schedule to keep."

The emperor shooed away his advisor. "I will be exploring your city tomorrow," he said, "although I am not interested in a second parade. Perhaps you could suggest something more diverting."

Sibylla recalled a book extolling Caligo's hidden beauties. "There's Hoxley Tower in the west, the palace gardens if your imperial majesty somehow missed them, or St Harailt's rectory if you're interested in seeing her royal majesty's divine implements." Sibylla paused. "Though perhaps not. I propose either the library in Stalwerch, Marlowe's Menagerie, or the museum of medical oddities in Hiddle's Park."

Sibylla's braid had slipped free from her coat collar, and the emperor trapped the flapping ribbon ends with his hand. "If I wanted a list, I would read a book."

This was a man who could ruin a nation. One she wanted to impress, she reminded herself. She'd do better to put some thought into it. So far, Emperor Timur had shown an interest in the lower classes and relished a good meal. She could point him to a hotchpotch or a woman like Dame Angeline. Her cousins seemed to enjoy her establishment, and they had mentioned a new ingénue.

She tugged her braid free and tucked it back inside her collar. "If your imperial majesty would like, I'm sure our Minister of Foreign Affairs would merrily show you any corner of Caligo, even places a lady such as myself could not attend." With growing concern, Sibylla realized she didn't know which direction the emperor needed to be pointed.

"Please, call me Timur."

"Timur. As I said, a minister might better understand your needs. I'm afraid I can only tell you what interests me."

"Then do."

Sibylla hesitated. She couldn't imagine what would dazzle him most, so she settled on the one place she'd longed to visit since returning from Helmscliff. "Crosswitch Bridge. Its imported black stone is beautiful and its structure unique. Not to mention, cart peddlers have sold wares on its segmented arches for centuries, and as a child I was fond of a woman there who sold fresh bread stuffed with dates and olives. I haven't been back for some years, however."

"Your Minister of Foreign Affairs looks like a cross between an overbaked sheet of seaweed and a splatted egg. I'd prefer you take me. Though if he's my only way of stealing your company, then I'll happily arrange an outing for three." The emperor's smile elicited an unexpected flutter in her stomach.

Sibylla nodded her head toward the vice-admiral with crossed arms. "I'd much rather go on our own as well, but the palace will no doubt insist on following protocol." As it was, she'd snuck out during the guard change to avoid an army of maids and chaperones following her as she performed secret cleansing rites.

The emperor laughed. "I will not be asking permission. And neither will you."

Sibylla could hardly point to any attendants as proof of needing consent, and both the vice-admiral and Dr Kaishuk seemed miles away and annoyed. For the first time, she considered whether the queen would truly accept Emperor Timur as a suitor, even after she'd succeeded in soothing national egos. Unlike her cousin, he wasn't some dynastic conclusion. The emperor had no need of Sibylla's lineage or her title.

In the crypts beneath St Myrtle's, sealed urns of the magicked nobility dating back to Saint-Queen Ingrid were kept, each with its own family record illuminated in Old Myrcnian script on vellum. When Sibylla died, her body would be exsanguinated, her whistle-click, inking, and glow cataloged, and her urn filled with her blood, and placed in front of her parents. This way the church ensured none of the magic would be bred out by accident, and, when necessary, certain pairings could be "encouraged."

Marrying Timur would allow her to escape all that; she might not even be entombed beneath the church at all. She studied his appearance. He had a strong, graceful build and a manner not entirely repugnant. Their children might inherit his chin and her lips, but they would not receive her magic. Her offspring would need a magicked father to inherit her gifts. Surely a safe Myrcnian border was more important than passing on the royal glow.

"The queen won't approve," said Sibylla. To the emperor, it sounded as though she meant the free-style courting, but in her head, it was more.

No matter the political consequences, Sibylla hadn't once believed the queen would truly discard her granddaughter into a magicless match. And only one man had ever made Sibylla think of running away.

"Are good relations not what your queen wants?" The emperor's voice held a note of challenge.

"It's the execution she'd disapprove of."

"And what do *you* want?"

She didn't know. She could smell him on the cold breeze – rowanberry spirits, Khalishkan leather, and vegetal amber. He could be an ally, or he could be a trap.

"Then let's see what happens when someone dares dictate my actions." Emperor Timur held his arms behind his back. "Tomorrow after breakfast, the seditious cicada and I will meet on the terrace and go to see a bridge. I think I am not company you can deny."

He wasn't company she could accept either. No matter how pleasant he smelled or how he intrigued her, the queen did not allow Myrcnian nobles to marry outsiders even when she invited them herself.

Sibylla unpinned her hat upon entering Malmouth Palace and unraveled her braid into a messy bun at the nape of her neck. The palace staff had begun preparations for the Royal Heritage Ball in four days' time, and every spare hand was busy with the related activities.

Harrod could evade her indefinitely, having gotten Roger's prerogative of service with nary an inquiry from her. Only two days remained until the Binding ceremony – two days to decide, after hearing his crimes, whether Roger Weathersby deserved this stay of execution. Rupert the Webbed had taken two days to spare Angus the Foul, and so it followed for every Straybound since. She rubbed the temples of her forehead.

Turning the corner toward her bedroom, she inhaled sharply. Dr Lundfrigg reclined against the wall in silk trousers better suited for sleeping than making house calls. His dour jacket couldn't hide the lurid plaid waistcoat beneath.

"Back at last." Dr Lundfrigg pushed himself upright and tapped the floor with his medical cane. "Did you know the queen was looking for you? I politely explained that you had scheduled a physical this morning."

"And what prompted you to make up such a lie?" Exhausted by the day's events, she had little patience left to deal with the royal physician.

"I am keen to win your highness' good opinion." He waited for her to open the door to her room. "There's already an awful rumor circling that you've been pining after some lieutenant… or was it a captain?"

Addressing such nonsense hardly seemed worth the effort, but she did have a good idea of how to deal with Dr Lundfrigg. Until he achieved his goal, he'd continue to haunt her in this manner. It wouldn't be long before he asked the queen to compel her cooperation – no doubt in the name of her health. "Come inside, then."

"Have you finally decided to make a personal contribution?" Dr Lundfrigg brightened at the opportunity. "The number of cases one sees at St Colthorpe's on a daily basis is enough to unnerve even the most stout-hearted medical professional. All those illnesses, and only meager treatments available. I'm doing my best, but imagine if my patients had your highness' glow. I could stare right into a man's guts and discover the exact nature of his ailment."

Sibylla pulled off her overcoat. "You still want my blood then?"

From his medical cane, Dr Lundfrigg once again produced an empty glass vial while Sibylla took a seat on the chaise lounge, rolling up the sleeve of her blouse. Dr Lundfrigg stroked her arm, running his fingers up the inside of her wrist to the nook of her elbow, searching for a vein. Sibylla let her skin turn translucent, her blood glowing purple-violet. He wouldn't see what she did next.

"How thoughtful of your highness." Dr Lundfrigg pierced her skin with the needle. He folded his hands around her fingers until they'd compressed into a ball. "Keep your fist tight, and the procedure will be over soon."

As her blood flowed into the syringe's glass barrel, so too a thin line of ink made its way from her balled fingernails up her arm. Dr Lundfrigg might have noticed if not for her luminescence, which washed the surface of her translucent skin in a haze. A mild wave of nausea rippled through her stomach as she directed the ink into the vial. Her fingers prickled, but sure enough once the vial had been stoppered there was no discernible sign her "sample" had been contaminated.

"Extraordinary times we live in, are they not? Shaking the timbers of society with the brilliance of the human mind." Dr Lundfrigg spoke with an enthusiasm that reminded Sibylla of Roger. Perhaps because of her lightheadedness, the lingering uncertainty over Roger's convictions soured her stomach.

Fortunately, Dr Lundfrigg had finished and removed the syringe. He applied gauze to the pindrop of blood on her arm and began reassembling his cane. Having concluded his strange business, he bowed before exiting. Now he might leave her alone for a while. At least until he discovered she'd muddied his results with ink.

Sibylla eased back into the chaise lounge, resting her head against the cushion. If she completed the Binding, blood extractions would become a daily part of her life – a necessary burden to keep her Straybound alive. She wondered what Dr Lundfrigg would make of the devotional, a holy rite that required the consumption of blood. The royal physician seemed to think he'd find the answers to men's illnesses inside their veins, but Sibylla knew magic could no more fit in his glass vials than inside a teacup.

A hematologist wouldn't unravel the divine mysteries any more than a botanist could forever banish weeds from a garden or an engineer pull water from a well in the sky. Even the church couldn't explain *why* the blood binding worked, only that it did, and by the grace of the Divine Lady of the Stream. Let fools chase explanations that didn't exist, as Sibylla had to live in the practical world.

She cradled her throbbing head in her hands. She might not endure a week of Straybound devotionals if she felt as she did now. She needed to look Roger in the face to know he didn't kill those women. It wasn't enough for Harrod to profess his innocence then hide like a coward; she'd perform her own examination of Roger Weathersby and determine: man of science or murderer.

22

At half past seven in the evening, Roger found his way to the Anathema Club on Brocade Circle. He'd often overheard wild tales at Eldridge's from the lucky stiffs who'd scored an invite – it was where the biggest names in Myrcnian science sipped port, swapped theories, and bloodied one another at the tallycracker table. Roger had once fancied sneaking in disguised as a medical student, but never made it past the porter. Yet here he stood, invitation in hand, and a genuine un-forged one at that.

Dawson had dressed him in castoffs from his own wardrobe: a brown frock-coat, satin waistcoat, and charcoal wool trousers. Although Roger had taken care to wrap a burgundy cravat around his high, starched shirt-collar, he still felt like an imposter.

He was no imposter, he reminded himself. As a man of science, he belonged here as much as any physician, geologist, or astronomer. Besides, his presence here was no act of self-aggrandizement. He wanted to secure a hospital bed for Celeste and inquire about her condition. If he could make a good impression and be taken for a professional man on top of that, well, that would merely be a bonus.

A servant in a black tailcoat craned his head out the front door. "I'm afraid the club forbids loitering, man." He'd already pegged Roger, despite his dapper getup, as working class.

"I've an appointment with Sir Finch S Lundfrigg, MD." Roger thrust forward the letter as evidence.

"Why didn't you say so? Follow me."

Roger gazed slack-jawed as he stepped into a vast entrance hall. Pillars of mottled marble braced a domed roof, and across the ceiling a parade of skeletons cavorted, both human and beast. A staircase with a red runner ascended before him, then split into left and right wings.

"Dr Lundfrigg is in the library," said the servant as he escorted Roger up the stairs. As they passed various chambers, Roger glimpsed men playing tallycracker under canopies of cigar smoke, and solitary gents nursing books or glasses of rye. Another wall featured pinned multicolored insects, their glassy wings splayed. The preserved kraken tentacle from Sibet's history book, lopped off the writhing Kettlebay monster a century ago, revolved inside a massive glass jar.

The servant halted outside a set of large oak doors. "Be sure to show respect, young man. That's her royal majesty's physician in there. You still haven't removed your hat."

Flustered, Roger wrested open the massive doors and entered the library. A skeleton of brass staircases spiraled up three stories of shelves, and crisscrossing bridges connected various upper balconies. The far wall exhibited a massive shale slab containing the fossil of some toothy sea creature.

Emotionally charged voices filled the room as two individuals argued beneath the fossil. Roger approached with his hat clasped in hand and waited at a polite distance. He couldn't help overhearing snippets of the discussion.

"…It appears my trust in the reputed progressiveness of your country's surgery has been misplaced, seeing as dissection of the dead is all but taboo here. We have abolished the archaic practice of bloodletting entirely, yet your knowledge of Physick is a century behind ours…" said one of the figures in an irate, feminine voice. She spoke fluently, but with a thick accent. "…do you not agree that one corpse might benefit a dozen living patients?" The speaker wore a foreign belted tunic-like dress and had gathered her hair in an unruly bundle at the back of her head. Roger remembered a Khalishkan girl from one of the cookshops on Goatmonger Street with that same striking staccato to her voice. "…Then of all we've discussed, to reach consensus on that single item is better than none at all."

The second individual, presumably Dr Lundfrigg, listened to this diatribe while tapping a cane against his leg, muttering about "poisonous powders" and "Khalishkan snake-oil."

The woman flicked her gloved hand dismissively and turned to leave. For a moment her eyes locked with Roger's, and the brunt of her displeasure transferred onto him.

"Is this another Myrcnian bloodletter come to lecture me?" she snarled as Roger sidestepped from her path and bowed. "I do carry my own ammonia carbonate. Should I faint from the exertion of leaving your little boys' club, please do not fret. I shall happily revive myself. Good day, sir." She disappeared into the corridor, leaving a faint whiff of carbolic powder.

"And you are?" Sir Finch S Lundfrigg, MD looked Roger up and down, but did not extend a hand. Though not young, Dr Lundfrigg appeared sprightly compared to the wizened Dr Eldridge, and he quivered with the energy of a coiled spring. He sported the dandiest pastel suit Roger had ever seen and must have been a hit with the tailors on Amanita Row. A small shield-shaped pin with a purple sunburst adorned his lapel – the only visible indication of his knighthood.

"Roger Starkley at your service, Sir Finch," he said with as deep and graceful a bow as he'd ever accomplished without falling over. "You do me much honor, invitin' me."

Dr Lundfrigg winced at Roger's unpolished accent. "There must be a mistake. I was led to believe that Roger Starkley was the brother of Captain Harrod Starkley, and a medical man, but I can hear for myself that is not the case."

The words stung like a slap, but Roger hadn't come all this way to be dismissed out of hand. Words tumbled from his mouth as he stood wringing his hat, his head awkwardly bowed.

"It's true that I'm no proper gentleman, sir, nor surgeon neither. But if you ever stuck your nose into the lecture hall at Eldridge's college, you've seen my handiwork on the slab. I were the dissectionist for the recent course on circulation – the guest lecturer praised my scalpel work. I flayed and waxed an arm for him after, to add to his personal collection."

"I attended that lecture," said Dr Lundfrigg after a thoughtful pause. "I do recall a lovely specimen with the arteries dyed red and the veins blue. Solid workmanship indeed. What is your method?"

Roger's voice quavered. "I use an injection needle fixed by tubes to a water-pump operated with a foot pedal. I flush the blood vessels with hot water and prepare my wax with artists' pigment. Cobalt and rose madder work best."

"Your suturing, too," continued Dr Lundfrigg, "was as tight and neat as any practitioner's on Mouthstreet. But I suppose you can't scrape up the surgeoning fees. Dr Eldridge is notoriously tight-fisted."

Roger took a breath. It was now or never. "Truth is, sir, I quit him. He never paid me what I was worth. Now that we've had a falling out, I can't go back to Mouthstreet. But if an honest man like yourself might give me a chance, sir, I've brought with me—"

Dr Lundfrigg held up a hand. Roger fell silent and bowed again, certain his gamble had failed. Yet when he looked up, Dr Lundfrigg had extended his arm, flashing a perfect porcelain smile.

"Please, we're all men of science here." He squeezed Roger's hand with strong surgeon's fingers. "You may dispense with the 'yes sir, no sir.' 'Dr Lundfrigg' will do. Within these walls, I prefer to be known by my profession." He motioned Roger to a nearby chair.

"I… Thank you, doctor." Roger sat on the edge of the cushion and folded his hands on his hat. He focused on keeping his tapping foot still.

"Please don't mistake my intentions." Dr Lundfrigg seated himself opposite Roger. "I understand you have read my work in *The Speculum* and would care to present an interesting medical case. What do you think of hematology?" He paused, as if testing Roger's comprehension.

"I find blood fascinating myself, sir… ah, doctor," said Roger, hating how eager he sounded. "Some days ago I were witness to a puzzling disease of the blood. Perhaps I could ask you a few questions about a curious case—"

The doctor slapped the arm of his chair. "Ah, but I haven't anything to drink. There's a decanter of whiskey on the sideboard. Aifric single malt. Do pour me a tumbler, young man. And why not have a jot yourself, for your pains."

Roger splashed the amber liquid into cut-crystal glasses.

"Before you regale me with your 'curious case,' allow me to make a few educated guesses," said Dr Lundfrigg as he accepted a glass. "First, you tried to treat some 'poor widow' without a license, and second, that the poor widow is actually a whore. Perhaps you're even in love with her. How many did I get right?"

Roger stared at his own glass. This was not going as smoothly as he'd hoped. "Please admit her to your ward, doctor. That's all I ask."

"I suppose you've come to me grasping at straws, now that you've exhausted all your own medical 'tricks' to help this suffering doxy."

Roger nearly sloshed whiskey in his lap. "That would be illegal, now wouldn't it?"

"In the eyes of the law, yes. But there are no secrets at the Anathema Club. We men of science take care of our own. What kind of medicine have you practiced?"

Roger drained his tumbler in several gulps. The whiskey was a far cry from Nail's preservative spirits with its notes of pinesap, oranges, even nutmeg.

"Nothing like real surgery. I bled a few chaps: students, an undertaker's apprentice with the grippe – just practice. I pull teeth. All my patients recovered, and I weren't paid for it. I work with stiffs mostly, but I knows them inside and out."

"I see." Dr Lundfrigg held out his glass for Roger to refill. "You're no stranger to the lancet. Then perhaps a demonstration." He opened a little case containing linen strips, vials, and a thumb-sized folding blade.

"Might I ask why, sir?" Roger's heart sank. Dr Lundfrigg couldn't even spare a breath for Celeste.

Dr Lundfrigg stopped short and his mouth twitched into a smile. "Because I like you. Now bare your arm and come here by me."

Roger removed his coat and rolled up his shirtsleeve, despite Dr Lundfrigg's condescending tone. He crouched and balanced his outstretched arm on his knee.

Dr Lundfrigg bound a linen strip above his elbow as a tourniquet. "A surgeon's worth is in how he holds the blade." He handed Roger the thumb-lancet. "Just enough to fill a vial halfway, then."

Roger made a fist and found a suitable vein. After setting his empty glass on the floor, he nicked his skin in one deft movement. The pain was sharp and brief, and a bright red stream spurted into the whiskey glass below.

"Not bad, eh, doctor?" Roger lifted the glass to his arm so the blood wouldn't spatter. Dr Lundfrigg's impressed half-smile sent an energetic jolt through him, and for a moment he forgot he was an anointed Straybound. "You could use a surgeon's assistant in one of your hospitals, no? I could wash down the slabs and rinse the tools, or–"

"By the Merciful Mother, I don't need that much blood. Put a compress on it before you stain the carpet." The doctor slapped a folded linen square on Roger's arm.

While Roger bandaged himself, Dr Lundfrigg poured blood from the glass into his vial. Then he added a few drops of some solution and observed it closely. "Your blood looks bright and healthy, and perfectly ordinary. You can't ask for more than that." Then he lifted the crystal glass to the light and swirled the remaining blood. "Tell you what, lad. If you toast her royal majesty and drain this glass, I'll try you out for a job."

Roger shuddered, certain Dr Lundfrigg must have seen the revulsion on his face. He regained his composure with a breath and met the other man's eyes. "You serious?"

"As an aneurism."

Roger took the glass and eyed the half an inch of blood at the bottom. He could never swallow it. Could he? He might bluff, at least. Thumping his chest with one hand, he raised the glass. "To her majesty."

Just as the crystal met his lips, Dr Lundfrigg caught his wrist.

"I'll give you a try, Mr Starkley. For a day. I just wanted to see how badly you wanted that job."

Roger smiled weakly. "Doctor, that case I wrote you about–"

"Here." Dr Lundfrigg pressed a fresh glass of whiskey into his hand. "That should settle your stomach. Sit."

Roger obeyed, letting the alcohol scorch his throat. "You said my blood were healthy. But suppose it were dark, and sluggish like treacle. What sort of malady might that be?"

"It could be any number of things. Perhaps there's a buildup of impurities in the bloodstream, or tumors within the body. I take it you bled your doxy friend?"

Roger nodded.

"Then there is little more you could have done."

"There must be something. Won't you at least admit her to hospital?"

"There is no point, my lad, even if the queen's law didn't forbid it. Based on this evidence, she's at death's door. Remember that a physician is not a magician, and neither are you. But as nature's mysteries reveal themselves, someday we may reclaim the human body from sickness, if not death."

Roger wouldn't win Dr Lundfrigg over with words so he pulled his gin flask containing Celeste's blood from his coat pocket. He downed his whiskey, then poured Celeste's blood into the glass, still as dark and treacly as when he'd collected it. Dr Lundfrigg leaned forward with interest.

"Take a look, sir."

The doctor swirled the glass. "This is your doxy's blood?"

Roger nodded. "Curious, no?"

Dr Lundfrigg brought the glass to the edge of his nose, and as though testing a fine wine, took a long whiff. Roger hadn't thought to smell the blood.

"Very distinct. I'd like to keep this for further tests. I'll admit you've intrigued me, Mr Starkley, if that is your true name. Had I not known better, I'd have mistaken you for a surgeon after all."

Roger grinned.

"Tell me, what exactly is your true relationship to Captain Starkley?"

"I'm his lackey, sir." Unused to the heavy drink, Roger's thoughts had begun to ripple and blur, as if filtered through ancient glass.

The doctor laughed. "Well, that explains that. Now, about the job. Is tomorrow too early? If I like what I see, I'll consider hiring you full time. Will you be available?"

No, in two days he'd become Straybound to a princess. On the other hand, he had nothing to lose. And he might still convince Dr Lundfrigg to take on Celeste.

Roger nodded. "If I might have a note in your handwriting, my master won't detain me."

"Then it's settled. I shall see you at St Colthorpe's at eight tomorrow morning." He scribbled on a scrap of paper and handed it over.

"I'm at your service." Roger stood and tucked the note away.

"You needn't leave just yet. It would be remiss of me to send you off without giving you the proper Anathema Club tour. Who knows if you'll set foot here again. Is there anything you wish to see?"

Roger thought for a moment. "I heard tell of an *ether-frolic*. Is that a mythical beast around here or no, doctor?"

"Ether-frolic?" Dr Lundfrigg rubbed his palms together. "Oh yes, our prize-winning students and knighted scientists alike frolic regularly in the smoking room, in the company of nitrous oxide, diethyl ether, and some newer, more exciting substances. Would you care to look, or are you a man who wishes to experience for himself?"

Roger's glee matched only Ada's when she'd wielded a scalpel over Mrs Carver's soon-to-be-jellied veal.

Dr Lundfrigg took Roger by the elbow and steered him to a seat at the smoking room table, built to withstand vigorous rounds of tallycracker. A pair of medical students, identifiable by their iodine-stained fingers and the bottle of Skullflash gin between them, took turns sniffing from the neck of an apothecary's decanter. At the sight of the newcomers, the students gave cheery cries of "Hullo, Finchy," and, "Bring us anything, you raspy old bone-knocker?" They didn't even bother standing to greet a Knight of the Realm.

Dr Lundfrigg, to Roger's surprise, beamed and clapped the students vigorously on their shoulders. "Sidney, Cato. Which of you young lancets swiped ether-spirits from the royal infirmary again?" He leaned in for a sniff from the decanter. "My naughty lads."

Roger, feeling ill from the whiskey, propped himself up on his elbows while the table pitched slightly. He was used to cheap, watered-down spirits.

Dr Lundfrigg nodded at the Skullflash gin. "Pour him a dram, Cato."

Cato studied Roger's face. "Hullo, aren't you old Eldridge's chap?"

Roger stiffened, expecting cries of "Greyanchor Strangler!" but none came. Either the student couldn't connect his face to a name, or Dr Eldridge had hushed up his arrest at the college.

Cato slid the unstoppered decanter under Roger's nose. The fumes smelled like plum-infused port cut with a more corrosive tipple.

"Barely recognized you in those togs," said Sidney, the student with sandy hair. "Maybe it's just the shock of seeing your face in natural light, ha ha. You helped me pass my suturing exam last year, remember?"

"And you paid me with an old anatomy text," Roger replied between inhalations. "Er... much obliged." His eyes watered from the fumes, but he didn't yet feel the fabled twinge. The phrase "ether-frolic" promised pub-style Tyanny dancing on the tabletops, but so far the experience proved disappointing. A sip of the Skullflash gin jolted him upright with a bright spark behind his eyeballs. The others laughed.

Dr Lundfrigg corked the ether decanter. "You had asked if I'd brought something better, my lancets. As it happens, I have." He pulled a lavender handkerchief from his breast pocket and unfolded it with care to reveal a bundle of mushrooms.

Cato and Sidney leaned forward.

"You got more of that good stuff from last time, sawbones?" asked Cato. "Or will we need to shuffle across a bearskin rug to feel a shock?"

"Oh, I believe this batch is better than the last," said Dr Lundfrigg. "See the extensive gilling here, and that bluish partial veil? I changed up the soils, as it were. Experimented with the nutrients I had on hand. Horticulture is a most calming hobby, though I don't have as much time to dabble as I'd like."

Sidney unfolded a jeweler's loupe and studied the specimen with interest. "I can even see the spore dust on my fingers."

"Are you looking to cure some ailment?" asked Roger. He knew common herbs could treat certain illnesses and heal wounds.

"In a manner of speaking, all of them," said Dr Lundfrigg. "Eventually. For now, let's just have some fun."

Roger didn't see much to be excited about. He looked from the dried stuff in the handkerchief to the corked decanter at Dr Lundfrigg's elbow and sighed. He had a lot to learn about gentlemen's clubs.

"Are they quite... exciting, then?"

"Exciting, man?" Sidney peered at Roger, his eye grotesquely magnified through his loupe. "These mushrooms may well be the highlight of my week. Considering I'm sitting through Dr Eldridge's lectures on the female specimen, that should tell you something."

"I suppose he's not yet a student of mycology," added Cato with a chuckle. "He'll learn. With old Finchy's permission, I'll cut you a sample."

At Dr Lundfrigg's nudge, Roger presented his hand. "I quite like plants myself," he said defensively. "Especially the snap-traps that eat flies."

"That's botany." Cato placed a button-sized mushroom cap in each of their hands. "A different vat of eels altogether."

"Now, gentlemen." Dr Lundfrigg moved to the head of the table and cleared his throat. "You are holding a portion of variant ES1, my latest attempt to hybridize the common ghostcandle mushroom – purely in the name of medical advancement, of course." He winked at Roger. "I can't overstate how thrilled I am by these results; however, bear in mind that this is but a stepping-stone. The process is what excites me, not the recreational benefits you'll soon enjoy. Once I've become more practiced in manipulating my mycological specimens, I foresee a treasure-trove of groundbreaking developments. And you, my dear lancets, will say you once shared a glass with the father of a new Scientific Age."

The students and Roger indulged him with hearty applause.

Dr Lundfrigg beamed. "Now then. Are we all good and tipsy? Another round of Skullflash for the table? Don't fall over, if you can help it. Before we start, you may wish to loosen your cravats. Remove rings and spectacles. Step away from the furniture. There's no saying what could happen. Ready, then? Three, two, one..."

Dr Lundfrigg and the students placed their mushroom caps on their tongues. Roger followed suit.

"Don't swallow," Cato told him. "Don't chew, just let it sit. Something is bound to happen any–"

He didn't finish his sentence. A bubble emerged from his mouth with a gurgle and floated in the air like a blob of animated jelly.

"That's not an ordinary bubble, is it?" managed Sidney before a similar blob emerged from his own mouth. He stabbed it with his finger, and it disintegrated. The remnants splattered on the carpet. "It's like a normal air bubble, but it's full of water. Impossible!"

Dr Lundfrigg stood grinning at them, then parted his lips and blew a ring-shaped water bubble.

"Look sharp, the sawbones has been practicing." Cato tried to laugh, but only bubbles emerged.

A strange pressure built in Roger's chest, and his breath escaped in a rush. A cloud of tiny bubbles fizzed from his mouth to form a dense, foamy cloud. Meanwhile the others entertained themselves trying to create the biggest bubble, made difficult by their drunken laughter.

Roger had seen this before. When he was a palace scullion, a cursing Lady Esther had spewed furious, terrifying bubbles from her mouth when she caught him and Sibet playing hog-the-wash with her skivvies. Somehow, Dr Lundfrigg had given common, drunken medical students this same ability. Magic for the common man.

A strangled laugh escaped his lips along with the bubbles. Harrod and his unimaginative ilk insisted some magic spark in noble blood marked them as "divine." But now Roger had seen "magic" reproduced in a mushroom from Dr Lundfrigg's garden. If anyone had magic, then anyone could rule. No more chapels or Saint-Queens, royal miracles or spark shows. Myrcnia could finally shuck off its obsolete faerie-tales for the Scientific Age. An odd feeling of limitless opportunity swelled his chest, and he wanted to shake Dr Lundfrigg's hand.

Instead, Roger coughed out another swarm of little bubbles, each no bigger than a barley groat. By now the medical students had noticed his difficulty.

"Pretend it's a smoke ring," Cato said. "But don't concentrate so hard."

Dr Lundfrigg put a hand on Roger's shoulder. "I think I know the problem." He assembled a stethoscope from his medical cane. "Unbutton your shirt, young man. Let's see how well I know my auscultation."

Roger removed his jacket and unbuttoned the top half of his shirt, careful to keep his cravat in place over his bandaged neck.

Dr Lundfrigg pressed the cold metal bell of his scope to Roger's chest. "Deep breaths. Very good." He moved the bell in a line across Roger's skin. "Just aim those bubbles away from my head. Aha. Just as I thought."

He disassembled the stethoscope, and Roger buttoned up again. The effects of the mushroom had finally worn off.

"Have you ever had the romantic disease?"

"Doctor?" Roger hoped this wasn't a test.

"The graceful cough. The flooded lung. Consumption."

"Not as such. My mother did."

"Well, allow me to extend my congratulations. You've had it also, a mere primary infection, that is. Most people with a primary infection never know they have it unless secondary complications set in. You've survived, and it's unlikely to flare up again after all this time. There's some scar tissue – I can hear it when you breathe, and it's shredding those bubbles most impressively. My poet friends would be jealous." Dr Lundfrigg took out a small notebook and jotted something down. "Finally, we are getting somewhere. I suspect the particular characteristics of ghostcandle variant ES1 could be a handy diagnostic tool for pre-symptomatic consumptive infections. Early treatment could revolutionize our approach to a disease that kills one out of every seven Myrcnians. Observe, gentlemen. Scientific progress has advanced under your very noses. This is only the beginning."

The medical students cheered.

Roger spat out the remaining scrap of bluish mushroom and studied it in his palm. He wished he could transport it to his mother, before her first consumptive cough. Something might have been done to save her.

"This calls for a celebratory drink." Dr Lundfrigg waved away the Skullflash. "Send a servant for the finest double-cask, silver-ribbon whiskey to be found this side of Khalishka."

As Roger sipped his drink, an uneasy feeling settled in his gut. Dr Lundfrigg had used science to manufacture – no, cultivate – a power like the royal family's smoke-and-mirror magic. A line had been crossed, connecting science to magic in unprecedented ways that could revolutionize Myrcnian society… or unravel it altogether.

23

By missing breakfast, Sibylla spared herself familial inquiries and instead read up on the history of Crosswitch Bridge. At a quarter to ten she grabbed her hat. Adjusting her veil, she made her way to the Great Gallery where Edgar stood seething in the front entry.

"I won't allow you to go with that… *foreigner*." His cadence made the word sound more like an insult than a descriptor. "Have you no concern over the damage to your reputation? There are already rumors of your friendliness with certain officers and my–"

Sibylla cut him off, taking two steps in. "That *foreigner* can injure our economy, invade our borders, or, if he chooses, take me out for a treat. After your dinner performance the other night, I doubt he fears Myrcnian royals. So by all means, tell the Emperor of Khalishka you won't allow it."

"Our marriage has been intended since the day I was born."

"Then I suggest you take these concerns to Grandmother."

Sibylla brushed past Edgar, leaving him fuming on the terrace while she joined Emperor Timur at the bottom of the steps. If the queen didn't want Sibylla soothing diplomatic relations, then let her do something about it. The church's genealogy charts weren't the only measure of a person's value, and the emperor had more to recommend him than magic.

To further provoke her cousin, she leaned close to the emperor and straightened his olive overcoat's collar. "Lovely morning, Timur. Did you enjoy a good Myrcnian breakfast? It can be a tad heavy if you're not accustomed."

The corner of the emperor's mouth tilted in amusement. He glanced at Edgar, who stood glaring on the terrace as if that might make Sibylla return to him. "I've noticed you avoid breakfast with your family."

Sibylla followed his gaze. "I recommend everyone do so."

"Excellent choice."

Emperor Timur extended his right arm toward the carriage. This vehicle had neither embellishments nor emblems, just a driver and two Khalishkan footmen. Only the nervous groomsmen worked for the palace.

Sibylla gave the driver directions to Crosswitch Bridge via the scenic route through Glasspon Gardens. They departed the hilltop palace and headed for the lower city. As they traveled, she struck up a conversation about the bridge's construction while the emperor peppered her with absurd questions. How many Caligo men were needed to move a single wagon of stone? Did any bats reside beneath the arch? Had Celia the Devout cemented the severed heads of traitors into its walkway? Sibylla checked for a smirk on his face, certain he must be teasing.

When she pointed to a police station as an example of uneven Masonist style, he removed a notebook and charcoal stick to sketch it.

"Allow me," said Sibylla, shaking off her right glove.

Without touching the notebook, she replicated the building's disproportionate windows and rusticated stone walls in black ink. The emperor's finger traced the lines as they dried. He flipped to a new page and pointed toward the red brick university. She continued to indulge him, enjoying his attentions, until the carriage halted on the west bank of Crosswitch Bridge.

They disembarked while his attendants stayed behind. Whether they stood out more than the average Myrcnian with a good income, she couldn't say. Even unveiled, Sibylla doubted she'd be recognized here. Since her return from Helmscliff, she'd made one official appearance at the emperor's greeting ceremony, and she no longer resembled the apple-cheeked princess who appeared on nougat tins and commemorative pie plates. In fact, the emperor, despite dressing to blend in, with his shorter beard, foreign eyes, and nimble build seemed to draw more attention.

Sibylla spotted a bread-vendor manning a wooden cart. Driven by her empty stomach and the smell of fresh baked goods, she took the emperor by the elbow and encouraged him to hurry.

At the front of the line, she requested two of each kind of bread. She glanced at the emperor while the baker wrapped the small loaves in beeswax paper. She hoped she hadn't been too quick to order for him. Men often took umbrage to a lady who did the choosing. Instead, he leaned over the bridge rail to admire its black stonework.

She'd purchased five kinds of bread: date-stuffed buns, curry rolls, wheat with dried apple slices, marbled rye, and a white bread that looked fluffy enough to melt like ice shavings. Sibylla offered a curry roll first. The emperor examined its fried exterior, then sunk his teeth in.

Steam rose off the white slices. Not waiting for them to cool, Sibylla shoved half of one piece into her mouth and chewed. "A little saltier than I remember." The soft center dissolved on her tongue. "We timed our visit well – still hot from the oven." She grinned between bites. "I could eat a shell's worth."

The emperor's remaining half-roll disappeared inside his mouth. "As a Myrcnian lady, you've an uncommonly healthy appetite."

Embarrassed, Sibylla swallowed her last chunk of bread.

The emperor continued, "If you'd be so generous, I've a mind to experience more of your tastes this evening. Perhaps we might also enjoy some other pleasures."

She gasped, the wheat loaf slipping from her hand. It tumbled over the bridge's rail and landed with a splash in the Mudtyne. Flustered and unable to breathe at the implications, she watched the small loaf ride the current before sinking beneath the murky waters. She gripped the rail to calm herself and faced the emperor. He loosened his scarf, exposing his neck to the cold wind blowing off the river.

What kind of pleasure?

A night with the emperor might lead to a marriage that would promise a prosperous future for Myrcnia, but she'd be risking her status and the queen's wrath. Endless concertina lessons, bloody fingers and no supper would be just the beginning. Dorinda had done far worse to her own husbands – rat poison and drownings – and if the queen preferred Sibylla to marry Edgar then Dorinda would ensure it happened. If nothing else, Straybound were the perfect instruments to express royal disapproval. Sibylla gazed out over the city rooftops, steepled and flat.

Even though she enjoyed Emperor Timur's company, a part of her was reminded of Roger. Some day the emperor might also entice a flickering glow from her veins, and when he did, she might fall for him as well. Then, as with Roger, the queen would have her way. Despite their promises, the steaming bread shared on cold mornings, and his intriguing smile, the emperor, too, would disappear.

"This is another fiction," said Sibylla in a fit of pique. Propping her hands on the bridge, she bent over the edge and limply smiled. "Just like the sharks in the Mudtyne. They don't exist."

"Do you know why you're presently my favorite liaison?" The emperor removed his hat, and long strands of his hair flickered in the wind.

Sibylla stared down the river currents. "I don't."

"Because my interest in you angers more people than it pleases. But I have no desire in attending to people who think themselves less than what they clearly could be."

Sibylla laughed. She had never been told she thought less of herself than she should. "And you have an understanding of what I could be?"

Tentatively, the emperor tucked a strand of loose hair behind her ear. "An equal. For example, if you tell me you are already engaged this evening, I would believe you are engaged. And if you say you are not, then you are not."

Sibylla studied the emperor, certain he spoke of more than evening entertainments. "And if I needed this afternoon to pursue another matter?"

The emperor stared into the Mudtyne's murky waters. "Then I would consider that a small price for a private dinner. The time it takes to weigh one's fortune against those of others."

Another opportunity before the Binding ceremony would never present itself. Come typhoon or earth-tremor, tomorrow Roger would be bound. Sibylla had little more than a day to learn how he'd become the Greyanchor Strangler before she settled a contract that would join them to each other for as long as she lived.

Smoothing her gloves, she moved with intent. "I'll instruct your driver on where we'll meet for dinner. You mentioned wanting to try Caligo's famous stews. I know a spot even the older residents don't. And you really should see Marlowe's Menagerie in the meantime."

"While I respect your autonomy," the emperor began haltingly, "I fear I would face severe censure by leaving you unguarded. Caligo is a dangerous city, more so than any in Khalishka, and it is my pleasure to accompany you. Unless, that is, the cicada has some other defensive trick up her sleeve?" He tilted his head in curiosity, but when she offered no response he signaled to a nearby attendant to ready the carriage.

"Really, that is not necessary." Sibylla racked her brain for some excuse to go alone, but the emperor was already heading to the carriage. She stared at his retreating back. He had enabled her to leave the palace unsupervised, and she could hardly bargain her way out of his company now. At least he seemed adept at keeping secrets.

Uncertain but having no other recourse, Sibylla gave the address for Harrod's townhome in Burkeshire Gardens to the carriage driver, though she didn't have much hope of Roger being lodged there. Between the initial Rite of Contract and the Binding, Straybound were kept in cells.

Emperor Timur helped her into the carriage, and her face heated at the brief contact of his hand upon her elbow. An icy breeze whipped the windows as she adjusted her skirts to give the emperor room to join her. Sibylla intended to minimize how much she revealed in front of him, and so as a distraction she peppered him with questions. Did Khalishkans really burn dolls of the Myrcnian royal family? Had he ever been to the reed gardens in Lipthveria? And did he play any instruments?

Fortunately, when they arrived at 13 Burkeshire Gardens the emperor seemed content to admire the townhomes from the carriage while Sibylla questioned Harrod's butler Dawson. Not only was Roger *not* living in a cell, but he had also taken up residence in Harrod's house. And against all sensibilities, he'd gone to work somewhere in the medical district, apprenticed to – as Dawson called him – "a most distinguished gentleman." Apparently, after lying to her, Harrod had lost his remaining wits. If the archbishop learned any of this, she'd need another prerogative of service to prevent a second hanging.

Back in the carriage, Sibylla squeezed her hands together to reassure herself. She had misjudged Harrod's fondness for his brother, enough that she wondered if Harrod might have been blinded to Roger's guilt.

She turned to the emperor. "Are you familiar with Caligo's medical district?"

The emperor shook his head no. "I hear from Dr Kaishuk that it's quite historical, in both the architecture and scientific attitudes."

So far, the emperor had not pried into her affairs, but a knot of guilt over whether she should tell him some version of the truth had lodged in her throat. If she continued this pursuit of Roger without explanation, the emperor would likely draw his own conclusions.

"Before we go, I shall tell you something. As a child, I tutored a boy who worked in the palace kitchens." Sibylla paused to see whether this revelation had offended the emperor. He gave nothing away, so she continued, "I've since learned he's become a doctor of some repute." Certainly being named the Greyanchor Strangler counted as repute. "And I'd like to introduce him to the royal physician now that I've returned to the city. After all, he was very bright once." Sibylla stopped, as anything more would turn to lies.

The emperor considered her words, then replied, "You really *are* a seditious cicada."

They arrived in Caligo's medical district where tincture vendors, barbers, surgeons, and well-to-do purveyors of medicine occupied every shop front along Mouthstreet. Royal public service warnings against dishonest quacks and poisonous "health potions" were pasted over advertisements for Dr Groady's Droop Serum – for "when even the princess can't help your performance." Though the emperor chuckled, Sibylla didn't find the slogan amusing.

She hopped from the carriage to question a peddler, who took one look at her lace veil and pearl-studded traveling dress and laughed in her face.

"What's a lady doin' lookin' fer a surgeon? I've got a good idea…" He trailed off into another ugly laugh.

Putting on the sacrosanct air she used to deliver benedictions, Sibylla glared blackly at the peddler through her gauzy veil, then produced two winkles as further incentive. "I'm looking for a man. He goes by Roger Weathersby." The peddler's face remained blank, so she added, "A man of science. He's a surgeon… or studying to be one."

"Roger Weathersby. Weathersby…" The man jiggered his wig. "I know the name. A lusty fella, right? Got you in a bit o' trouble, did he?" He hollered to another peddler. "You heard of a surgeon named Weathersby?"

"A surgeon? Naw, only Weathersby 'round here were that corpse fornicator. The one what sold his victims to anatomists. Old Eldridge were a customer, though he paid to keep his name from the papers." Then, he began to sing. "A miscreant named Weathersby, who murders girls…"

"Where can I find this Eldridge?" Sibylla interrupted, all too aware of the emperor standing at a watchful distance. At this rate, he'd think her a scandal-chaser. Or worse.

The peddlers pointed toward the large Hospital of Gastronomical Revelations, and instructed her to keep going until it smelled like poverty and piss.

The emperor couldn't help but comment: "This old pupil of yours has an interesting reputation."

"So it would seem." Sibylla hardly blamed his skepticism, and it was too late to amend her story.

"Clearly, the cicada favors men with colorful histories. I fear I will need to commit some scandal by sunset to pinion your wings."

Sibylla held his hand to climb into the carriage. "Perhaps we'll come upon a sea lion for you to wrestle."

Three blocks west of the medical district's major intersection stood Eldridge's College of Barber-Surgeons. A faded sign swung on a squeaky bar. Sibylla knocked on the door. Unable to persuade the emperor to stay behind, as he'd an interest in meeting a "typical Myrcnian bloodletter," they waited side by side until a beleaguered physician appeared.

"Hello, sir." Sibylla lifted her veil so he could see her face. Dr Eldridge squinted but made no sign of recognition. "It's my understanding you employ a Roger Weathersby here."

Dr Eldridge's eye twitched. "Don't know him. This is a reputable school for aspiring young surgeons, not whatever you've heard!"

Sibylla tried to get out, "I'm a relative—" as Dr Eldridge shut the door. "A wealthy relative!" she yelled from the stoop. The emperor feigned disinterest by pretending to birdwatch, though she saw no birds. She'd turned to leave when the door opened a crack on whining hinges.

"Wealthy?" Dr Eldridge pressed his face into the gap.

Sibylla leaned close to the door, and in a hushed voice said, "*Very.*"

The old man swung the door wide again. "How can I be of assistance?"

Sibylla blotted her eyes with the silk kerchief Mr Maokin had given her, holding it so Dr Eldridge could see its fine embroidery. "I've news of a dead uncle, and the fortune he's left sweet Roger. Do you know where he might be working now, or at least where he lives? He's always been so fond of the medicals. I'm sure he'll be making donations soon."

Sibylla dared to face the emperor, not quite able to meet his eyes. The emperor hung his head in sorrow to match hers. At least *he* was having fun. What a fool she was to play-act in front of him, surely destroying her chance to secure a Khalishkan alliance for the sake of a probable murderer. Her eyes misted with only the tiniest effort.

"Oh—oh, you poor dear." Dr Eldridge offered his own kerchief, which she used to blot her cheeks. "But I'm afraid Mr Weathersby resigned some days ago."

Sibylla shook her head in pity, then gracefully returned the doctor's kerchief with a full shell coin tucked inside. "For your troubles. Any hint of where I might find him will do."

Dr Eldridge felt the heft of gold wrapped in cotton, and his eyes brightened. "I don't know his living arrangements, but he worked at Grausam's Undertaking for a time." Dr Eldridge's eyes seemed to scour the creases of Sibylla's clothing for loose change. "And if you see the lad, remind him that Eldridge's College of Barber-Surgeons accepts anonymous donations, even from those with… grim reputations."

Upon their departure, a pit of apprehension took root in Sibylla's stomach, and she squeezed her hands into fists to stop from nervously filling the carriage with ink-bees. She couldn't make sense of it. Roger had never mentioned working as an undertaker, and Harrod could have paid for his apprenticeship at any of the city's medical colleges.

For his part, the emperor remained silent, though undoubtedly his opinion of her lessened with each stop. When they arrived in Grausam's neighborhood – an unsavory spot of taxidermy, dental transplant, and boil lancing services – Sibylla held onto the fantastic hope Timur might stay behind this time. He did not.

Instead, he paused outside the undertaker's shop to admire the upright coffins leaning against its brick exterior. "What an interesting practice." His hand lingered on a cast-iron theft-proof model. "We don't bury our raw dead in Khalishka, only their bone's ash."

On any other day, Sibylla might have enjoyed a discussion of differing funerary customs, but today her skin prickled with foreboding. A part of her hoped to find Roger as she'd always imagined him: smartly dressed with a satchel of instruments in one hand and a basket of fruit, gifted by a grateful patient, in the other. Unfortunately, reality had no intention of cooperating.

As they entered the shop, a drippy redheaded youth shrugged on an official countenance that failed to put her at ease. "How may I be of service, my lovely?"

"Are you Mr Grausam?" asked Sibylla.

"Sorry, he's just popped out. But would you care to view our newest model of lead-lined coffin? Just in from our supplier–"

Sibylla broke in, uninterested in spending more time than necessary inside this establishment that smelled of astringent and wood rot. "I'm looking for Roger Weathersby. He worked here some time ago."

"I can assure you, we don't employ no-good malefactors here."

Perhaps sensing her discomfort, or because he also found the smell displeasing, the emperor intervened. "We have no interest in bringing harm to your friend."

At the word "friend," the youth threw up his arms in protest. "I'm no friend of this Weathersby. He may make love to jammy tarts on public thoroughfares wearing pinched silken hats just to hide his horns – knocking 'em off so he can do in-dekorus things to their lady bits – but I can assure you here at Grausam's Undertaking and Coffining Services, we never allow such defecation of our clients. We treat the deceased with the utmost care. Else your burial expense is on us."

"But you *do* know where he hangs his… silken hat. Don't you?" Sibylla pressed.

"More like where he hangs his filthy gravesnatcher's mask."

"Simply give us an address." The emperor undid his coat to reveal a silver pistol and short sword in the Khalishkan style, guardless and slightly curved. "And we'll be on our way."

The redhead dropped any pretense of withholding information. "Suet Street. Butcher shop, topmost floor, just follow the flies." A salesman's grin reappeared on his face. "Please come again. At Grausam's, you kick the bucket, an' we do the rest."

Outside the shop, Sibylla gulped fresh air.

There were no more chances after this. If Roger couldn't be found on Suet Street, she wouldn't risk offending the emperor by asking to postpone dinner.

The emperor caught her arm as she stepped off the footpath and spun her out of the way of an oncoming brougham. He loosened his grip at once, then helped her regain her footing. "Mind the path you travel, lest the shadows overtake you with ghost-breath."

Her heart hammered from the close call. "Lin's *Parade of a Thousand Sins*."

"A favorite of mine, also." His deep voice cut through the noise and bustle of the street.

Sibylla caught herself staring into his eyes, and her face warmed with shame and embarrassment. She'd taken the Emperor of Khalishka, a man who defined continents, to see Caligo's nostrum salesmen, weathered medical institutions, even the local undertaker. If she'd been a spy sent to undermine his opinion of Myrcnia, no doubt she'd have earned a ribbon. Her grandmother would never forgive her, let alone the people of Myrcnia. She'd only be so lucky to return to Helmscliff now. It wasn't too late. She didn't have to climb the stairs to Roger's abode. She could spare herself the sight of his plummeting worth, but if she turned back now, she'd never know how far he'd fallen.

24

"St Colthorpe's Charity Hospital," said Dr Lundfrigg as he led the way down a corridor, "is a most modern institution for the merciful treatment of Caligo's poorest citizens. It is funded entirely from the royal coffers. I like to keep a presence here, as one of my many responsibilities as royal physician to the queen. "

"Modern" was not the word Roger would have chosen to describe the gothic arched windows and occasional arrow slit that ventilated the tunnel-like corridor. He struggled to keep up with Dr Lundfrigg's flapping coattails. Residual effects from the Skullflash still sparkled behind Roger's eyes, despite a self-prescribed glass of sodium bicarbonate in water. A haze still blurred his memories of last night – he recalled bruising his jaw in a free-form tallycracker game, but not Dawson dragging him home. Luckily, Harrod had been so impressed with Dr Lundfrigg's offer that he agreed to let Roger go, to fulfill his final day of probation: service.

"Three hundred years ago this was a fortress," continued Dr Lundfrigg, "two hundred years ago an abbey, one hundred years ago a prison for lunatics, and now the main chapel houses the men's medical ward. Women and children are treated in the annex, while the madmen have been relegated to the dun... downstairs. I have a specialist who knows procedures to turn even the most violent maniac as gentle as a lamb. This is, after all, the cusp of the Scientific Age."

"There's no end to the wonder of science," said Roger, unable to believe he would be making the rounds in an actual ward. "I hope to learn as much as I can."

A few civilians nodded to him as they passed, almost as if he was a real surgeon. None of his old mates would recognize him now.

Dr Lundfrigg paused outside a door. "Before we enter the ward, Mr Starkley, I want you to remember two things. First, a good surgeon cuts slowly enough to see what he's doing."

Roger nodded intently.

"Second, a *great* surgeon cuts with such speed, the patient doesn't have time to realize pain. It's better to act too hastily than too slowly. You don't want your patients throwing you to the ground and leaving a trail of blood as they flee. Understood?"

"Yes, doctor."

Dr Lundfrigg opened the door with a grand sweep of his arm. "Impress me, Mr Starkley."

The ward was a high-ceilinged room lined with iron beds, not unlike the misdemeanors' bay in Old Grim. Some of the patients' families had set up camp around their respective invalids. Many had brought children, picnic baskets, bedding, and one woman stirred a pot of broth on a portable tin stove.

"The beds only cost a winkle a night, but families must provide their own rations," explained Dr Lundfrigg. "I'd like your thoughts on the patient in bed number three."

Roger approached a metal-frame cot where a boy of about thirteen lay fidgeting, as if waiting for permission to join his friends playing dash-the-can in the streets. A brother, by the look of him, held down the younger boy's shoulders.

Roger crouched by the bed so that his head was on the same level as the younger brother. "What's your name, lad?"

"Joe," said the boy. "Joe Brash. An' I'll pummel you soon as look at you if you touch my leg."

"And what happened to your leg?"

Joe lifted the blanket, and Roger's eyes were drawn to the unnatural arc in the shin, almost like a second ankle.

"He were a porter," interjected the older brother. "He followed the omnibuses and cabs, chased 'em from one end of Caligo to the other, and got paid fer helping nobs with their trunks."

"Aye," said Joe. "Until that day I didn't run fast enough. Coach and pair clipped me."

"They near flattened you, numbskull." The brother tried to push Joe back on his pillow when he reached for the crutch propped against the bedpost.

"When did this happen?" asked Roger. "Does it hurt?"

"It don't hurt so much now." Joe gave his brother a shove, then flopped back on his pillow. "But I can't run. It happened months and months ago."

"You didn't have it looked at right away?" Roger held a tentative hand over the boy's leg. With a nod from Joe, he ran his fingers over the lump of badly healed bone.

"Physicians are fer toffs," said Joe matter-of-factly. "Had a mate who saw a physician once. He took a healing powder fer jaundice that knocked him dead like a poisoned rat.

"He don't mean that," the older brother interjected. "Begging yer pardon, sir, but them's all exaggerations. You prescribe yer healing potion, I'll pay for it myself, and Joe here'll be cured."

Aware of Dr Lundfrigg listening to all this, Roger chose a tactful response. "St Colthorpe's is open to all. Perhaps you should pass that news 'round your tenement."

The brother leaned close to Roger's ear. "Someone told him this is where they send the medical students to botch operations on folks as can't afford better. But you look sober, and you sound like one of us."

"Well," said Roger, directing his words to the reluctant Joe, "you'll not do much running unless you can trust me to fix this leg."

Dr Lundfrigg cleared his throat. "And how do you plan to go about that, Mr Starkley?"

"Hear that?" shouted Joe. "Mister! He's not even a doctor!"

Roger focused on Dr Lundfrigg's question. He'd seen the broken bones of the dead, both fresh traumas and long-knitted fractures from early youth. "I'm afraid there's no such thing as a magic healing potion. Bone will heal itself, but it must be set proper and splinted. I can't bend bone that's fused crooked. Which means the tibia – your shin bone – must be broken again, then splinted and braced."

Joe blanched and tried to wriggle from his brother's grasp. "I won't do it!" he screamed. "You lot of poxy bastards will eat shit first!"

The brother stammered apologies to Dr Lundfrigg and tossed a murderous look at Roger, who still crouched by the bed.

Dr Lundfrigg nudged Roger with his knee. "Well? Does the lad truly understand what's best for him? Can he choose to reject your treatment?"

"He's old enough to be hanged for making the choice to steal," said Roger. "But he only understands that medical treatment will hurt like blazes." He placed a firm hand on the boy's head. "Joe, look at me. Think about your life since the injury. Can you still work as before? Do you get by?"

Tears dripped from the boy's chin as he shook his head. "I can't even keep up with the costermonger's cart, can't carry nothing, neither. Now I paste labels on bottles of shoe blacking, and my brother must buy me suppers. I ain't no good, sir."

Roger blinked. This was the second time in five minutes he'd been called sir. It must be a record. "If you let me reset your tibia – your shin bone," he told Joe, "you'll have a chance to chase coaches as before. But maybe you're just another wet-eared ninny. You want to live under your brother's thumb forever?"

"I told you I'd pummel you."

"Spoken like a mustard-colored cowardling," Roger bluffed. "Are you scared more of the crunching, or the grinding?" He rose and turned to Dr Lundfrigg. "I'll see the next patient, doctor."

"Wait!" Joe grabbed Roger's sleeve. "I ain't no cowardling. I'll take yer crunching, grinding, and I'll throw it right back in yer face."

Roger shrugged off the boy's hand, pretending to be unconvinced by his change of heart – he wanted to be certain of the lad's commitment to this horrid procedure.

"Don't we have none of that ether to spare, doctor?" he whispered.

Dr Lundfrigg shook his head. "Not unless you want to dip into your own expense account." He raised an eyebrow, perhaps probing the depth of Roger's generosity. "Otherwise there's always hypnosis."

"I'll just use my all-purpose surgeon's fluid." Roger produced his flask – this time refilled with actual gin skimmed from Harrod's cabinet – and encouraged Joe to tip some down his throat. A thickset orderly arrived with an instrument cart, and showed the older brother how to help restrain the boy. After taking a slug of gin himself, Roger selected a wooden mallet from the cart.

Dr Lundfrigg hovered close by. "Remember my words from before, Roger, my sharp young lancet. The best surgeon is a quick one."

The orderly held Joe's leg steady while the brother had the foresight to tie his own neckerchief around the boy's eyes. Roger found the knob of badly knitted broken bone, and tapped it once with his hammer. Gritting his teeth, he reminded himself that a boy with a crooked leg would never have a normal life. At least this way, the lad had a chance of healing enough to walk without a crutch. He swung and heard a crack like ice splitting on a pond. Then Joe's howls filled the ward. No time to think. Roger gripped Joe's knee in one hand and ankle in the other, then pulled the ends of the tibia outward. He fought the withered yet contracted calf muscle until the two halves settled into a shape more resembling a straight line.

"Splint!" shouted Roger. Someone thrust a scrap of wood into his hands, along with some strips of linen. As he secured the splint, he noticed the boy had fainted. Roger showed the brother how to tie up the splint and advised him to make Joe wear it for two months at least.

The brother looked doubtful. "This'll cure him?"

Roger hesitated. If the brothers followed his advice, in theory the bone should knit. But it was difficult to trust in forces you couldn't see; no wonder people preferred "magical" healing elixirs to surgery.

Dr Lundfrigg spoke up. "He has a one-in-five chance of healing, provided the leg is kept straight."

"Is that good?" asked the brother, and Dr Lundfrigg gave a wan smile.

"Time to move on, Mr Starkley. Bed five, tumorous growth on the clavicle. I want to see how well you wield a knife."

As Roger turned to follow, the brother grasped Roger's hand. "Thanks for trying, sir. I'll do my best to keep him knocked out for the next few days." It didn't sound like a joke.

Roger spent the better part of the morning on one routine case after another: a small tumor, an ingrown toenail, plantar warts, and a putrefied finger Roger lopped off with only the slightest hesitation. They bypassed a patient in the late stages of consumption. "Nothing for us to do here," murmured the doctor, and pulled Roger past with barely a glance.

"I've seen enough of the simple procedures," said Dr Lundfrigg at last. "Let's take a turn through the women's ward, shall we? Perhaps we'll find a more interesting case."

They entered a wide sunlit hall in the annex where rows of female patients lay side by side. The hall seemed somehow emptier than the male ward. With husbands at work and children under the care of neighbors, fewer families accompanied the ailing women.

Roger felt a sudden swell of emotion. He knew this room. For how many hours had he sat here, years ago, holding his mother's hand until she passed?

With one step, then another, some subconscious force pulled him in the direction of the bed where she'd lain.

Dr Lundfrigg held him fast by one arm. "I forgot to mention that I took the liberty of arranging that matter we spoke of last night. Your... widow is here in the women's ward under my personal supervision."

Roger could have kissed his hand.

A familiar face peered up at him from one of the pillows and managed a feeble smile.

"Celeste?" Roger approached cautiously, afraid a show of emotion might give her away. Ada's mother lay under a coarse gray blanket. She'd changed even more since his last house call. Her now-bluish skin was stretched over nothing more than a skeleton, and she struggled to pull herself into a sitting position against the iron rails of the bed. His breath caught in his throat. "Ma," he croaked before he could catch himself. He squeezed his eyes shut for good measure before opening them again.

"Dr Weathersby," she said in a hoarse, dry voice. "Thank you."

Roger cringed at the sound of his real name, but of course she wouldn't know.

"I'm Mr Starkley today, a mere surgeon," he said, hoping Dr Lundfrigg hadn't overheard. "And I suppose you must have another name too, Mrs…"

"Smith," said Celeste in her raspy undertone, with a hint of a smile. "The law-abiding widowed charwoman. Dr Lundfrigg knows, but no one else. He's a charitable man. Not unlike you."

Roger knelt by her bed. "Is there anything I can do?"

She gripped his bloodstained hand with withered, talon-like fingers. "Get it out of me."

"I… I don't think anyone can."

"Then bleed me. Bleed it out. You can do that."

Glancing over his shoulder, Roger noticed that Dr Lundfrigg watched him with an alert intensity that seemed different from their time in the male ward.

"You've had another look, Mr Starkley. What are your thoughts?"

"I…" Roger's voice failed him. The wasted image of Celeste blurred into how he remembered his mother. "She should be kept comfortable. She asked to be bled, and I don't see the harm if it puts her mind at ease." Again he wished he could afford ether, or another round of laudanum.

Dr Lundfrigg stared thoughtfully into space. "Well," he said at last, "the Khalishkans say bleeding is an obsolete travesty to science. I don't entirely agree, but I have an alternative we might administer instead. It's purely experimental but… you can see she has nothing to lose."

"Experimental?" asked Roger. "Like your mushrooms?"

He remembered how he'd huddled at the foot of his mother's bed during the last night of her life, overwhelmed by a misplaced conviction that he could save her, if only he could find the right tincture. During her final hours he'd dashed to druggists and apothecaries, but deep down he'd known miracles only existed in faerie stories. Of course no fanciful magic haddock would appear in a charity ward to grant him three wishes. They trafficked their magic with royal twits who didn't need it.

"You know how these things are," said Dr Lundfrigg with a frown, and swiveled off the top of his cane to produce a vial of some blood-colored substance and a syringe. "Medical research is an investment in the future. She can't be saved, but perhaps in the years to come, others will."

Roger nodded. He couldn't save his mother. He couldn't save Celeste. Even young Joe's recovery was uncertain. But perhaps, someday, he'd have a patient he could cure. Who knew what latent power might hide inside Dr Lundfrigg's vial? Experimentation brought advancements: ether anesthetics, fruit drops for scurvy, and inoculations against the pox. If he could contribute one thing to science, Roger wanted to ensure Ada would never die to the same illness as her ma.

Dr. Lundfrigg squeezed his shoulder. "Now, can you demonstrate proper preoperative procedure?"

Roger gathered his supplies: wool soaked in wine spirits, a linen tourniquet for finding the vein, and lint for swabbing blood. Celeste waved away his offer of gin. She extended her arm with a flicker of a smile.

"Does Ada know you're here?" he asked, binding the linen tightly around her upper arm. "When was the last time you saw her?"

"I forbid you to tell Ada where I am."

"But you're her mother." Roger took extra care to pierce the evasive vein at her elbow with his first jab. She winced as he pushed the plunger, injecting the tincture into her bloodstream.

"I won't have her see me like this." Celeste stroked strands of brittle hair from her face. "She should remember me as I was. Not carry this image with her for the rest of her life." Her ribcage, as substantial as a wicker birdcage draped in linen, rose and fell as she sighed. "I'd rather she forgot me as quickly as possible. You make sure she does that, Dr Weathersby. If she quits her place at the laundry, give her a good smack and say it was me from beyond the grave." Her twisted, haunting smile and glinting eyes were Ada's. "Promise me. Promise! Or she won't be the only ghost haunting you."

Roger nodded, unable to find his voice. He withdrew the needle. Thick, black blood trickled down her arm.

"This may sting." He swabbed her arm with the wine spirits.

"I feel better already," she murmured.

"You should." Dr Lundfrigg's voice was pinched with excitement. "My young lancet here doesn't believe in magic. But perhaps he'll be eating his words in the days to come."

25

"Not all acquaintances are worth revisiting," remarked the emperor as they arrived in Suet Street. He assisted Sibylla out of the carriage. She had no grounds to argue, and so remained silent.

The setting sun cast gloomy shadows across the shopfronts. She looked up at the face of the butcher's shop. The building tilted to the right, and rivulets of bloodied water collected in cracks along the footpath. She took care to step over a red puddle. A string of piglets dangled in the window, cut from snout to tail and splayed to show their cavernous, eviscerated bellies.

The emperor followed her to a side door and shoved it open. It made a sound like wood being forced through a cheese grater. In the gloom, they could make out the bottom of a staircase. Sibylla covered her nose. The smell of old meat wafted through chinks in the wood, and the stairs, green with mold, hadn't known soap and water in decades.

Just as Sibylla considered brightening her blood into its soft blue glow, the emperor lit a match. He ascended the stairs until he found a rat-gnawed candle in a broken sconce. He grimaced, then turned toward her with a reassuring smile. Sibylla had been afraid she'd never find Roger. Now she wasn't sure she wanted to. Still, she had an obligation. She'd sworn never to take a Straybound, and she needed to know she'd broken her promise to save the life of an innocent man.

Sibylla led the way up stairs so narrow her skirts scraped the walls on either side. When they reached the uppermost landing, the emperor squeezed past her.

"Allow me."

As no thief would have bothered with such a place, the emperor had little trouble forcing entry into the tiny attic room. Sibylla gathered her skirts against her body, not wanting to touch a thing. The last gasps of light from a filthy window revealed a sloped ceiling streaked with mold. Wads of soiled clothing lay strewn on a tiny cot beside a jumble of rubbish that belonged in a burn pit.

"How amusing." The emperor's fingers brushed the grip of his sword.

Sibylla saw nothing amusing in the absolute disrepair of the cramped garret. Amorphous shapes floating in apothecary jars lined makeshift shelves. As her eyes swept the darkest corner, her body tensed, and her tongue curled to whistle-click. A dark thing loomed in the shadow – some faceless creature.

It perched on a table made of old crates, with a mop of tar-black hair half-concealing a pinched, skeletal face. If not for the threadbare dress, the malnourished body could have been mistaken for a boy's. A corpse? Sibylla covered her mouth and fought down a retch. She spun about and hoisted her skirts to flee.

"You don't want to ask her questions?" The emperor pointed at the creature, his eyebrows raised.

Sibylla's eyes popped wide. "You mean it's…" She looked again. The thing tossed its head, swinging its hair back. It looked ready to spring at them.

The emperor drew his sword, a curious smile on his lips. He winked at Sibylla and approached the girl. "There's one sure way to test for ghosts."

"Wait." Sibylla threw out her hands as the emperor pointed the blade at the girl's feet.

The girl shrieked, banging her head against the slanted roof. She sprang off the crates on nimble limbs and scurried to the corner behind the cot. Her eyes locked on the window but the emperor blocked her escape.

"So this is a Myrcnian dormouse." Having brought the girl to life, the emperor moved to a flanking position.

The girl bared her teeth and hissed. Her eyes darted from Sibylla to the emperor, as if intent on avoiding the fate of the slaughtered pigs downstairs. Anxious that this grimy pixie might attack her next, Sibylla grabbed one of the stout apothecary jars and hefted it over her head.

The girl's wild eyes fastened onto Sibylla. "Put down that jar!" she screeched. "Don't hurt it!" She crouched with her hands before her face.

"Hurt what?" Sibylla paused, ensuring the girl wasn't somehow tricking her, then peered at the jar. A shape undulated inside, like a lady's bell-sleeve in a breeze. A faint blue glow shone through the glass.

"The moonstar jelly."

A blue ripple of Sibylla's own light moved down the length of her arm. Her skin prickled. She concentrated and imagined stuffing the glow in a clay jug and hammering in the cork. The prickle subsided. Disaster averted.

She lowered the jar, and her nerves relaxed. "Why in the world would he collect something like this?"

The girl snatched the jar away and replaced it on the shelf with care. "Well, he ain't here. We ain't got nothing to steal neither."

"That one can tell by the look of the place," the emperor offered politely.

Sibylla stepped closer. Despite the girl's bravado, her shiver betrayed real fear. "You're too clever to belong to Roger. And too old."

"I don't belong to no one."

"Not by the look of it, you don't. Is this where you live?"

"I haunt the sack-'em-up man. Plus folks fool enough to stop by."

"The sack-'em-up man? That's what you call him. How delightful." Sibylla gave a sardonic smile. "Do you know when this… sack-'em-up man will return?"

The girl shrugged.

After all her efforts, Sibylla had ruined everything to gain utterly nothing. She readjusted a raven skull that teetered on the edge of the shelf. Still, there was something of Roger here amongst this collection of curiosities, which included the girl.

"He was a scullion at your age, you know. He worked in a kitchen," she added, registering the girl's confusion. "He would crawl inside the biggest pots to get them clean, and even scrubbed a floor or two. Though you wouldn't guess by the look of this place, would you?"

"He always cleans the blood off his tools. Cleans 'em twice, once in water and once in gin. Also his teeth. He's got a jar of teeth up there. New ones get a good scrubbing when he brings 'em home. And sometimes he has hot cross buns."

Sibylla was at a loss. This Roger, the one with books and curiosities, who gave away food and shelter to a starving girl, was the one she wanted to remember. Yet, the disgusting room, the frightful mask, the bones and teeth and corpses… That Roger troubled her. Even now, she didn't know which she'd be Binding tomorrow.

A man or a murderer.

She pushed the thought away. A mosaic of seashells caught her eye, cockleshells and limpets pushed into the surface of a clay pot. That was the kind of thing that belonged to the Roger she remembered.

"He could never say no to whelks," she said aloud.

"Say no to what?" The girl had come up beside her and tapped a fingernail on one of the seashells. "What's whelks? Are they a bun?"

"Pickled whelks. A whelk lives in the sea in a shell like a palace, and fishermen catch them in baskets. We used to stuff our faces with them on Fraycable Street, by the pier. Yams, too. He could always pick the sweetest ones, even when the vendor tried to coax him to choose differently. I thought it was his magical gift for a while. But then, he can be pretty lost in his head most of the time. Is that why you're alone here?"

"He hasn't come in a while."

"Perhaps it's better that way." Guilty or not, a Straybound wasn't the proper caretaker for a child.

The girl timidly stroked a fold of Sibylla's gown. "Are you Queen of the Crumpets?"

"More of a princess than a queen," explained Sibylla, as the emperor coughed over his laugh. At least one person had been entertained this afternoon. "Though I do like a nice buttery crumpet."

"Should I tell him you stopped by?"

238

Sibylla studied her again but couldn't find much of Roger in her face. The waif looked one biscuit away from starvation. But was she really too old to be his? Sibylla hadn't spent enough time around children to tell their ages.

She pulled the locket Harrod had given her from her bodice and held it, suspended by its silver chain. She let a glow well up from her inner core to the surface of her skin. Now they could see despite the growing dusk.

The girl backed away from Sibylla's intensifying glow, but then inched forward, arm outstretched. "You're a moonstar," she whispered, and dared to touch the skin of Sibylla's hand.

Sibylla opened the locket to show the girl a bit of parchment framed inside – an inked portrait.

"That's the sack-'em-up man." The girl leaned in to get a better look. "'Cept he never looked so pretty, not no ways, not even after a shave."

"Perhaps I embellished a little," Sibylla wanly smiled. She took the girl's arm, feeling her tremble though she didn't scream. Snapping the locket shut, Sibylla placed it in the girl's hand.

The girl stared wide-eyed like she'd met a ghost. "You're giving this to me?" She scrunched her brow. "Why?"

"Because I want to." Sibylla had spent the afternoon looking for someone who might say a kind word about Roger, and she'd found only one. She straightened herself, nodding to the emperor to signal her intent to depart. "I won't be angry if you pawn it. Would you tell me your name?"

The girl couldn't decide where to look. "It's Ada, miss, but the sack-'em-up man calls me Ghostofmary."

The yellow smudge of a gaslamp shone in from the street below. The emperor no doubt had witnessed everything for what it was. A princess would never have set foot inside this garret for a boy she'd merely tutored. She'd given away her secrets, and her own reputation. Perhaps Mr Maokin's orchid water, meant to lay bare her concealments, was magic after all.

Sibylla wiped grime from the girl's cheek. "You shouldn't stay here, Ada. You'll get dirty."

"I'm fine, miss."

Sibylla tucked a rogue strand of Ada's hair behind her ear. She could barely keep her voice even as she forced her eyes to meet the emperor's. "We should go."

Ada gave the emperor a wide berth as he escorted Sibylla from the room. The glow in Sibylla's skin had faded, but the candle provided light enough for her to lead the way down the narrow stairwell. At the sound of creaking footfalls on the landing below, she stopped.

A man ascended toward her, carrying a candle that illuminated his face.

Roger.

She steadied her hand against the wall. Sideburns outlined his jaw, and his unruly hair had fallen over his forehead. Fading bruises marred his nose and cheek, and his jinxed eyes. Lost in thought, he looked straight past her. Had he always looked so frowzy? No, he'd been dashing and kind once.

"Mr Weathersby, home at last." She swallowed the bile of her resentment. Why lose her temper now? Yet her face flared hot.

The stairs were only wide enough for one. Roger paused a few steps below her. His eyes focused and his brow creased – the look of a man hunting the stacks of a dusty library for the volume to complete his mental encyclopedia.

"Sibet?"

"Do I look like the butcher's daughter?"

Roger glanced past her at the emperor, who stood on the stairs behind her. "If I'd known you was gracing my humble abode, I'd have cleaned it up some." His insolent grin faltered. "Or, you know, burned it down."

The stale air around her grew pungent with gin. How dare he make light of everything! She wanted explanations and apologies, not glib jokes better suited for old schoolmates. In her pursuit of him, she'd lost more than she cared to admit. If the emperor let one word slip to the queen, Sibylla would be hauled off to the dungeon in Hangman's Tower, left to molder beside the bones of Celia the Devout's apostate sister. She'd come looking for a medical student, unfairly accused, not this man dredged from the Mudtyne. They were not friends. This was not a social visit.

"You must know all that I've seen and heard." Sibylla's words came out in a furious rasp. "Horrors on horrors. And all centered on you. I wanted to look you in the eyes before the Binding, and now I rather wish I hadn't."

Roger's candle guttered in the gale of her words. The shadows deepened on his face. He was a stranger to her.

"What lies has Harrod been feeding you?" His eyes flashed for a moment, then he ducked his head in a half-bow as if to make up for his impertinence. "I honor my debts. I am your humble servant, Sibet." He did not sound humble at all.

"You're no servant of mine," Sibylla hissed. "Truly innocent men don't rob graves so they can visit prostitutes. Or keep stray girls as pets. Or have ballads written about their disgusting crimes. No, Dodge. You did something to get where you are, a murderer in name or deed, tied to me by a contract signed in blood. But I don't want a broken tool."

"A murderer? A tool?" he spat. "I might be many things – foolish, rash, penniless – but I'm no murderer. I set a lad's shin today, and tonight I'll be drudging on my hands and knees to polish Harrod's floor. Now you ride up on your high horse and presume to mock my situation? After all I've been through?" His gestures had taken on a wild, almost threatening quality. "What a priggish thing to say." He stopped. His tone changed as if a new thought had hit him. "My letter. Is that what this is about? You think I'm guilty. And here I thought you knew me better than that." He swayed, and for a moment she thought he might fall to his knees. "You should have just let me hang."

"Oh, that will come," she snapped. "Perhaps if I'd known what you'd become, I'd never have let Harrod talk me into signing that prerogative." *No.* She unclenched her hands, but her breaths came short and rapid. No, she couldn't have brought herself to act otherwise. Even if Harrod had told her the truth, she'd have done the same.

"Then why don't you pair of carps send me back to Old Grim and get it over with?"

"Because Harrod and I…" What could she say? That they loved him?

That *she* loved him? *Had* loved him. She stared at Roger's contused face, his rumpled clothes, and unruly hair. She'd wanted so badly to see him again and now it choked her. "I thought you were a decent man."

With a desperate look in his eyes, Roger reached for her hand – a reckless, futile gesture. In an instant the emperor nudged Sibylla aside. She heard the scrape of his short sword leaving its scabbard and felt the whish of air as he leapt past her and held his blade to Roger's chin. Roger wobbled back, but the emperor grabbed his shirtfront and held him fast.

"You're done here," he said, allowing the blade to nick Roger's skin.

Roger put a hand to his jaw. His fingers came away tinged with blood. "Call off your dog, Sibet," he growled. "You've gone too far."

Sibylla clung to the rail in shock. Not once all day had the emperor's eyes sharpened as they did now. She couldn't coax words from her lips, but it didn't matter. He had no obligation to follow her commands.

The emperor eased his blade off Roger's throat, unable to keep a steady grip from laughing. "I'm no one's dog, Mr Weathersby, and you're just a pup." He sheathed his blade, then wiped the thin trickle of blood from Roger's jaw with his thumb. "You may wish to consider whom you're addressing next time you speak. We all serve our masters, whether they be of mind or heart. And isn't she yours either way?" He patted Roger's cheek.

Sibylla risked touching the emperor's arm.

He turned to her with a smile so pleasant she thought she'd been drugged. "Your highness." He bowed his head, then made room for her to pass by, jamming Roger against the wall.

As she squeezed past, Sibylla risked a glance at her Straybound's face, his jinxed eyes glassed, refusing to meet hers. She bit her lip. Hesitating now would do more harm than good. As she left the building, the bitter night air hit her face. Rounding the corner as fast as her hitched skirts would allow, she almost stumbled into a man who stood contemplating the carcasses in the shop window.

Harrod bowed deeply from the waist and held the position, staring at the pavement. "Your highness." He'd thrown on an overcoat to cover

242

his uniform and conspicuous medal and looked more like a constable than a naval officer.

"Why are you here?" She'd had enough of smug, self-satisfied men pretending to be humble. He'd been avoiding her for days, and only when he knew she'd found Roger did he show himself.

Harrod lifted his head. "I've come to explain."

"You." She slapped his face. The impact sent a wave of pins and needles up her arm. Everything she'd stoppered up inside began to spill forth. "I trusted you, Harrod. I believed everything you told me like some maundering fool."

Wearing the red after-stain of her smack, he remained obeisant before her. "I couldn't let him hang."

"You bloody fool, stop bowing already."

"Sibylla." Harrod's arm twitched toward her.

"Don't." Warm wet ink pooled at her fingertips, staining her gloves. She flung a black cloud between them.

"I wanted to explain the matter privately."

"You had plenty of opportunity."

"I didn't know how to tell you. He's a wretch, a malefactor even, but not a murderer. I took him into my household. My plan was to make him fit for service to your highness, but he's proved more of a challenge than—"

"And what of the child?" Sibylla interrupted. "His pet poltergeist, more alive than dead."

"She's not his."

Relief trickled through her but did nothing to quell her anger. She fumed at his detached response. "How can you be certain? Tell me, *captain*. Do you know where Edgar is this very moment? Edmund? Or Edward? Don't your locating talents only extend to your closest blood relations? Myself, Roger, our father. Maybe your own little bastards." Her entire body shook with rage. "How could you do this? You're my brother, the only one I have. I adored you, but you used me without consideration or regret."

Harrod cleared his throat and nodded toward the emperor. "Your highness is obviously unsettled."

She didn't know how long the emperor had been standing there, and she didn't care. She peeled off her ink-stained glove and dropped it on Harrod's shiny boot. Obviously, Harrod cared more for his half-brother than Sibylla – his half-sister. She'd humiliated herself today for him, and for Roger. Now, she had nothing left to hold onto.

"You tricked me into signing that vile contract. Even when faced with the queen and Dorinda, I was loyal to you. I've spent my life afraid someone would find you out; the thought made me sick to the bones. But here you are, so busy saving his life, you never once considered how I'd feel in the matter." She turned to leave, but Harrod reached for her arm through the ink. A whistle-click sent him reeling. His shoulder smashed against the brick exterior of the shop, and he cupped his ear in pain. Harrod either didn't have the courage to follow her, or feared she'd do worse the second time.

Inside the carriage, Sibylla stared at the fog-shrouded buildings, watching the last lamps being lit for the night. The emperor sat with her in silence, a reminder of her impropriety and foolhardiness. She'd made a grave mistake in coming here.

Shaking off her remaining glove, she forced her mouth into a smile. Harrod and Roger had each taken a dinner knife to her heart, and now she hadn't the lungs to breathe. "Do you wish to return to the palace?"

"My preference is unchanged." The emperor reached into his coat pocket, and produced his small notebook. He flipped through the pages she'd inked earlier that day, and stopped on a blank sheet. "A map for the driver," he said. "Wherever the cicada instructs, I will attend."

Regardless of what the emperor may have heard, she might still blur his memory with a lively evening out, to include a sampling of Myrcnia's strongest liquors. Ink pooled beneath her fingernails as streets formed on the page. After all, she'd made an agreement with Timur. Even if it killed her, she intended to uphold her end of the bargain. The emperor would at least have Caligo's famous beef and kidney stew to look upon fondly. The rest she'd handle tomorrow.

26

Roger stumbled upstairs to his garret. Nausea at the princess' cutting remarks brought him to his knees just inside the door, and he retched into the pail that still smelled of dead cat. Hot tears dribbled down his nose and chin.

So she'd seen him for what he truly was, then. Somehow she'd known he'd kissed doxies, and unearthed corpses, and had neglected poor Ada. And though he knew he wasn't a murderer, now that she'd called him one to his face, he almost believed it.

To think he hadn't recognized her with her hair pinned up and the face of a sun-starved morel – a far cry from the impish apple-cheeked girl he remembered, the one with the insatiable sweet tooth.

He'd surely changed in her eyes, too, but to far worse effect. That austere glare of hers invited no flippant teasing, or kisses in the servants' passage behind the sunfish hanging. She didn't even smile, not once.

"You look right sozzled." Ada's small hand smoothed back the hair that had fallen in his face. "You should water your gin more. That's what my ma says when she's in a state."

Roger glanced at the girl, registering the smudged face, bird-thin elbows, and her blood-smeared smock that told him she'd helped Mrs Carver with the boning, tying, and grinding down in the shop. At least she looked better than her mother. "What a sod I am, Ada," he said in a choked voice. "Why do you stay on in this hole? You'd be better off in one of them charity workhouses than with me." He retched again, and she patted his back.

"Poor sack-'em-up man. I don't need no taking care of." Ada daubed his face with a damp cloth. "I heard you get a lamming on the stairs. That man were a weasel. But I liked the moonstar lady."

"Well, they can both rot in hell." He must have looked like a slug in need of a salt-dousing to the princess. She might as well have squeezed lemons into his wounds, waltzing in as she had in that gauzy faerie-dress just to remind him her place was the aether, and his the mud. Roger closed his eyes until he'd regained most of his composure. Then he felt in his coat pockets and pulled out a sad little flattened package. "Blast. I brought you teacakes from Harrod's, but they was mashed to crumbs."

Roger slumped back over his bucket, trying to push Sibet from his mind. Best not to dwell on the princess. He drowned out her uppish voice in his head with a long swig from his flask. He didn't need the reminder that he wasn't a good man.

Besides, he told himself firmly, he had bigger things to worry about. In defiance of her mother's wishes, Roger had returned to take Ada to the hospital. Let Celeste haunt him. Her shade couldn't possibly be as trying as her flesh-and-blood daughter. His own mother, on that final day, had kneaded his hand with her brittle fingers as if to say – *I can't face death alone.*

His heart sank knowing where he intended to bring her. At least a promise of food might coax her out of the garret. Roger hauled himself to his feet and put on his hat. "Come on then, Ghost. Tonight the young lady gets her pick of pie at the Fox & Weasel."

"I ain't no lady," she said. "But I'll take your pie. Maybe tomorrow we can get whelks? Pickled whelks?"

"Pickled whelks? No one likes pickled whelks." Roger had been working over in his brain how to broach the topic of her mother, but every expression sounded lame, or false, or cruel. He wrapped a scarf around her neck, and they tiptoed down the stairs so as not to draw Mrs Carver's attention.

"But you like 'em."

"They're something ghastly. Like chewing bits of soap soaked in kerosene."

"Are they really?"

"To me they are. I only ever knew one person who liked the blasted things. Whenever she wanted 'em, I had to run all the way to Beadle Street for the pricey ones. I got quite good at choking 'em down with a grin."

"How daft."

"Of course it were daft. I loved her."

"Then why ain't you with her?"

Ada's voice rang in his head. There were plenty of reasons, but none he cared to share.

While Ada curled up next to her mother, Roger observed the deterioration of Celeste's body. As with Lady Margalotte and Claudine, her belly had the same soft mounds dotting her stomach. During his earlier evaluations, he'd suspected gallstones or cirrhosis of the liver, but that hardly accounted for the current amount of swelling. While some bloating of the deceased was normal, Celeste still lived to whisper in her daughter's ear. It didn't seem right.

With Ada's head tucked under her mother's chin, Roger palpated the stomach, examining the soft protruding spots in her abdominal wall. They had been concave divots the first time he'd examined her in Will-o'-the-Wisp Lane. Now he guessed a tumor – or a host of them – had expanded among her organs. She wouldn't be strangled, or buried alive, like the other victims of this disease. Whether that was a mercy, he was no longer certain.

Celeste's uneven breath caught in her throat as she and Ada whispered beneath the tented sheet – a ghostly foreshadowing Roger couldn't bear to watch. He left the women's ward for the quiet corridor, not wishing to intrude on Ada's grief, and afraid of Celeste confronting him for going against her wishes.

He stalked the halls of St Colthorpe's like a phantom himself, unwilling to leave Ada behind, but unsure of his role – what was he to her, anyway? An unreliable source of buns and teacakes at most.

Despising this feeling of helplessness, he sought out the physician on duty to ask about the official diagnosis and whether Dr Lundfrigg had left any patient notes regarding his experiment. At the very least, Roger would search the mortuary for any other potential victims.

As Roger approached the door to the storage bay where he'd once made nocturnal deliveries, the senior physician on night duty exited one of the side offices to intercept him.

"This area is off limits," snapped the physician. Roger recognized a recent graduate; single young men often got stuck with the night shift. "I won't have the likes of you skulking about our hospital. You're to shove off, or I'll send for the constables."

"I need to know the diagnosis for the patient in bed nineteen. I work here." Roger inwardly cursed his roughed-up face. No one trusted him by sight. "Dr Lundfrigg – Sir Finch – gives his blessing. I've been doing rounds as his assistant."

"Well, I would hardly know it to look at you. Why should I trust your words?" He sucked his lips in revulsion. "You could be the Greyanchor Strangler for all I know. Such a clever villain, thinking you could toady up to the royal physician himself." The doctor caught Roger by the lapels and collared him. "But I'll wager your neck brand that you're nothing but a common criminal looking to snatch a stiff out from under my nose." He tried to get his fingers under Roger's cravat.

If the doctor glimpsed his Straybound Stigma, he'd swing from the gallows. Sod that.

Roger clapped the doctor's ear with the flat of his hand. The man lurched sideways and grappled at Roger's throat to catch himself. Such an amateur move. Roger's pulse hammered – his first fair fight in weeks! He might never knock a practiced pugilist like Harrod cold, but he could still scrap as well as any streetwise lad. He thrust an arm between the doctor's wrists and wrenched himself free. With one swift kick, his opponent toppled.

"You'll be in the bag for this!" shrieked the doctor from the floor. "Show your face here again, I dare you."

The sound of running footsteps echoed down the corridor – orderlies and morgue assistants must have heard the struggle. No reason to press his luck. Roger fled into the still-dark streets. Let Ada have her space. He'd keep the promise he'd made Harrod to return after his hospital shift, which he'd planned all along to say had run late. Roger didn't fancy being arrested and hanged the night before his Binding, and since he hadn't figured a way to get out of it, he'd let them wave their incense sticks and pronounce him "bewitched." He had never feared any of that religious tripe, and tomorrow would be no different.

27

"I hear you kept his imperial majesty out until the wee hours, Sibylla dear," said Lady Esther, setting down her breakfast plate. Her aunt's shrill voice echoed in Sibylla's skull. The emperor had insisted on that second bottle of Greenkills Sap Liquor, and, because of her mood, she'd slugged down more than her share. By the time their carriage had returned to Malmouth, she couldn't tell whether she was slumped against the carriage box or the emperor's shoulder.

The royal family and a smattering of bleary-eyed Khalishkan dignitaries served themselves tarragon potatoes and caviar-stuffed boiled eggs from large silver chafing dishes. Sibylla, who had chosen a seat with vacancies on either side so she could avoid conversation this early in the morning, flinched. Shading her eyes from the sunlight, she bit into her sourdough toast.

"And yet," continued Lady Esther, "you shamelessly show your face among us. No child of mine was ever so impertinent."

"No child of yours is much of anything." The queen, who approved of buffets in theory yet insisted that three footmen serve food to her personally, rebuked Lady Esther with a look.

"Your majesty!" Lady Esther brought her fork down sharply. "Just this morning, Edgar assisted Dorinda in inspecting the footmen's livery for the Royal Heritage Ball, and Edmund and Edward…" Her voice fizzled, but the queen's brow arced in expectation. "Well, they haven't been out all night unattended, with no proper chaperone to keep their behavior in check." Then with a whisper deliberate in its volume, she added, "Why, I heard her highness' breath smelled so strongly of pine sap that one of the palace dogs nearly mistook her for a tree."

Having had her fill of breakfast insults, Sibylla meant to defend both herself and the emperor. Enough rumors of her supposed dalliances had spread throughout the palace. No doubt Lady Esther continued to have a hand in the cholera-like epidemic of gossip. Edgar and his mother could both go shrivel like coalfish in the sun for as much as she cared to hear their opinions.

Sibylla raised her voice above the general chatter. "His imperial majesty desired a tour of our city, and I can think of no more gentlemanly a companion. What ill-mannered individual would refuse such a request? I'm shocked to think someone would deny his imperial majesty a meal at one of Caligo's finest eateries." Sibylla sipped her tea and mustered an innocent smile. "After all, he is our invited guest. Why, returning by midnight when Myrcnia has so many cherished diversions is nearly insulting. How nice it would have been to watch the sun rise together."

"Butter wouldn't melt in your mouth, would it dearie?" Lady Esther lowered her voice to elude the queen's sharp ears. "It seems his imperial majesty is too exhausted by your escapades to join us for breakfast. I'd have stayed in bed myself, had I not been led to believe our presence this morning was mandatory. If our puffed-up princess were not such a delightful dollop of cream, I'd think she had soured the man to our ways."

Sibylla chased a remnant of caper omelet across her plate. "And if my aunt weren't such a happily married matron, I'd say she was a jealous old trout."

Lady Esther gripped the lacy edge of the tablecloth and stared hard into Sibylla's eyes. "You poor, silly girl. Did you actually believe Lady Brigitte when she said you could marry the Emperor of Khalishka? We've all known for weeks. Your return to Caligo is nothing more than a pretense to lowering cheese tariffs." Sibylla's gaze slipped to the head of the table where the queen sat finishing her plate. "Go ahead. Ask her majesty if you dare. We both know what her answer will be. You'll be engaged to Edgar the very second that Cabbage King crosses the border for home."

Dropping her napkin onto her plate, Sibylla stood to address the queen. "Your royal majesty, might I be excused?"

"Run along, Sibet." The queen waved her off without looking up from her ham. Clearly Sibylla's meager status hadn't changed among the royal family, and none of the Khalishkan dignitaries paid her any mind. Only Lady Esther, with her gloating smile, observed her exit.

A pang of uncertainty over Lady Esther's words now lodged between head throbs. The emperor had not attended breakfast, and though Sibylla herself often skipped morning meals, she wondered whether his absence had to do with her behavior the previous day, or merely implied that the ministers had finally settled on the price of Highspits blue cheese.

Under the guise of being useful, Sibylla summoned the steward to prepare a wheeled cart of breakfast delicacies for Emperor Timur. She carefully selected her favorite biscuits – spiced orange and burnt caramel, and a lemon leek pancake drizzled with thyme syrup. She'd barely slept that night, recalling the emperor's scent, redolent of a larch forest, and the speed at which he placed a sword to Roger's throat. Neither could she forget Roger's eyes as he reached for her hand, and the smell of gin on his breath when she squeezed past him on the stairs. If she could repeat yesterday, she'd have foregone the medical district and Roger's grimy garret in favor of curiosities at Marlowe's Menagerie. But such time-bending magic didn't exist in this world, and now she had to face the consequences of her sizeable misjudgment.

Sibylla carried a silver teapot while the steward wheeled the breakfast cart up a ramp built to accommodate private meal deliveries. They continued to the wing where the higher Khalishkan dignitaries had been housed. The furniture here was more expensive, curated to impress visitors. Tapestries of seascapes covered the walls, illustrating *The Prison of the Lobster Prince* and other tales from Myrcnian lore.

As they neared the emperor's chambers, Sibylla's nerves betrayed her and a glow crept up her fingers, glinting off the silver teapot. She tightened her grip on the linen napkin she held over the teapot's spout so the hot water wouldn't slosh onto the carpet.

"I'll handle the cart from here, thank you." She set the teapot next to the biscuits and smoothed her skirts.

The steward looked half-ready to argue, but, glancing at her glowing skin, he reconsidered. "Ma'am." He bowed and hurried away.

Sibylla hesitated before the bedroom door, inventing an explanation for why a Myrcnian princess might know the Greyanchor Strangler. She also needed to convey gratitude to the emperor for keeping silent over her associations, and then somehow convince him she was still a worthy marriage partner. A hysterical laugh escaped her lips. Her head was a mess. Resting her back against the door, she stared headlong at Old Claude.

The suit of armor stood watch from across the hall. Its helmet of polished steel neighbored a painting of a rosy-cheeked young woman in a red gown, her hair woven through with gold laurels. As Sibylla studied the woman's eyes, she suddenly recognized her aunt – a shapely, smooth-faced Lady Esther from decades ago. An ermine stole draped over one gauzy sleeve, and behind her, a mirrored reflection of a bespectacled figure in heavy brown coat. So even this circus-like image of Lady Esther juggling globes of blue water like round rubber balls would be witness to her failures now.

At least it wasn't the woman herself. Sibylla rapped on the door with trembling knuckles and held her breath. She wasn't sure she wanted the emperor to answer. When the door did open, she started.

"Harrod?" Her brow scrunched in confusion.

Over his shoulder sat the emperor along with Mr Maokin and a figure obscured by Harrod's chest. None looked up from their discussion, but the older minister tapped his middle two fingers against the table where a series of documents lay.

With a quarter half-turn, Harrod bowed to the emperor. "Your imperial majesty," he uttered before pushing Sibylla back into the hallway. He shut the door behind him and sighed – the color drained from his face.

"Why were you meeting with the emperor? And what were they discussing? Are you here because of Roger?"

"Roger?" Harrod regained his bearings and waved her questions off. "Security arrangements for tomorrow's Royal Heritage Ball."

"Since when does a naval captain with the Ordnance Board discuss security?"

"Ceremonial concerns. Order of the Kraken and all that." His jaw clenched. "Let's discuss this elsewhere." He offered his arm to lead her down the corridor.

"But what about the emperor's breakfast?" Sibylla gestured toward the silver domes.

"Easily cared for." Harrod flagged down a passing footman who dared glower his way, and left the breakfast in the confused man's custody.

Out of habit, Sibylla tugged Harrod closer, despite her residual anger over his recent wrongdoings. "Did the emperor say anything?" she pressed. "You look ill."

Harrod rubbed the side of his ear. "Your highness' tongue-lashings pack a wallop worse than McCleary's left hook."

"If you're expecting an apology…"

He shook his head. "I deserved worse."

Sibylla hated the stab of sympathy he evoked from her. "I shouldn't have done that to you. I blame Roger for getting me brined up. Here I'm saving him from dying a miserable death, yet when I see him, he offers only insults. After he abandoned me, I always assumed he'd make something of himself, but he's gone terribly wrong – hasn't he? My blood still boils when I think of that insolent smirk."

"We're of the same mind there," said Harrod. "But I'm afraid time is running short. His probation period is up, and your highness must make a final decision about his future forthwith."

They entered a high-ceilinged atrium where a cluster of ministers and foreign delegates discussed policy and culture beneath the domed glass and gray Caligo sky.

"Then you still believe he's innocent," said Sibylla, straightening the Kraken medal on Harrod's chest. "You may not have lied as blatantly as your brother, but you did hide the truth. And now you've foisted Roger upon me. I never knew you to be so soft."

Harrod clasped her hands in view of all. It wasn't like him to ignore their surroundings. "I'm doing all I can. By the Merciful Mother, I'd have done more if it were in my power. Unfortunately, yours was the only such authority at my disposal."

"Authority?" Sibylla scoffed. The last few days hadn't made her feel rife with command. "If you need the dinner menu changed, I'm certainly capable. Beyond that, I'm about as effective as a paper boat in a hurricane."

"Not in this case." Harrod squeezed her fingers. "He's alive because of that mark on his neck. And if he doesn't complete the Binding, he'll be returned to Old Grim and hanged by the archbishop, as per the terms of his probation. You know as well as I: without a patron, his contract is void." Harrod straightened. "But perhaps it's for the best."

"Don't pretend you think I'd let Roger hang. I only wish you'd have come clean to me before I signed that contract." She gave a bitter laugh. "Maybe Edgar would have taken him. He loves acquiring my former belongings."

Harrod grimaced. "The poor sap. He's much better off with you. But your ink, as they say, has been spilt."

Sibylla longed for the magic to conjure a lovely flame under the seat of Harrod's breeches. A Straybound Binding was worse than the countless archaic rituals she'd been forced to attend, and required more participation than merely a long afternoon coughing on incense in a darkened church. Afterward, Roger would remain by her side until she breathed her last, and then he'd follow her unto death. The idea of his daily maintenance wrung her chest. But her feelings didn't matter now, and neither did his. She would commit to the ritual and spare his life, whether they both regretted it or not.

"So you do consent to have him hanged?" Harrod sounded so chipper she nearly believed he meant it. Nearly.

"Why waste good arrangements?"

"Then we'll meet at your personal chapel at the cathedral of St Myrtle the Chased in…" He consulted his watch fob. "…in two hours." He pressed her hand to his mouth. "Your highness."

A disapproving murmur rose above the gurgling fountain. Sibylla exhaled through her teeth. Very well. Taking a Straybound came at a cost, and she would suffer it. Roger might not have her power or privilege, but he could still be useful to society, and to her. If she had to toe the line, then so did he.

28

The hired cab hit a bump, jostling Roger against his brother. His skin glowed pink from a chilly morning bath and a fresh shave, yet his mind remained clouded by nerves and a lack of sleep. He wore only a plain, freshly-pressed shirt and breeches, and he shivered in his state of undress, wishing Dawson hadn't reclaimed his loaned waistcoat and hat. Harrod leaned on the window as if he could whip the horses faster with his glare. Every few seconds, a flurry of instructions fell from his lips, too fast for Roger to keep up.

"Speak only when spoken to. Cast your eyes downward, follow all instructions to the letter, kneel when you are told, and for the love of Queen Mildred keep your titles straight. Archbishop Tittlebury of Cropspin is 'your grace' and her highness is 'your merciful highness', emphasis on the merciful. Can you remember that, Roger? The cathedral of St Myrtle is just ahead. Are you even listening?"

In fact, Roger had been silently agonizing over how he might still escape his Binding. "It's not too late, Harrod." He deliberately dropped his brother's title to stoke some flame of fraternal empathy. "I know more about the real Strangler now than I did before. We might still convince the archbishop I don't deserve this. You're better with that ritual legal tosh than me. You have clout. You're a Kraken. They might listen to you, if you'll just listen to me."

"It's the law that's placed you here." Harrod sighed. "Once Archbishop Tittlebury commuted your sentence, you'd never stand trial again. There is no higher authority than the Queen's Exalted Bench, and divine interventions are never overturned. Even if this… strangler you're so sure exists were to walk into the church and confess on his knees, you would still be guilty of his crimes. I can't make it any simpler for you. Now, as I've done everything in my power to help you, you might agree that keeping your manhood intact, along with your neck, is a reasonable trade for the mere clipping of your wings."

Roger sat fuming in silence. Harrod was determined to see this through, and if his own brother wouldn't help him, the list of those who still could was a short one indeed.

Harrod then explained how Roger should exit the carriage with his palms facing upward. "A mere formality." He'd repeated the phrase many times in the last quarter-hour. Each time, a feeling of dread twisted Roger's entrails like the hand of an overeager medical student. "A mere formality" was also how he described the pair of robed men with truncheons and masks styled like blindfolds who looked on as Roger descended from the cab. Likewise, the braided silk noose placed over Roger's head, which Harrod deemed "purely symbolic."

"You are a murderer in the eyes of the law," Harrod reminded him as he escorted Roger up the stairs of St Myrtle's. The main entrance had been barred to the public, but a robed acolyte admitted them with a deferential bow. Inside the vestibule, the acolyte bound Roger's eyes with a red silk sash.

"What are you lot? Bricklayers?" Roger protested.

Harrod thwacked him on the skull with his palm before handing him off to the acolyte, who guided him further into the cathedral. The air smelled of incense and snuffed candles. The acolyte must have worn soft slippers for his feet made no sound. Roger's own footsteps clunked in a nave so massive it took several seconds for the echo to return. Unless Harrod had slipped off his boots and accompanied them barefoot, he had remained behind.

"Kneel, Straybound, before Her Precious Blood."

"You have the wrong man," Roger shouted. His voice echoed loudly in his ears. "If only you'd give me one more day–"

A blast of incense smoke into his mouth silenced him, and strong arms forced him to his knees. Soft lips brushed his forehead, and then a thumb traced the symbol of the Blood Line along his brow.

"The officer charged with your probation, one Captain Starkley, has deemed you of sufficient humility and compliance to face the Rite of Binding. What say you?"

He could see nothing through his blindfold, nor could he tell how many stood around him. This time Roger chose more diplomatic phrasing. "I am her merciful highness' to command." A shudder ran through him.

He remembered his brief time as a palace footman. Seventeen year-old Sibet had returned late from an evening romp in the royal gardens, soaking from an unexpected summer storm. He'd ruined his livery unbuttoning her mud-caked boots. As she stifled a fit of giggles, he hoisted the barefoot princess into his arms and carried her up the stairs to her chambers. Her maid had gone to bed, so he peeled the sodden wrap from her shoulders and unhooked her dress to prevent her catching cold. With an impish grin, he cast aside his mud-stained coat. How unfair that he had glimpsed her petticoats – she must pull off his shirt and then they'd be even. She had never seen a shirtless man before and made him turn in a circle. That image of her shivering in a pale, otherworldly glow had not faded with the years.

Now the archbishop clipped those memories short. "Accept Her Exalted Highness as your savior in all things, give Her your mind and body so that you may be cleansed. Confess now to your criminal deeds and wipe clean the slate of your ruined soul."

Roger cared little for the faerie magic of souls. Hundreds of dissections had failed to produce even the tiniest gauzy remnant, nor had he glimpsed the fabled golden orb floating skyward from a deathbed – not even his mother's. The tip of a blade pricked the back of his skull, held by a steady hand. Now seemed a bad time to protest his fitness for some secret religious order.

"You can tell her worshipfulness that I'm every bit the horror she imagines." Bull-headed honesty was all Roger had left. He let the words fall bitterly off his tongue. "I traffic in corpses. I visit doxies. I pose as a man of science without legal license; I act and dress above my rightful station; I let folks take advantage of my labor; I spend faster than I earn. I've disgraced the only girl I ever loved and abandoned the only child to rely on me. I'm too quick to trust, and too easy to buy." He paused, "And I kissed Dorinda by the ash, by my own choosing. Tell her that, as she's waited years to hear me admit it. For all these things, I'm sorry." Behind him, the knife-holder cleared their throat. Did that mean he was meant to confess to that Smith woman's murder? "As I'm honest in my way, I resist feeling shamed by my way of life. But let her mercifulness know that I am not nor never will be a murderer. *That* I swear by my own neck."

Light filtered through his blindfold, creating a red glow.

"Ah, but we are only as others perceive us to be," replied the archbishop. "Even if your inner slate were clean – and it certainly is not – your surface is forever stained. Remember it well, Straybound, as you go forth into your mercifully lengthened life, should you be humble enough to receive Her blessing."

The steady hand removed the dagger from his neck, and Roger bowed his head in silence. He didn't feel bewitched. Was that all? A confession and he was free to go? It seemed an impractical method for dealing with pardoned murderers. Perhaps the archbishop believed in his innocence and chose to be lenient after all.

"The Straybound will now be born anew." Archbishop Tittlebury's voice reverberated off the cathedral's high ceilings.

Strong hands lifted Roger to his feet as someone ripped the blindfold from his eyes. He stood in one of the side chapels of St Myrtle's, cluttered with dripping red candles and their ornate fixtures. Set in an alcove, a statue of the princess in crown, veil, and halo gazed upward at the stained glass rose windows – or perhaps she was rolling her eyes in contempt. Then the real Princess Sibylla crossed in front of him to stand before the jeweled monstrance containing her blood. She brandished a golden dagger in one hand.

"Bugger me sideways," he said. The archbishop gave a scornful hiss and Roger corrected himself. "I mean… your merciful highness."

Coolly, she returned his gaze. "Ironically, there is a distinct lack of mercy in most Myrcnian tradition. I shall try to make this as painless as I can. We have both suffered enough, I think." She nodded to the archbishop. "I am ready."

Archbishop Tittlebury kissed his fingertips and waved them in the air. "To be reborn a Straybound, you must first die a man."

One of the guards tied Roger's hands behind his back while the other yanked the "symbolic" noose so tight he choked. They dragged him backward to a massive column and knotted it to a ring on the end of a longer rope that hung from a hook jutting from the stone, about ten feet high.

Roger tried to shout, but he couldn't breathe. To his horror, the men began to haul on the rope, forcing him onto his tiptoes. The silk cut into his jaw. While Sibet struggled to push a gold-colored stepladder to the base of the column, his toes left the ground.

The archbishop began to chant in Old Myrcnian. Roger, swinging a foot above the ground, recognized it as a dirge sung by mourners during funeral possessions. Horror cloaked him like a hood and he thrashed, fighting for air that would not come. He was going to die.

"I, Sibylla Celia Ingrid Muir of Alabeth, daughter of Prince Henry Leopold Louis Muir of Alabeth..."

Sibet's face appeared inches from his own. She must have climbed up the ladder. Her lips moved quickly. Was that her voice, tinny and distant? A strange euphoria washed through him, and his vision flickered. He relaxed.

"...being of sound mind and sacred blood, on this, the day of consumption, do hereby, with the blessing of the divine Priest-King Rupert, solemnly absolve Roger..." Her voice faded.

Had he died?

But then she squeaked out, "Roger... Xenophanes, Roger Xenophanes Weathersby."

His lungs burned, yet his oxygen-starved brain latched onto the most idiotic thoughts. He had no middle name. She'd made that up. The X was just his old mark, from before he could write his name.

A bright light flared before his eyes. He heard a blade scrape and scrape at the braided silk. The light shrank, like a window rushing into the distance, became a pinprick, then disappeared.

He regained consciousness sprawled on his back. His hands clutched a severed piece of cord. On the ceiling above him a mural depicted Saint Myrtle in her mythic flight across the moors. A dozen wolfhounds appeared to leap over the stone ribs of architectural struts, frozen in pursuit. In the corner of his eye he saw Sibet sheathe her blade.

The quavering voice of the ancient archbishop rose in a singsong chant.

"May the blessings of our merciful daughter fall upon her servant,
newly born to share her bonds, her burdens and her blood.
Let us remember Saint Myrtle the Chased, princess of old who fled
her most divine obligation of marriage and was torn asunder by dogs.
May she be a reminder to the Straybound of the fate that awaits
the defiant and the shirker, be one a pauper or princess."

The burly men propped a shaking Roger onto his hands and knees. They tugged off his cravat and neck bandage, tore open his shirt, and removed the pewter physician's medal he wore against his skin.

The archbishop kissed his two fingers, and again drew the Blood Line across Roger's forehead. "From this day forth, you shall have no other allegiance, nor master."

An acolyte approached, carrying a gold tray of various vessels.

"Your highness," intoned the archbishop, "consecrate your instrument so that he may be bound to you for eternity. His is an oath only his master may sunder by means of the blade. He is yours in all things, and on the day of your death, he too shall die."

Roger gasped, afraid he might start laughing manically, partly from lightheadedness but mostly at the archbishop's rubbish. "Please." Air scorched his bruised windpipe as he spoke. "There's a real Greyanchor Strangler. I'm here, but he's the one that should be. If your lot can do all this, then help–" His voice broke off in pain as Sibet dabbed a finger in one of the vessels and bent down to smear unguent on his Straybound tattoo. It burned the raw, wounded skin of his throat. He hissed through his teeth.

"And now," announced the archbishop, "let us bind the blood."

Sibet lifted a gold chalice from the tray and held it under Roger's nose. "Drink, Straybound, from the cup of my mercy," she recited in a practiced voice as if he hadn't spoken a word to her.

It was half-full of a blackish substance that smelled, to his experienced nose, of old blood mixed with ambergris and preserving spirits. He turned his head and gagged.

"It's almost over," she whispered. "This is the worst part – the loyalty test. Those masked men expect you to fail. They want to see your throat slit. But you won't fail me. Not this time."

Roger managed to take the cup in hand, making every effort not to inhale. He squeezed his eyes shut and swallowed the entirety in three gulps. He very nearly retched. When the substance hit his stomach, he felt the fizz of some alchemical reaction. Pinpricks spread throughout his body until the underside of his skin itched worse than measles. Yet to scratch, he'd have to flay himself alive.

The archbishop clapped his hands and beamed. "You may take the hand of your master and rejoice. You are now and forevermore Straybound reborn."

When Sibet held out her hand, he kissed it desperately, unable to form words, his reason nearly gone. This must be the bewitchment. He felt pulled to her by some primeval urge in his very arteries, deeper than lust. The faintest voice of the man of science within him called out, as if from the bottom of a well. *Your blood has been meddled with, Roger. And not just yours. Blood connects everything: Claudine, Margalotte, even Celeste. They've been meddled with, too. Their blood speckled black. You need to find out how, and why.*

He gulped down air as he regained his bearings. Even bewitchment wouldn't prevent him from catching the Greyanchor Strangler before the murderer struck again. After all, now he had a princess of Myrcnia at his side, even if she hated him.

While Archbishop Tittlebury hunted the sacristy for a book of devotionals to bestow on the new Straybound, Sibylla seated herself on the pew beside Roger. He hunkered in silence, head in hands. The slender nick across her thumb, from drawing the Blood Line on his forehead, reduced years of memories to a scrape. She didn't know which of them had borne it worse – him or her. By looks alone: him.

"Well," she said at last. "It's fortunate our feelings for each other have run their course. Otherwise, this would be an awkward situation. How's your throat?" The sight of what the ritual had done to him made her stomach churn. Still, she'd be steel for them both and treat his Binding to her as nothing more than a paper cut.

"Attached, your merciful highness." He spoke into his hands.

Sibylla slid closer along the bench, unsure if holding the knife to Roger's back or watching him thrash in the air had chased away her resentment. Only a cooling pang remained. "If I know you at all, right now you're cooking up a pot of Dodge's famous rage stew, to be eaten in sullen silence and passive aggression. I hardly blame you, but our emotions won't change our fate." She stared down at the dagger in its sheath – for use at her discretion, the archbishop had advised, should she ever wish to sunder her Straybound's oath.

Roger lifted his chin, his eyes bloodshot, but didn't reply. Had it not been highly inappropriate, Sibylla might have laid a hand on his shoulder. "I suppose there was as much a chance of you rising from graverobber to respectable surgeon as there was for me becoming an architect of embassies." She looked up at Saint Myrtle the Chased being pursued by wolfhounds.

"If only I'd had a chance to do a proper autopsy, then I'd have seen what's been done to them." He seemed to be having a conversation with himself.

Sibylla placed her hand on his thigh, then pulled it away when her face grew hot.

Roger's shoulders tremored as he finished buttoning his shirt. "I'm no Strangler, just some idiot scapegoat, cross my heart. A blighter with bad luck."

"Is that so?" Sibylla stuffed her emotions into a box. This was no space to be vulnerable. "Then, however did we get here?"

"You have to listen to me, Sibet. I may be a resurrectionist by trade, but that don't make me a murderer. At least two women have been done in the same way, and they weren't strangled. They had something put into them, causing peculiar changes to their stomachs. First the chocolate shop owner, then the lady actress, both took ill *before* they was strangled. If they was strangled at all. Now a doxy is dying at St Colthorpe's with similar symptoms. I've examined her blood and it's a horrific black syrup. Contaminated, I'm sure."

When she didn't grant him the reaction he wanted, he cut off his medical diatribe with a frustrated wave of his hands.

"See, there's the rub. There is no simple explanation. No constable in his right mind would listen to my madman's rant. But if you don't help me, there'll be more murders. The Strangler must have his reasons – or hers. And I mean to find out what they are."

Sibylla unsheathed her knife and studied Roger's eyes. She wouldn't give up either. Even if she never impressed the queen, she could still answer two prayers.

Claudine Walston, Margalotte Remley, Emma Jane. A litany of victims, and Sibylla, in consigning all related records to the sacred flames, had erased all but their names from their headstones. Someone had invented a wraith and framed Roger as the Greyanchor Strangler. When the real culprit murdered again, he'd inspire a horrific new ballad: The Throat Mangler or Corpse Lover. Whip up a public frenzy about some killer on the loose, and facts were no longer facts. Who cared if things didn't add up, so long as a suitable miscreant got what he deserved?

Well, she cared – for Mabel, and that other shopgirl, and the poor Straybound sitting next to her.

"Well, I didn't think you'd entirely lost your mind." Sibylla stared at her gold knife. "I'm not doubting your prowess at sleuthing, but any drunkard off the street would have worked as a scapegoat. There must be some reason you were arrested for Claudine Walston's murder. She wasn't the first victim, or the last. Even if you don't know it, she's the reason you became the Greyanchor Strangler. Whatever possessed you to dig her up?"

She'd read the court records out loud before setting them ablaze in the "sacred cleansing fire," but they'd only given evidence of Roger's guilt, including his alleged defilement of Ms Walston's corpse – scandalous like some winkle tale, but hardly an investigation.

"We don't all have a train of servants jumping to our every wish. Medical schools need stiffs, and a resurrectionist needs cash. I didn't dirty my hands unearthing her, though. A crypt without night guards is easiest for a lone wolf like me."

Sibylla wrinkled her nose. "You really must take care, Dodge. Claudine was interred with her husband. As in buried in the ground, beneath the dirt." She closed her eyes to remember the detail from the court paperwork. "Plot 715: Claudine, wife of Daniel Walston – strangled and buried beside her beloved husband."

"I think I'd remember digging her out of the ground," Roger snapped. He seemed to realize his insolence and lowered his eyes. "Your highness. She weren't buried as a Walston either."

Sibylla's fingers twitched, and an inky bee floated up between the pews. Roger stared at it, mesmerized. "Now that is strange." She flicked a second bee into the air. "Placed in a grave that wasn't her own, and 'resurrected' by an unlucky gravesnatcher." Another bee drifted up. "I'd swear I was reading a Salston play. And that hatpin you sent me, and which I politely returned. It belonged to her?"

Roger split the bee with his fingertip and studied the ink on his fingers. "I didn't lie. Not about that. She weren't the only one. I saw one on another blonde lass. An actress, pretty as jam and laid out on a bed of lilies."

Margalotte. Sibylla dispersed a bee, and sent its two halves floating in opposite directions. Margalotte Remley, an actress of repute, understudied the role of Madam Barstowe, first made famous by Dame Angeline.

"If I may speak plainly, your highness… Why do fine ladies insist on taking valuables to the grave? It's a waste and causes undue temptation for the resurrectionist. Better in the pockets of paupers, if you ask me." With a solemn dip of his head, he added, "Assuming there are no orphaned daughters to inherit." He winced as he wound his cravat around his throat, where the silk noose had left a red line.

"Let me help." Sibylla took the ends of his cravat from his hands and tied an elegant knot. "You've given me an idea. Those women, I believe they share one person in common *besides* the Greyanchor Strangler."

"You mean that salon lady, don't you? Dame Angeline." Roger combed his fingers through his hair. "It's true Claudine and Margalotte worked there before. And… someone else I know. It's possible all the Greyanchor's victims do."

"Then it's time I see this salon for myself." Sibylla swiped the last bee from the air. "There may be no hope for either of us. You and I are like poor Myrtle up there, our fates are sealed, but I'm not going to ignore this. Dead women don't wander into stranger's crypts without a helping hand. And if both these women were Angeline girls, then maybe…" Sibylla's voice trailed off. Perhaps she had recited one too many declamations, or awakened some undiscovered desire within her. For once, she wanted to crush someone else.

Harrod and Archbishop Tittlebury met them in the vestibule where Harrod presented Roger with crimson livery fitted with gold lace and tail pleats, and the archbishop handed him a gilded book of devotionals. Roger's ineffectual attempt to hide his grimace with a bow aside, Sibylla's thoughts returned to the strangler stalking the streets of Caligo, a pit of culpability settling in her knotted stomach.

The archbishop placed his hand on Roger's head. "Now my lad, for each morning of the year, you must recite a specific vow from this book. The recitation will invite her highness to grace you with Her divine and precious blood. You mustn't fall lax on your duties or divine punishment shall be Her will."

Roger nodded, looking flummoxed.

"He means you'll die," Harrod helpfully interjected.

Roger appeared unconvinced, so Sibylla lay a hand on his shoulder and lowered her voice in his ear. "It's not the devotionals so much as the schedule. You must keep to it or else the Binding will kill you."

"That bewitchment." He pulled at his cravat, and his lip curled. "I'll reckon it's just poison, and she supplies the antidote."

Archbishop Tittlebury sucked in his breath. "Young man, Lady

Sibylla is a divinity. Divine beings do not poison their subjects." He turned to Sibylla. "Your highness may have need of that dagger within the next few days. I do suggest you keep it upon your person until this instrument fully accepts his deliverance."

"Your grace is too kind." Sibylla glared at Roger darkly. She had no interest in eliciting a pious tirade from the ancient archbishop, who smiled brightly before asking, "Will your highness do me the honor of a dance at tomorrow's ball? I shall be wearing my holy hat, as it were, and these vestments tend to intimidate the young ladies."

"It would be my pleasure." Sibylla had nearly forgotten the Royal Heritage Ball, and after this morning's breakfast would have preferred not to attend. However, if she intended to stay in Caligo, she couldn't upset the queen. Even Harrod had been roped into some sort of security detail. Still, the real Greyanchor Strangler wouldn't politely wait out a formal dance before striking again. In the meantime, Sibylla would do all she could to find him.

She gestured for Roger to follow as Harrod took her arm to escort her down the steps leading to the street below.

"All affairs in order, then?" Harrod raised one curious eyebrow. "I thought it might take a bit longer."

"Perhaps you'd like a Straybound of your own?" Sibylla prodded Harrod with the hilt of her dagger. "I'm sure you can find another princess to subdue."

"Sounds like a lot of bother. I'll settle for making it through the ball."

Behind her, Roger made a sound almost like a growl. His eyes drilled into his brother's back – no doubt biting his tongue with enormous effort. He didn't seem to know how lucky he was to have a brother who'd merrily lie on his behalf.

Not to mention, she'd be the one enduring physical hardship – bleeding herself once a day so he could live – and for years to come. Yet by the look on Roger's face, he suffered alone. The resentment she'd buried bubbled up. She, too, wanted to sulk. Except no amount of wringing would undye this wool. Perhaps if she handled her own heart, then she could manage his.

"What do you say, Roger?" She'd keep her composure in the face of this mare's nest. "Meet any good chaps in prison for Harrod to take on?"

"I wouldn't wish this on my worst enemy," Roger muttered. "Not even my brother."

"No one's having a good time here," she said, but Roger remained sullen. Well, she was no tyrant. This could be a true rebirth. Even innocent men deserved benevolence. "I always liked seeing you at your studies. We can start them up again. A new name, a new life. Why don't you visit your garret one last time, and pack up any possessions you wish to keep? If the guards give you trouble, bare the tattoo on your neck."

"No one is changing my good name," said Roger with a snarl.

"Your highness can't mean to allow…" Harrod trailed off as her eyes darkened to express how little patience she had for his opinion on the matter.

Sibylla loosely shrugged. "Drop the name change if you must, Roger, but I expect you to return with your pixie ward."

"I can try, your highness. I don't exactly own her."

"Still not clear on the Straybound thing, hm?" Perhaps she should have Dorinda explain things to him. How sordid. She sighed. "Just retrieve your ward and meet me at my chambers before breakfast tomorrow. I dine at seven with my family. You can arrive with the tea at half past six and do your morning devotional."

"Don't be late," added Harrod gravely. "Or you'll invoke the dreaded Straybound Curse. You'll find yourself begging to be locked in my coal room, should that happen."

"Enough. I swear you two are nearly as ridiculous as my cousins," Sibylla snapped. "But yes, Roger, don't be late. This won't be like your old writing lessons where I punished tardiness with a run to Beadle Street for pickled whelks and a slap on the wrist."

After Roger bowed himself from their presence, Harrod paced back and forth, searching for the cab he'd sent a messenger boy to summon. He adjusted his hat no less than four times and dug the heel of his boot into the steps like he couldn't contain himself. "He'll need tighter supervision, your highness. Mark my words. You'll be asking me to drag him back to you by afternoon tea tomorrow, but I'll be buried in security meetings and Khalishkan dignitaries."

"Let us hope not," Sibylla said. "For all our sakes."

29

Roger felt like an interloper amid the daytime bustle. He banished thoughts of Straybound curses and crowds as he hurried toward the hospital, and Ada. What were the chances Celeste had survived the night? The detached surgeon part of him knew – not likely. He'd failed to cure his first real patient, blundering unprofessional fool that he was. But even with Dr Lundfrigg's help, he had no positive diagnosis for her malady. There was only one thing left to do: perform a postmortem examination. Perhaps he could still save others.

A pair of women with parasols eyed him askance. He glanced at his reflection in a window and saw a roughed-up rogue with bloodshot eyes, clad incongruously in fine crimson livery. With trembling hands, he removed his gaudy coat and offered it to a bewildered passing youth in exchange for his threadbare jacket. At least now he fit in with his surroundings.

Chill air filled his lungs and soothed his throbbing head. Pangs of nausea accompanied foggy memories of a golden dagger and the scuff of his knees on stone. Once, catching a glimpse of the princess in a sweetshop advertisement, a rush of gratitude for her sent him staggering into a gentleman passerby. That elixir of blood must have addled him good. Damn faerie magic.

He leaned against the facade of a medical instruments shop, his cap pulled low, and eyed the front of St Colthorpe's. Sibet had told him to fetch Ada, so fetch her he would. She hadn't expressly forbidden him from performing autopsies on the side.

The night-shift physician must have reported last night's skirmish, for a pair of constables flanked the entryway. Crossing the street, Roger headed for the back alley. The hospital's rear corridors wouldn't be as closely watched. If he was lucky, Dr Lundfrigg would be doing his morning rounds. Once Roger explained himself, the royal physician would surely call off the police. Perhaps he'd even lend Roger a scalpel and his microscope.

Roger slipped through the hospital's rear morgue entrance. A pair of stiffs lay under sheets on slabs. A quick check proved neither were Celeste, though both bore tags with instructions for burial: an adolescent boy to be given a third-class funeral by his surviving family, and an unclaimed old woman, destined to be buried in a sack at the Tenderbone Interment Ground for paupers. By Roger's reckoning, the stiffs were worth nine and seven shells, respectively. Remembering Ada, he pulled himself away.

Roger traversed the maze of corridors, ducking into doorways at the slightest noise. Approaching the women's annex, he was five paces from the ward door when it opened. The sight of a blue uniform stopped Roger in his tracks. A constable emerged with a truncheon tucked under one arm, followed by the same young physician from the night-shift, bleary-eyed and stubble-faced, but with no apparent injuries from their row.

"That's him," shrilled the physician, pointing at Roger. "The man from my report."

Roger backed away, intending to run, and collided with the solid chest of an orderly who had come up behind him. Hands like forceps gripped Roger's shoulders. The strong-armed orderly regularly held down unwilling surgical patients and knew what pressure points to employ.

"You sure you recognize him, Dr Foley?" asked the constable. His thick muttonchops extended to his chin.

"Without a doubt." Dr Foley rubbed the side of his head where Roger had cuffed him earlier. "He assaulted me when I thwarted his criminal intentions last night. Back to take care of unfinished business, are you?"

The constable approached Roger, halting close enough that the toes of their boots nearly touched.

"You do look familiar," said the constable, and Roger recognized him from his arrest at Eldridge's. "I've nicked you before."

"Oh, I'll wager he's a bodysnatcher," said the physician with a nasty grin. "Might even be the Greyanchor Strangler's apprentice."

Roger raised his hands in protest, wishing he'd socked the young doctor in the eye when he'd had the chance. The orderly pushed Roger face-first against the wall so the constable could pat him down.

A calm came over Roger. All the nooses in the world couldn't scare him now. He pressed his palms against the brick while that gloating weasel of a doctor looked on. By now a second constable and a small crowd of hospital staff had come to gawk. Where was Dr Lundfrigg?

"What do you have to say for yourself?" asked the first constable.

"Ain't the royal physician here?"

Dr Foley crossed his arms. "Never came in to relieve me. Must be held up at Malmouth."

"I've a girl what depends on me." Roger mustered his confidence and continued, "Her mother's ill, yet I were booted from the premises for attending her."

"You were a person of suspicion in a restricted area," retorted Dr Foley. "The girl was but a convenient alibi."

Roger ignored him and addressed the two constables. "You can take me away after I've seen her. She'll be in that ward there."

The physician spat. "You mean the feral beast who swung a curette at a nurse and nearly gouged out an eye? I locked the horrid creature in a linen cupboard."

Roger clenched his jaw and craned his neck to look the man in the eye. "You pisspot."

Dr Foley turned to the constables. "I want slander and libel added to his assault charges. He has a prison brand on his neck. I saw it."

Roger pounded his fist on the brick. "Go bugger a goat." Ada would be safest at the palace, if only he could get her there. If he made a big enough scene, Dr Lundfrigg would have to get involved. "Is this what you're looking for?" Ripping off his cravat, he bared his wounded neck and raised his chin so that little prick and the constables could get an eyeful. "If I'm to be arrested for drubbing a tosser like that who abuses a grieving child, I'd like to at least black his lamps first."

Roger braced himself, expecting the orderly to smash his face against the wall. Silence. One of the constables stepped forward to make the orderly release Roger's shoulders. Roger gaped at the lawmen, who bore sheepish looks.

"Our sincerest apologies," said the first constable, and shooed the orderly away. "We won't detain you any longer, sir."

Roger shook his head in disbelief.

"What are you doing?" Dr Foley cut in. "Why aren't you arresting him?"

The second constable tipped his helmet to Roger. "A good day to you," he said, and slipped away.

"Have you lost your bleeding mind?"

The remaining constable coughed to get Roger's attention. "I believe you said you were going to 'black his lamps,' sir?"

What witchcraft was this? Roger touched his neck. During his probation he'd taken care to bandage and hide his mark, for fear he'd be turned in and executed. But the constables had no interest in arresting him after his Binding. Apparently a Straybound had much more authority than a prisoner on parole. Sibet had said they did dirty work for royals, legal and otherwise, and were an abuse of royal authority. Still, Roger didn't care to pass up his newfound powers. The constable prodded the equally confounded young doctor in Roger's direction with his truncheon.

Such an opportunity might never come again. Roger spat into his hand and wound up for a wallop.

Dr Foley winced and raised his hands in self-defense. At the last second, Roger pulled his punch and let his arm drop to his side. He couldn't hit a physician like this, even if the man deserved it.

"Show me to the cupboard where you locked the girl. The sergeant here will come along."

Roger re-tied his cravat. So this was how being Straybound worked. Maybe shop owners would give him free pies if he flashed his neck their way. Or he might steal one, and the constables would pretend it never happened. A dishonest man could murder as he pleased. Roger shuddered. Imagine if he'd really been the Greyanchor Strangler. Still, there had to be a catch. His bewitchment, as far as he could tell, relied on Sibet. Just the thought of pleasing her warmed his blood. Bewitchment? No, he'd always felt that way.

He hadn't the time to wrap his head around Straybound particulars. He would ask Sibet in the morning at his devotional – that frightful yet unavoidable ritual. But for now he had bigger eels to pickle.

Dr Foley, his face glistening with sweat, led Roger and the constable down an adjacent corridor. The constable hung back, deferring to Roger with a meekness unusual for the law.

"She's in there." Dr Foley pointed. "The back of the storeroom."

"Poor thing," said a nurse, heading for the storeroom with a stack of linens. "We chased her into the cupboard there an' locked it. We had no choice. Kept screaming and carrying on, she did. Nearly took out my eye."

Roger took a breath and placed an ear to the door. All was quiet. He knocked.

"Ghost? You in there?" He tried the door, but it was locked.

"Dr Foley has the key," said the nurse.

He patted his pockets. "Not anymore. I told her I'd toss it out a window if she didn't shut her trap."

Even the constable looked ready to punch him.

"She tried to stab my foot with a trocar. If you had seen–"

The cupboard doors rattled, accompanied by a high-pitched wail.

"Stay calm, Ghost," Roger called out. "I'm here. You'll be free in two shakes."

A faint whimper answered.

The constable offered up his truncheon to bash in the door, but Roger turned it down. Another cupboard with glass doors held cases of surgical instruments. He selected one ivory-handled knife with a thin, angled blade similar in shape to the hooked lock pick in his personal collection.

"This should do it. Won't brain her by accident, neither. Now leave me," he told the constable. "And if you book that man there for assault, I won't complain to no one."

The constable doffed his hat and led the doctor away by the arm.

The lock proved little hindrance to an expert like Roger who'd cracked crypts with far better security. He jiggered the door, half-afraid of what he'd find inside.

Light from the window cast a pale triangle into the cupboard. Shredded gauze and linen lay tangled with a broken broom handle and a ripped surgeon's apron. For a moment, Roger thought Ada must have escaped. She'd curled herself so tightly that at first he mistook her for a crumpled wad of bandages.

Roger crouched and reached a tentative hand toward her. But she didn't launch at him with teeth bared. She did worse. She lay still.

He could guess what had become of Ada's mother in his absence, but couldn't think of how to comfort the girl. Had she been locked in here for nearly a day? Guilt sat heavy as a tumor in his chest.

He took her hand. "Come on, then. Let's get you home." Home? The garret, of course. Taking her to the palace would be unthinkable in her current state. But he had until tomorrow morning. Ada would need some time alone with some charcoal for drawing, or perhaps a pickled pig's heart to chop to bits.

"They took her," Ada wept. She pushed away his hand. "They took her away."

"They take us all away, at some point." Roger loathed the usual niceties overheard at funerals. *She's in a better place. Her soul has found rest. Saint Mildred has led her to the quiet seas.* He could never bring himself to speak such rot. "Our world has been around longer than you could imagine. Your ma lived in her time and you live in yours. You both lined up for a good nine years. What are the chances of that, in all of human time? Near impossible. Count yourself lucky."

Ada threw herself on him and sobbed into his chest. He sat and held her until the sobs changed to dry, heaving breaths.

"Roger," she whispered in his ear. It was the first time she'd said his real name. "A man came and took her. Said she were headed to a pauper's grave on account of having no family as could pay. They chased me off. I tried…" She swallowed a sob. "Roger, when the man took her away, she were *still alive*."

"She was in her last hours. Sometimes they look alive still, right after. But there was nothing anyone could do." Roger stared at the tiny square storeroom window, his thoughts a stew of undercooked scraps. Ada still seemed to be in denial. He should have stayed with her. "We don't like letting go of people we love. Sometimes we tell ourselves tales when we see things we don't want to believe–"

"It ain't no tale. She were alive."

Roger thought it best not to disagree. Besides, something didn't add up. The body would have been taken to the hospital morgue, but he'd seen the stiffs for himself, and neither was Celeste. One of them had also been destined for the pauper's burial plot, but the man who drove the cart would only make a trip every few days. Some rival resurrectionist could have taken Celeste, but that, too, didn't add up. Why take her when the young male corpse with barely a blemish would have fetched a higher price?

"I know a sack-'em-up man don't care much for feelings," Ada said, wiping snot from her nose. "You'll think it's rubbish. But I wanted to put her next door to Sir Bentley Morris. In the empty velvet-lined coffin where I used to sleep."

Roger squeezed her hand. "Well, I have all night, and certain professional knowledge. I'll find her for you." Roger had already some idea of where to look.

"And if you get caught? They'll hang you proper this time, sack-'em-up man. And then... I won't have no one."

Roger rose to his feet and brushed himself off. "Don't you worry about that, Ghost. I'm... well, let's just say I've built up an immunity to hanging. So long as I've finished by dawn tomorrow."

"You're daft, you are," Ada snuffled into the sleeve of her worn dress but showed the first signs of a smile.

Roger lifted Ada onto her feet. "I'll set out after dark, some time near midnight just to be safe. You head off to Mrs Carver's, cut up some meat if it makes you feel better. Then go scrounge up a candle or two, and some flowers to pay our respects, and I'll meet you outside Sir Bentley Morris' crypt when the bells of St Myrtle's strike two."

30

Lieutenant Calloway grumbled all the way to Dame Angeline's salon. As the carriage bounced and creaked along a stretch of old cobblestone road, Sibylla caught wisps of his muttered objections: "such an indecorous endeavor… impossible to bring a princess there… she's being too cruel," and a particularly shrill, "ruined by foreign influence!" Sibylla knew her ploy to enlist his aid hadn't been above board, but then she'd never asked the man to profess his love in ink. Besides, there were lives at stake.

Personal correspondence made for fine blackmail. As it turned out, Lieutenant Calloway had *not* considered what his father General Calloway, a close friend to the crown prince, would make of his son's love letter to Prince Edgar's intended. The moment it dawned on him that Sibylla aimed to show his beautifully penned correspondence to his father, his brazen veneer melted into blubbering protestations. He'd be flogged, beheaded, or worse – disowned! Once he'd wiped his tears on a silk handkerchief, he agreed to help her enter Dame Angeline's salon.

Sibylla insisted she only wished to see inside the salon out of curiosity, yet he continued stewing. This would not do.

"Do you remember what Mr Counselvice says to the barnmaid after he rescues her from the opera singer?"

"Sorry for the intrusion. This'll only take an intermission," answered Lieutenant Calloway, adopting a waggish accent.

She knew it! He *had* read her Salston plays, and probably kept them stashed inside his trunk. She clapped the side of his arm as if a fellow cavalryman. "Come along then, man. We'll be back in time for your evening calisthenics. Just be your cheerful self."

Arriving at the salon, Sibylla alighted from the cab assisted by Lieutenant Calloway in all his gold-braided crimson finery. Now she only required the lieutenant's formal introduction to Dame Angeline.

"Welcome to Dame Angeline's Salon, the diamond in Brocade Circle's crown," said the servant who took their coats and hats at the door.

Though she had yet to be recognized about town, Sibylla had rouged her lips, brushed her eyelashes with soot, then borrowed a dress from one of the maids. Pale ink freckles dotted her nose and cheeks to further obfuscate her appearance, and she wore her hair loose like some country ingenue.

"I say," Lieutenant Calloway called out to no one in particular. "I've brought a young duck with me. She has potential running out of her like grease from a pear-mince pudding. To whom must we speak, the dame herself? We demand an audience!"

Though the lieutenant had sworn he'd only visited the salon once or twice, women filtered out of the adjoining rooms to greet him. A lady dressed like a chrysanthemum in yellow ruffles beckoned them to follow. As they glided along the corridor, familiar voices cackled from inside one of the drawing rooms. She glanced through the door. Her cousins Edmund and Edward lounged in settees, attended to by cheerful young women.

"Should Dame Angeline accept you, beware of the princes," said the chrysanthemum matter-of-factly. "They particularly like new flowers. As regular as the fogs of Caligo, those two."

Her cousins would make terrible sport of finding Sibylla here, no doubt informing Grandmother straightaway. She hurried past to avoid them. She didn't need to give the queen any more reasons to doubt her worth. When they finally ascended the stairs to the salon's upper floor, Sibylla was thankful to leave the sound of her cousins' laughter below.

Sibylla and Lieutenant Calloway entered a plush sitting room forested with ferns and potted ficus. Paintings in gilded frames, of bare women draped suggestively in vibrant silks, adorned the walls.

"Ah, Lieutenant Calloway. One of our favored guests." A long-legged, handsome woman stood to greet them. Folds of black and crimson satin sloped around her body so that she looked almost volcanic. A pendant hung suspended from her throat. "You've brought me a protégée? Whatever flight of fancy possessed you to think you had an eye for spotting jewels?"

Lieutenant Calloway hesitated, looking to Sibylla first, then answered. "Isla here is my second cousin thrice removed... and she begged me to."

"She begged you, did she?" Angeline gave Sibylla a knowing wink. "Isla, was it?"

Sibylla curtsied. "Isla Lindley."

"I'm unsure what he told you, but we are most particular about the breeding of our girls, Isla." A familiar peach-blossom hatpin affixed her little feathered hat to her swept-up hair. "Even with a gentleman's introduction, there is no guarantee of admittance to our salon."

"I understand."

Angeline scrutinized Sibylla's body, dress, and posture. Thankfully her discerning eye could not read minds. "Have you no dowry? Is your father destitute from playing the ponies? Or have you perhaps suffered a compromising situation with a low-class lover?"

How many unfortunate girls came to this woman because they hadn't the means to go elsewhere? Sibylla forced a smile. "I'm the youngest of seven, mistress, and but one of my sisters is married. I no longer wish to be a burden on my family."

Angeline nodded. "A thoughtful sentiment. I can tell you if you pass the physical exam – and very few do – you'll need to work on that posture. With your crooked shoulders and sagging back, you'd be booted from the royal court in an instant. In my salon, the girls must give the impression of royalty. They must convince each client he is entertained by – no, in love with and hopefully marrying – nothing less than a princess. Although I will say, your imitation of a North Caligoan parlance is nearly passable. Did someone tutor you?"

Sibylla nodded in the direction of Lieutenant Calloway.

"Ah, of course. Now I'd like a moment alone with Isla. There may follow some discussion of delicate matters."

Lieutenant Calloway glanced questioningly at Sibylla. Hiding a hand behind her back so Angeline wouldn't see, she shooed him off. "I shall be quite all right," she said. "But don't go too far."

After the lieutenant had left, Angeline closed the door to the parlor. She circled Sibylla, raking her with her eyes. Still, her examination proved bearable. Sibylla had endured far worse under the queen's gaze.

"Do you know what makes my salon girls so special?" Angeline lifted a tress of Sibylla's hair to inspect its texture and weight.

This was probably a bad time to bring up the deaths of Claudine and Margalotte. She shook her head no.

Angeline moved behind Sibylla to clasp her waist with both hands. A strong centifolia perfume filled the air. "My girls promote sophisticated conversation and diversions among educated gentlemen and ladies." Her fingers crept up Sibylla's stomach. "That is no small part of it, but we cater to gentlemen, not ladies, and men crave the exotic and rare." With a quick, practiced movement she squeezed Sibylla's breasts. "Good, good."

Sibylla jumped, then caught her breath. This wasn't entirely new – seamstresses and lady's maids had done no better, in her experience. Now Angeline took her hand and pried her fist open. She should mention Claudine now lest this farce go further.

Before she could make up her mind, Angeline whipped the hatpin from her hair and pricked the pad of Sibylla's finger. Sibylla cried out more from shock than pain as a red bead appeared on her skin.

Angeline wrapped Sibylla's bleeding finger in white raw silk, then replaced her hat and pin. After a moment, Angeline removed the silk and rolled it into a small fabric scroll. She retrieved a vial of clear liquid from an apothecary cabinet, then slid the silk inside the vial. After placing it on the table, she settled herself gracefully on the divan.

"Please come sit, my dear." Angeline patted the cushion. "You have somewhat more potential about you than I first surmised, though that posture of yours makes me wince. However, I warn you that nothing is promised. Your wit and talent count for little here if you don't have the right blood in your veins."

Sibylla studied the vial on the table. "What are you looking for?" If all Angeline's girls had passed this test, then so had Claudine. What *was* so special about them that they'd attracted the attention of the strangler?

The liquid in the vial turned a powder blue, and the corners of Angeline's mouth curled into a smile. "A hundred girls may walk through that door, but rarely is more than one of them asked to remain. You, my dear Isla, are the exception. There is magic in your veins."

Sibylla laughed. "Some charlatan must have taken you in. Only the church understands the intricacies of divine bloodlines. There is no test for magical gifts. And there never has been." Which was why male bastards with half a mind could hide their talents and not be thrown down the well.

Angeline snapped her fingers. "You misunderstand. I'm not saying you *are* a princess. Conventional wisdom holds that either one *is* or *is not* magicked, and you'd catch the royal eye if you had any talent to produce sparklers or rust. Should that happen, you'd soon find you might not have a head. That is true for men. But with us, you see, there's a third type: outwardly mundane, yet magicked within. Girls like you." Dame Angeline lifted the vial off the table. "And this tells me you're unlike most."

"I've always wondered how this particular establishment is so remarkably popular with the gentlemen, when there are plenty of others like it in neighboring streets. But even if this… test is true, one cannot bottle magic in a vial. What good would it be locked away inside of a girl?"

"We Myrcnian women must play the social game. We must be married. And, with the right credentials, we might even gain class, rank, or wealth. A girl like yourself with latent talent, should she marry a gifted man, may produce gifted children. But such women are difficult to find, and genealogy lists are not as accurate as one might like. Magic travels in the blood. Latent or not, it is now detectable. The nobleman bachelor need no longer chance an unmagical pairing, and subsequent loss of title, as here exists a marketplace where he might find a lovely, accomplished wife to bear the offspring he desires. These days even the professional class of men desires quality women like ourselves, though they hardly benefit. We are quite the fad."

Now Sibylla realized what made Claudine special; a nobleman with magic, should he take a wife here, could be assured of magicked offspring. Harrod's mother, a palace chambermaid, must have been like these Angeline girls. Her son Harrod had inherited his father's magic, while Roger, the son of a cook, had none.

Sibylla pointed to the vial in her hand. "And you use *that* to see which mares to breed."

Angeline tsked. "Really, what Highspits cheese farm did you spring from? You poor thing. Yes. Isn't it wonderful? Aren't we blessed to live in such modern times?"

Sibylla didn't think this miracle test originated from modern times so much as a singular modern man. Her jaw clenched. "Does the queen know you perform these tests?"

"Her royal majesty would lump us in with those unfortunate women who only ply the trade between their legs." Angeline's face tightened. "She's an old biddy, but a formidable one. Fortunately, we have our own supporters in the royal family, the least of whom are the young princes you might have seen downstairs."

"What other supporters? Lady Esther? Crown Prince Elfred?" Sibylla asked. Then so as not to sound too obvious, she added, "Lady Brigitte?"

Angeline gave a deep, throaty laugh. "When you've earned your place, perhaps I might tell. Really, are all country girls as suspicious as you? Or have you heard one too many tales of the Greyanchor Strangler?" She stood up to ring the bell. "I'll have one of my grisettes prepare a contract…"

Sibylla had played her part long enough. She needed to confirm if her suspicions were correct on who had provided Angeline with her liquid concoctions, and which of her family members knew of its existence.

As Angeline reached for the calling bell, Sibylla grabbed Angeline's wrist. "I must confess that I've met you once before."

Angeline tilted her head in displeasure. "Well, I can't say I remember your face… love." Angeline glared at Sibylla's hand to indicate she expected its removal. When Sibylla didn't let go, she added, "I must have made quite the impression."

Sibylla smiled. "You signed my autograph book after your debut in *The Housewench of the Haunted Hearth*. You wore the most beautiful costume and a pendant much like that one. I expect this one is real, isn't it?"

Angeline's face darkened. "Perhaps I should reconsider my offer. I signed only two autographs that night, one to the owner of the theatre, Sir Lyle, and the other–"

"Looked like this?" Sibylla's fingernails blackened as she flexed her fingers, and ink appeared as though Angeline was signing the air: *To my dearest highness, the sweetest drama critic I've ever met, Humbly yours with affection, Angeline Lareine.*

Angeline gaped. "Why this farce? Wait… You've come to elope!" she exclaimed with more animation than her performance of the haunted hearth's demonic fire dance.

Apparently, *everyone* thought Sibylla intended to cause one scandal or another. She may have kissed a kitchen boy once or twice, but she hadn't run off with him. Who did Angeline think she'd come here to run away with?

"Lieutenant Calloway?"

Angeline clasped Sibylla's hand and squeezed. "I know a man who can arrange safe sea passage to Lipthveria. I can conceal your highness here until preparations are made." She sighed. "Ah! To be young and in love with a beautiful boy."

If Sibylla continued letting Angeline helm the conversation, she'd soon find herself sailing the milky seas of Andorna. She interrupted whatever fanciful fiction the salon owner might say next. "Does Dr Lundfrigg provide you with these vials?"

Angeline frowned. "I couldn't say."

Sibylla had suffered Angeline's opinions, her prodding and fondling, and finally her lies. Now she'd reached the end of her patience. She twisted her fingers from the woman's grasp. "Do you know what really makes royal blood so special?"

Angeline took a step back.

"It's the spark, you see," Sibylla said. "My great-grandfather once shattered a man's spine with nothing more than his whistle. And we all know the tale of King Roderick's electric globes that caused fried geese to plummet from the sky. Do you suppose inking and glowing are my only gifts? Or do you refuse to answer my question because you're curious to see what else I can do?"

Angeline seemed to weigh the risk of Sibylla igniting her dress in some oily inferno versus whatever alliances she hid in the wings. Nervously, she adjusted her gown. "Dr Lundfrigg brings me the vials to test the girls, but there's nothing illegal in them."

"And how did you come by this interesting arrangement?" Sibylla prompted. "With the royal physician, no less."

Angeline gave a weary smile. "That's where you're mistaken. He was no royal physician when we met. I first glimpsed him sodden with dew in a field, netting butterflies and foraging for chanterelles. He was merely Finchy then, and I a young girl with an ambition."

Sibylla attempted to imagine Dr Lundfrigg in such a state, but could not. She knew he'd been knighted somewhat recently, after providing some private medical service to the queen. "So he helped you open a salon?"

"He did, and with the science to vouch for my girls," said Angeline proudly. "Only after Lady Esther came looking for him did he become the royal physician. Why she needed him, I know not, nor do I care to learn. He continues to supply me with the means to test my girls, and I'm able to assure the gentlemen who walk through my doors of their premium quality."

Whatever bargain Lady Esther had brought to Dr Lundfrigg had earned his loyalty.

This thoughtless woman before Sibylla showed no concern for the welfare of her wares. Angeline was nothing more than a merchant, trading on the commodity of poor women whose blood happened to turn a clear liquid powder blue. How could she be so callous? Sibylla's jaw tightened. "Lately, their premium quality hasn't brought them old age."

"If your highness is speaking of Margalotte, Dr Lundfrigg did all he could for her. He may be the royal physician, but he still sees to our care. He even asked for a list to check on those who'd left the salon."

So Angeline had given her list to Dr Lundfrigg and thought about it no further. How that led to those women being strangled Sibylla had yet to discover. "I want to see one of those vials," Sibylla said, crossing her arms. As Angeline moved to the apothecary cabinet, she added, "Perhaps two more."

Angeline handed over the vials with a bitter twist to her mouth, then insisted on escorting Sibylla out.

They found Lieutenant Calloway ensconced in a settee with an Angeline girl trying to sit in his lap while the princes plied him with drinks. Sibylla averted her eyes. The thought of sharing a bloodline with those two ninnies made her seethe.

Edmund and Edward squinted up at Sibylla, until Edmund erupted in a fit of giggles.

"You've done it at last, Dame!" Edmund declared. "The spitting image of Weed-eyes."

"Come here, lass," Edward slurred. "I want to see what it's like to kiss my cousin."

"I knew it. I knew you were jealous of Edgar."

"Edgar? That fop wouldn't know the backside of a gilt, let alone our Sibylla."

"Dear me," Angeline cooed. "You boys are fiery today." She seemed to enjoy how Sibylla, unwilling to reveal herself, cringed.

A sudden curiosity struck Sibylla. "Do you ever test the gentlemen?" she whispered to Angeline.

Angeline looked aghast. "Certainly not. They're our clientele. Naturally, we accept men of modest birth with the means to afford our services, but true gentlemen are particularly welcome here."

"But you could. For example, my cousins – you could test them."

"What good would that do? Your blood is as blue as theirs. And furthermore, they are my guests… your highness."

Her cousins pulled at Lieutenant Calloway's sleeve to hold him back when he tried to rejoin her. She needed those two idiots' blood to prove her suspicion. "I understand your salon has a reputation for its thrilling rounds of tallycracker. They say nowhere else compares."

Angeline eyed her shrewdly. "That is so."

"I wouldn't mind viewing a match just once. It may even be worth an invitation to tomorrow's royal ball – I assume you aren't on the invitation list."

"I am not," Angeline answered. Sibylla waited to see whether she would bite. Angeline snapped her fingers and the chrysanthemum appeared. "Anabelle, prepare the table."

Soon a four-legged oak table had been moved to the middle of the drawing room, its surface polished and slick, while one of the girls shuffled the special deck of cards. Lieutenant Calloway found his way to Sibylla's side, eyeing the room as though any moment he'd be reprimanded.

"What's going on?"

"I need you to make sure they bleed," Sibylla whispered, handing him the scuffed wooden chase-puck.

The lieutenant's attention darted to the two youngest princes. "Your highness?" His cheeks colored.

Sibylla grabbed ahold of his scarlet uniform. "Have at it. I'll return your letter, cross my heart, and," she added pointedly, "forget all I've seen here. Or will you let a pair of royal smolts beat you at a man's game?"

Lieutenant Calloway's eyes darkened. "I always win."

31

Roger donned his beaked physician's mask and pulled up his hood against the freezing rain. He leapt the iron fence into the Tenderbone Internment Ground, and scraped at a patch of recently-filled earth where the newest stiffs were buried. What he'd give for the roof of a well-made crypt to protect him from the wind's lash.

A foot of dirt separated the uppermost stiffs from the night air. Tenderbone was not a cemetery so much as a series of trenches packed with corpses in nothing but gunnysack shrouds. The rain had churned the grounds to mud, and Roger's spade revealed its newest additions – a row of small bundled children. He stayed in the trench just long enough to confirm the only adult buried that day was a soot-blackened chimney sweep.

As he clambered out of the trench, he doubled over. No amount of garlic could keep him from retching into the bushes. He must have lost the steel lining in his resurrectionist's stomach from lack of use.

The bell of St Myrtle's Cathedral tolled the hour – one in the morning. He'd promised to meet Ada at Sir Bentley Morris' tomb at two, but so far his search of Tenderbone and Greyweight paupers' grounds had come up empty.

Even if Ada had seen her mother taken away alive, Celeste would not have survived into the night. But suppose someone had a reason for removing her from the hospital before her time? He'd seen one instance of premature burial before – Claudine Walston, another former salon girl from Dame Angeline's. If Claudine hadn't been a Smith, but ended up in a Smith crypt, then maybe Celeste, who wasn't a Smith either, had joined her.

The sunken Dolorous Avenue descended before him. If nothing else, the rain kept the watchmen at home. Down he went, the foliage above him smudging out the sky. The stony fortress of the Smith crypt loomed ahead, its stone queen in command.

"Still the pretty biscuit, you are," he murmured. "If I told you I were made a Straybound, would you give up your secrets?"

The statue proved too coy to respond.

Roger had left his good lockpick set at Harrod's, but he'd scrounged an old torsion wrench and half-diamond pick from his garret. The second cracking of a lock always went easier than the first, and the crypt's mechanism gave way in less than a minute under Roger's expert manipulation.

Fishing his last shriveled bit of garlic from his pocket, he placed the clove between his teeth. The crypt door swung outward. He held his hooded lamp aloft and peered into the dark, half-expecting to see Ghostofmary emerge, floured and coal-faced. The interior of the crypt appeared similar to his memory: dusty caskets stacked to the ceiling, the older embellished elm boxes toward the back and newer ones of cheap pine near the front. Claudine's coffin was still sealed like he'd left it, but now an identical coffin lay stacked on its lid.

A third new pine box sat next to it, open and with its lid propped upright against one of the stacks. Roger craned forward. Except for a thin layer of sawdust at the bottom, this coffin lay empty.

He sunk his teeth through the clove of garlic. "May the were-bats that screech in the burial vaults fly to dust in the face of reason," he whispered. The mask muffled his voice, which veered into falsetto when something brushed his hand. He jumped, nearly knocking over the propped-up lid.

Cobwebs.

He felt like an idiot as he flapped his arms anyway.

Who – or what – might be in that coffin on top of Claudine's? The wood was pale and fresh.

Roger set down his lamp. It cast just enough dull orange light for him to find the cheap metal rings nailed into the sides of the coffin. He swung the unwieldy box to the floor without too much of a ruckus.

"Please be Celeste."

Taking a pair of iron nippers from his coat, he prised the nails from the lid until he could wrench it up a few inches. He'd have submitted to another Straybound hanging for just one swig of gin.

A fruity stink nearly knocked him down, despite his mask. At first he saw only darkness within. Then he noticed a constellation of tiny glowing lights, pinkish through the lenses of his mask, in the center of the dark. He jimmied the lid open further.

Lamplight fell on the thing within, and Roger struggled not to scream. He thrust the nippers forward, in case it leapt at his face.

The remains of a blonde-haired woman lay inside, her face sunken from a week of decay, her eyes empty sockets. The lips curled back from her teeth in a frozen scream. Her red burial gown tented up at the abdomen, and through the fabric glowed dim points of light – the "constellation" he'd seen.

Just as he'd suspected. The dead women's insides held the secret.

His hands shook as he opened his clasp knife to slit the fabric in a long, horizontal line as if conducting some macabre surgery. Mushroom caps – glowing with blue and green light – sprung from the incision in the gown. He recoiled with a shout. Their tall, slender stalks had pierced through her dead skin like needles.

Roger slammed the lid and darted for the crypt door. Hands on knees, he drew deep, cleansing breaths of damp night air. At last he righted himself. He had seen that stiff before. Lady Margalotte the actress, with her lengthy will stipulating no fewer than ten mutes, looking more asleep than dead in a fancy elm coffin. How had she come to be interred here?

Roger had helped bury her in a plot up on the ridge. He'd seen Nail install a mortsafe. He hadn't managed to resurrect her himself, but apparently someone else had.

But he had no time to worry about it now. Not while Ada waited for him. Roger planned to open every one of the Smith crypt's dozen residences until he found her mother. Claudine's came next. This one should be empty – he'd already robbed it once.

But no. Claudine lay inside, bare and lying on top of the clothing Roger had stripped during that first job. He recognized the plaiting of her hair, and the marks about her neck, but like Margalotte her eyes were dark holes. She seemed to have shriveled and dried, and the cavity from her sternum to her pelvis was a hollowed pit of mangled organ sections.

But Roger noticed one very important difference. Unlike Lady Margalotte's corpse, Claudine had only a single glowing mushroom cap growing from her withered abdomen. And, judging by the dead stems that wilted nearby, it was clear that the rest… had been harvested?

This human mushroom-patch was by far one of the oddest things he'd ever observed as a surgeon. But the mushrooms made a kind of sense. All those divots in their stomachs, that had become bumps, had burst forth with glowing mushrooms. The strangler had done these women in and hidden them away so that no one would know of the gardens they'd nourished inside them.

He clamped the coffin lid shut and crouched, trying to steady his spinning head. How many more of these women would he find? At least two dozen coffins rested here, some old and gilded, the newer ones cheap pine. This frightful collection had been here all along. His hunch was right. The killing didn't matter to the strangler. Only the mushrooms did. And Roger wasn't about to let him reap Celeste.

He picked up his nippers and, in a burst of righteous fury, pried at the nails on the lid of the first pine coffin in the next row back, the only one not in a stack.

He'd determined the gruesome pattern. This would be another wasted garden bed for mushrooms, reduced to bones and dust.

"Bloody hell!" This time, he was wrong.

Before him laid the gaunt, bearded, mummified face of his old master – Mr Grausam of Grausam's Undertaking and Coffining Services. Before he could make any sense of it, a cold breeze swiped his neck. Behind him, the crypt door, which he'd left ajar, creaked. Hefting his iron nippers, Roger turned.

There stood Nail with a corpse-shaped bundle of sacking in his arms, his red hair aflame in the lamplight.

The apprentice – or was he? – wore no mask. With one look into the crypt, Nail dropped the corpse-shaped bundle near the threshold and flew at Roger, brandishing an undertaker's trocar.

"You vault-vacatin' vagabond!" cried Nail, thrusting like a fencer. "I'll perforate yer skull."

Roger dodged Nail's first blow by rolling behind a stack of coffins. His mask fell askew, and clumps of dried herbs from the beak fell into his mouth. He managed to knock the mask back in place before Nail caught up with him. Huffing, the redhead stabbed wildly at the air, but one well-aimed kick from Roger brought him to his knees. Roger scrambled over the apprentice to ensnare him in a headlock, using the iron nippers as a yoke. He tossed his mask to the floor.

"Nail," Roger gasped. "It's me, you daft bastard. Drop your weapon."

The trocar clattered on the stone and rolled away.

Nail raised his hands. "I'd ask what a known resurreck-shnist is doin' in my vault, but I think I know the answer."

"I'm not here to thieve," said Roger, invoking every calming thought to keep from choking the man. "Not in the usual way. But that don't matter. I've seen what you keep 'round here."

By now Nail's face matched the hue of his hair. His nose dripped blood. "Ain't hardly nothin' here of mine. You might say I'm but a landlord."

"Then explain *that*." Roger grabbed a handful of Nail's hair and wrenched his head to the side, forcing him to look at the mummified Grausam. "Or so help me, I'll shove these nippers in your mouth and pull every last tooth I find."

"Steady on, friend." Nail twisted his neck and attempted a grin. "That gentleman there – that sloughed and mortal husk – he buckled you, remember? Sent you straight for Ol' Grim, he did. His own apprentice! You should be pattin' my humble back. Such a busy man he were, always shut up with his books, and me doin' all the filthy labor. No soul has missed him these last months, neither you nor I, so long as I keep up appearances."

"You killed him?"

Nail tried to shrug. "It were a kindness, really. He had the dropsy. The shop would be bankrupt had I not stepped in."

Roger kept his firm hold on Nail's neck. "He were a strict master. Old-fashioned in his views, but honest. Never fobbed off them knot-holed boxes to the poor widows." He kneed Nail in the back. "And what of the girls? They've all got mushrooms growing out of 'em – and I'd be willing to bet if I dug up all the other strangled women, I'd find more of the same. What say you?"

"You're the man of science, so you'll know more about experry-mints than me." Nail's voice had regained energy with the prospect of shunting his captor's fury elsewhere. "I'd have nothin' to do with it, if not for the handsome earnings. Like the humble farmer, I box, I harvest, and I get my pay. He says it's all in the name of reason – you should be the last to fault me fer that."

"Who hired you?"

"Smith, of course. You think he'd give his true name? I just do as I'm paid, an' don't ask no questions."

Nothing Nail said made any sense. Farms? Reason? Roger had to break this stalemate. "Then let's bargain. You give me that bundled stiff you brought–"

"And you'll let me go without surgeonizin' me?"

"Perhaps." Roger pushed Nail away and pocketed the nippers. "But you'll need to tap your terrible memory first."

"You're a good friend, Weathersby." Nail rubbed his neck and thumped Roger's arm with a chummy, sheepish grin.

Roger pulled away. "I'm no friend of yours. You ain't telling me half of what you know. You must see the man who pays and instructs you. What does he look like? Where do you meet?"

"That's no way to question your mate." Nail pulled out his flask and unstoppered it. "Calm down, surgeon-man, and have a drink. I'll answer you when my whistle's wet. To stiffs, to science, to silver coin, an' you not surgeonizin' me."

Roger had no desire to drink to anything Nail might bring forward. "Shove off," he said, and pushed the flask away.

Just as the metal touched his fingertips, Nail whisked the flask in an upward arc, splashing spirits in Roger's eyes. Blinded, Roger lashed out to throttle the redhead, but his assailant had leapt out of the range of his windmilling arms.

Pain sparked along his back – Nail must have jabbed him with the trocar. His overcoat bore the brunt of the attack, or else he'd be breathing blood. Through a hazy lens of tears, he made out Nail's silhouette. Roger lurched forward and tripped on something – Nail's outstretched leg? He tumbled face-first into the empty open coffin. The layer of sawdust mixed with rosemary, meant to sop up putrid fluids, broke his fall.

Then darkness descended with a clap like thunder. Nail had shut the coffin lid.

Roger shouted and kicked and clawed at the sawdust. The steady bam-bam-bam of a hammer answered him. Roger's head grew light, and he panted like an overheated dog. He couldn't even roll onto his back within the narrow space. Wood scraped on stone as Nail dragged one of the other coffins across the floor. A creak, a grunt, the groan of wood…

Nail was stacking the boxed-up corpses on top of him.

"That were your cleverest joke yet, you scab!" Roger shouted into the sawdust. "You hear me laughing? Now let me out."

He writhed in the tight space of a coffin built for a smaller frame, choking on the wood shavings. Nail dragged something across the floor with a scrape. Then the crypt door shut with a clang.

Nail! He had no head for the science but made a perfect accomplice for murder. An undertaker had access to the necropolis and could move stiffs about at his convenience. Nail had brought the murder victims to the Smith crypt, then served as their caretaker. He'd likely told the truth about being paid by a Mr Smith. Some other person – or persons – must be the real Strangler. But as it turned out, Nail *was* just the sort to bury a man alive. Roger's throat tightened as he remembered the look on Claudine's face when he first came upon her, and her coffin's lining torn to shreds.

"Nail!" Roger shouted in one last futile breath. But all had fallen quiet in the crypt beyond.

32

Her morning tea arrived but her Straybound did not. Sibylla, Archbishop Tittlebury, and Harrod had all been clear about the consequence of missing a devotional. Failing to refresh his bonds, by drinking a cup of Sibylla's blood, would result in Roger being struck with divine punishment. The slow and painful process might last a day or two, but always ended the same: death. By now, her family would be enjoying their breakfast of walnut-peppermint scones and poached eggs while Sibylla, pacing anxiously about her room, inked a swarm of bees.

She had set out preparations for Roger's first devotional on the table beside her bed. She'd even arranged for the glass cupping instruments to be warmed. A frightening-looking scarificator with its spring-loaded steel blades sat beside a gold bloodletting bowl with etched lines for measuring. Sibylla fiddled with the mechanism inside the brass box, adjusting the depth to which the blades would cut – just deep enough to breathe the veins.

Archbishop Tittlebury had assured her the royal constitution was made of hardier stuff than that of commoners, but she only partially believed him. Aside from her skin healing quickly after bloodlettings at the chapel, she had no experience with daily benefactions. Supposedly by changing the place they cut weekly, her thumb marking would be her only permanent scar. None of these concerns mattered, however, if Roger intended to run away. Surely he wasn't so stupid.

She squeezed her eyes shut. Though he might groan and protest, she couldn't imagine Roger purposely taking his own life. Another bee escaped her thumb. And yet his innocence, professed or otherwise, didn't change the fact he was Straybound. As such, missing a devotional was its own execution sentence.

To distract herself before she filled her entire room with inked insects, she removed two lacy handkerchiefs from her writing desk, each stained with dried blood. The one with the blue embroidery belonged to Edmund, while the other was Edward's. Or rather, they belonged to the Angeline girls who had wiped the blood from her cousins' faces after Lieutenant Calloway trounced them in tallycracker.

With a pair of silver scissors, she snipped scraps of the bloodied parts from each. She'd intended to wait for Roger, as the man who wanted to be a surgeon might find the strange demonstration interesting, but now she shoved each scrap into a vial of Dr Lundfrigg's clear liquid and waited. And waited. Her own vial had turned powder blue within a few breaths of conversation. Maybe men's blood took longer.

She picked up one of the vials and shook it several times, but the scrap had already dispersed its red traces throughout the liquid without effect. Had Angeline cleverly switched the vials and given Sibylla gin instead? Sibylla took a whiff but detected nothing peculiar. She went to retrieve the scarificator with its six spring-loaded blades for quick, efficient bloodletting. Setting aside the vial, she cocked the blades inside the box. As the sharpened steel razors extended through the narrow slits in its brass body, she deliberately sliced her skin.

Wincing, she held her thumb over the vial. Her blood mingled with the sopping scrap of kerchief inside, and she impatiently waited for the results of her experiment. With every passing second, her pride over yesterday's threats, which had gotten her these vials, dissipated.

Until at last the liquid changed to powder blue. She sank onto her bed, pulling her morning robe tightly around her. So Edmund's blood wasn't like hers, after all. Then, perhaps his mother Lady Esther hadn't the right blood in her veins to begin with. Impossible. All royal marriages were strenuously checked. The church's crypt beneath St Myrtle's, dedicated to meticulous recordkeeping, ensured that, and Lady Esther came from the distinguished Gusets – water blowers who when angered spewed river-like streams from their nostrils. Sibylla had received plenty of her aunt's watery tirades. Yet her imperious and unruly cousins, she'd barely witnessed perform… parlor tricks.

Her cousins were bastards.

She shot up from the bed. Edmund, Edward, Edgar: they never glowed, or sparked, or rusted, not like her. First Edgar's disappointing dinner performance, and now these vials. Lady Esther had had an affair, three by her count, and not with a Calloway or Cornin, either – those sons would have gained magic from their fathers.

Sibylla squeezed the bedpost. Should the queen discover the not-so-magical paternal origins of Sibylla's cousins, she'd never let them inherit the throne. But unless Sibylla wanted to condemn her cousins to death by revealing matters, her grandmother might never know the truth. How could Lady Esther have done this? Myrcnia relied on the magical legitimacy of the Muir line – they'd shepherded the country through famine, snowstorms, and war.

Sibylla dropped her hands in uncertainty.

Unless… All this time Lady Esther and Edgar had insisted on Sibylla marrying her cousin out of tradition, but perhaps they simply couldn't stomach smiting a thousand-year dynasty. Given time, they'd have surely invited a Calloway to bed her.

A brisk knock on the door broke her reverie. She had no time to hide the bloodletting devices that littered her room. Two maids entered carrying a silver dress. Beautiful white silk flowers adorned the skirt, and the sleeves were light and airy like the wings of a dragonfly. She blinked at the brocade bust with its intricate seaming, not quite sure why it had been brought to her room. Then, as if a heavy wooden block had fallen on her chest, she remembered. The Royal Heritage Ball.

The younger maid gasped, noticing Sibylla's collection on the bedside table. She dropped the hem of the gown as she clapped a hand to her mouth. The senior maid, for her part, wore a stoic expression that demonstrated a familiarity with any manner of curious objects. No doubt she'd seen the queen's items kept for Dorinda.

There was no avoiding the dress and ball. And the Muir dynasty could survive another day while a certain wayward Straybound would not.

"I need to speak with the steward straightaway," said Sibylla. The palace steward oversaw the ball's arrangements, and he would know where to find Harrod. And Harrod, Divine Maiden willing, could retrieve Roger before he faced an excruciating death.

The older maid nodded to the younger, who left in a hurry.

"Your headpiece will arrive shortly, ma'am." The maid curtsied. "Lunch will be served in the main dining hall soon, but I could send up a cart if you're otherwise disposed."

"Thank you," Sibylla nodded.

Better to stew in her bedroom than suffer the company of her relations, especially now that she had guessed a certain secret. Little escaped the queen's eyes, yet her cousins remained alive and in line to inherit the crown. Sibylla needed to act with care. While she had no fondness for Edgar, Edmund, or Edward, it was not their fault their mother had strayed, and the bastards' well had no need of more bones. She'd decide her course after she found Harrod. Time pressed. Without his talents, she'd be less one Straybound.

33

Roger lay facedown in a coffin so narrow that his shoulders were wedged between the sides. He had stopped struggling. The pine "eternity box" might be cheap but it wasn't flimsy, and his attempts to kick himself free had left him sweaty and exhausted. Sawdust filled his nose and mouth. The walls of the coffin trapped his hands up by his ears. The iron nippers in his coat pocket dug into his hip, but he couldn't bend his arms to reach them.

Betrayed by Nail! Roger cursed into the sawdust. He'd survived a hanging only to be buried alive – this time with no princess standing by on her little golden stepladder to spare his life.

As a hanged criminal his body would have gone to the anatomists in Mouthstreet, to be sliced and flayed by scalpels, and held in general awe. At least he'd have been among friends there, contributing to greater human knowledge one last time. But here… After he suffocated, his organs would start to liquefy, and patches of mold would sprout from his rain-soaked garments, as if he were an aged cheese. Freshly dead, he guessed he'd be worth ten shells. Once the rot set in, he'd be worth nothing.

Roger shivered, the moisture from the rain and sweat cooling on his clothes and skin. He jerked his head from side to side, pushing the shavings away from his face so he had a pocket of air to breathe. With his hands pinned against the coffin sides, he tore at the flimsy fabric lining. Pine coffins were cheap because they often contained knotholes that let in the damp, and which a less honest undertaker might try to hide. Sure enough, his fingers found a thumb-sized hole near his right ear. He extended his neck and pressed his nose close. If only he could reach those nippers!

Rocking his body, he pushed deeper into the sawdust until he rolled himself partway onto his side. From here, he could grab the front of his coat with one hand and reel it up, like a fishnet. The iron nippers slid up his body until they lay against his ribs. With one last teeth-grinding contortion, he had them in his hand. He couldn't open the nippers in the narrow space, but he managed to scratch the clamp-end against the rim of the knothole. The wood splintered. He scraped and scraped.

This would take all night. Ada must be missing him by now, but Sir Bentley Morris' tomb was a good ten minutes from here. Even if she somehow thought to look for him at the Smith crypt, Nail had surely locked the door. Crypt locks were engineered to ward off all but the most stubborn and practiced bodysnatchers. Not even a ghost could pass through.

What of Sibet? She'd discover him missing come morning when he didn't show. She might send for Harrod, who claimed to know Roger's every move. But that had all been a bluff to scare him. Harrod had washed his hands of him now, anyway.

The knothole widened by a quarter inch. Roger passed his fingers over the mutilated wood around the gap and kept scraping. So far he'd managed not to let his mind drift to the horrors that lay above him, separated by a few inches of wood and sawdust. Now thoughts of the "gardens" crept back into his brain.

He scraped faster. Who could be paying Nail to play farmer for a mushroom patch?

His hand stopped. He already knew the answer, though he'd nearly forgotten since he'd been so drunk at the time. A gentleman with an uncommon interest in strange mycology, Dr Lundfrigg had brought mushrooms to the Anathema Club to share with his favorite students. Mushrooms that, when eaten, created magic-like side-effects that could revolutionize medical science. The man whose hand he'd wanted to shake. But that didn't mean he grew his "hobby" mushrooms in the bellies of murdered women… did it? To think he'd placed one of those mushrooms on his own tongue.

Roger dug his elbow into the sawdust, then pounded his implement against the side of the coffin.

No. The royal physician, Dr Lundfrigg, whom Roger had wished to emulate and impress, could not possibly be the kind of man to grow mushrooms in corpses.

But who else made sense? Not Nail. It required a man of experimentation and science. The medical students at the Anathema Club had mentioned no one else. He had let his own future prospects with Dr Lundfrigg bias his thoughts.

He spat out a mouthful of sawdust and thought through everything he knew about the strangled corpses and his interactions with Dr Lundfrigg. At St Colthorpe's he had, at the physician's direction, emptied a syringe into Celeste's vein. He had wondered about its purpose at the time, but had trusted the more experienced man and stupidly gone along with his direction. Whatever he'd given her had probably hastened her death. Nail wasn't his only accomplice now.

He remembered that she'd been given a morelle mauvingnon by a customer. Perhaps it hadn't been just wine, but spores and a solution to help their growth. Still, why use a human to grow mushrooms when all you needed was inexpensive peat? Something about Celeste had been special, as Estella had shared the wine without developing the same symptoms. What if the bodies of the women somehow accounted for the spore's ability to infest the blood and infuse the mushrooms' magic-like properties? Roger had read enough of Dr Lundfrigg's articles in *The Speculum* to know the physician believed blood could be exchanged between people. If salon women weren't magical, but the blood-like substance he'd injected into Celeste was… Then, it might not have been an "experimental treatment" but a catalyst for magic – even royal blood itself. If Roger escaped, he vowed to beat the man into the pavement with his bare fists.

At last Roger had a theory for how the "Strangler" murdered. First the women – Celeste for certain, and likely Claudine, Margalotte and the rest of them – were given some form of mushroom spore to ingest, and over time the fungi spores began to germinate. Not in the stomach, but by moving into the bloodstream, then the kidneys and liver, and the other organs supplied by the blood. Under the microscope, he'd observed black specks – the spores – in Celeste's blood. Dr Lundfrigg would have wanted to keep the true cause of death a secret. Killing, or having Nail kill, the women by strangulation would have created the sensational wounds to distract from the symptoms that had already ended their lives in a horrible fashion. Murder also kept the women and their precious cargo in the city in case they sought out the healing baths in Fillsbirth, as Claudine had.

Science truly had managed to create, or at least imitate, magic. If such a thing could be proved to the Myrcnian masses, the social fabric itself might rupture. Divine rule would be no more. The royal family deposed… beheaded? Revolutions had started over less.

Sibet. He choked – maybe on the sawdust, or some other mawkish tripe. His very blood tingled at imagining her harmed. Allowing himself to worry about her hurt his concentration. He needed to focus. He wouldn't let himself jump to these alarming conclusions about political upheaval until he could escape. Though if he let his mind wander too far in the other direction, he'd be neck deep in her imaginary petticoats and ruffles, and that might cause complications of a different sort.

He must have scraped at the coffin for hours, working along the wood grain. The hole elongated slowly, until at last a loud crack startled him. The wooden side splintered outward as the weight of the stacked coffins above pushed down on the lid.

Forcing the nippers through the split in the side, Roger levered the opening wider. The plank wrenched free. He bashed his fist against the weakened coffin side. Weighted from above, it ruptured in a slow crescendo of popping, crackling wood. He tumbled forth with a crash as the entire coffin stack collapsed around him.

Escape!

Roger's elation lasted barely a second. He sat up in the dark. Blue, glowing blobs lay scattered around him. Margalotte's coffin must have splintered open when it hit the floor, sending mushroom pieces flying. Their dim glow barely penetrated the darkness. Roger patted down his pockets for a shard of flint or match. He had none. Groping on hands and knees in search of his kit, he found only spongy bits of mushroom and corpseflesh.

Where was the door? He crawled along the wall and found it with a few bumps to his head. As he'd already guessed, Nail had locked it from the outside. Roger bashed it with the iron nippers, even shouted at the door to give way. He shivered and sweat. To have escaped the coffin, only to die inches from open air!

In his fevered mind, the desiccated husks of Margalotte, Claudine, and Grausam twitched and sat up in their desecrated boxes. He could feel their dark eye-sockets watching, waiting for him to join their little party. Jaws clicked, dry bone on bone. He had no more garlic to protect him.

He awoke on his back with an aching head. Had he fainted? How long ago? Turning his head to the side, his gaze lingered on the blue glow of a mushroom cap a few inches away.

Sitting up, he rubbed feeling into his tingling legs. It must be past morning now, though no daylight shone in anywhere. So much for his morning devotionals. That promised "curse" for missing them had been an empty threat – he hadn't been struck by lightning or chased by wolfhounds. The corpses, too, had left him alone.

Still, he felt a bit… odd. The tips of his fingers and toes had gone numb, as if from frostbite, and now the tingle was spreading past the arches of his feet and the knuckles of his hands. His elbows and jaw and spine seemed stiffer than usual, harder to move, as if they'd been gummed with sap.

"I must get out," he said to the darkness.

EAT ME.

The mushrooms seemed to whisper, and he wondered if their spores had embedded in his brain, or had he finally gone mad? Eat them? He remembered the medical students at the Anathema Club recounting tales of zapping one another with electric jolts, or turning their skin various colorful shades for seconds at a time. He tried not to think about what had nourished the fungi as he reached for a mushroom cap. Breaking off a tiny piece, he placed it in his mouth. The rest went into his pocket.

How long until he'd feel the effects? Would he shoot fire from his fingers, or electricity from his palms? Or summon the strength of five horses to deliver a fatal kick to the door's solid iron hinges? Ha, no chance of that. What good were tricks like faerie-sparks or electric shocks, or floating water bubbles? If he could make a spark, maybe he could light a small flame, at least. He waited a minute, then two, then five. A quarter hour must have passed for all he knew before he admitted these mushrooms were a dud batch.

He reached for his nippers, thinking he might try bashing at the door hinges once more. The iron fizzed in his palm. Heat prickled on his skin, and then crumbled bits of dust collapsed into his fist. The parts of the implement that did not touch his skin fell away and clinked on the floor. He jumped to his feet as if an electric eel had sparked him.

This power wouldn't last much longer. Roger threw himself at the door.

It was solid and several inches thick, but he knew the weakness would be the locking mechanism. It had held up under his physical assault earlier, but now as he pressed his hands against the first wide latch, it crumbled to dust within a minute. He found the other three latches, all connected to the central lock, and ran his fingers along them.

The numbing in his feet crept up his calves toward his stomach. This must be the Straybound curse, activated through his blood after his missed devotional.

Roger rammed his shoulder against the damaged door, once, twice, and on the third strike it swung open. He tumbled out of the crypt and landed under the entryway portico. Somewhere above, the sun shone, though only a dull gray light filtered through the low mist that engulfed Dolorous Avenue. When he looked over his shoulder into the crypt, he realized that the bundle Nail had brought – surely Celeste – was missing.

Now his legs below the thighs turned wooden. He collapsed to the ground. Pulling himself forward on his elbows, he crawled down the flagstone path to the avenue. There the mud was rutted and thick, but he bellied through it, fingers clawed, teeth gritted. He tried to shout, but managed only a parched rattle, as if his throat had been stuffed with straw. When he at last emerged from the trench-like road to a wide hilltop covered in more commonplace tombstones, he felt like he'd swum the full width of the Mudtyne.

He pulled himself on to one of the memorial stones and sat looking out over the vast acres of Greyanchor Necropolis. No one living could be seen.

With clumsy hands, he extracted the Straybound's devotional pamphlet from his pocket and let it fall open at random. He tried to read, forming the words with his lips, but no sound came out. No good. All feeling in his limbs had gone, and now his pulse slowed, his blood oozing through his veins like treacle.

Roger toppled backward off the gravestone and lay in the grass, his legs still angled up against the granite, and stared at the rain-heavy clouds. He would have laughed if he could. His heartbeat stuttered in his chest.

Was he moving? His eyes had frozen open, and he watched the necropolis stones creep past his face. Someone had removed his greatcoat and was using it like a sled to drag him. He couldn't call out. A faint reflection on the polished granite stones revealed a slender figure.

Ada had found him. By the sound of her sniffling, she thought him dead.

34

Lady Brigitte stepped back to examine Sibylla. "Beautiful," she breathed. Pride adorned her eyes, and she clapped her hands in delight.

"I need to speak with Father."

"He should be here soon. It *is* almost time."

"Harrod is missing." Sibylla strained to remain calm. She didn't care about the ball. The private parlor, where she and her family had assembled to await the procession into the grand ballroom, was as stifling as a casket.

"Ah, yes." Lady Brigitte adjusted the floral hairpiece on Sibylla's head. "You needn't worry."

After Roger missed his morning devotional, Sibylla had sent for Harrod, only to have the palace steward report back that Harrod was not, and had never been, involved in the ball's security. Panicked, she'd dispatched footmen to the Ordnance Board, his home in Burkeshire Gardens, and finally, in one last desperate attempt, to the Admiral of the Fleet himself. None had seen Captain Harrod Starkley all day. Without his particular talents, she would never find Roger.

Sibylla clutched at her stomach. "I can't attend. I'm going to be ill." Let the ballroom sink in a whirlpool, she'd uncover Roger somehow.

"Those are nerves, Sibet… or lies. You are getting better at telling them." Sibylla detected a hint of admiration in her mother's voice.

"I won't be dancing a step until I've seen Harrod, which is why I need to see Father first." Like a salmon in search of its stream, Prince Henry and Harrod shared the same ability to sense where their closest blood relations were hiding – a gift far more useful than her whistle-click. Discovering Roger on her own in a vast city would be insurmountable. For now, she'd focus on the missing naval captain. Prince Henry would tell her where to locate Harrod, and then Harrod would tell her where to find Roger. A sensible and simple plan. She wouldn't lose her wits now.

"Oh, you mustn't worry about the captain." Lady Brigitte sighed, then added more softly, "He is indisposed, but I promise you'll be together soon. I hope you two practiced the proper waltzes at Helmscliff."

"But I need him *now*."

"That's enough, Sibet." Lady Brigitte usually demonstrated such snappishness only after spending time alone with the queen.

Sibylla wished she had time to be patient, but the effects of Roger missing his devotional would be on him now: a living death, to prolong the disobedient's mortal suffering, preceded the eventual stopping of his heart. By midnight, if not sooner, he'd no longer be of this world.

As she opened her mouth to object a third time, her cousin Edgar intruded, dressed for the ball in a dapper coat embroidered in silver and a narrow frown. "Lady Brigitte."

"Edgar, dear." Lady Brigitte smiled despite her nephew's coldness. "Always the smart dresser."

"As are you," said Edgar. "That hairpiece – another Ibnovan gift?" His half-accusation hung in the air. Before Lady Brigitte could respond, Prince Henry startled them all by sneaking up behind his wife to place a kiss on the crown of her head.

"Such displays are revolting, don't you think?" Edgar whispered to Sibylla.

Sibylla thought of sharing something truly revolting, but instead she dragged her father aside.

"Where's Harrod?"

Prince Henry rolled his eyes before answering. "I'm afraid that is quite the story."

"There's no time." Sibylla gripped her father's arm so hard that he struggled to pry her fingers open. "Just tell me where he is."

"Yes, well. You'll have to wait with the rest." He leaned in with a devilish smile and tapped the crown of her head. "But for my cuttlefish, I'll give you a hint. The Sea Swallow's Lament."

That odious waltz in the middle of the ball. How did he expect her to glean anything from that? Lady Brigitte pulled him away to speak to the general in charge of the queen's Black Stallions, but Sibylla had no intention of letting him escape. She attempted to sidestep Edgar, but he boxed her in with a sneer. Unfortunately, her whistle-click would draw unwanted attention.

"Once the foreign pests depart, Grandmother will be planning our wedding. You should reconsider how you treat me." Edgar looked down his nose at her. "I've always thought of you as my–"

"Look at that footman's hideous stockings!" exclaimed Sibylla, pointing to a yellowed pair of silks.

Edgar narrowed his eyes at the footman standing beside the parlor's blue curtains, then stalked over to fire him as loudly as possible. Sibylla swore she'd reinstate the poor man later. Having diverted Edgar, she avoided a listing Crown Prince Elfred and chased after Prince Henry who'd wandered to the other side of the room. Edmund and Edward, in matching coats and their hair parted identically, bobbed into her path and stood there looking more like twins than brothers separated by a year.

"My deepest condolences, Weed-eyes. Our mother can't stop crowing over your soon-to-be nuptials. She overheard Dorinda placing an order for a burial veil once the Khalishkans have been thrown out of the palace."

"You mean bridal shroud," chimed in his brother.

"Same thing. If only you'd taken better care to sharpen the emperor's knife." The boys grinned wickedly, and she could barely tell one from the other. Now might be the time to whistle-click a chandelier down.

"Come, come now, Edmund. Isn't it better to keep her in the family?"

"A kiss from a cousin never hurt. If she doesn't mind a few mistresses…"

"Maybe when she gets cold, I'll come for a warming visit."

They snickered. Sibylla had to bite her tongue, or the secret of their blood might spill from her mouth out of spite.

"Will the pair of you never cease your teasing?"

"I think we upset her."

"Better stop, Edmund. Edgar might take away your favorite badminton racket next." Edward shoved an elbow into his brother's side.

Sibylla's tongue curled, and only the chime of the arrival bell saved her cousins' eardrums.

The queen turned heads as she entered the parlor, resplendent in a gown of silver silk and lace with a plum-sized diamond pendant above her décolletage. Worried creases rimmed the queen's eyes. But when she caught sight of Sibylla, her worry was replaced by a pleased smile – not the reaction Sibylla expected. Now if Sibylla wanted another word with Prince Henry, she had no choice but attend the opening ceremony.

Resigned, Sibylla found her assigned place within the processional line and fell in behind Lady Brigitte. A fanfare of trumpets announced their entrance, and the crowd hushed. First the queen, then the crown prince and his family, passed through the parlor's doors and into the majestic ballroom. Light from numerous candlelit chandeliers glinted off so many mirrored surfaces that Sibylla thought a gem had swallowed the room whole. Lady Brigitte winked over her shoulder, but Sibylla was searching the faces of the crowd. Harrod must be here. She couldn't wait for some silly waltz. For once, she would ferret him out first.

The queen began her welcome speech, and as her voice dipped and rose, the crowd parted. The emperor entered at the far side of the ballroom, wearing a formal dress uniform in elegant cream with pitch-black epaulets and an uncrowned topknot. On his chest glittered a silver star, the center of which held a winged horse. Sibylla's pulse quickened. As they joined one another on the dais, the emperor and queen stood on an even footing.

However, instead of introducing the traditional first waltz, the queen raised a hand for silence. She turned to motion Sibylla forward.

An uncomfortable stillness filled the room to its vaulted ceiling, and Sibylla shivered. As she stepped between Edward and Edmund, she nearly stumbled into them. She hadn't been warned she'd be performing any divine demonstrations. No one had told her anything. Glimpsing Edgar's bewildered face, she realized none of them knew what the queen had in store either. Hands mortared against her stomach, Sibylla took her place beside the queen. She felt the weight of so many eyes on her, their curiosity almost palpable.

"On this occasion," the queen began, her voice wavering momentarily. "It pleases us to announce the engagement of our granddaughter, Princess Sibylla Celia Ingrid of Alabeth, to His Most Imperial Majesty, Emperor Timur of Khalishka. May this prosperous match strengthen, not only the bonds between our countries, but also the prosperity within and beyond our borders."

The collective gasp of the audience rose, and a smattering of applause radiated outward, followed by a shaky cheer. Sibylla dug her palms into her abdomen. She couldn't move. Betrothals happened quietly, in a garden or drawing room, between two people. Hers had taken place in a ballroom with an audience and had caught her completely by surprise. Her mind went numb as though she'd fallen into a heavy slumber, except her eyes kept blinking. *But he never asked.* Her face prickled in shock. How could the queen announce an engagement when Timur had never proposed?

"To mark this momentous day, may the dancing begin."

The custom of inviting the guests to dance was as tested and old as the Dams of Fourth Height, but when the queen took Archbishop Tittlebury's hand for the first waltz, Sibylla felt her reality start to slip. The queen whirled as though ten years younger, floating on her frothy skirts from one end of the ballroom to the other. She moved so gracefully, yet the floor seemed unsteady beneath Sibylla's own feet.

A heady pall of perfume, spiced orchid and cinnamon, announced Lady Esther's presence. She tugged Sibylla's arm, pulling her away from the dance floor.

"What did you do?" Lady Esther's eyes brimmed with venom.

"I don't understand," Sibylla choked. There hadn't been time for seeds to blossom in the Khalishkan's heart or branches to break in her own. She'd known for years the narrative of her future marriage, thanks to frequent reminders from the queen, Lady Esther, and Edgar himself.

Even Archbishop Tittlebury had sanctified pairing the cousins. Yet, here they stood.

"How did you seduce him?" Lady Esther demanded, as if Sibylla could bend the Emperor of Khalishka to her will, or convince the queen to give up reinforcing tradition.

"I didn't. That night on the town, we had kidney-beef stew and discussed Marlowe's Menagerie's collection of vultures." And marriage pledges didn't typically follow "romantic" outings to undertakers and butcher shop garrets, either.

"If I'm to believe he fell for you because of stew and squawking birds, Helmscliff has made you mad. Khalishkans see us as nothing more than wand-waving magicians, claiming our right to rule while pulling doves from hats, and here you've managed to enspell one." Lady Esther's needle-like fingernails dug into Sibylla's skin. "Did your mother teach you some trick?"

"My mother?" Sibylla wrenched her arm free, shoving Lady Esther back. Her hand curled into a fist. Then someone touched her upper back, fingers hot against her bare skin. The emperor had snuck up behind her like a cat on silent paws.

Lady Esther's eyes widened. She stumbled on her words. "My congratulations," she stuttered, "though your imperial majesty might wish to change his mind after so hasty an announcement."

His hand lingering on Sibylla's back, Emperor Timur inclined his head with a smile. "I am surprised your aunt thinks so little of you, dear cicada, to suggest I would not have fallen of my own accord. I am a man of deep conviction." His fingertips danced on the back of her neck, sending prickles – and a rippling light – down her arms. "Myrcnians are a most peculiar lot," he continued as he scanned the dancers stepping in time to the waltz. "Why do you all insist on making each other so miserable?"

"You..." Lady Esther jabbed a finger at the emperor. "You... you cabbage-fed reprobate!"

"Lady Esther," Sibylla coldly admonished. "I do believe you've forgotten with whom you speak. Perhaps you should get yourself some punch before you cause any further humiliations."

Lady Esther flinched as though Sibylla had struck her. She retreated, first backing into Crown Prince Elfred and then Edgar, while the emperor laughed. Edgar caught hold of his mother, and a small giggle of hysteria escaped Sibylla's own lips. No Harrod, no Roger, but somehow she'd managed an engagement to the Emperor of Khalishka. She masked her mouth with her hand. As she stifled her outburst, Timur produced a velvet-lined jewelry box and opened it before her eyes.

"Consider this my pledge," he said, fastening a delicate chain around Sibylla's throat. "Something worthy of my betrothed."

She turned the pendant in her hand – a black and white onyx goshawk set in an oval of blue enamel. Gold and diamond florets made a glittering border. Sibylla suspected the cost of it could fund the construction of a small bridge. A pinch at the base of her neck made her jump.

Still holding the pendant dumbstruck, she asked, "Why would you do this?"

Timur gazed in Edgar's direction. "Look at his face, crushed like the pulp of a stem tomato. Yours, on the other hand, is a lovely shade. Did you secure more pine liquor for us?"

"Engaged…" She hadn't yet come to terms with having a Straybound, and now this. "You might have asked me before announcing to the world." She wasn't certain she could have refused, or that she would have.

"When you first smiled at me, I was uncertain. You proved more convincing after a night of drinking. With that Myrcnian glow of yours, your song is quite clear for any man with eyes. Although I may need to arrange a few lessons in guarding secrets." He teasingly entwined his fingers with hers, and she looked down at the bluish glimmer along her wrists. "Your lack of discretion certainly gave me the advantage in negotiations with the queen."

Timur had seen many things the day they spent together, but surely nothing to convince the queen to commit her granddaughter to a foreign alliance. Sibylla's stomach turned queasy over what she may have said. He let go of her hand, allowing her to breathe again. Inches from her, well groomed and self-possessed, he intimidated her. She couldn't manage one man, let alone a second.

Still, the betrothal couldn't last. Sibylla bitterly regretted not telling the queen of her cousins' non-royal bloodline that morning. Soon, she would quash the engagement with one fell secret. Could Myrcnia even weather such a calamity?

"I have something else for you, from Lady Brigitte." He handed her a dance engagement card in the shape of a hand fan and decorated with names to indicate her partners for each dance. A flicker of satisfaction crossed his face. "I've made sure I'm your last."

Sibylla had no desire to dance. She intended to throw the fan aside when her eye noticed Lady Brigitte's hand – or rather her ink – had crossed out one gentleman and replaced him with another. There, number twelve... Harrod's name had been inked in.

She stared at the fan in indecision. Harrod was the only guarantee she had of saving Roger, and he had been handed to her on a dance card. It wasn't ideal, but it would have to do. She could manage her other concerns later. For now, she prayed Roger could survive a few more waltzes.

35

"Open up." Someone clenched Roger's jaw and forced it open.

Roger snapped back into himself. He still couldn't move even an eyelid. A lit lamp sat in the grass near his feet. Reins jingled nearby as a browsing horse shook its head. When had the sun set?

Fatigue saturated him, as if he'd been submerged in a bog. Someone had propped him up with his back against a cold stone. The Necropolis Hill sloped to overlook the starry glints of Caligo's gaslamps, and beyond them the flat, black sea.

A woman leaned over him, concealed in shadow. She tipped the contents of a globe-shaped bottle down his throat, and he choked on the bitter iron taste of blood. With effort, he pivoted his head away. His neck felt stiff as a rusty hinge. Cold blood sloshed his chin and waistcoat.

Where was Ada? His last memory had been of her dragging him down the path. His lips formed words, but it took three tries to break the seal of his bottled voice.

"Sibet?"

"Is that your pet name for your duckling of a patroness?" Light angled across the woman's face as she leaned back. A severe bun pulled her face tight. She wore a trim riding habit with a high collar like a constable's, yet had darkened her eyes with kohl as doxies often did. He knew that mocking voice from somewhere, years ago.

"What a stallion you must be, to have earned her reprieve," the woman continued. "We are chosen to serve for our particular skills. As you have not the look of a cold killer, your talents evidently lie elsewhere."

"We?" Roger rasped. "You're Straybound, too?"

"Have a care." Her eyes glinted as she placed a finger to his lips. Her leathered gloves smelled of horse and sweat. "It is impolite to speak such words. Never flaunt your station. We are but replaceable pawns in their grand schemes. Announce your position at your own peril. Now, one more swallow." She pinched his nose and held the bottle to his lips. "Behold, the blessing of the Divine Maiden Sibylla." Her voice twisted mordantly. "Receive it with humility to save your own miserable life, lest I slash your throat and feed you through the slit."

Roger obeyed with a shudder. He recognized the glass bottle, faceted like a cut ruby, as the centerpiece of the monstrance in Sibylla's chapel. His stomach contracted. He had to drink it if he wanted to live long enough to reveal his findings. It took all his concentration not to spew the stuff right back in this woman's face – and invite a shivving, no doubt.

Warmth trickled back into his limbs.

"Adulterated as this stuff is, you might make it to morning," she said. "Usually the blood is warm and fresh. You'll learn to crave it soon enough."

Roger squinted to see clearer in the dim light. "I remember you. The queen's maid. Dorinda."

"Roger, was it?"

"Aye, you remember well. But I can't loll about here sharing memories. I must see the princess." He shook his legs to get the blood moving, still too weak to attempt standing.

"I never forget the mouths I've kissed in service of her royal majesty," said Dorinda as she packed the monstrance's centerpiece away in her satchel. She did not share Roger's desire to move quickly. "Such a willing young buck you were, as if you couldn't wait to get her highness' taste off your tongue."

Roger's face grew hot. "I could never have her. That were clear enough, but just knowing don't douse the flames. Hush money ain't no pail of cold water."

"Neither was the flogging nor prison, apparently. But now I suppose she can lock you away in her boudoir, as I can't imagine you're good for anything else. Indeed, her highness is most merciful." Dorinda looked him up and down. "I trust her taste is just a shade... necrophilic."

Roger ran an unsteady hand through his hair, knocking out bits of sawdust. Mud caked his front, and his clothes gave off the mildewed reek of the tomb. He still couldn't stand, but she didn't seem inclined to help him to his feet.

"I must thank you for the timely rescue." With a grimace, he once again tried and failed to pull himself up to a standing position using the gravestone for support.

Dorinda frowned. "I'd have let you die. It is tradition after the Binding for the unrepentant man to learn the consequences of defying his patron. But I had orders. A certain naval captain implored her royal majesty on your behalf. Captain Starkley even told me where to find you. He certainly has great sway over her royal majesty's feelings."

So Harrod had come through after all. Roger vowed to try to thank him the next time they met. First, he had to make it back to the palace. Then he'd expose Dr Lundfrigg for the monster that he was, to Sibylla, the queen, and anyone else who might listen. He just needed to regain control of his legs.

A faint wail rose from the stones behind them, carried by the wind. The horse huffed through widened nostrils and skittered off into the dark. Roger craned his neck to see over the gravestone. A shadowy figure came bounding over the hill, wailing and keening as it wove between the stones. A long lace veil billowed out behind.

Ada! Roger sank back with relief against the headstone. He knew that sound well enough.

"Get your hands off my sack-'em-up man!" Ada shrieked, bounding onto one of the headstones, where she balanced with outstretched arms. "I am Ghostofmary. I shall lop off your fingers and stick 'em up your nose if you dare resurrect him!"

Dorinda's icy line of a mouth split into a grin. "Ah, but I already have."

Ada brandished a hand-trowel like a sword. She leaped from the stone and, skidding up to Roger, pounded his chest. Pale lines streaked her cheeks where tears had washed away the grime.

"I thought you was dead." She bundled her long lace train and laid it on the ground between them. "See? I ran up to my crypt to fetch your shroud." Then she held up the trowel. "And after I wrapped you, I planned to bury you right here. You're the kind that likes a good view."

"That were right thoughtful of you, Ghost," said Roger, and pressed her thin hand to his cheek. Some feeling had returned to his skin despite the numbing wind.

Ada dabbed at the blood on his chin with the corner of the shroud. "Though if I were bigger and stronger, I'd have sold you to the sawbones in Mouthstreet for the price of a 'gazy pie."

"How touching." A man's baritone startled them both. The speaker stepped out of the darkness, his spectacles glinting in the lamplight. Roger recognized him with a start – the barrister Mr Murray, a bogeyman from the past. At least, his arrest felt distant now. Roger tried to stand but slumped sideways against the headstone. Where had Dorinda gone? Her lamp remained, set on the base of an ornate stone urn, and he could hear the jingle of her horse's bridle somewhere down the hill.

"I've been looking for you, Weathersby," said Mr Murray. His manicured sideburns looked like two black cleavers on his chiseled face. "I knew I would find you. I shouldn't be surprised you made off with the bonnets. Where are they?"

Ada placed herself between them like a guard dog.

"Bonnets? What rubbish are you spouting off this time?" Roger pulled himself to his feet and took a wobbly step forward. "I don't bloody well care about your ladies' hats. How did you find me here?" He'd figured out Dr Lundfrigg's and Nail's part in the murders but had forgotten the lawyer who'd ensured his conviction as the Greyanchor Strangler. This bastard was in on it, too.

Mr Murray pointed to the muddy path where Ada had dragged him. "You left a track wider than an ox cart." He pulled the fur collar of his expensive coat tight against the wind. "First you resurrect a body you never should have, then you return to the scene of the crime for the rest of it. Enough games. Whoever your patron is, they've lost. Now, the mushrooms. Nail told me he had killed a thief, but when I arrived I found the door open and the prize stock missing. Tell me where you stashed it before I'm forced to do something unpleasant."

Always the opportunist, Nail must have absconded with Celeste intending to pin the theft on him.

"I never took your mushrooms," Roger spat. "Best you ask Nail. He's told me plenty of lies already, and now he's told you some, too. I wouldn't be surprised if he was halfway to Khalishka."

"You're the only liar here, but I'll have you screaming the truth soon enough." Mr Murray advanced, a thin, silver pen-like implement in one hand.

Roger puffed up his chest. "Did Dr Lundfrigg put an advertisement in *The Speculum* for lackeys and lickspittles? Just how many of you blighters work for him? Even if I knew where Nail took your bonnets, I'd sooner tear out my own tongue than help you."

"Is that what you've managed to put together?" Mr Murray tucked his chin behind the fur collar of his coat and advanced against the wind. "*Dr Lundfrigg* is the one working for *us*."

"That makes no sense. What does a lawyer need with magic-inducing mushrooms?"

"This will be your final opportunity," said Mr Murray, almost upon him now. The silver implement Roger had mistaken for a pen was in fact a thin blade. "Now tell me where you hid the stock. Thief!"

"Ada, run!" Roger had lost track of the girl in the dark. With effort, he raised his fists. The cumbersome blocks of wood that were his feet stumbled in the mud. Mr Murray's blade thrust toward him and Roger could only throw himself out of the way. He tried to knock the lawyer's legs out from under him, but the man was too nimble. Mr Murray lunged again, his stiletto aimed for Roger's eye.

"Tell me where!"

The lawyer stopped short. He arched his back and howled. Ada had hurled herself at him from behind, pulling a strip of the lace shroud tight around his throat.

"You feral bitch!" Mr Murray screamed. He tried to shake her off, but she pulled tighter, cutting off his voice. Roger pushed himself to his hands and knees and scrabbled forward, but just as he caught one of Mr Murray's shoes, the lawyer flung Ada to the ground. She landed with a thud and struggled to her feet, but he pulled her to him by the hair and held the blade to her throat.

"If you don't talk now, Weathersby, this wild beast never will again, either."

"But I—"

"Threatening a child." Dorinda's voice echoed among the stones. "Have you no shame?"

Mr Murray turned in a circle, still holding Ada, searching for the source of the voice. "Who's there? Show yourself at once," he demanded of the dark.

Roger took advantage of this distraction to haul himself onto unsteady feet. He could sense Dorinda's shadow orbiting the circle of lamplight. Her movements made no sound.

"Unfortunately for us both, I'm charged with returning this man alive." Her voice now seemed to come from the opposite side as before.

"I assure you, ma'am," said Mr Murray, a quaver in his voice, "this is no business you wish to be involved in."

A chuckle answered him, and the lawyer shielded his eyes as if it might help him see in the dark.

"That's where you're wrong, Bruce Isles. I'd have caught up with you eventually." Dorinda used a name Roger had never heard. "You've only saved me some trouble. Two birds with one stone, as they say." She sounded gleeful, her breezy voice playing tricks with their ears.

"How do you know that name?" Mr Murray's voice tripped up an octave.

"It may have taken this long, but we've ferreted you out at last. Did you think your affair of the heart with Lady Esther would stay hidden forever? Did you think *you* would stay hidden?" Dorinda's laugh cut like a lancet. "But many buried secrets have started coming into the light. Sons are often disappointing, no?"

Mr Murray's face blanched as though it had endured a good boiling. The deliberation he'd shown earlier had gone, and the stiletto fell from his hands. Not to waste an opportunity, Roger caught Ada's eye.

She nodded, and he shoved Mr Murray aside. His grip on Ada's hair loosened. The girl ducked free, then vanished into the dark.

Mr Murray's eyes widened. "How much? How much does the queen know?"

"Her royal majesty knows *everything*. The years-long affair. Your three not-so-royal bastards. And their not-so-magical father."

Their petty squabble didn't interest Roger. "Who cares about bastards when you've been murdering women? Did you strangle them, or Nail, or did Dr Lundfrigg do it himself?"

"What's this?" Dorinda's shadowed form appeared behind the lawyer. She touched her hat, and Roger caught the flash of something pretty and red in her hand – a hatpin with a carnelian bead. "Have you been killing again?" she asked, alerting Mr Murray too late of her presence. She embraced him from behind. One arm wrapped around his waist, and the other pressed her hatpin to his jugular.

Roger's heart pounded in his chest at this sudden reversal. "I'll ask again. What does a lawyer need with magic-inducing mushrooms?"

Desperation cracked Mr Murray's cool demeanor. "Why should the queen care if some tarts die? Yes, I strangled them, all but one. Nail tried to handle that chocolate shop girl alone and flubbed it. My sons need magic, and Dr Lundfrigg offered his services in exchange for access to the royal family. Things were looking up until you got your corpse-thieving hands involved."

Dorinda eyed him with scorn. "If Lady Esther had wanted to keep her triplet of bastards, she should have ensured their father had the right blood in his veins, instead of bedding a common knave like you."

Before Mr Murray could respond, she stabbed him through the neck, again and again, until blood fountained from him in thin streams, too many for Roger to count. Mr Murray crumpled to the ground and writhed facedown in the muck.

Blood dripped from Dorinda's dagger-like hatpin. Roger stumbled to the wounded man and rolled him on his back. He clamped his hands tight around Mr Murray's starched cravat to staunch the flow, but the man spluttered and gurgled, drowning in his own blood. Before long Mr Murray would be decaying flesh and bone, like the stiffs resting all around them. Roger kept his hands pressed to the lawyer's neck long after he'd gurgled his last.

Dorinda wiped her hatpin with a black lace kerchief. "Stop your whimpering." She looked down at Roger. "You're as theatrical as your owner."

"You just killed a man." Roger grit his teeth. "Killed him as easy as pinning your hat."

Dorinda cocked her head. "A man? That?" She slid the hatpin with its shiny red bead back into her hat. "Take a closer look." She tapped her own neck, and then pointed to Mr Murray's blood-soaked cravat.

Roger peeled the material back. There among the puncture wounds he found a familiar Stigma – a Muir rose topped with a coronet and outlined in shining gold pigment.

"You can't murder a condemned man." Dorinda adjusted her riding gloves. "A lesson you would do well to remember."

Roger stared at his bloody hands.

"And I thought you'd be pleased to see the man who sent you to prison, dead before your eyes." Dorinda smiled. "Roger, you disappoint yet again." She threw the reins over her horse's head and mounted. "Well, I have revived you. My duty is completed. Good day."

"Wait," Roger called out, as she kicked her horse and trotted down the grassy slope. "How am I supposed to get to the palace?" He shambled after her, still unbalanced from his ordeal, then stopped, too out of breath to continue.

"Not my problem," she shouted back. "Your princess patron should take better care next time."

Roger felt a tug on his hand and looked down.

"I've got a shelling saved from the butcher's," said Ada, slipping a coin into his palm. "You could hire a nag from Ol' Brindleburn on Goatmonger Street. Come on, I'll hold you so you don't fall. Then after, you'll owe me…" she counted on her fingers "…a dozen hot cross buns and a 'gazy pie."

36

Roger's horse was foaming and out of breath when they reached the top of Broadbriar Street and the brightly lit Malmouth Palace. As he approached the side gate used by servants and delivery carts, the guards shouted at him to halt and lowered their bayonets. Roger unraveled his cravat, spat on it, and wiped the mud from his Straybound Stigma. It was enough to get inside, but unless he wanted every household attendant between him and the princess calling the guards to check his credentials, he'd need to find a way to blend in.

He dismounted at the couriers' stables and headed for the main palace building. Music hit his ear in spurts, and glistening coaches flashed in the lamplight of the ballroom's entrance. The Royal Heritage Ball had been the talk of the town for weeks. Large events often required the head steward to hire temporary staff, so an unfamiliar face would not be noticed, assuming he looked the part. Fortunately, he'd been a palace footman once upon a time, and he knew his way around.

He shed most of his clothes and leapt into the horse trough, scrubbing himself with a currycomb until one of the grooms chased him off – politely enough, since he mistook Roger for a drunkard who'd wandered out of the ball. Next, he climbed over a hedge and through an unlatched window into the head steward's office. Roger left his soaked trousers and shirt hanging by the steward's banked fireplace and dressed himself in the best-fitting livery he could find.

The stiff new fabric of the red livery tailcoat and knee-breeches chafed his skin. With his tattoos covered, his damp hair slicked back, and his chin still passably smooth, he presented well enough. By keeping his chin tucked to his chest and his eyes cast downward, he hoped to hide his old bruises. He made his way to the large servants' hall located directly below the ballroom where a contingent of junior footmen sat at a long table, frantically shining hundreds of crystal flutes. All around them maids and hallboys bustled about with napkins, silverware, winter roses, and greased rags.

Roger slid right into the bustle as if he belonged there, setting flutes onto silver trays. Playing footman would get him inside the grand ballroom quickly and clear a path to the princess. No one paid much attention to the servants during these grand events. He lined up with the other footmen and accepted a tray of sparkling wine. Hushed whispers informed him the queen was about to make her second big announcement of the evening, and there would be a celebratory toast. When the head butler dropped his hand, they were to circulate the ballroom.

A peppery rose scent bubbled from the silver-rimmed flutes, and Roger followed the footman in front of him. They breezed into the ballroom like red and gold confetti. He stood stiffly at the edge of the dance floor as the crowd hushed and waited for the signal. A horn blared, drawing the crowd's attention to the queen on the dais. As she began to speak, Roger searched for Sibet among the gilded frocks.

"On so joyous an evening, we wish to convey the greatest of tidings. Many years ago, our youngest son, Prince Henry, and his dearest wife Lady Brigitte, gave birth to a baby boy while abroad. Tragedy befell them during their passage across the Green Sea from Salancia to Caligo, and the baby was tossed overboard during a storm that nearly sunk their ship. Unwilling to burden our nation with their grief, they mourned in private. Now, it gives us the greatest joy to announce their son, thought lost, has been found."

The crowd gasped as if an airless bell jar had been placed over the ballroom. Roger couldn't stomach more royal secrets. He skirted the edge of the dance floor, scanning the dancers for a woman in silver. Only the royals wore that color in winter. Finding Sibet should be simple enough.

"Washed ashore at Fillsbirth, and raised in ignorance of his true parentage, he chose to serve his country at an early age, returning to the sea as a midshipman. His blood is now confirmed by Archbishop Tittlebury to be of the divine Muir line. It pleases us to present our grandson, Prince Harrod."

Harrod... Roger glanced at the dais. There stood his brother, as solemn and motionless as the necropolis queen. A silver sash accented his uniform, along with a fur-trimmed cape and enough silver braiding to rig a sail. Sweat glistened on his brow, and he looked ready to retch.

Harrod, a royal prince washed ashore? What utter bollocks. If he had to be royal, then he must be a royal bastard. They shared the same mother, of that he was certain. Harrod might be Prince Henry's son, but he didn't belong to Lady Brigitte. Still, the idea of Sibet and Harrod being related made Roger's insides churn. She'd always been quick to take Harrod's side, and now he knew why. He ought to be angry with her for keeping this secret from him, but his head kept making excuses on her behalf.

Harrod bowed his head to the audience. Excitement gripped the crowd, as if the queen squeezed them in her fists. A lady swooned. Men of all stations whooped. Then, as one, the entire assembled crowd bowed to their prince, all except Roger who stood rigid until a fellow footman elbowed him in the ribs.

If the royals wanted Harrod, they could have him. Roger only cared about finding Sibet.

He circulated through the crowd, offering ball-goers sparkling wine to toast the newly-anointed prince. His last glass was snatched up by a man with a shapely mustache and flushed cheeks, wearing a dandy red uniform to match.

The crowd raised their flutes to the queen and her newly rediscovered grandson.

"To the prince!" they cried in one voice.

After the toast, Harrod descended the steps behind the queen, and a crowd queued to formally greet him. A whole line of toffs bowing to his brother! Roger couldn't spot Sibet among them. He might as well be searching for a silver lancet in a pile of lockpicks.

"It's quite amusing, no?" A Khalishkan dignitary in a striking white uniform cuffed Roger's arm.

"Just another day in Caligo," said Roger, then clamped his mouth shut. He added hastily, "Sir." Giving opinions to guests was a massive breach of protocol, and the last thing he wanted was to draw unwanted attention.

The chamber orchestra held a long tuning note, and the crowd shifted to allow a better view of the dancers. Roger risked a glance over his shoulder.

"Are you looking for someone in particular?" asked the foreign gentleman in his rich accent. Perhaps Khalishkans weren't as stuck-up as the average Myrcnian. Or maybe the man hadn't realized Roger was a servant.

Roger knew enough of upper crust gentlemen not to be tricked into thinking they cared to hear him speak. "I'm only a footman, sir. If you was looking for a partner, I'm a terrible dancer. Please ask someone else." He bowed deeply, hoping the Khalishkan might leave him alone.

"You *are* droll, aren't you, Mr Weathersby?"

"I try." Roger's mouth went dry at the sound of his name. He studied the man's face. It had been too dark in the stairwell to see his assailant properly, yet here was the man who had held a sword to his neck. At the time he'd assumed Sibylla had acquired a foreign bodyguard. This man was a toff through and through.

The Khalishkan pointed to the far end of the dance floor. "I'm afraid the only partner I fancy is her. At least we have one thing in common."

Roger followed the direction of the man's pointed finger, and his heart thumped in his chest. There she was at last! Sibet stood with her back half-turned, consulting a fan-shaped dance card. Her white-silver gown reflected every glint of light in the room. He'd finally found her.

As couples paired up for the next dance, Sibylla linked elbows with a man in an absinthe-green tailcoat and violet cravat. *Dr Lundfrigg*. A surge in Roger's blood made him sway. That man – that human cesspit who murdered women in unspeakable ways – snaked his arm around Sibet's waist like an eager ponce.

"What are you doing? Your tray is empty." A sneering, freckle-faced footman jostled Roger's shoulder.

Roger didn't give a damn about his tray. Across the floor, the royal physician spun Sibet in a sickly swirl of white skirts. His mouth went dry. She needed to know with whom she was dancing. Now.

Roger dodged left, but the overbearing Khalishkan had swiveled nimbly into his path. "A polite gentleman doesn't disrupt a lady's dance card," he persisted, ever the pleasantest of blowhards. "I'd hoped you might tell me a bit more about the princess, what with you being a great favorite of hers for so long…"

By the Lady's nethers, no! Fuming inwardly, Roger ducked his head. By now a few bystanders had taken notice and whispered to one another behind their hands. He pivoted about-face to see the freckled footman now stood beside the palace steward and gesticulated at Roger's empty tray. He couldn't go that way, either. He spun back around, but the Khalishkan gentleman hadn't budged.

Bugger the lot of them. With one mad push, he knocked the Khalishkan off-balance. Free at last, he dashed into the crowd. First, he hurried toward the dance floor, but a handful of guards and footmen advanced to intercept him. Roger backtracked, veering for the empty dais instead. He had to separate Sibet from Dr Lundfrigg. An idea struck him, and he dug in his pocket for the mushroom he'd kept to show her.

If he couldn't get to the princess, then he'd bring the princess to him.

This crowd of toffs was about to see something they'd never seen before – a lowborn man performing "divine" magic. He gripped the silver tray like some mythic shield. It was metal, just like the locks on the crypt door. The queen would be forced to acknowledge Dr Lundfrigg's crimes or let the foundations of her authority crumble. And if Dorinda took a hatpin to his neck? Then he'd die knowing he'd avenged Ada and her mother. Tried to, anyway.

37

Sibylla cursed under her breath as Roger ascended the dais with his tray. She knew that look on his face better than anyone: brave and bold and stupid. She spun behind Dr Lundfrigg, using the waltz's partner exchange to make her escape. Lifting the front of her ballgown, she set off in Roger's direction. He'd already shoved an emperor, and now he intended to get himself shot.

Having reached the top of the dais, the suicidal idiot held up the shining silver tray and began shouting.

"Sibylla! Fellow Myrcnians! Listen to me. That Lundfrigg chap there, Sir Finch to you, has faked royal magic and hoodwinked you all." He cut a dashing figure in his footman's livery, at least.

All conversation died away, though the orchestra played on in the background. The entire assembly had their eyes turned toward this raving footman who was sure to be shot, beaten, and sacked, though perhaps not in that order.

Roger's arm wavered. Sibylla, standing close now, just behind Lady Esther, could see the silver tray beneath his hands blacken like dark gravy spilling across its surface. She didn't know what he'd intended, but he seemed to be waiting for something much more dramatic. Who could see tarnish from thirty feet away? If it were iron, perhaps, iron crumbled, but silver... Silver tarnished.

The crown prince's magic.

But how was this possible? Crown Prince Elfred had been banned from using his gift at the dinner table, having ruined one too many salad forks, and Roger – despite all reason telling her otherwise – was somehow using his magic, but didn't realize the difference between iron and silver.

The crowd's shock wore off and turned to titters of laughter. A nervous young bodyguard moved to intercept him, but Harrod held up a hand indicating he should not. Sibylla locked eyes with Harrod. If only they could get Roger out of here without anyone intervening.

In desperation, Roger changed his tactics. "Dr Lundfrigg." He pointed at the royal physician who stood at Sibylla's shoulder with a smug grin on his face. "You're the real Greyanchor Strangler, and I know why you've done it. You killed those women for your experiments. Made 'em sick with infecting spores. All so you can grow this!" He raised something in his hand – a mushroom? "But the Greyanchor Strangler isn't you alone. The undertaker Nail, the lawyer Murray – you fiends hid your murders behind an innocent scapegoat and kept on killing. Seeing as I'm already damned, I've come to show my fellow Myrcnians how you've grown magic from the dead."

Through his speech, most of the crowd gawked, motionless. A few people laughed, and one poor sod even clapped.

Roger leapt from the dais, perhaps emboldened to apprehend Dr Lundfrigg with his own hands, or bash his brains out.

From the corner of her eye, Sibylla caught the queen nodding to Dorinda, her patience for this display at an end. A flash of something red appeared in Dorinda's hand, and Sibylla knew whatever Roger intended to reveal would get him murdered in a most striking fashion to prevent him saying more.

"Merciful Mother." She had to protect him. Her fingers twitched first. Black ink pooled beneath her fingernails – something, anything to block Roger's words from the throng and keep Dorinda safely at bay. Sibylla spread her fingers, flattened her palms. Thick trunks of black ink trees sprouted from the polished parquet floor. A forest took shape around them, a circular copse. Her ink trees grew in height until their branches spread in watercolor streaks like a mourning canopy, black leaves unmoving above their heads. She had never created such a massive, intricate painting at once. A few speckles of ink marred the silver of her dress but that couldn't be helped. The rest of her ink would diffuse into the air as soon as she lost concentration.

The ink muffled the exclamations from outside the copse, and Sibylla spread her fingers wide, her arms outstretched. She'd caught Roger in her inky net, at least, and Dr Lundfrigg at her side. Harrod as well, thank the Lady of the Stream. Lady Esther and the emperor were the only unintended bystanders. She didn't know whether she could move without disrupting her inking, so she remained like some terrible water sprite trapped at its center.

"Roger? Harrod?" she called out. The sudden inky canopy enveloped them in shadow. If any of them blundered headfirst through the black walls, they'd encounter Dorinda, the queen, and the contingent of royal guards within the grand ballroom.

Sibylla drew a long, steady breath. Inking and glowing at the same time was like singing while playing the concertina – annoying at best and impossible at worst. Still, she let her skin turn translucent until the eerie glow of her blood lit all their faces with a ghostly pallor. One problem solved, but now she needed to think of a better idea than hide.

"How is this possible?" Lady Esther touched a trunk, staining the tip of her finger black. "I demand you stop this."

Sibylla's creations had always been small, like ink-bees, but this was true Muir magic, grand and spectacular. Sweat trickled down the back of her neck as she thickened the ink all around them. Countless days of inking thousands upon thousands of insects and clouds had not prepared her for this feat of endurance. Lady Esther pressed her lips together as though blowing out a candle. A bubble took shape from her mouth, and with speed headed toward one of the tree trunks. Sibylla tightened her jaw, unable to prevent the collision.

Pop!

The bubble burst in a tiny splash, slurring a small portion of the ink gray.

Lady Esther's strained mouth appeared moments away from shrieking, "This has nothing to do with me."

Ink was not stone. If Lady Esther wanted to cover herself in black, she could leave whenever she wished. The emperor laughed into his fist while Harrod offered Lady Esther his hand.

"Don't touch me, you degenerate rake," Lady Esther snapped.

A loud clang caught their attention.

Dr Lundfrigg lay curled on the ground.

Roger stood over him, chest heaving, the silver tray gripped in his hands. "I spent a night on your little mushroom farm," he roared. "To think I trusted you. But you lie, your magic lies, this entire bloody country is built on lies."

Dr Lundfrigg lurched to his knees. His voice cracked. "Do you know how close I am? With Princess Sibylla's blood and this new batch of mushrooms, I might achieve medical marvels no other doctor could dream into existence. With the royal glow, I could peer through a patient's skin without scalpel or pain. Remember the broken-legged boy. Imagine if we could see his bone healing with our own eyes, allowing us to make the perfect adjustments so he could run again. And at what cost? A few moments of the royal family's precious time, to provide a service far more valuable than a pointless ceremony. What good are spectacles to the bedridden invalid? Think how we could bring about the Scientific Age."

Roger looked ready to trounce him a second time, and Dr Lundfrigg shielded his face with his arms.

"A mushroom farm?" Rivulets of black ink streaked down Sibylla's fingers, shading the blue-violet glow in her hands as she struggled to hold the tree copse together around them.

Roger brandished the tray. "I'm thinking of a girl who's got no mother because of you. But I've stared death in the face three times over, and I'll even give him one last glim if only I take you with me."

His face contorted into an expression she'd never seen, not even during their worst rows. He'd missed his devotional, and yet here he was, alive if not exactly well. Now he seemed ready to throw himself into a volley of rifle-fire. Sibylla bit her lip. A day ago, she'd sent him to fetch that odd pixie girl that haunted his garret. She couldn't imagine what horrors he'd encountered to make him risk his life.

Dr Lundfrigg clambered to his feet. "Look around." His arms flailed toward the swaying inky walls. "You can't spread your lies in here." He nodded to Sibylla as though she'd assisted him. Now she wanted to strike him, too.

"Please, Sibet," Roger choked. "In Myrcnia, it only matters how people see you, not who you really are."

"If you tell me what's happened, I'll help." The strain in her neck spread down her back, and the ink seemed to churn within her, replenishing itself.

"This man," cried Roger, as he grabbed Dr Lundfrigg by the lapels and shook him, "grows mycological magic in specially chosen stiffs."

"Enough," Harrod barked. "This farce must end here."

"I believe him, Harrod." Sibylla had already measured Dr Lundfrigg's character for herself. Not only had he taken great pains to acquire samples of royal blood, including her own, but she also knew he had a list of former salon girls provided by an unwitting Dame Angeline – many of whom she'd learned, from reading court records, now lay dead. As for the magic, Sibylla had seen her cousins faking small displays all week. Her stomach turned at all the times the royal physician had talked to her of gardening. "Dr Lundfrigg is a traitor."

Sibylla had to think. She couldn't keep her wall up much longer: glistening ink gloved her forearms to her elbows. How could she end this without Roger winding up dead?

"You believe him?" Harrod gaped at her.

"Your highness!" Dr Lundfrigg exclaimed like a petulant child caught stealing licorice sticks. "If I'm guilty, so is this man. I hired him. Tried him out. He followed orders without question."

"You lying sack of bonemeal." Roger raised the tray above his head. "The only ones working for you are that two-faced pox of an undertaker's assistant and the dead lawyer what tried to frame me for your crimes."

"You're all daft." As Harrod raised his hands in defeat, Lady Esther abruptly snatched his pistol – an engraved silver pepperbox he'd concealed beneath his ornamental fur cape.

She trained the barrel at Roger's nose. "Did you kill Mr Murray? Did you kill my Bruce?"

For a second, Sibylla imagined she was standing in a stage production of *The Barnmaid of Bareth*. Pain stabbed behind her eyes. Lady Esther intended to shoot. The serving tray clattered to the floor, and the emperor's hands gripped Sibylla's waist, pulling her out of the way.

"I didn't kill him." Roger raised his hands. "I killed no one–"

"Ma'am, give me–"

"You scum." Lady Esther's bosom heaved beneath her gown. Tears trickled down her nose and water bubbled from her mouth. The gun shook in her grasp. The trigger chinked.

Crack.

Sibylla released her hold on the inky trees as she fell. The upper branches disintegrated, ink raining on their heads. Bright light shone through the thinning, lacy trees. An applause greeted them – mistaken delight at Sibylla's creation. Then screams filled the ballroom. The emperor left Sibylla safely on the ground. He leapt at Lady Esther, who brandished the pepperbox while wiping ink-smears from her face. People jostled back and forth, unsure if they should flee or run to the aid of their new prince bleeding out on the floor.

"Harrod!" Sibylla's legs buckled.

It couldn't be. Lady Esther had aimed at Roger and fired at point-blank range! Harrod must have thrust him out of the way – that damnable hero. Steady arms caught her as she attempted to stand and held her upright. She blinked at a blurry face, unable to stop the translucence of her skin, or her glowing blood beneath.

A blond mustache, a scarlet uniform… Lieutenant Calloway. He held her, squeezing the breath from her chest, and turned her face away. She struggled, but he refused to let go.

"Please," she gasped into his shoulder. "He's my brother."

The words seemed to resonate with him, as he loosened his grip for her to slip away.

"If he dies," Sibylla seethed to Lady Esther as she passed, "you'll soon follow."

Edgar and Crown Prince Elfred hovered close, neither daring to help Lady Esther. Not even the queen herself would intervene now. Not while the emperor pinned Lady Esther's arms behind her back with one hand and wrestled away the gun in the other. Khalishkan officials stood close, hands on the hilts of their guardless swords. Lady Esther slumped, shattered on the inside, perhaps never to be mended.

Sibylla landed on her knees at Harrod's side in a crinoline puff. She cared nothing for her ink-spattered dress or the crowd that hung back as if a bullet wound were infectious. Blood drenched Harrod's dress uniform, and the kraken medal on his chest. Her throat tightened. She couldn't breathe. Her entire body felt heavy and numb, like she might disappear completely, leaving only her blood on the floor.

"Sibet." Roger's voice came to her through an ocean. Not an ocean, but tears – her own. She blinked. "Sibet! Sibet, he'll be all right." He sounded so calm, so confident, as though certain of his words.

Roger stripped off his neckcloth, exposing his Straybound tattoo and the red rope-wound around his neck. He cinched the cloth around Harrod's upper arm as a tourniquet, stemming the flow of blood.

"Bring me gin!"

For a moment Sibylla thought he wanted a drink, but Dr Kaishuk dashed forward with the leather bag she seemed to take everywhere and handed him a bottle of some medical tincture, instead. With scissors she cut the heavy fabric of Harrod's sleeve from cuff to collar, splitting the shirt in half, while Roger drenched his hands in fluid before beginning his inspection of the wound in Harrod's left arm. Harrod gave a blood-curdling scream that trailed off when Dr Kaishuk placed a wet cloth over his mouth and nose. Roger worked at the wound and Sibylla looked away.

Harrod's fingers found hers, slippery with sweat. She looked down with a start, then squeezed them back, exhaling stale air she'd been holding in her chest.

"Damn it all," Roger said. Sibylla didn't have the stomach to look. "The bullet's torn down the length of his forearm and lodged in his elbow. Nothing but boneshards. There's but one thing to do, though I'm certain he'd near kill me first."

"We should move him," said Dr Kaishuk, her voice husky over the crowd. "Leave this to the *real* professionals."

"Filthy surgeon," Harrod mumbled as a litter was brought, and half a dozen men lifted him onto it.

"You're lucky the bullet missed your lung, brother." Roger's voice was full of bravado, but the sweat on his forehead told a different story.

Sibylla gripped Roger's elbow as they watched Harrod being carted off with Dr Kaishuk dancing attendance.

"That poor livery. There's no chance of getting it clean now." She tugged on his shirt. His sleeves, shoved to his elbows, were splattered with blood. He'd wiped his hands on his breeches, leaving wide red streaks. Even his white stockings matched the dark red of his coat.

"Brother." He repeated the word softly, so only she could hear. "I suppose I can't be calling him that now."

"I'm sorry, Dodge." Sibylla slipped her fingers into his and squeezed. Holding his hand was dangerous. Behind him, Dorinda lingered near the Khalishkan dignitaries and royal guards. If she dared move closer, they'd both discover whether Sibylla's whistle-click could rupture a skull.

"I'm no royal physician, but do you think they'd let me help change his dressings?" Roger's arms fell limp at his sides.

"You can try."

Sibylla didn't have the heart to tell him that no raving lunatic of a footman would be allowed near the new prince. Straybound or not.

38

Throughout the night, servants brought Sibylla updates on Harrod's condition while she inked in her bedroom, unable to sleep. By morning, Harrod had shouted off all the physicians brought to his chamber – first the Khalishkans followed by the Myrcnian doctors, until only Roger remained to tend his wounds. Thanks to a timely amputation, early indicators pointed to a steady recovery, no doubt helped by the magic blood in her half-brother's veins.

At seven the next morning, Sibylla steeled her guts upon entering the dining hall. A glance about the room revealed no footmen, guards, or family members – only the queen. To her right, an expansive spread of browned toast, poached eggs, baked beans, bacon quiche tarts, and five varieties of sausage waited in silver serving dishes.

"Be a dear and fix me a plate."

Sibylla walked down the row of delicacies, selecting one of each item save for the baked beans she knew the queen detested, and brought the plate to her. Attempting to replicate a palace footman's meticulous skills, she swooped the plate onto the table. Sibylla pulled out the queen's chair and eased her into it.

The queen clucked in disapproval. "Aren't you forgetting something?"

Sibylla stiffened, clasping her hands behind her back. "Ma'am?"

"Your fry-up, Sibet. You'll never adjust to devotionals if you perform them on an empty stomach."

The matter of Roger as her Straybound hadn't escaped the queen's notice after all. Fortunately, Dorinda hadn't murdered him yet, either. Sibylla hastened to the serving dishes and returned with a full plate, save for the black pudding.

The queen skewered a poached egg with her fork, sopping up the spilt yolk with her bread. Sibylla scoured her memory for the last time she'd been alone with her grandmother – when she'd been asked to glow in practice for the emperor's greeting ceremony. In some ways, her future had been clearer then, without a Straybound or an engagement. She had more to care for now, with so little idea of how to do so. She forced a bite of dry toast down her throat. This food was too heavy for her knotted stomach to manage so early in the morning.

The queen's silence eroded her restraint, and Sibylla opened her mouth first. "Did your royal majesty sleep well?"

The queen snorted. "Did I sleep well? You mean after all that fuss you caused. Did you think that was an appropriate way to celebrate your betrothal?"

Sibylla's grip tightened on her fork. "Has the emperor decided to break off the engagement?" She didn't know what answer she'd rather hear. While she might happily marry Timur one day, she had no idea how to be an empress.

"I believe he finds it all rather charming." The queen rotated a brown sausage on her fork. "And a man with his temperament, after going through such trouble, won't readily change his mind over a few ink-stains."

Sibylla halted, a fork of baked beans halfway between the plate and her mouth. "What trouble?"

"Privately, I made it very clear that while we wanted to smooth relations with Khalishka, Myrcnia wasn't in the position to offer her our divine granddaughter. Not as my suspicions concerning your... not-cousins had come to a head." The queen wiped a bit of gristle from the corner of her mouth. "Do you know what Emperor Timur said?"

Sibylla hunted for the answer, then admitted defeat. "Not a clue."

"That he'd be taking a princess while providing a prince."

"Harrod?" Sibylla's fork slipped from her fingers.

"I never would have uncovered that Captain Starkley was Prince

Henry's son if not for the emperor. Though how he came into possession of such coveted knowledge, he wouldn't say."

Outside of Roger's garret, Sibylla had been out of her mind with anger and careless with her words. The emperor had used her spilling the delicate details of her family relationships to bargain with the queen over her granddaughter's hand. Now, Sibylla recoiled to think how he might have used her secret if he hadn't wanted to marry her.

"Men like him are excessively dangerous." The queen picked through her plate as she spoke. "He had papers drawn, and convinced even Lady Brigitte to the charade."

The morning Sibylla tried to deliver a breakfast cart to the emperor she'd been shocked to find Harrod there along with Mr Maokin, a mysterious figure, and a stack of papers. Now she began to understand how much the emperor had done to set forth their engagement. While she and Roger were on the trail of a killer, Timur and her grandmother had rewritten history.

"But do be mindful not to stray too far. That… *attachment* of yours will only entertain him for so long."

The queen seemed to imply the emperor already knew of her feelings for Roger, past and present. Sibylla *had* seen them conversing at the ball, up until Roger had the gall to shove the emperor aside. Roger should thank the man for not beheading him then and there. Sibylla shifted in her chair but couldn't find the strength to argue with the queen.

She flattened her hands on the table. "I promise not to make the same mistakes as Aunt Esther."

"There's a difference, Sibylla. Lady Esther *fell* in love with her Straybound, she wasn't already *in* love with him."

"I'm not. Not anymore."

The queen's laugh filled the dining hall. "If you can convince one person of that lie, make it yourself. As for Lady Esther, she'll be enjoying her stay in Saint Myrtle's convent soon enough."

At the enclosed religious order of Saint Myrtle's, the sisters adhered to strict covenants of extreme poverty and repentance. Lady Esther would soon trudge the fields barefoot in prayer, far from her accustomed lavish balls and breakfast buffets.

"Her sons, meanwhile, will have left the country if they have one complete brain among the three of them."

Sibylla fidgeted as the queen chewed the tough casing of a black sausage. "And Dr Lundfrigg?"

A sharp smile split the queen's lips. "Terrible tragedy. Dorinda discovered him just this morning – dead of a poisonous bite. The single needle-tooth of his own syringe, perhaps, but I prefer to think that a viper slithered into his bed and gave him a deathly kiss. It's more poetic that way, don't you think?" The casual tone of the queen's voice elicited a shiver.

Once the queen had cleaned her plate, she rang a bell for the footmen. Sibylla waited until she stood, then followed.

The queen bestowed a significant look. "Take note, dear girl, the emperor isn't known for his mercy – as I am."

"Yes, ma'am." Sibylla curtsied, though her reservations grew. She'd gained an engagement to escape a family that no longer seemed so frightening.

The queen reached across and patted Sibylla's cheek with soft, papery fingers. "Off you go then. Try to remember, it's customary to keep one's Straybound from killing too many their first year, and I don't mean through surgery, either."

39

Sibylla crumpled the paper, setting it atop a mound on her desk. Since seeing Roger take the dais at the ball, bullheaded and dashing in red and gold, she'd been producing likenesses of him – his shoulders, the length of his hand, the scruff on his face. Now, she had enough sketch fragments of the man to build a paper replica.

Standing in the center of her bedroom, ink pooled beneath her fingernails as a life-sized image of her Straybound took shape in the air. Unlike the living man, he didn't look away when she smiled.

"Hello, Dodge." She doffed an imaginary hat. "Is that a knighthood I see? My apologies, Sir Roger. I had no idea your medical practice was near the palace. How fortunate. I've recently suffered a terrible injury. Shall I tell you where it hurts?" She spun to face the window, as if this silent, grinning Roger might tease her for her burning cheeks. She lay a finger on her lips. "Here, and…" Her voice trailed off as her hand moved toward her heart.

The pendant around her neck – the emperor's betrothal gift – sat heavier on her chest than the locket she'd given that waif, with Roger's picture inside. This was her future, not doctor's calls with Roger.

Holes formed in his ink-body first, dissolving outward as she let his image slip away until only his face remained. Yet still, she yearned to kiss the back of his neck until he cracked a smile and scooped her into his arms.

"This will never do." She leaned close as if to kiss his mouth. Then with a puff, she blew the ink away.

A thump at her door sent her heart racing. As she waited for the last black droplets to diffuse, she cleared her throat so that when she spoke, her voice rang like cold crystal.

"Come in."

Roger entered the princess' room with an awkward bow, a tea tray balanced in his hands. Through the windows the gaslamps of Caligo mapped the city like a star chart, waiting for the late winter sunrise. Sibet crossed her arms with the same feigned impatience he remembered from her writing lessons when she would scold him for being late and demand a kiss. He waited, hoping she'd point to her cheek, her neck, even her hand, but she didn't move. Then his eyes flitted to the table of bloodletting instruments laid out for him, and his stomach dropped.

She stood in the center of the room, her fingernails black with ink, and raised an eyebrow at Roger's tea tray. "When I said come with my morning tea, I meant you should arrive at the same time, not serve it yourself. Though I suppose the position of a footman would be a handy cover for a Straybound."

Roger ducked his head. Already he felt like a fool in her presence. "As Straybound I serve your highness in all things." The archbishop had made him memorize the line. He was glad – he couldn't think of anything witty to make her laugh. While she made herself comfortable on a chaise lounge, he poured hot water from the silver pot over an infuser of Ibnovan rosehip tea leaves. Roger counted out three sugar cubes into the princess' cup. He added a splash of cream, then stirred exactly once, enough to break up the sugar yet leave a sweet, clear slurry on the bottom.

"Your highness," he tried again, placing the cup in her hand. "I reckon I've not made my gratefulness clear enough."

"Gratefulness?" She knitted her brow.

"For the–" Roger waggled his fingers, unable to invoke words for that strange, inky jungle that had shot from her hands. "And, you know." He clasped his throat and made a face.

His heart pounded as she laughed and raised the teacup to her lips.

"By the Lady," she spluttered. "You've upended the sugar bowl in here."

"But it's the way you like it. I still remember." He quickly took her cup and poured it out over a potted heliotrope.

Sibet shook her head. "I wasn't permitted sugar at Helmscliff. But thanks to Captain Starkley I developed a taste for chicory."

At the mention of Harrod, Roger averted his eyes. He had no words to discuss the new prince. "I'll make you another without sugar," he said. To change the subject he added, "I brought you something, your highness." He placed a jar and a silver skewer on the table before her.

She turned the jar and plucked at the plaid fabric covering the lid. "Are these... pickled whelks?"

"From old Sourjam's on the wharf. The ones with juniper and star anise in the brine."

"I haven't tasted whelks in years. And Sourjam's were always the best." Her eyes met his with a playful spark. "I would turn the clocks forward before your lessons, just so you'd be tardy and I could send you for them. I kept thinking you'd catch on, and that one day you wouldn't return." Her gaze shifted out the window, a sad smile on her lips. "Then again, I suppose that's exactly how it happened – you didn't return."

All this time he thought he'd done her a favor with his disappearing act. What romantic future could she have envisioned for a princess and a servant? Not this. But no alternative happy ending sprung to mind. It was his fault, forgetting she'd believed in those faerie stories all along. He bit his tongue until she took pity on him and broke the suffocating silence.

"But when could you possibly have had the time to fetch these whelks? I was told you never left Harrod's side all night."

Roger shrugged as casually as his tight new waistcoat allowed. "Adelaide brought 'em, your highness. I sent a constable 'round to Suet Street to coax her here. It only took a basket of hot cross buns. She's taking her breakfast in the kitchens. The whelks was her idea." That last bit was a lie. Best to hide his shameful sentiment.

"Be sure to thank her for me." Sibet twisted the lid open. "I'm glad to hear you aren't afraid to use your new authority. Is there any word on the girl's mother?"

Roger nodded. The same constable who had found Ada had also, thanks to a tip from Roger, found certain damning evidence in the cellar at Grausam's Undertaking and Coffining Services. By now the apprentice would be in a cell in Old Grim. "I'm arranging her funeral tomorrow. A quiet interment with a sealed iron coffin, next door to Sir Bentley Morris." Though he deplored such measures normally, Celeste deserved an undisturbed eternal rest. "Ada would like you to come, if you can find the time."

"I'd be glad to, though my presence isn't generally considered comforting."

Another awkward silence. Both he and Sibet were stalling. She must be as anxious about devotionals as he. He tried to remember the archbishop's advice for initiating the ceremony. Sinking to his knees before her chair, he worked his fingers through the knot of his cravat and bared his neck. If only he could tear off his waistcoat and shirt as well, let her tousle him on the downy covers of her bed. A shiver passed over him.

"I… I can't remember what I'm to say, your highness."

Sibet tilted back in her chair, clutching the jar to her chest. "Don't you want one of these first?" She skewered a whelk and held up the dripping glob. "We should each have one. To fortify us for… for the ordeal. I remember how much you liked them."

Roger's first impulse was to make up some excuse about needing to fast before choking down three jiggers of her blood. But whelks no longer seemed so disgusting by comparison. Before, he'd eaten them to impress her and because she might reward him with a kiss. Now he had to stop himself from moving toward her out of habit.

"They're not mine to eat."

"Oh." She shrugged, popped the whelk in her mouth, and set the jar aside. "Well then, let's get this over with. I think I remember how to start." She slit her thumb with her ceremonial dagger and, after letting a bead of blood well to the surface, smeared the sign of the Blood Line on Roger's forehead. Her fingers trailed for a moment over his tattoo. He sucked in his breath as another tremor passed through him. Closing his eyes, he kissed the bloody tip of her outstretched thumb, meant to seal the bond or some such nonsense. He longed for her mouth. But even her thumb was better than nothing.

"As Straybound I serve your highness in all things," he recited.

She grimaced, though he couldn't tell whether she disapproved of his words or the object in her hand. She pushed a small, brass box – a scarificator – toward him, then hitched her skirts to expose her calf. A look of vulnerability flitted over her features before she seemed to harden herself against feeling anything at all. He hadn't given much thought to her end of the Straybound bargain until now. Seeing Sibet offer her body like some church wafer, it finally sunk in that she would have to suffer this ordeal every day. For *him*.

Roger wiped blood from the cupping glass used to complete his first proper devotional. Sibet recovered on the faded green chaise lounge, one bared leg elevated on an ottoman, and a blood-tinged wet towel wrapped around her calf. The scarificator had been simple enough to operate, but its six blades had cut too deep and Roger found the application of the cup more messy and awkward than expected. A simple fleam and basin would have been less painful, but she had seemed determined to follow the strictures set out for her. The scarificator, with its cocked-trigger mechanism, could be used by a surgical novice, and Sibet insisted she learn to use it herself.

"Are you all right? Not lightheaded?" Roger rinsed the tools in an ornamental basin and lay them on the bedside table to dry. The blood sat heavy and sour in his stomach, but a tingling warmth had begun to seep through him. Dorinda was wrong. He could never crave this, not unless he turned into something monstrous like her.

Sibet massaged her temples. "I hate you seeing me like this."

"Nothing I haven't seen before." His pulse quickened as he watched her from the corner of his eye. Hopefully she hadn't noticed how his gaze lingered on the smooth line of her shin. "Besides, I'm a professional."

"At least you're finally dressed like one. Thank the Merciful Mother for Butterwick's Emporium for Gentlemen, and the palace steward for getting them to open their doors in the middle of the night." Sibet handed him the towel and applied a folded square of linen to her calf, pulling up her stocking to hold it in place. "It seems he got your measurements right."

Roger ran a hand over his new waistcoat in black and burgundy brocade. His neck chafed under a high starched collar, held in place by a silken cravat. He'd never been so well-dressed in his life. A week ago he'd have given his eyeteeth for such quality threads. Now that he understood their price, he'd have traded them for his old bloodstained shirts in a breath.

"But I'm no proper surgeon, your highness. Even if you wave your magical hands and make it so, I haven't the training."

"Yet. You haven't the proper training yet. I have something for you." Sibet pulled a bound stack of papers from under the settee. "I had this prepared. It's a copy of the exam required for your bachelor's in surgery. It is unmarked, but I believe you'll find shelves of medical texts in my old tutor's classroom, which you may access with this key. You sit for your exams a week from today, both written and practical. You've already proved yourself capable. I still don't know how you talked your way into the surgery, but I understand Harrod made it through the night without catching fever. They're saying taking his arm is what saved him."

In fact, it hadn't been difficult. The surgeon summoned to perform the amputation had gladly deferred to Roger – perhaps because last year he'd paid Roger to complete his amputation practicum on one of Dr Eldridge's stiffs, and gotten perfect marks.

But Roger wouldn't tell the princess this. He bowed. "I won't disappoint your highness."

"You do have a certain history, Dodge." Her voice took on an icy edge. "I'm not sure I want you calling me your highness. In fact, I'd prefer you address me as Sibylla when we're alone."

"It's not my place, your highness."

"But neither of us has ever enjoyed such formalities. A trait we still have in common, no?"

"Plenty of bad blood has passed between us since those days."

"And plenty more shall pass yet. But I do like to think we've arrived at some understanding. It's not my design to torture you. We've both had enough heartache these last few years. I should have forgiven you then, when things weren't so… this."

"If I know anything about wounds, your highness, it's that they scar, even as they heal." Roger wanted to explain further that he'd only done what was necessary to get by, but the words in his head sounded futile now. He clamped his jaw shut and looked on in silence as she stirred her tea, her spoon clinking on porcelain.

She took a sip. "If you insist on using titles, then I won't stop you."

Their eyes met, the glance of two songbirds in separate cages.

Her gaze exhumed yearnings he'd long ago buried. Tried to, anyway. "Your highness, I heard that a Stray… that a man such as I were meant for one particular use, but I gather you have something else in mind?" Since he was no steely-eyed killer, Dorinda had implied Sibet might use him as a lover. So he hoped, yet he couldn't bring himself to ask. Let Sibet tell him herself.

"A particular use? Do you mean assassination, or laundry?" She pinched the handle of her teacup in thought.

"I never minded wringing out your petticoats," he admitted. As she shifted in her seat, he glimpsed her white stocking. His fingers brushed her skirt. "Or unbuttoning your boots if your highness prefers."

Her eyes lingered on him for an excruciating moment before she firmly set the teacup aside. "You might offer your felicitations." Her back straightened with each word she spoke.

Roger didn't see anything to celebrate yet, and so settled on delivering a safe retort. "That a new gown, your highness? It makes your arms look long. In a nice way."

"On my engagement."

Engagement? Roger opened his mouth, then closed it again. His heart split in a gory mess of confusion. "Not… not to Harrod?" That made as much sense as anything.

Sibet raised a troubled eyebrow. "Harrod really *is* my brother. That wasn't some pretense, and we royals don't marry our siblings, half as they may be." Was she mocking him? He pretended to adjust a cufflink so she wouldn't see his distress. "I suppose you missed the announcement.

And what with Harrod being named prince, then shot… ha, I suppose that's one way to stop gossip about me – give them something else to talk about."

Roger wet his lips. He couldn't process everything at once – devotionals, newfound princes, secret Straybound lovers – or had he only imagined that last one? "Apologies, your highness. I'm not feeling my sharpest. Go on. The announcement?"

"I'm betrothed to the Emperor of Khalishka." Sibylla thumbed the pendant hanging at her neck. "Sorry, I thought you knew. I saw the pair of you chumming it up and just assumed–"

"I were chumming it up with an Emperor of Khalishka?" Roger stood, stricken, and tried to think of the ball, but Harrod's blood tinged his memories. "There were that lady physician, and that sword-swinging bearded bloke who got the shove he deserved–" He bit his lip. All became clear. "Bloody hell."

"Have you considered what this means?"

"That I'll be murdered in my sleep, your highness." That settled it. He hadn't slept all night, and his vision had started to cloud and tremble. He would never sleep again.

He must have made some too-brash movement because she reached out to him.

"We're going to Khalishka, you and I. As my Straybound, you'll finally leave Caligo. We may even see the whitefish before Lake Nagova freezes over. A few weeks from now, we depart."

The room spun as her words sunk in at last. He looked from her still-stained fingernails to his scrubbed hands, then let them flop to his sides. "Your highness. I can't… I mean, it ain't possible that I–"

"It is indeed possible. As it were, his imperial majesty has made a most generous offer." Her face clouded before continuing, and he wondered how much say she'd had in these arrangements. He detected a falter in her cool tone. "He's allowed for the appointment of a Myrcnian personal guard to ensure my confidence in taking up residence in his somewhat hostile nation. A very formal way of saying I can bring along a few people of my choosing. And yes, my surgeon will be a key member of my retinue. Dr Kaishuk was sufficiently impressed with your swift actions in the ballroom yesterday that she even offered to take you on as an apprentice of sorts when we reach Khalishka."

The generous offer did nothing to ease Roger's mind. Worry for Ada consumed him. Useless guardian that he'd been, at least she'd had someone. If he left the city – no, the country – what might become of her? Prostitution, thievery, poison, or worse.

"That girl Adelaide, your highness." What had Sibet called her? "My pixie ward. She comes with me or I stay here."

Sibet gave a wry grin. "I believe your staying would be equally futile."

"I won't leave Caligo without her." He dropped to one knee. He had to make her understand. "I've lost everything else." It came out in a whisper. "My garret. Dr Eldridge's. My brother. *Sibet*."

She pressed a hand to his cheek. His breath caught in his throat as her palm warmed his face, and light shone through her skin like a sun flare. As he reached for her hand, she flinched and tucked her hands out of sight, until her otherworldly glow had faded.

"Here, take this." She tossed him a brand-new book of Straybound devotionals to replace the one he'd lost. "Recite today's passage, and your pixie ward shall be welcomed into our Khalishkan contingent. This month's devotional subject is 'tractability.'"

Roger followed an endless strip of blue carpet down a vast gallery. The eyes of portraits seemed to follow his every step. He passed knots of liveried footmen gossiping in whispers about the rumored annulment of Lady Esther and Crown Prince Elfred's marriage – and probably the new Straybound surgeon, for all he knew. The guards never glanced his way, but some of the senior footmen turned their heads to stare.

The old tutor's key clicked in the lock, and Roger stepped into the classroom. It remained as he remembered from the days when Mr Coverley had sent him to fetch various biological materials for the princes and Sibet to study. Dusty books lined the walls, and to one side lay the vast laboratory table for conducting experiments. A cabinet with a glass door contained flasks, tools, trays, and chemical jars.

A map of Myrcnia and the greater continent was tacked to the wall above the table. Roger knew little of geography, and after much searching he found the eastern portion of Khalishka. The rest of the empire's lands fell off the map. Myrcnia itself appeared far larger than Roger had imagined, the city of Caligo immense enough that he had never left it.

His finger passed over the leather spines of several books before selecting *Moore's Manual of Phlebotomy and Hematology*. Sibet had said he might pack a trunk with these books and equipment to bring on the journey. The sight of so much knowledge terrified him – to think he knew none of it. Even blood, the stuff that spattered him, soaked his clothes, flowed through his veins, and now bound him, remained a mystery.

Still, he had a theory. Claudine, Margalotte, Celeste, they were not much different from Straybound. They'd been given some fungus or pathogen that rooted through them, sent them into a deathlike sleep, and finally killed them. He had to take that same sort of blood mixture or risk his heart bursting. So might some similar infection lurk within his own veins? Whatever the case, he was convinced his "Binding" was not entirely magic.

And if not magic, it might be understood.

And cured.

Roger found a brass microscope and a box of glass slides in one of the cabinets. Taking a thumb-lancet from his pocket – the one he'd failed to convince the princess to use – he jabbed his finger and smeared one of the slides with blood that looked thicker and darker than he remembered. Then, turning up the flame of the nearby lamp, he bent over the eyepiece and brought the slide into focus.

ACKNOWLEDGEMENTS

First and foremost, we want to thank our agent Caitlin McDonald for falling in love with our characters and championing *Resurrectionist* through murky submission waters, and the Donald Maass Literary Agency team who helped make this publication possible.

To our entire Angry Robot team, especially Marc Gascoigne for believing in us and this book, Lottie Llewelyn-Wells for her eagle editorial eye, Penny Reeve for her tireless enthusiasm and organization, Gemma Creffield for helping us navigate the intimidating publicity waters, Nick Tyler for his behind-the-scenes wizardry, Paul Simpson for wrangling resistant typos, and countless others at Watkins Media who helped ensure this book went out into the world as well-dressed and polished as we could make it. We'd also like to extend a hearty thank you to John Coulthart for the gorgeous cover.

And where would we be without our Pitch Wars mentor Michelle Hauck? This manuscript would have a hundred more rhetorical questions for starters. Among her many magical talents, she gravitated straight to the emotional heart of the book and helped us balance those big feelings with a tighter plot. Thank you!

We also want to give a special shout-out to Jaida Temperly, who ushered us through a rigorous structural edit that made the story pop, and to Joanna Volpe, who gave us a helping hand in uncertain times.

Last but not least, thank you Brenda Drake and the greater Pitch Wars community for your support, enthusiasm, and commiseration over the many hills and valleys on the road to publication. We wish you the best.

Wendy:
Resurrectionist has come a long way since its initial germination – to be precise, the moment when Alicia talked (coerced!) me into trading some fictional letters as a joint writing exercise "just for fun", and plied me with froufrou coffee. Thanks for being an epic friend, collaborator, writer, and productivity whipping-mistress. I'm glad we embarked on this crazy experiment together.

I also owe a huge debt of thanks to my spouse and partner-in-crime M, who has never wavered in support for me, and helped me carve out precious writing time. Also to my son and the rest of my family for their general enthusiasm, and their tolerance for my weird, obscure writerly obsessions.

Numerous other people have helped shape my writing over the years. Thank you to my classmates and faculty at Vermont College of Fine Arts, especially my mentors Ellen, Joshilyn, Clint and Domenic. To Sally, Johnnye and the Nebraska Writers Workshop. To Megan, for gamely reading everything I've thrown at you.

And thank you Mom for always inspiring me to take risks, creatively and throughout life. I miss you, and I wish you could have read this book.

Alicia:
To my mom: you always tell me what a creative, bright, intelligent person I am, and even if you're contractually obligated, I believe you at least half the time. To my dad, though you're no longer with me, I know how proud you would have been to see this book in print. And to my big brother, you've always looked out for me, no matter how bratty I'm being or how much I hate the sun. I'd be remiss not to thank Kyle, who kept telling me about this other writer I just had to go hang out with. This other writer turned into a coauthor.

So lastly, I want to thank my literary other half, Wendy, whose endless obsession with feelz haunts me every time I sit down to write. May your characters always suffer; I know you wouldn't stand for it otherwise.

ANGRY ROBOT

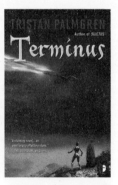

We are Angry Robot

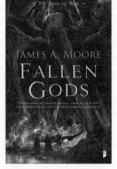

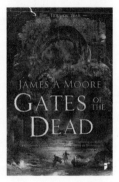

angryrobotbooks.com

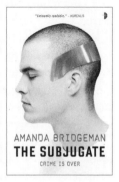

Science Fiction, Fantasy and WTF?!

@angryrobotbooks